The Revenge

Also by Tijan

The Damaged
The Insiders

The Revenge

An Insiders Novel

TIJAN

ST. MARTIN'S GRIFFIN
NEW YORK

First published in the United States by St. Martin's Griffin, an imprint of St. Martin's Publishing Group

www.stmartins.com

Library of Congress Cataloging-in-Publication Data

Names: Tijan, author.
Title: The revenge : an insiders novel / Tijan.
Description: First edition. | New York : St. Martin's Griffin, 2022.
Identifiers: LCCN 2022010191 | ISBN 9781250210814
    (trade paperback) | ISBN 9781250852717 (ebook)
Subjects: LCGFT: Novels.
Classification: LCC PS3620.I49 R48 2022 | DDC 813/.6—dc23/
    eng/20220303
LC record available at https://lccn.loc.gov/2022010191

Our books may be purchased in bulk for promotional, educational, or business use. Please contact your local bookseller or the Macmillan Corporate and Premium Sales Department at 1-800-221-7945, extension 5442, or by email at MacmillanSpecialMarkets@macmillan.com.

First Edition: 2022

10 9 8 7 6 5 4 3 2 1

To all the readers who love the Insiders trilogy.
I hope you enjoy *The Revenge* as well!

Thank you for your support!

The Revenge

ONE

Kash

There was someone in my apartment.

I didn't know this because of some sixth sense. I knew this because I'd received ten different alerts. The guy tripped the back perimeter alarm with the first door he opened. That was the first one sent to my phone. Second alarm was the security team picking him up on the video feeds. Third alarm was when the intruder got into the building. Fourth alarm, when they went up the back exit stairs. Fifth alarm, when they got to the sixteenth floor. Sixth alarm, when they went through the door to my floor.

Seventh alarm, when they got through my front door.

The eighth went off when he stepped inside the apartment door.

I checked my phone once it buzzed again.

That was the ninth alarm, and they were in the back bedroom.

Tenth alarm, they were in the walk-in closet.

"You sure about this?" Josh, a security guard who was fast becoming my right-hand man, asked. He was somewhat replacing Erik, who asked for a leave of absence because of his own family.

I didn't say a word, but I looked up to the back camera and saw the green light was on. He was watching, and I mouthed up at him, "*Shut. Up.*"

He laughed in my ear. "Just reminding you that you do have an entire detail of guards back here, waiting on your command. They'll rush in, immobilize the guy, and you can waltz in like fucking Batman."

I rolled my eyes.

Josh was on a kick about the caped crusader, and it never made sense to me. My phone went off again.

"We have eyes on him," he said. All cameras were turned on if there was a breach in security. He continued, his tone cold and professional now, "He's moving to the bedroom door. He'll be there in three, two . . ."

I turned.

"One."

The living room light was off.

The bedroom door they were approaching was just beyond it. Bailey preferred a smaller, cozier layout in our apartment. I had downgraded with her in mind after her second kidnapping attempt. All the doors and rooms made her uneasy, and sometimes less was easier to handle, so we went down to a two-bedroom place. Our bedroom and an office were on the other side of the kitchen.

My phone buzzed again. "He's opening the door."

I could hear it in real time, but I didn't look.

If they'd had a weapon, I wouldn't have allowed them access to the building. They would've been captured after the first perimeter was broken. But security had done a scan and nothing was on them. All they had were their phones and a set of keys. We couldn't be sure if the intruder was male or female at this point, but we did know they didn't have a wallet—thank you, full-body sensors installed on each set of doors.

I left my phone, wallet, keys, everything in my pocket.

With my head down, I walked through the living room and went right at them.

"They eased back. They're behind the bedroom door," Josh said in my ear.

I went in.

A normal person would be worked up.

I knew they were there. I knew where they were. I knew as much about them as I could.

What I did not know was why they were there.

I did not know their intentions after making their presence known.

I did not know if they were going to attack me or jump out and yell "Surprise!" I doubted it was the latter.

What *they* did not know was that I knew they were there.

So going through that door, I was the one with the element of surprise.

While I appeared calm and my heartbeat said I was, I *was not calm.*

I was the opposite of fucking calm.

I cleared the door, and Josh's voice sounded. "Now!"

I whirled.

They were lunging for me. I could finally see them; the intruder was male. A weapon flashed in his hands, a weapon that had *not* been flagged by the full-body scanners.

He didn't come from behind me.

He was right in front, and my hands were up.

I reached for him first, using my elbow to slam the weapon out of his hand. As his eyes met mine, they went wide, and I body-slammed him down to the floor.

I could not let up.

Not for one second.

I went down with him, knees to his chest, but he was twisting, trying to get free.

I let him go, but as he started to stand up, I tackled him again. A full body slam any lineman would be proud of, and I flipped him around so he was facedown. My arm went around his neck. My whole body went on top of him, securing the chokehold.

He couldn't move.

But he tried. He fought. He tried to twist. He tried to throw me off. He tried to find a weakness. He tried to knock out my legs.

I never gave an inch. I only tightened my hold.

And then, as blood rushed through my body, my eardrums feeling as though they were about to pop, my vision blurring at the edges, his entire body jerked, strained, squeezed, and then he began to go limp.

I still waited.

There was always a lull, a time when they tried to pretend they were unconscious. I didn't fall for it, and this time it proved true, because he came alive suddenly. He thrashed harder, more violently, rougher, and with a choking, gurgling sound, he went limp for the final time.

I released him, seeing the door opening from the corner of my eye.

Josh walked in, his weapon drawn. A line of men trailed behind him, and all came to stand in a circle as I got to my feet. It was only then that I kicked his body over and got a good look at him.

He was still breathing. His chest was rising steadily.

Josh glanced across the room. "Scanners didn't pick up that switchblade."

I grunted and knelt down.

I reached for the bottom of his ski mask and took hold.

"You think he knew about the security measures?" Josh asked.

I paused and looked up. "What do you mean?"

"We scanned for weapons. He was only allowed inside because it showed he didn't have any. That blade must've been well hidden on his body to get through. I'm saying maybe he knew you knew he was coming. That's why he only had that blade on him."

It was food for thought.

My blood was still pumping fast and hot inside, and it didn't matter. I wanted answers, and I needed another hard workout with the boxing bag because this hadn't been enough for me. It hadn't quenched the fury really building inside of me, simmering there all my life.

I didn't answer Josh.

I whisked off the ski mask and stepped back.

The men grunted, a few stepped back.

And me . . . I was looking at me.

TWO

Bailey

Three weeks later

The dress was itchy.

It was made of some super-strength alien fabric that hugged my body like latex, but it looked like gaudy cloth fabric. And it was plaid. Holiday break and all, and my friend Tamara, the hairdresser extraordinaire, swore I had to wear this red, black, and silver plaid dress contraption.

I hated it.

If I was going to mourn my mother, at least let me do it in comfort. This Lycra bodysuit invention gone wrong was adding insult to injury here. Chrissy Hayes would've thrown a fit at seeing her in this.

Her.

Crap. I was doing it again.

I winced, because here I was, thinking of myself in third person once more. It'd become a habit I picked up over the last three weeks, ever since I had to report in detail to the cops how I witnessed my mother's murder. Chrissy Hayes's murder.

Seraphina asked if I wanted something to drink the other night, and I'd responded with, "Yes, Bailey would love something to zonk her out. A valium and vodka, please."

My little sister had nodded, turned to fill my order, then stopped. She turned back.

I cringed, catching what I had said, but she only asked, "Vodka and valium?"

Crap.

I coughed and covered, "I mean an orange juice please. Maybe some champagne with it?"

She nodded and went to do it, accepting that drink order instead. Mimosas were almost the norm in the rich, high-society world that Seraphina had grown up in. I was newer, coming into the family this past summer, after a kidnapping attempt because I was Peter Francis's illegitimate child. Shock and awe to me because, one, I had no clue my childhood hero was actually my father; and two, Chrissy Hayes had a whole lie set in place that my dad had been killed in the line of duty. She'd even enlisted help from a few veterans at the local VFW. I'd been livid when I found out. Now I started crying because I would take more of her lies with actors and accomplices and a whole universe created to back up her story if that meant she were alive.

But fast-forward from that first kidnapping attempt, because life happened at breakneck speed after that.

I had left Chrissy behind, thinking it was for her own safety, and moved into the villa of my dad's right hand and somewhat adopted son, Kashton Colello. Who was hella hot, with smoldering cognac eyes, a jawline that made my knees weak on a regular basis, and those high and chiseled cheekbones. Kash wasn't really adopted, but he'd been taken under Peter's wing and, feeling all sorts of gratefulness, Kash dedicated his life to taking care of the entire Francis family in return.

He went above and beyond, bringing me into his own home.

He had me tell my new siblings (I had always been an only child, and voilà, now I had three) that I was a friend of his and most definitely *not* their sister.

Yeah. See. He went above and beyond. I'm not all the way meaning that in the positive way, but it was beyond, for sure.

Lucky me, my brother Matt figured it out before long. Then I had a friend and an actual brother. And while I was dealing with the new life situation, the hotness of Kashton Colello had started to burn inside of me.

It blazed hot. Boiled over. And yep, he and I ended up in bed together.

There were kisses. Hot nights. Climactic nights.

During all that time, I fell in love and *bam!*—then I found out who Kashton Colello actually was, and thinking he'd been brought in under my dad's wing was an understatement. Peter had kept him from the entire world because he was hiding out in his own way, from an evil, sadistic, murdering grandfather named Calhoun Bastian.

Kash had lost both his parents to his grandfather, and he'd been terrified that Calhoun would kill the rest of the Francis family. It'd been the main reason I was left out in the cold, so to speak. My father knew about Calhoun and thought it'd be safer for me if no one knew I was his daughter. Hence the father I never knew I had, and ironically, I had inherited his brain and his looks. We had the same dark hair that was so black that in a certain light it looked like there were streaks of blue. Honey-brown eyes.

I'd also inherited his computer skills.

That meant I could hack my way into almost anything, including looking up and violating a dozen firewalls if I wanted to find my father. So the whole veteran-accompanying witness testimonials that were fed to me had been needed, since I was given a name of a real guy that did die.

I hadn't hacked my way into finding out the truth. I wish I had, now.

I sucked in my breath, the plaid fabric scratching my stomach, just over my ribs, and I cursed in a hiss.

I really hated plaid.

I hated the look. I hated the feel of it. I hated even the smell of it. And yes, it definitely had a smell. Stale death. Bottle that crap up and someone would make a fortune in a nasty prank sort of gift. Can you imagine? Instead of sending a bag of dicks or an envelope stuffed with exploding glitter, you send a can of perfume and they open it to smell stale death?

I'm a genius, I tell ya.

Though maybe it's just me, since I've *only* been smelling stale death for the last three weeks.

It was that long ago when we put the closed casket of Chrissy Hayes six feet under. Everyone had come out in droves. My graduate school classmates. My new friends. Professors from Hawking, classmates and teachers from undergraduate, and even people from high school. Then again, almost the entire town of Brookley showed up. Chrissy Hayes was a community legend. A nurse in the local hospital, who kicked ass in the Christmas ugly sweater competitions year after year. She was looked at like a daughter by most of the vets from the VFW, or a sister, or they just wanted to fuck her. 'Cause my mom got a lot of that, too. She was hella hot, if I do say so myself.

So there were a lot of those guys at the funeral. Guys who had dated her. Guys who wished they had dated her. Most looked at her fondly, and if they didn't, they pretended for the day, because they took one look at the thirty-plus security guards stationed around the church, wake, cemetery and they got fake real quick. I don't think there were a lot of those anyway.

Neighbor Carla came.

And my family.

So many of my family members came.

My grandma and grandpa. Aunt Sarah. My uncles. All my cousins. Most of them were giving Kash, Peter, and Matt stink eye, but then Seraphina and Cyclone came forward to meet the other side of my family and all of them melted. You'd have to be the psychopath who put a bullet through my mother's brain not to soften at the sight of my little sister and brother. By the end of the weekend, Cyclone didn't move from my grandma's side and Seraphina walked hand in hand with my grandpa, only switching out to hold my Uncle Rich's hand, too.

They weren't the only family who came.

Peter's side came, too.

His two brothers, their wives, their ex-wives, and their children. Peter's parents had passed long ago, so it made sense why Seraphina and Cyclone took to my own grandparents so fast. And thank God I didn't know anything about their mother's parents, because either someone said something or maybe Payton, their aunt, had slunk away somewhere for the last month. She wasn't there when Kash said he thought it was best if we moved into the Chesapeake estates' main house—not just his villa but the actual house—and I hadn't seen her since. Marie and Theresa had stepped up, and I was just glad Marie was there. Marie, who had been my first nemesis at the family's estate, and now she'd been the glue holding everything together. Theresa ran the kitchen, but she was the second glue. She was like a crown molding.

Or maybe for me.

Maybe they'd both been the glue holding *me* together.

I didn't know. That was too much thinking, something I was trying not to do so much, because when I started thinking, I started remembering, and want to know a smart person's personal nightmare? Having a photographic memory and replaying your entire childhood, where you were raised by your recently buried mother, over and over and over and . . . You get my drift.

So, yeah.

Not thinking. Another habit I was trying to pick up.

It worked some of the days. Most days, not so much.

"Bailey."

Ah. There they were. It was the latest person Kash sent.

I've been standing in a room, by myself, staring out the window, not talking to someone, and there was always a timer. It wasn't just my family, but it was my friends, too. Torie. Tamara. Even Melissa and Scott. They were around, taking turns checking on me. The only one who was in tune with me, who knew I'd probably stepped away so I wouldn't lose my mind, was Kash.

My man.

I loved him.

Thinking back to the girl I'd been when I first met him—she never stood a chance. It was like her job was to fall for Kash. It was written in the stars. It was inevitable. But all the shit that came afterward hadn't been included in the fine print. She had no clue that choosing her father over her mother, choosing to fall in love with Kashton Colello, would eventually make her lose the one person who'd been there all her life.

Brain, shut off.

That was my own checkout.

When I started thinking thoughts like that, I automatically shut down. It was a door closing, and on the other side was a mess of catastrophe, hysteria, panic, hatred, loathing, and just so many emotions.

The girl (see, still talking in third person here) needed to go into zombie mode. So that's what I did.

It was at the same time that the person chosen to check on me stepped next to me, and I turned even before they spoke another word. It was Matt. His face was closed off, but there was a distant hint of concern in his eyes. He had a glass of bourbon in hand, but to be honest, he rarely went without it lately, and he took one look at me, sighed, put his free hand in his suit pants pocket, and then turned to look out the window with me.

He murmured, right before taking a sip, "I don't blame you one bit."

I was hiding.

He knew it.

I now knew he knew it, and just like that, without another word spoken, we both looked out the window. I had no clue where we were. That was another given these days. I rarely knew what we were doing, where we were going. I just went. I showed up. I stood around. I sat around. I rarely spoke, and then eventually Kash would come get me, or he'd send someone for me, and then we'd go home and we'd repeat it the next day.

Today I asked, "Where are we?"

I felt Matt's perusal more than I heard his silence before he responded, quietly, "We're at an event at your school. Dad donated that seventy million."

That would explain why I saw one of my classmates earlier. And why I was in a dress that itched.

"Oh. Okay."

That was it. That was all I had in me.

So, back to the window.

It was a good window.

I just never saw the window.

THREE

Kash

"She's not doing good."

I grunted at Peter's statement, turning to him. "No shit."

We were standing in a banquet room, surrounded by Bailey's professors and Hawking higher-ups, and both of us were watching our girl standing at the window. Matt was with her now. Neither spoke a word, but I was glad he was there. Her brother had tuned in to how to be with her, because if you pushed her, Bailey would bolt. She couldn't handle much, and I had actually sat and watched her turn herself off too many times to count.

"I'm glad you guys moved into the house."

I hated it. "It's good for Bailey to be around you guys right now."

"That, and your apartment wasn't safe."

She was thinner since Chrissy's death. Bailey always looked beautiful to me, always would, but there was a sadness that emanated from her. She looked lost at the same time. I watched as she began rubbing her chest, her finger scratching her dress, and I was feeling the same itch. Maybe it was because of my background, knowing why my parents had been murdered, who had had them murdered, and the fact he was still out there, but

I hated living in a house like Peter's. It was a mansion, but we were put up in our own section.

We were supposed to have privacy.

That wasn't the truth.

Seraphina. Cyclone. Even Matt. Marie. Theresa. They were all stopping by, all checking on Bailey, and I couldn't blame them. I'd have done the same if I wasn't the one holding her in my arms. But I hated that building. Give me an apartment building with a clear escape route next to me, or my own place like the villa, and I was happy. I'd been staying at the villa almost since I first moved in with the Francis family.

I've always been like this. Wired. Always feeling in a corner. Waiting for my grandfather to come.

It was now.

Calhoun Bastian had delivered a devastating blow, and I hadn't been able to fire back, not yet, but I knew I had to. God. My chest burned. I was thinking it, and it would take me away from Bailey.

And fuck my grandfather because he did his research.

He came to her school.

I thought it was about trying to scare me, to show me how close he could get to Bailey. It hadn't been about that, and I knew it now. I knew it too late. He'd been testing me. He'd been gauging me, seeing how much I cared for her, and I showed him. Freely. Willingly. I pushed back on him, hard, and it'd been a mistake. He saw how in love with her I was.

She was my weakness. Not the Francis family anymore, but Bailey.

I wanted to hunt him down *now*, stop him *now*.

"We haven't talked about . . ."

I let Peter's statement hang between us. No. We hadn't talked. Peter had fallen in love with Chrissy Hayes, and my grandfather had taken his woman away. What was there to talk about? I heard his tone, how he was trying to warm up to the real conversation. And that he wanted to do it here, in a fucking college building. I wasn't angry at Peter, but I *was* angry.

I was angry at everyone, everything.

I was angry because the real person I wanted to tear apart would require me to leave the woman I had hurt, the woman I loved, and I wasn't sure if that's what she actually needed more than anything.

God.

"Kash—"

"Don't," I gutted out, cutting him off.

"Kash." He tried again.

I turned to him. "I said don't."

Peter swallowed. His chin firmed. He was taking what I was showing. I shook my head and turned back to watch Bailey, like I'd done a thousand times over the last three weeks.

"I need to go and you know it," I said.

I heard his swift inhale. "She needs you."

"She needs me to kill him more."

The decision was made. I had to go. The sooner the better.

He frowned. "Kash."

I shook my head. "No. You know I'm right. I've been fighting him using board moves. I set up chess pieces and *still* never saw him coming. He took her mother out. He took your woman, and that's on *me*."

"It's not—"

"It *is!*"

I seared him with a look. He shouldn't be fighting me on this. He *knew*. He knew more than anyone how this was my fault, how he hadn't brought her into the family in the first place because of me, because of who I shared blood with.

My men were stationed around the entire room, and at the sharp exchange, I saw Josh separate from the wall. He was coming to me. I looked at him, shaking my head to tell him to stay back, but he kept coming. It was then that I saw he had his finger to his ear and was listening to something being said in his earpiece. A resolved look came over him, making his hard face seem even harder, and he never slowed. He didn't falter one bit.

Something was happening, and he was coming to tell me.

Making eye contact with Scott, Fitz, and Derek; all three of them were watching Josh's movements.

Fuck. This was the call I set in motion three months ago when I took Bailey to Burriotle. She was getting a lunch, but I was meeting an old friend, Robbie, preparing for *this* call.

Josh stopped next to me.

"What is it?"

"They made contact."

My chest swelled and I clipped my head down. "Fine."

No. It wasn't fine. It was good.

I had to go.

"How is she going to sleep at night?" Peter asked.

I gave him a sharp look. "You got cameras in our room?"

He'd been paying more attention than I thought he had been.

"I have cameras in the hallways. She paces at night. You come and get her. She doesn't leave again after you do that." He stepped closer, dropping his voice. "I know you help her sleep. How's she going to sleep now?"

How could I kill my grandfather if I couldn't leave her side?

"I can't take her with me."

He stared at me.

I stared back.

Neither of us said a word.

Then, a break, and Peter nodded. He stepped back. "Fine. I can see if Seraphina will stay with her."

Seraphina was twelve, and she loved Chrissy, too, but she was more worried about losing her new big sister. Because of that,

Bailey would not let that happen. No one would be allowed in her room at night, but he was right. Bailey had to sleep.

And I had to go and kill my grandfather.

I would not take her, so she was in more danger.

Shit. Shit. Shit.

"I'll be back as soon as I can." I took a step away, but rounded back. "I will send for her if I can, but only if she'll be safe."

Peter gave me a sharp nod. "My daughter won't come back to us if she can't rest."

Yeah. Fuck. Yeah.

I gave Josh the signal, and he separated, going to give out my orders.

Josh had been a part of the first security detail my grandfather had hired. I had infiltrated that team, setting up my men to be his. They acted as spies, but I knew there would be a time when they would have to unveil whose side they were on. I did it earlier in our war because I wanted my grandfather to think when he hired a second team that there was no way I could've gotten to any of them.

He thought wrong.

I reached out to a team in Brazil, guessing who my grandfather would approach. They had a reputation he would want. They were known for being committed to the end, being ruthless where it wasn't necessary.

They were *exactly* the guys he would want to hire.

Calhoun reached out on the very afternoon I pulled my first team from him. I got to them first. And since then, under my orders, those men had been guarding him.

They were instructed to call when my grandfather was about to strike.

They had not called before Chrissy Hayes was murdered.

They called now.

But first, Bailey.

I went to her, nodding to Matt, who saw my approach. His eyes flashed, a guardedness and hardness flaring before he ducked his head. I didn't consider Matt's emotions. If he was angry at me, it made sense. I was angry at me, too.

I touched her elbow, knowing she already knew I was there. She adjusted her footing. She always did, whether it was consciously or unconsciously done, and she moved closer to me.

"I have to go."

She looked at me. "Hmm?"

I flinched, seeing the glazed and almost glassy look in her eyes.

Bending, brushing my lips over hers, I murmured again, "I have to go." I tucked a strand of her hair behind her ear, my hand lingering. Jesus. I loved her. The warmth in me shoved all the shit emotions aside, filled me with the need to take her in my arms, to never let her go, to know she'd be safe there no matter what.

I fought that down.

I applied pressure on her lips, feeling her breath and taking it in. My eyes closed. I trailed my hand down the side of her face, cupping her neck before I pulled back. "I love you. I'll call later, when I know you're home."

Some of the glazed look faded. She was refocusing, seeing me a bit more clearly. "You're leaving?"

I nodded, knowing she'd been in shut-off mode. It took this long to get through. "I'm going to get some answers and then I'll be back."

She stared at me. Her eyes sharpened. I saw her brain turn on. Emotions flitted over her, and then a wildness, a panicked look flared tight, and she sucked in her breath. She shut down again. Little by little, the alertness softened, then disappeared. The glazed expression came back. Her face smoothed out until she was a walking corpse, and her hand fell from my chest. I hadn't even realized it was there until it was gone.

I wanted that touch back.

I rested my forehead to hers. "I love you. I'll be back."

She turned for the window. "Oh. Okay."

That was it.

She was gone.

I looked for Matt, and he'd been waiting. He stepped away from a pocket of people who'd been trying to talk with him. He came over, his eyes on her. "You gotta go?"

"I gotta go."

His shoulders rose. His chest lifted. One long fucking deep breath and he exhaled, saying, "Okay. I'll sleep outside her room."

"That might be best."

His eyes met mine, and that hardness from before came back. "I don't know what you're doing, where you're going, but I'm hoping it's bringing you one step closer to putting that fucker in the ground. Kill him, Kash. Kill him for Chrissy."

I would, but I'd be killing him for Bailey. I didn't say that to Matt, just nodded and left.

Josh had the car waiting for me.

FOUR

Kash

When we landed, it was at a private air strip in a small town in Montana. The nearest lights were twenty miles away, and we could only see the smallest glimmer of them in the night sky.

"Why'd we pick this place for the meet?"

One, it was fucking cold. These guys were mostly based out of South America. They were used to heat and humidity, not frigid temps. And two, because it was on the north end of the States. They had to make the trek around and through Canada, and I had friends up there. They were looking out for me, so I'd been getting reports on their progress.

I didn't say any of that to Josh, instead saying, "Because I wanted to inconvenience them."

He grunted, going before me as we left the plane. We arrived early on purpose, and as soon as we touched down, a fleet of cars were leaving Missoula and would be arriving in thirty minutes.

Josh glanced at me, frowning. "I know you keep things close to your chest, but maybe share the connections here? You're Mr. Badass in fighting, but I am one of your guards. You die, I'm out of a job." A dry grin was on his face when I frowned at him. "Humor me?"

My frown deepened, but he was right. I had been keeping things too close to my chest.

"I grew up with these two guys from my mom's family's neighborhood. Robbie and Ace Mistroni."

"The fighter?"

"He has a manager that is a retired military guy. He specialized in covert op missions, worked as a mercenary for a long time, and has connections deep into that world."

"And that's how you got in touch with the guys who were doing security for your grandfather?"

I nodded.

The night was clear, but cold. We had men positioned around the airport by now, and we could see the faint glow of headlights approaching from the north. I was guessing those were the guys we were meeting, but my men were coming from the west and they'd be coming in dark.

Josh shivered, blowing on his hands and shifting his weight. "Fuck. I didn't think it could get colder than Chicago." He paused a second. "Wait. What's this guy's name? The leader."

"Harden."

"Mike Harden?"

I raised an eyebrow. "You've heard of him?"

He whistled, nodding. "If you have him on your side, you're good to go. He's known to be the best of the best, if you get my drift."

I did. It was why I reached out to him.

"Why are we meeting with him now?"

Josh wasn't usually this inquisitive, but the cars were nearing the airstrip from the road. I stepped forward, my hands coming out of my pockets, and I waited to approach as the cars pulled one by one onto the airstrip. It was small and private, so they drove right up to us. Three trucks in all. All black. The doors opened on each one of them, an entire team of men stepping out. They were large, muscled, and each wore a bulletproof vest with visible shoulder holsters.

One of the guys from the last truck moved forward. He wore a hard face, dead eyes, and he was just as large and imposing as the others.

He was also their leader. "You're Colello."

"Harden."

He nodded, looking around, scanning the perimeter. Then he faced front, his hands going to the sides of his vest. "We weren't alerted when Bastian moved on your woman's mom. We made the trip to let you know that in person. Clocking your second security team trying to sneak up on us is insulting, but we're still here. We're trying to impress upon you that we didn't double-cross you. That should say everything to you."

His jaw clenched. His eyes flashed.

A few of his men shifted in their stances, similar expressions on their faces.

It was telling me they didn't like hearing how their target killed an unarmed woman on their watch, because it was their watch. It was the whole fucking reason we were having this meet.

"You are a member of my grandfather's security team. I understood that and understand that's why it took this long for a face-to-face, but I'd like to know how you got away from him for this meeting?"

His eyes narrowed on me, staring long and hard. "I'll say this much. We didn't like your grandfather before you reached out. Now that we've been working for him, we actively *despise* him. Your mission to take him down has become our mission, too, but it's not that simple. He's got multiple teams of security. We were dispatched because someone from your grandfather's family cut free. This was all kept under wraps. When we were roped in, it was thirty-six hours ago, and we were told that the men higher than us on Calhoun's trusted list tried to contain the situation. They failed and they were letting us loose to search him out." His eyes were steady, tracking my every movement, the slightest emotion I let through. He wasn't reading anything from me, and his mouth turned down. "Why do I think you already know about this person?"

Fuck that.

I tipped my head back. "I didn't just call this meeting to look you in the eye and ask why my grandfather was able to murder my woman's mother." I indicated his men. "I know how you came into the country, what roads you used in Canada to get to this country. I know the airport you arrived at, the day you flew out of Rio. I knew all this because the second reason for this meeting is that while I'm getting reports on you, I'm also getting reports on my grandfather. And since you've been gone, he's done no moves. None. If he didn't trust you, he would've been concerned. He's not. He's doing nothing except waiting for you to return to him. That tells me that he trusts you, and that was the point of *everything*."

"What?"

It took a second.

"This whole meet was to test your grandfather's alliance with us?" His hands went to his gun, but held there. His men reacted to him, going on alert. But by that time my own security team was coming up from behind us. And they were coming in dark. The vehicles would've been left behind, and they were walking in.

Harden jerked toward me, then caught movement behind me and stepped back. His hands went up. His men's, too.

He swung his gaze back to mine, livid. "What the fuck is this?"

"You told me you knew I had security coming."

His nostrils flared. "I was bullshitting you. I didn't actually know you had men coming in."

They walked past the line of security guards who had flown

with me. They walked past me, past Josh, and they spread out. They made a circle around Harden's men, who were outnumbered now.

All of *them* were eyeing my new guys warily.

"Relax."

At my command, the new team lowered their weapons but remained exactly where they stood.

Harden had been noting all of this, and he swung back to me. He muttered a curse, rubbing a hand over his jaw before spitting to the side. "Can you explain what the hell is going on here?"

"The third reason I asked for this meet." I nodded to the new guys. "These men are going to go with you."

"What?" He went still, his eyes bulging out. "I can't do that. Your grandfather's really fucking paranoid."

"Exactly." I stepped closer. "You are gone right now. You brought with you the rest of my men. He still has men with him that aren't mine, and I'm a selfish bastard. I want to control everyone around him. To do that, I will leak information back to him, making him think the current team with him right now is turning on him. I will keep at it, and when you return with the coordinates for the person he sent you to search for, he will then promote you. He will tell you to get more men. You will bring in mine." There was no room for kindness in this world. I wanted to choke the life out of my grandfather. "I want every goddamn man surrounding him to be mine first. Got it?"

He stared at me, long and hard.

Five seconds.

Ten.

Thirty.

A minute passed before his mouth thinned. He abruptly nodded, his neck looking stiff. "I'm assuming you've arranged travel for all your men?"

"You assume correct." I nodded to Scott, who came forward,

pulling a folder from his bag. He handed it over to Harden. "That's everything. Instructions are all in there."

He leafed through the file before handing it over to one of his men. Turning back to me, his eyebrows were pinched together. "You said you were watching Calhoun? You partly pulled us out to test him? See if he trusted us or not."

"I did. He's paranoid, and he hasn't sent anyone to watch you. That means he trusts you enough not to double-cross him. It also tells me he's stretched to the point where he doesn't have anyone to send after you." Which gave me the best satisfaction.

It told me Chrissy's murder was the ace in his sleeve and he was hurting.

It was time to set the trap, to draw him in, and then to close it while he was inside. I was salivating over that meeting.

"You didn't need to do this face-to-face."

I shook my head. "A part of me needed to look you in the eye. You reached out right after Chrissy Hayes's murder and reassured me you were not in the loop on that one. It was a small team project and was kept quiet from everyone. I wanted to believe you, but I couldn't know for sure. I saw your reaction to Chrissy's death. You reacted. So did your men."

"We're not in the business of murdering innocent women."

I nodded. "Take care of the rest of my men. They're about to become your brothers down there."

Scott was debriefed on the way here, so he approached, giving Harden and the new team further instructions. Josh went with me, following me back into the small plane. He took his seat, watching me, and after a few moments of silence, he whistled under his breath.

"What?"

"I heard stories about your grandfather. Being in our business, you can't not hear about him. The rumors are all true. I've seen enough firsthand. But *you*. No one's ready for you. You're going to make a lot of powerful people very nervous."

He was right.

I didn't care.

I shifted back in my seat, took my phone out, and texted Bailey.

Coming back. Are you sleeping?

Her response came through right as we were circling to start taxiing for liftoff.

Waiting for you.

FIVE

Bailey

I woke to an empty bed.

The good news: I woke. That meant I had slept. The bad news: Kash was gone after only just returning late last night.

I rolled over, pulling up the blankets, snuggling in. I'd give myself only a second, because I'd learned that if I didn't move right away I would space on time. That meant that if I said five minutes, I could remain there for hours.

With the two kidnapping attempts, I thought I knew trauma. I did not.

I never lost complete moments of time before. But now, after my mom, I could lose an entire day and not know it. Then, at other moments, I couldn't get my brain to stop thinking and rest. I would go into an altered state of mind where I was me, I was here, but I wasn't. There was an edge of irrationality, a biting feel to my brain, and I would only know if I was in that state when I *left* that state. It was exhausting and perplexing. Simple things. Like now, I was giving myself just a beat before I pushed back the blankets and got up.

Padding barefoot, I went to the bathroom first.

I washed my hands.

I forgot to flush the toilet, one second.

I was back.

I rewashed my hands.

I dried my hands.

I brushed my teeth.

I put my toothbrush back. I recapped the toothpaste.

I turned the sink back on, testing it. Making sure it was luke-warm.

And bending, I wet my face.

I reached for my face cleanser, lathered it on my hands and then applied to my face.

Slow circles, tracing my entire face.

My eyes were closed, and I worked around them.

I cleaned behind my ears. A little down my neck. Under my chin.

Over my lips.

The bridge between my eyes.

Over my forehead, lingering on my temples, and I applied pressure. That felt good, but I released and the pressure from inside built up again.

I sighed, reaching and testing the water once more. It was still lukewarm.

I bent, and this time I splashed my face. I cleaned most of the cleanser off, reaching for the washcloth to get the rest. When that was done, I put the washcloth aside and reached for the towel. Everything had been in the same spot for the last three weeks.

I could move around this bathroom without opening my eyes, not once, and I would know where it all was.

I touched the towel, snaking it off the rack, and I dried my face.

That was done.

I stopped, regrouping. My mind was still not turned on, so I went through the motions.

Oh. I forgot.

I laid out the washcloth so it would dry, and then I turned and folded the towel back over the rack. It was a little damp, so I spread it all out. Later I would come in and fold it back up. I would match the corners to line up together perfectly.

My arm was reaching as soon as I was done with the towel. I snagged my hair comb and, turning from the sink, I brought it through my hair.

No snarls.

No knots.

I put the comb back down, back into its spot. I patted it, making sure it was in the right place.

Then, with another sigh, I reached up and began parting my hair. Three different sections. Starting at the base of my forehead, I moved the right section under the center, over the left. I swung the left under the center and over the right. I kept moving, just like that, all the way down to the ends of my hair. Grabbing a tie, I wrapped it three times around the end of my braid, and when that was done, I went to my closet.

Simple things. Simple movements.

I didn't know the day. I rarely did these days, but I knew I couldn't do schoolwork. I couldn't work on the computer, and Kash was gone, so that meant Matt might be around. Or Seraphina. Or Cyclone. Or I might wander down to the kitchen, have Theresa put me to work and help out. I could do dishes. She always balked, but I didn't care.

The motion of cleaning, of spraying away the dirt, of putting the dishes through the dishwasher, of pulling them out the other end and knowing they were clean gave me satisfaction. I didn't know why, but I wasn't going to question it.

I knew there would be a time when I would.

I would look back at all these little routines I did now, that got me through each day, and I would analyze the reason I did them, the reason they helped me, but for now, I didn't do any of that.

I grabbed jeans, a shirt, a sweater, and I put on socks and sneakers. I was comfortable, ready for anything, and only then, after snagging my phone and putting it in my pocket, did I leave the room.

I never once looked in the mirror.

"We should day drink today."

Matt found me in the kitchen corner, cutting board in front of me, knife in my hand, and thirty carrots spread out, ready to be chopped. I'd just been victorious in getting Theresa to let me use the knife. She kept worrying I was going to miss the carrot and cut a finger off.

"Nope." I waved the knife in the air. "I'm good here."

Matt cocked an eyebrow, leaning against the counter beside me. His arms crossed over his chest and he hooked one ankle over the other. He took me in, the knife, the cutting board, the carrots, the knife, the rest of the room, Theresa, and back to the knife.

He murmured, "Uh-huh. Yeah."

I shot him a grin, lining up the first carrot. "Thirty minutes."

"You'll be done in thirty minutes?"

I shook my head, making the first slice through the middle of the carrot. "That's how long it took me to talk Theresa into letting me help prepare lunch."

"Theresa." Matt turned to her.

She was standing beside another line cook, who was chopping up the rest of the vegetables for the soup. She didn't look up, just started shaking her head. "Nope. Not going to happen." She raised a hand up, pointing at me. "She came in this morning and started doing dishes. I kicked her out. She came back ten minutes later and started making coffee for everyone. I kicked her out again. Came back and you're now seeing our compromise. She wanted to man the grill, and no way am I letting one of you Francis children near that grill.

You all are good staying out of my kitchen, thank you very much."

Matt gestured to me. "But she's in here."

"Yeah, 'cause she wouldn't stop coming in—"

I spoke up, looking down. "It's because I'm a Hayes."

The other chopping stopped.

The guy at the grill stopped scraping.

The dishes were held suspended.

Theresa didn't talk.

Matt didn't say a word.

The only sound that filled the room was water boiling on the stove and the dishwasher machine doing a load.

I could feel how pregnant that silence was, but I kept chopping all the while, and I could almost feel my mom patting my back, saying, "You tell 'em, Bailey. You tell 'em how we Hayeses handle ourselves."

I sucked in my breath, stopped seeing the carrot under my hand, felt the tears swelling up, but I'd gotten damn good at doing things without seeing. I sliced the carrot, moved it aside, and grabbed another. I lined it up and I was putting the knife through it when Matt coughed, clearing his throat.

He leaned in close and said quietly, "How about we go day drinking when you're done with the carrots?"

I couldn't do that.

I'd drink. Then I'd feel. Then I'd think.

I could handle it now, working, and feeling her. But if I started feeling my own emotions and then also feeling her, nope.

Not gonna happen.

But I couldn't tell him. I couldn't explain it like that.

My throat was swelling up, and I couldn't get any words out.

Theresa called, in that tone of hers, telling me she understood exactly what I was going through at this very moment. "Leave her be, Matthew. The time for day drinking will hit, but it ain't here yet."

Matt was quiet next to me.

I was tense, holding my breath, and then I heard him sigh, too. "Okay." He patted my shoulder. "Call if you want to hang. I'm going to Naveah then."

He left.

Those tears didn't fall.

I never stopped cutting the carrots.

That seemed important to me for some reason.

Kash

I was leaving a meeting and going to another meeting when my phone started ringing. Glancing down, seeing it was Matt calling, and knowing he was back at the Chesapeake, I answered just as I was sliding into the back of the SUV.

"Yeah?"

Josh shut my door and went around to the front passenger side. I was alone in the back and I heard a biting greeting: "She's cutting carrots, Kash."

I frowned.

"Bailey?"

He snapped, "No. Payton. *Yes*, Bailey. I wanted her to go to Naveah with me today, and she wouldn't stop cutting those fucking carrots. Carrots. She's begging to work in the kitchen. Theresa couldn't get rid of her this morning, so she put her to work. My sister, who is one of the smartest people I know—and I come from a family of geniuses—is dicing through carrots like her life depends on it. *What the fuck, Kash? What the fuck?*"

I sighed on the inside.

On the inside, I wanted to swear with him, rage on the phone.

On the inside, I wanted to go back to the Chesapeake and hold Bailey until she could start feeling again.

But all I did was murmur quietly, resting my head back

against the seat, because suddenly I was fucking wiped. "She's in mourning."

"Yeah." Another biting word from him. "Three weeks ago. Chrissy died three weeks ago. She—Bailey—she should—"

"He waited."

Matt swallowed his words. He was silent.

I said again, "He waited, Matt. He waited until she could see and then he killed Chrissy. Bailey knows this. She's done the math in her head. She is probably haunted by that day every minute of every hour. She has a photographic memory. She is a genius—"

"I know!"

Another sigh, from me. "She needs time."

He was silent again.

Then a strained, "I can't lose my sister. I just got her."

"I know." My head was too heavy to rest. I let it hang. I let my shoulders slump. "I know."

"I want her back."

I did, too.

"I'm going to get wasted today," he said. "Like, you better send a full detail on me, because I'm letting you know ahead of time. I'm drinking. I'll probably fuck a few girls today, maybe a few more tonight. I'll try and not do drugs, but I can't make promises. I can only promise that I'm going to be stupid today. I need it, Kash." He was breathing heavily into the phone. I could hear his restraint slipping. "Watching Bailey choose to remain a zombie every day is killing me. And I liked Chrissy. I really liked her, too, but I can't handle this shit. It's too close. It's just like . . ."

It was just like when his own mother died.

Matt was a brother to me. My meetings weren't saving lives today. I had done as much as I could today in regard to my war against Calhoun.

I squared my shoulders up and addressed Josh. "Cancel the rest of my meetings for the day and take me to Naveah."

Matt stopped talking on his end. "You serious?"

I heard his happiness and my gut shifted.

I'd been neglecting someone I considered a brother.

"I'm coming to you."

"What about Bailey?" His voice had grown hoarse.

"Bailey is doing what Bailey can do right now. She'd be happy that I'm coming to you."

"Thank you." Still hoarse. I heard something else there, a tone that had me blinking my eyes rapidly. "I'll have a drink ready for you, man."

I grinned into the phone. "Someone's gotta make sure you don't do something too stupid today."

"You're right. That was always your job."

We hung up and I sent off an email to my assistant. She would reschedule the meetings that Josh didn't know about. Two different worlds that I was walking between. The business world and the shadow world. I went over the line daily, and one of these days there'd be a time when I would only exist in one.

Moves. One at a time. I was making them.

I was finding my grandfather.

I was tracking my grandfather.

I was cornering my grandfather. He just didn't know it, but when he did, when everything was lined up, then and *only* then I would cross that line for the last time.

I only hoped I'd be able to return to this world.

I also called Torie. "I want you to take Tamara and Melissa and go to the Chesapeake. I'm coming to Naveah to spend the day with Matt, so I'd like you to be at the house with Bailey."

There was no hesitation on her end, just the background music playing. "You got it. We're just hanging?"

"Spend time with her. Meet her where she's at. Right now, she's cutting carrots."

"Carrots?"

I grinned. "Carrots. Try and make her laugh. Be there, pull in Seraphina and Cyclone if you can."

"Got it. Maybe I'll wash the potatoes."

A brief chuckle, but that's all I had in me. "I'm sure Theresa has that under wraps, but you can force the issue if you'd like."

"Take Theresa on? I don't think so." She snorted. "I'll take care of your girl, boss. I care about her, too."

"I know."

We hung up, and then I texted Bailey.

Love you. With Matt today. Check in later, please.

But I knew she wouldn't. She had started not carrying her phone with her, so I handed mine to Josh when we pulled up to Naveah. I wasn't here to work, for once.

SIX

Bailey

A week later

Kash was holding me.

He was kissing me. I was kissing him back.

Then he was sliding inside, and I stopped wanting to cry.

Another week later

I was sitting on the couches by the bowling lanes.

Seraphina shrieked with laughter and fell to the floor just as she let loose the bowling ball. It went right into the gutter, but she turned her face toward Tony—Matt's dickhead friend Tony. He had said something that made her laugh, and he was laughing, too. He held a hand down, helping her stand back up.

They were both chuckling as they returned to the couches.

I didn't like that, for some reason. I didn't know why.

I noted who else was there.

Friends. Guy. Chester. Torie. Tamara. Melissa was on the end, tucked next to Matt, who was whispering into her ear.

I frowned at that. I thought that was done with?

Then I felt the absence beside me and looked. Where was Kash?

There he was. He was coming back into the room, putting his phone away. He looked up, meeting my gaze, and he faltered in his step.

He smiled, then frowned, his head cocked to the side.

Three weeks later . . . or maybe four?

"She needs to go back to counseling! This is enough."

I was awake and sitting in an office. That was Peter, yelling on the other side of the door.

"No, she doesn't." That was Kash.

It was dark, with no lights on in here. The glow of the light from their side shone under the door.

"Bailey?"

A whisper from the side and I turned. Seraphina was pushing open a different door, peering in, biting her lip.

"I'm here." I waved her over, patting the couch beside me. I had a blanket. I didn't know why it was there but it was, and I lifted up an end of it. "Come cuddle with your sister."

She'd taken a step toward me, her eyes worried, still chewing on her lip. Her hands were twisted around each other, but at my last suggestion, her eyes lit up. She stopped biting her lip, and her hands came free from each other. "Yeah?" She grinned, almost literally brightening up the room.

"Yeah." I could smile. I noticed it then. It didn't hurt my cheeks, and when she slipped under my blanket, I drew her to me.

I liked this.

Kash had my back on the other side of the door. I wasn't worried, and I had my little sister in my arms.

My shoulders seemed a little lighter.

Five weeks later

I was straddling Kash.

My legs around his waist.

He was sitting up against the bed's headboard, his hand to my neck, and he angled his head, taking my mouth harder. He was thrusting up into me. I was riding him. My hands were bracing against the headboard behind him.

It was hot.

Everything was buzzing.

Good. Not good.

I was—I was writhing. I was needing.

I was feeling.

Then I was screaming and I was climaxing, and my body began shaking.

My body wouldn't stop shaking.

I was crying.

Kash was holding me, cradling me to his chest.

I was lying down.

He was smoothing back my hair.

He was whispering to me, telling me he loved me.

I felt safe in his arms.

Loved.

Warm.

I didn't want to feel warm.

Why didn't I want to feel warm again?

Six weeks later

Kash

She was waking up.

I could tell. It was small, but it was significant. A little bit, every day.

I was the only one who noticed. No, that wasn't true. Seraphina had noticed. She was smiling more around Bailey, drawn to her, reaching for her hand and hugging her more often.

That was good.

And one night at the dinner table, Bailey turned to me, tears in her eyes, and asked, "Do you know where my laptop is?"

Matt dropped his fork. It clattered on his plate.

Seraphina gasped.

Marie had been pouring some milk into Cyclone's glass and cursed. "Dios!"

Cyclone looked up, squinting at Bailey.

Peter's eyes filled with tears. His hand covered his mouth.

I smiled back at her. "I'll get it for you after dinner."

She smiled back. "Thank you."

She was waking up.

SEVEN

Bailey

Holy fucking hell, my chest hurt.

I woke and everything hurt. Everything *ached*.

My eyeballs. My arms. The hairs on my fingers. The nails on my toes. Even the nuclei in my cells. They were pounding in agony.

I jerked upright and I gasped for breath, bending over, my hands clutching at my chest.

Christ.

I felt like I was having a heart attack.

God.

Jesus.

What the ever-loving fuck was happening to me?

But I knew.

The bed was empty. I looked over, saw it was three in the morning, and I was having so many different types of flashbacks all at once. I was panting and gritting my teeth just to get through wave after wave of slicing pain. And the other flashback—the bed was empty. Kash had been here. He'd come to bed with me, so I knew he wasn't gone on another business trip. He would've woken me and told me if he had to leave last minute.

I ignored all the extra aches cutting into every orifice on my body.

Padding barefoot, I went to the bathroom and used some mouthwash super quick. Raking my fingers through my hair, I grabbed one of Kash's sweatshirts. He had these large ones that dwarfed me. I could've stopped and grabbed some pajama pants or sweats, but I kept with my sleeping shorts. His sweatshirt fell almost to my knees. It was fine. And then, without taking the time to realize my feet were cold and I should grab some socks or at least some slippers, I headed out.

I didn't recognize the night guard, but he straightened from the wall where he was positioned when I stepped into the hallway.

"Where is he?" I asked, before he could say anything.

His hands came together in front of him and he stood even taller. He nodded forward. "In the basement gym, ma'am."

Ma'am.

I grinned at that, literally hearing Chrissy chuckling next to me. *"You're just like me now, girly. Ma'am. What a hoot."*

Yeah. A hoot.

I padded past him and headed for the elevator that went past the main section of the house. Going inside, I hit the basement floor, and there were two guards waiting for me.

I paused, seeing Josh as he was eyeing me. "Don't you ever sleep?"

He grinned. "I sleep when your man sleeps."

I narrowed my eyes.

His grin deepened. "So that's rarely, ma'am."

I bared my teeth. "Don't you start with that 'ma'am' shit."

He just laughed. "Would never entertain the thought, ma—"

I growled.

He amended, still chuckling, "Bailey."

I scoffed, "Better."

If anyone had asked me last summer where the gym was on

the Chesapeake estates, I wouldn't have had a clue. I would've rolled my eyes and said something sarcastic like, *"Of course there's a gym; it's alongside the Olympic-sized pool,"* but now I knew exactly where it was, and it *was* right next to an Olympic-sized pool, though the pool was only two lanes wide. It wasn't built for playing and horsing around, not like the pool outside, which had a complete slide with it.

Heading farther toward the gym, I was shocked to not hear sounds of grunting and punching from inside. Instead, the door to the pool was open.

"He had some extra energy to work off."

I glanced sideways, not having heard Josh walking beside me. "I honestly don't think he's human."

Josh's mouth twitched. "You might be on to something, Bailey."

We came to the door and he stepped forward, checking the room before nodding for me to go ahead. I stepped inside, feeling the humidity and breathing in the chlorine before I noticed Josh shutting the door. A second later, I met his gaze through the door's window, and he gave me another polite smile before pressing a button. The window frosted over.

Looking to the corner, I saw the camera's light switch from green to red. Josh was giving us complete privacy, and only when that was all done did I seek out where Kash was.

He was at the far end, turning, flipping, and coming up a few paces away, heading my way.

I went to the edge and sat down, putting my feet in the water. I didn't have long to wait, enjoying the view as Kash's arms were cutting through the water, his shoulders and biceps bulging from the motion.

I forgot how he was a fish in water.

His head was perfectly in alignment with his shoulders, and every fourth arm swing he raised his mouth up for air and went back down. He went past me. I thought he was going to keep going, but at the last second, his hand snaked out. He latched on to my ankle and tugged me into the water.

I shrieked before I was eating chlorine. "Agh!"

He grinned, the water pulsating between us, and he maneuvered me back until I was against the pool wall. "What are you doing down here?" His eyes were alert, taking me in as he placed a hand on either side of me, trapping me.

The buoyancy kept me floating, but then Kash was moving his legs under me and I was completely resting over him. My legs straddled his, and he hooked one ankle around the other, tugging me to open even wider for him.

Heat flared in me, boiling my blood, but when I thought Kash would bend his head, finding my throat, he didn't. He moved his head back, sinking so he was on the same eye level as me, and he tugged at his sweatshirt. "Nice shirt."

I grinned, feeling a laziness intertwining with the warmth in me. "It was this or a robe. This was closer."

"Really?"

I nodded, enjoying the teasing look in his eyes. It was dark, but it was there. "Really." My voice hitched on a soft sigh with that one.

He grew sober, his head moving back so he could take me in more fully. "You look good." His eyebrows dipped down. "You look like you again." His hand moved, and he touched a wet finger beside my eye. "I see you again."

My throat swelled up, my chest filled with an ache that was bittersweet.

"Woke up."

"I can see that." His head cocked to the side, but he didn't say anything further. He was still holding me in place, and as he settled back, I knew he was waiting for me. He was waiting for whatever I was going to say or do, for whatever path I was going to put us on because that's what I felt in that moment.

I was awake.

I was angry.

I was remorseful.

And I was thinking more clearly.

I said, "I know you've been waiting for me."

That somber expression settled back on him, and his hand went back to the pool wall, trapping me in again.

"You let me mourn her, and I know that I'll always grieve my mother. I'll never forget what they did to her, what *he* did to her, but I wasn't myself. You gave me that time. You knew I would come back to me and I did. I'm here. Me. I'm ready for the next chapter."

Hunger licked my insides, lighting that fire again.

It grew, jumping up, and it was engulfing me.

I sunk down on Kash's legs, and the higher that blaze built in me, the more I wanted him. But I wanted more. I wanted blood.

"I know you've been making moves against your grandfather, but I want in. I deserve to be in now. He took her from me. I want to rip his heart out."

Kash's head lowered, his eyes still holding mine. They were growing more intense as I spoke. "I can't risk him getting his hands on you."

"He won't—"

"Yes!" His hand jerked from the pool wall but shook as he caught himself. Softening his touch, he traced a finger through my hair, following a strand and retucking it behind my ear. His eyes followed it, lingering on where he paused, his hand holding that piece of hair before he looked up to meet my gaze again. A hardness flashed there, one that I knew was in Kash, had seen in Kash, but he didn't vanquish it like he had the other times.

I saw him.

I saw behind the walls he showed to everyone else, to me, to even himself.

I was seeing the real him, and he was as hungry as I was—more, even.

My lips parted at that realization.

He couldn't have been, but no—I was thinking. I was remembering. Calhoun took both his parents from him. He had to remain hidden most of his life because of his grandfather, so in essence Calhoun had taken Kash's normalcy, his childhood, too.

Yeah. Kash wanted to kill his grandfather just as much as I did, but I didn't care. I wanted it for Chrissy. I needed it for Chrissy.

He dropped his hand to my shoulder, pushing the sweatshirt out of the way and then smoothing his hand down my arm. The sweatshirt was big enough that it trailed to my elbow, before a growl left Kash and he shifted. His other hand took hold of it from the other side and he whisked it up and off of me. It was tossed behind us and I was bare to him except for my sleeping shorts and tank top.

His hand continued its path, going over my arm, my hand. To my chest, down my chest. Lingering between my breasts. My top was nearly transparent, but the water swelled between us and he bent his head, his lips finding my shoulder at the same time that his hand pushed my top aside. He covered one of my breasts, his thumb rubbing over my nipple.

He moved in, his body more firmly cementing me against the wall, and I felt his heat. It melded with mine. "He can't touch you." He lifted his head, moving to my other shoulder, trailing to my throat. "He can't hurt you. He can't have you."

My whole body shivered, and I closed my eyes, my head falling back.

His mouth moved up my throat, lingering on my jawline before sweeping to rest just over my mouth. I opened my eyes, my eyelids heavy. I was aching for him, but I was also crying on the inside. There was such agony intertwined with what he was doing to me, what he was making me feel, how much I wanted him.

His lips pressed down and he breathed into me. "He can't

take you away from me." His hand closed over my hips, tugging me firmly into him. "I won't let him." His hands came up to cradle my neck, the side of my face. His thumb moved over my cheek, holding me for him, and he raised his head. His eyes lifted, meeting mine, holding mine. He looked as haunted as me, tortured, but there was a fierceness in him that took my breath away. "I will never let him near you. Ever." His hand started shaking, holding me captive, and he closed his eyes.

He was done.

I felt it.

He ground against me, my breath hitching at feeling how hard he was.

I always knew Kash had darkness in him. I always knew he was furious inside, but there was an animal in him. Or a monster in him, one created because of his relation to Calhoun, maybe. He had never let me see that side of him, but he was out now. The monster was before me, half unhinged but also in complete control, and his entire body was shaking in his urgency to remain in control.

I didn't want his control.

I hated his control, and I wanted to push him over the edge. I suddenly thirsted for it, desperate for it, and my legs locked around his waist.

Before he could do anything, I shoved a hand between us and pulled him out. My hand wrapped around him once, rubbing him. I lifted my hips. My shorts were whisked off, and I sank down, sheathing us together.

He cursed, reacting instantly. His mouth was on mine, hard.

Our movements weren't coordinated after that. There was too much rawness and realness brimming to the top. I commanded him. He demanded me. His thrusts were rough, almost violent, but it's what I wanted. It's what I needed. It sent me spinning, feeling alive, and I was gasping for breath as he continued fucking me.

He crushed me against the wall.

I knew there'd be abrasions over my skin from the pool side. I. Did. Not. Care.

I only felt him.

The climax tore through me, making me feel as if I broke my back with its force, and I cried out, my mouth tearing from his. A scream erupted from my throat, and then more, as Kash wasn't done. He grabbed my hips and stood, carrying me farther into the shallow end of the pool, which had a gradual slope in and out. He moved until we were almost out of the pool, then covered my entire body with his. I had to grab ahold of the pool side to hold my head up so I could get air, but then his mouth was on mine and it didn't matter.

Nothing mattered.

Then again, when I was with him like this, nothing much mattered anyway.

After he came, roaring, his body stiffening, jerking, I ran a hand down his back. It was meant to be soothing, but he knocked it aside. "No," he growled, his mouth opening over mine once again. And just like that, I was swept up again.

I grew aware of a door opening, closing.

Something was covering me, warming me.

A beep.

We were moving.

Another beep.

Someone coughed.

Feet were shuffling.

Then a door opening, and a voice saying, "Do I ask?"

Even half asleep, I heard my brother's tone. He was amused, but there was a hint of concern there, too.

Kash's arms tightened around me, his voice sounding from just above where my head was resting against his arm. "Do I ask about you, too? I know you just got home."

We were moving past Matt, so I tried to open one eye. I saw movement. He was straightening, but then we were past him.

His voice came from behind us, and sounded tired. "Let's just say I'm thinking we both needed to work out some demons to-night."

Kash stopped, his arms becoming like cement. He turned and ground out, "You didn't."

Matt just laughed in response. It was harsh and caustic sound-ing. "Don't throw stones, Kash. We're all a little dark inside. God's sakes, I know you are."

"It's not the same thing."

"Yeah." Matt sighed, his voice growing faint. "Just don't hurt my sister, okay? I'm not meaning in the bedroom, either."

A door closed after that.

Kash remained still before his chest rose, lifting me in its move-ments, and his head bent. He murmured against my ear, "Go to sleep. Your brother's okay."

That was enough.

My eyelids cemented closed, and I woke once more to bed-sheets and a hard body curling behind mine. It was like heaven.

TRIAL SET TO START FOR QUINN FRANCIS

Quinn Francis, who has reverted back to her maiden name, Callas, is set to begin trial this coming Tuesday. Her defense team is ready and eager to prove Ms. Callas's innocence.

"Miss Callas was wrongfully convicted. She is the victim of a series of complex and interweaving false narratives being spoken from the entire Francis family. She's better off away from them, even in her particular setting. She would take being charged with kidnapping and attempted murder over remaining in that household, and that says everything."

More to come for this story.

—*Inside Daily Press*

EIGHT

Bailey

I had lost time.

I know, I know. I was grieving. I had to mourn. But seriously. I. Lost. Time.

Kash was so far ahead of me, and I hated that. I woke the next morning when he was already at work.

"Whatcha thinking about?"

I started, my knee slammed up against the table.

Ah. Crap.

I scrambled, reaching, but nope. There went my coffee. It spilled over the entire breakfast table.

"Crap, crap, crap." I reached for some napkins, throwing them over the pile of hot liquid, and began dabbing. I was trying to smash that liquid with a fervor like no other.

Matt was frowning next to me. "Uh. Bailey?"

I almost had all the coffee soaked up. "Huh?"

"You've got half that mug running down your chest."

I looked down, and that's when the sizzling seeped through. I screamed, running from the table. "Crap-shit-shoot crap-shit-shoot crap-shit-shoot—"

"Okay." A wet washcloth smacked me in the center of my chest.

A strong hand was behind it, and I looked up to Marie's frowning face. Her other hand was on my shoulder, holding me firm as she soaked up the rest of the coffee from me. She moved me back into my chair, but in a whole gentle way that was authoritative at the same time. "Relax. Your coffee was lukewarm, if even."

Theresa came into the dining area and circled around. She ducked her head, laughing, her shoulders shaking. "Never dull around the Francis family, that's certainly true."

Matt threw her a cocky smirk, picking up his own coffee and pulling out a flask from his pocket. He uncapped it, pouring some booze into his coffee, and said, as he recapped and returned it, "And that's why we love you both and you put up with us."

Marie grunted, taking the washcloth from my chest. Most of the coffee had been absorbed into it, and Marie was right. I touched my chest. The sizzling had been the sound of sausage being fried from the kitchen. I gave her a sheepish look, sinking back in my seat. "Thanks, Marie. You're a chest saver."

Theresa started laughing, putting down a plate of toast and returning to the kitchen. "That's a new one I've never heard my mama called."

Marie was trying to look at me all stern-like, but at her daughter's joke, her eyes warmed and she couldn't keep half of her mouth from curving up in a grin.

A wave of jealousy washed through me.

It was abrupt and powerful, enough that it wiped everything out of me. A tear filled my eye, but I kept it back and looked down to my lap.

God.

I wanted that back.

Mom and daughter. In the same house. Teasing comments. A mother's pride at just hearing her daughter sounding happy. I wanted it, so bad.

I was biting my lip.

I was tired of crying. I was tired of being a zombie. I wanted to live again. I wanted to move forward, keep going, and damn it, that's what I was doing. And I was starting with eating a god-damn good breakfast. After that, I announced, "I'm going to Hawking today."

Conversation stopped.

Okay, there hadn't been much of a conversation going. Matt was on his phone, and he looked up. Marie was pouring some orange juice into two glasses and put the pitcher down, proba-bly more because both glasses were full, but still. The thought counted here.

I was counting it.

I looked between the two, not having a clue what day it was, what time it was, or where anyone except Kash was, but I said it again for dramatic effect. "I'm going to reenroll and finish my studies." I picked up the orange juice glass that Marie had put in front of me. "It's time."

Matt lifted an eyebrow. He and Marie exchanged a look be-fore he sat up in his chair. "You sure?"

"I'm sure." I gave Marie another sheepish grin. "This is really good orange juice."

She just frowned at me.

Matt coughed, leaning back in his chair. "I'll come with you today."

I looked at him. "Huh?"

"Today. School. You're going in to reenroll, right? Talk to them. I'd imagine there'd need to be some form of meeting, since they gave you extended leave from your studies." He shrugged, picking up his coffee. "I'll go with you. Team Batt." He winked, taking a sip.

Marie was looking between the two of us. "I agree with that idea. Matt will go with you. Team Batt . . ."

Matt just laughed. "You've no clue what that means."

She went past him to the kitchen, and as she did, she raised her hand, making a motion like she was going to smack the back of his head. She didn't actually hit him, but Matt followed her, turning his head so he could see her. Noting her implication, he just chuckled, and then he called out, "Fitzy!"

Fitz, my bodyguard-slash-driver, stepped in from the other hallway. "I heard."

Matt narrowed his eyes at my security guard, raising his coffee again. "I'm assuming you know what to do."

The subtext was to let Kash know my decision and probably to set in motion letting whoever else needed to know about my reentry into school, but I kept quiet about my other plans. For those, I figured it worked out best if Matt was the one coming with me, and not Kash himself.

"Okay." Matt saluted me with his coffee, right before he finished drinking it. "Meet you out front in twenty minutes?"

I nodded, reaching for and then downing my orange juice as he got up, going to his room.

It *was* really good orange juice.

NINE

Bailey

Turns out, it was a Wednesday and smack in the first week of February, so that meant classes were a go. That also meant my advisor thought I was nuts. She said it herself. Ms. Wells shook her head but went to work on her computer. "Okay. Are you sure you want to take last semester's finals this week, and then also try to catch up?"

"Yes."

I was firm. I was adamant.

She stopped typing and looked over my shoulder to where Matt was standing. He shuffled over, coming to sit next to me. He shrugged, shaking his head, and folded his arms over his chest. "She woke up with a mission today. Don't look at me to talk sense into her. She's the genius, not me."

"Have you—Was this run by your, er, Mr. Colello?"

I flushed. "I don't need permission from my boyfriend to start school again."

"I called him and he wasn't surprised by this turn of events. He said if she wants to learn, let her learn," Matt said, as if I hadn't spoken.

I heard another tone in his voice and slid my eyes sideways, but he wasn't looking at me. His gaze was firmly locked on my advisor's and the two seemed to be reading each other's minds. She confirmed this a second later. "Uh-huh. I see."

Typing it up, she handed me a note to take down to the registrar's office, and after we did that, I was reenrolled. Classes started tomorrow. Which, crap, I didn't have my books. But going through my list, I saw that only two required a textbook. The rest were online, and I smacked Matt's chest as we were walking through campus. "We gotta run by the school store fast."

Matt grunted, his chest deflating a second. "Ouch. You hit hard, woman. And what are you talking about?" He took my class list out of my hands, reading it. "MIS 545 Operations Management. MIS 516 Security Risk Management." He read my other two classes and frowned, absentmindedly rubbing where I'd hit him. "Just the titles of your courses give me a migraine. I don't get how you, Cy, and Dad are into this, and that you guys almost salivate over it." He handed the paper back to me. "You guys are super nerds. Not just nerds; *super* nerds."

I snatched it away. "Well, don't get your panties in a bunch. I've got a feeling you've got super nerd powers of your own, just haven't found 'em yet."

Matt threw his head back and laughed. "You serious?"

I frowned.

Fitz was walking ahead of us, and one of Matt's guards was behind us. We had two others covering us, but walking far away so students wouldn't automatically associate them with us. It didn't matter anymore. I was past wanting to be invisible. This was how life was going to be. Guards. People would recognize us, but as we were going back to my usual building, I realized that only a few people had paid attention to us. And even those people had just stopped, stared, frowned, and then continued on.

A few were glancing at Fitz and the other guards, but it wasn't the spectacle of last semester.

As if following my thoughts, Matt said, "We're old news."

"What?"

He gestured around us, his hands sliding into his back pockets. "You're looking around, right? Noticing no one noticing us?"

"Yeah."

He inclined his head. "We're old news. You've been gone, mourning your mom, and Kash isn't letting anyone take his picture. There was a spread of him and me at Naveah a while back, but you've gone to ground and so has he. People moved on. Some celebrity posted an image of himself and you could see his dick. Everyone was in an uproar about it."

Well.

That was nice.

Felt nice.

Normal.

And I was almost crying, because it was reminding me of a time before the first kidnapping attempt.

That was making me think of Chrissy, and yeah. No "almost" anymore. Huge tears were rolling down my face.

Matt looked over and cursed under his breath. "Come here." He put an arm around my shoulders and pulled me into him. We kept walking, but I was half tucked under my brother's arm, and by the time we got to my building, the size of the tears had shrunk. He patted my arm. "There you go. Look at you, learning the Francis way and getting in control of your robot side."

I laughed.

The tears were almost gone as Fitz held the doors for us and we stepped through. I used the backs of my hands to wipe my eyes clean.

That's when we ran into Hoda, my on-and-off nemesis from school.

Who used to work at Naveah, and who was the one to release an image of Kash and me in a compromising position. That Hoda.

Who was friends with our blogger nemesis.

I had a lot of nemeses.

She was coming out of an office, looking down at her phone.

Matt stopped and frowned. "Hey, isn't that—"

Hoda's head whipped up, saw us. Her eyes went wide, and she tried to go back into the office she'd just left.

"Hey!" I zipped out from under Matt's arms.

Hoda was still scrambling for the doorknob.

"Hey!" I grabbed her arm just as she got it open and started to go through.

I pulled her back out.

"What are you doing?" That was me, in her face. I was more confused, though. I thought we'd been okay before.

"Sorry." She moved aside, but she still seemed agitated. "I don't know why I did that."

Matt raised an eyebrow. "Conditioned response?" He flashed a cocky grin. "Makes me feel good that you instantly fear us." He smoothed a hand down his chest. "We're doing something right."

I stifled a grin.

Hoda glared at Matt. "So not funny." She looked at me. "And I am sorry. I was just, uh—" She realized she was still holding her phone, and she looked at it. Her face got beet red. Her hand jerked; she started to put it in her pocket.

Matt swooped in, plucking it out of her hand. "What's this?" He began reading her screen, then stopped abruptly.

Everything changed.

His slightly joking demeanor vanished and the air grew charged.

The hairs on the back of my neck stood up, right as he lifted his deadly serious and stormy eyes, locking on Hoda. "You want to explain this shit?"

She ducked her head, heaving a long dramatic breath. "Damn."

"Yeah," Matt clipped out. "Damn." He went back to the phone, clicking through it.

"Hey!" She tried for it. "That's private property."

He held it out of her reach, backtracking. "Not when you're texting with our enemy." He looked at me, gesturing to Hoda with his head. "She's still hanging out with Camille Story."

Camille Story, the blogger nemesis on whom we *still* needed to exact revenge, because she'd done all sorts of bad stuff against us.

"Good!"

He frowned at me.

Hoda twitched, doing a double take at my gush. "What?"

"Yeah." Matt's eyebrows pinched together, and he threw Hoda a scowl. "What?"

"No. That works out." I took the phone from him.

"Hey—hey!"

I moved away from Hoda, shrugging her off, and Matt stepped in, blocking her.

Hoda was *still* talking to Camille.

Hoda was *still* in a good relationship with her.

I read over their exchanges. It was normal messages between friends. Venting. Excited exclamations. Some OMGs and *Oh God!*s. They talked about guys. Whoa. Wait. They were talking about *Liam.* I threw Hoda a frown. "You have a thing for Liam?"

Liam was the jock nerd in our class.

He wasn't really a nerd, but he was a jock, and we're all big computer people, so the phrase stuck.

Her face was bright red now.

She was up against the wall, but Matt was still blocking her from leaving. She made a grab for her phone. Matt simply didn't let her move. She moved one way, he was right there in front of her. She went another way, he moved that way, too. He was enjoying that a bit too much, and Hoda threw him a dark look before falling back against the wall in defeat. "Yes. I mean, yeah. And he and I are going to move in together. It was his suggestion."

"*His suggestion?*" Matt's eyebrows arched high. "Did you hypnotize him one night or something?"

She flushed again, but by this point it was getting hard to tell. "No! Not that it's any of your business, but I can't stand Camille. That's me holding up my end of our promise." She turned to point at me. "You said you'd close out all the spying on me if I got you in her room. I tried, I really did, but she's so pretentious. I can't stand living with her. She's horrible. I'm allowed five times to use the bathroom and I can only use it for fifteen minutes in the morning, to get ready for the day. I have to sneak a shower after she leaves the apartment, and I swear she's got cameras inside the place, because she always gives me this look like she knows I showered. But she can't call me on it because then I'd question how she knew, because I wipe down every single time!"

She rolled her eyes, her hands going into her hair and fisting both sides before letting them drop back down. "So, yeah. That's me being fake, and I reacted because it was just instinct. *No!*" She slapped a hand to Matt's chest. "That does not mean I instantly fear you. I, just, I don't know. Wait!" She stopped, realization and horror coming to her face. Her mouth dropped before she caught herself. "Oh my God. Your mom. You're here. What are you doing here?" She was scanning my face, studying me more intently. "You look good. You look like yourself again."

Matt snorted.

She threw him another scowl. "You're really annoying. Has anyone told you that?"

"Just Kash, usually. And that's because I annoy him on purpose." The cocky smirk was back. He was giving her bedroom eyes. "If a chick calls me annoying, it's because she wants me but doesn't want to admit she wants me." He leaned against the wall. "How about it? You want me?"

Her phone buzzed in my hands.

Liam: Are we still on for the apartment?

I answered for her. "Uh, no. Remember." I showed Matt the phone. "She's got a thing for Liam."

He read the text, but his smirk didn't lessen. "The guy's in for a world of hurt."

She cursed, grabbing the phone this time. "You guys are both horrible human beings," she replied, then remembered. "Oh, shit. I didn't really mean that about you, Bailey. Just him." She threw Matt a look.

I didn't care.

I waited until she was done texting with Liam and had put the phone away, giving Matt a cautious look before sliding it all the way into her pocket. Once she was done, her shoulders straightened. She looked relieved.

"Great! Now we're going to go and get a drink somewhere and you're going to tell us all about Camille Story," I said.

She paled. "I am?"

I moved forward, linking my arm with hers. "Yep, and then we're going to figure out a way for you to get her out of her apartment and us into it. And we're doing it tonight."

"Tonight?"

Turns out Hoda sucked at being a spy.

She didn't know anything about Camille Story, aka Matt's obsessive past reject, aka psycho stalker of the world. I always thought Hoda was smart. She certainly had proclaimed herself to be in the past. But sitting across from her and taking in everything she could report on Camille Story, I had two theories—

she was either incredibly real-life stupid or she was lying to us. Based on the fear on her face and the loathing that flared in her eyes when she talked about her current roommate, I was going with option A.

She was just real-life dumb.

I leaned forward, my hand on the table. There were three drinks between us. "You suck at this type of work."

She flushed again. And this time I could tell, because she had settled back, her body returning to her normal color. She rolled her eyes, shoving back against her chair, and folded her arms over her chest. "I didn't exactly sign up to join the CIA with this job. I was bitter and jealous."

Matt grinned, picking up his whiskey. "See where that got you?"

Her eyes narrowed at him, and if looks could kill, Matt would've been a pile of dust, and *whoosh*, the wind would've swept him clean already.

He didn't care. "So let's get this straight. She reached out to you because you hated my adorable sister for a time." He bumped his shoulder next to mine.

Hoda's look of death lessened. It was more a look of injury now. "Yes, and I'm fully aware now how stupid I was."

Matt's eyes were twinkling. "Say it again."

She made a disgruntled growl before looking at me. "Can you shut him up? Why is he here?"

I opened my mouth.

Matt threw an arm around my shoulders, raising his chin up in pride. "We're Team Batt."

I closed my mouth. That pretty much said it all.

Hoda's eyes flicked harder to the ceiling. "Whatever. Look, I'm aware she worked me, because she did. She knows all about me and I learned nothing about her."

"How could you live in someone's place with them for months and not learn anything about that person?"

Matt was musing, but he was right.

Unless . . . "But she did."

They both looked at me.

"Think about it. You said she had no pictures on her walls?"

Hoda nodded.

I kept on. "That says she either doesn't like pictures or she doesn't have anyone close to her. Did people call her? Did it sound like she made plans to go out with friends or talk to people on the phone?"

Hoda thought about it, then shrugged. "She likes pictures. I know that's not the case. I did get a glimpse into her back room once and it was a mess. There were magazines everywhere, and the wall was plastered with them."

"With magazines?"

She answered Matt. "Yeah. I mean, she cut them out, but it was a brief glance. The door shut right away, but it reminded me of my high school locker when I was a freshman. I had a crush on Justin Bieber that wasn't healthy. Now it's more BTS. I've progressed."

Matt groaned, his head dropping to his hand. He rubbed at his forehead. "I didn't need to know that. Neither of us needed to know that."

"Whatever." Hoda's word and tone didn't match. She sat back, her shoulders loosening. She looked refreshed, relieved. She reached for her mojito and finished it, circling her straw around it. "This was good. I want another one."

Gah.

That was it. Everything was off her chest, and she was now feeling good about it.

I frowned. She still had one more thing to do for us. "Who does Camille like?"

"Besides Quinn?" Her shoulders grew tight again, just not as much as before. She darted a look at Matt. "I mean, your stepmother. I know she likes her, because that's the only call she takes. She'll gab for hours on the phone with her, but that's in her room. I've tried eavesdropping to hear what they say, but she's got her voice muffled inside there. It's like she has on a fan or something. The room's not soundproof, because I can still hear her in there."

"They talk for hours?" Matt asked, sounding in pain. "I don't even want to imagine what that bitch is saying to her."

Hoda was nodding. "She is a bitch, but make no mistake, Camille is smart, and cunning, and she's got the right amount of stalker tendencies to make her dangerous."

Matt's lips thinned.

I was pretty sure that's not who he meant.

"Yeah." He grunted. He tossed back the rest of his whiskey and looked up.

The waitress appeared out of nowhere, and I didn't want to wonder if she was just watching for him to ask for another or if she'd been going past us. Knowing my brother, knowing how he was with girls, it was probably the first choice.

The server took the glass from him and asked, all sugary sweet and in a sultry tone, "Want another?"

Matt's grin was slow back, slow and sly. "Make it a double, please?"

"Sure thing."

As soon as she was gone, he turned to Hoda. "Who does Camille have a thing for? We need to get her out of that room for a long period of time."

Hoda's mouth pressed tight together, and she visibly swallowed.

I inclined my head. "Who is it, Hoda?"

She squeaked, motioning to Matt. "It's still him. I mean, she doesn't come out and say it, but I know she's still got a thing for him." Her eyes went sideways for a beat before she refocused on us. Sitting up straight, as if coming to a decision, she continued. "Quinn only calls her Friday nights, and on Monday or Tuesday. So she wouldn't call her tonight. I could call Camille, tell her that I went out with a friend and we saw Matt here." She looked uncertain, her head almost lowering, the more she offered.

Matt was thoughtful, his head cocking to the side. "It'd have to be somewhere that Kash or my father don't own. If I'm in a Kash bar, she won't come in." He tipped his chin to her. "What friend would you be with?"

"Oh." She frowned. "Oh! I could call Liam. I could just say I want to talk some more about moving in together, iron out more details. He'd come. He's always down for a beer."

"And what? Bailey breaks in by herself? I don't like it."

Hoda's eyes were wide, skirting between us. "I don't know what else would work. It has to be you, and you have to be alone. If you're with someone else, she won't come."

"You didn't say that before."

"Because I just thought about that." She leaned over the table. "But I'll be there. Liam will be there. We'll have your back."

Matt was shaking his head. "Nope. That leaves Bailey unprotected."

Hoda's head turned and she looked from Fitz to Matt's guard, both positioned near us. "But how? She won't be *alone* alone. She'll have that guy; he's always around her. And I'm sure another guy will come."

I sighed.

I understood Matt's reluctance, but I had just woken up. This needed to be done and the time was now. Camille Story was connected to Quinn, and Quinn was connected to Calhoun. Kash wouldn't let me go with him on a trip against Calhoun, but this was here. This was local. This was me getting inside a room, and then inside a computer system. That was my wheelhouse.

It needed to be done, and I could see that Hoda wanted to be released from the hold I had on her accounts. I got it. I understood.

"I'll call Kash."

Hoda's eyebrows snapped up, all the way to her hairline. But she didn't say anything. She grabbed her drink and sucked down some of her ice.

Matt threw a quick scowl my way. "Like he'll allow you to do this. Come on. Team Batt. I should be going in that room with you, not Kash."

"You know it won't work if you're there. You're the bait. You have to draw her out and keep her out so I have time to get in and hack her, too."

He swore, low and dark and under his breath, all the while still glaring at me. "I do not like this plan."

"I'll tell Kash."

He snorted. "No, you won't. Kash won't let you anywhere near that apartment, and you know it. You continuing to say you'll call him is a load of bullshit. Who are you going to actually call?"

Well. Crap. He just called my bluff.

Another snort from him. "Like I don't know my sister by now. I know you, B. And you've got the Chrissy Hayes look in you."

That made me smile. It made me tear up, but the smile overshadowed the rest. I could handle the smile, and he was right. This was a total Chrissy Hayes move.

"I'll . . . I'll call . . ." Crap. Who could I call? He was right about Kash.

"You can't call Torie; she'll tell Kash. You can't call Tamara without Torie finding out. You can't call your friend Melissa, the cute little one. She'll faint at just the mention of breaking and entering. You need someone who's good at getting in places, who won't think twice about any of it, and who'll keep their damn mouth shut."

I blinked. "Who?"

He grinned, another one of those slow, spreading ones, and the hairs on the back of my neck stood right up. "I know someone."

TEN

Bailey

Tony.

I braked going around the corner to where Camille Story had her lair.

Tony?

"You're kidding me!"

Tony Cottweiler was one of Matt's friends, the wealthy asshole friend who liked to get away with any sort of sexual act while sitting next to me in their booth. That Tony.

I was instantly growling.

He grinned, leaning one shoulder against the wall, and slid his hands into his pockets. He was dressed for the job. All black. Black jeans. Black shoes. I noticed they were the ones Seraphina was raving about, since they weren't in stores yet, and he had on a black thermal shirt under a black leather jacket.

"What are you doing after this? Going straight to Naveah?"

His hair was even messily rumpled, and grrr . . . I wasn't happy about this change, not one bit.

He laughed, rubbing a hand over his jaw. "Man. Your reaction right there was more than enough to do this. Matt promised me you'd be pissed, but I think I just got a hard-on."

"Gross."

His shoulders kept shaking in laughter, but he grew somber a second later when Fitz came around the corner. Tony straightened from the wall. "What?" He motioned behind me. "We can't break into an apartment when you have a guard with you."

I looked over my shoulder.

Fitz hadn't spoken a word when we made up the plan or left for the plan, and now we were here to activate the plan. Not one word. I should've been worried about that, but I was also not in the mindset to look a gift horse in the mouth.

I just shrugged. "He won't say anything."

Tony let out a long, dramatic curse. "*Are you kidding me?* He probably called Kash while you guys were figuring out this whole plan in the first place."

I looked at Fitz. "Did you?"

He just looked down at me, not a blink.

I groaned.

Tony cursed again. "Fuck!"

Well, crappers.

I took a breath. "How long do we have?"

Now he talked. And he blinked. "Seven minutes, if even."

Tony pushed farther away from the wall, stalking over. "Is Kash coming himself?"

Fitz swung his head to Tony, but he was done talking. He had fulfilled his daily minimum apparently.

Tony flicked his eyes upward, his hand going to the back of his neck before he motioned to me. "I'm getting you in, then I'm taking off. I don't want to be here when Colello shows up. He'll rip me to pieces."

He turned, leading the way to Camille's door, and took out a set of keys.

I eyed him, trailing behind. "Do you do this often? Is that why Matt sent you?"

"What?"

I motioned from him to the door, and to his keys. "Breaking and entering. You do this often?"

He laughed. "My dad owns this building. Matt sent me because I have a universal key to every apartment and door."

Oh.

Oh!

Well, then. "Guess we're not really breaking and entering, then?"

"No, we are. I have no right to enter her apartment when she's renting it, but I know the security guys. Got 'em to turn off the cameras for the next three hours." He inserted the key. It fit. He paused and looked at me. "I mean it. I was going to stick around and wait, but if Lethal Boy Toy is on his way, no way am I sticking around."

"Seraphina has a crush on you."

He almost fell into the wall from my words. His eyes went wide. "And? A lot of chicks have crushes on me."

"She's too young for you."

"No shit." His face was clouding over, becoming more stormy as I kept on. "Why do you feel the need to make this an issue? I'm not into kiddie porn, if you get my drift."

"You're not a good idea."

His mouth opened and an aghast mewl came from him before he jerked his hand up. Keys dangled from his fingers and he raised them higher. "You wanna rethink pissing me off? I have one more door to open for you."

I narrowed my eyes. I wasn't intimidated by him one bit, and I stepped into his space. He was taller than me, so my head had to angle up, but I was hoping to make up for the fierceness of it with my words and by closing my eyes almost to slits.

"I remember the sex house party. You had girls jerk you off with me sitting next to you, knowing I couldn't leave the booth. You got a blowjob beside that same booth minutes earlier, and I might've been in a grief zombie state, but

I clicked back to the present. I saw you making Seraphina laugh at bowling."

His eyes were blazing, but he kept his mouth shut.

I kept on. "I don't want her to romanticize you. I get if you were just being nice, but she's young. She's impressionable." I half cringed because I could hear Chrissy Hayes speaking through me. "But you know she has a crush on you. Don't encourage it. That's all I'm asking."

His anger lessened as I spoke. His jaw wasn't as tight and his scowl eased. He was almost thoughtful by the end. He didn't respond right away, taking the time to rub his jaw once before letting a soft curse slip free. He turned, going through the apartment.

It was a simple layout.

Kitchen and dining room on our right. Living room straight ahead. Going past the living room, there was the bathroom. Two bedroom doors beyond. I noted the pile of blankets folded at the end of the couch. That must've been where Hoda stayed.

Tony tested one doorknob. Locked.

He tested the other; it opened to a bedroom.

Door number one it was.

Fitting his key into the doorknob, he paused before opening it. "If she's as anal as Matt suggested, she'll probably have an alarm on the other side of this door. You prepared for that?"

I wasn't too knowledgeable about door alarms or security alarms, but I had my backpack of gadgets. I hoisted it tighter on my back. "I'll improvise."

He scanned my face. "Right." A beat. Then, "And I hear you about Seraphina. I won't encourage it. That's my good deed for karma."

I cocked an eyebrow up. "*This* isn't your good deed?"

He flashed me a grin. "Matt owes me a surfing trip for this. We're taking your dad's jet next weekend." He opened the door, and a blaring horn pierced the air right afterward.

"Okay. My job's done. Lock up behind you if you don't get caught."

I didn't watch him leave but I heard the door shut. A second later, as I had pulled my bag off my back and was rifling through it, Fitz moved around me. He went to a plastic box set next to the doorframe.

"What are you—"

I stopped talking. It was pointless.

He took a knife out, jimmied open the box, and yanked out a cord. Lovely silence filled the room next.

"Thanks." I wasn't going to question him on how he knew to do that, either. Only made sense that security guards Kash employed would have special breaking and entering skills. I had a feeling they had a whole lot more skills to go with that—more than normal guards would have.

"She could've rigged that to send an alarm to her phone. I'll call Matt, see if he can play distraction from her phone, too." He motioned to her computer. "I'd get working on that ASAP, because even though I don't like Tony, he wasn't wrong about Kash. He'll be here in three minutes, and he's pissed." He paused. "At both of us."

He stepped back, his phone in hand, and I hurried to Camille's computer.

ELEVEN

Kash

Camille Story's building didn't have an elevator, and she lived on the fifth floor. I took two to three steps at a time, loping up. Josh was right behind me; so were a couple others. Fitz knew we were coming. He had called it in, and instead of reporting what was happening, he just put me on a different channel.

I listened to the entire conversation.

Fitz asked later for my orders, but I told him to let Bailey proceed. I intended to get here before she got inside, but I hadn't counted on Matt calling in the building owner's son, who would have a key and would have no qualm letting Bailey illegally enter an apartment. A call to their security staff reassured me that Tony had thought ahead and had the feeds pulled, so at least there'd be no record of Bailey even being present.

Fitz was waiting for us in the hallway when we topped the last set of stairs.

He jerked his head backward. "She's inside, doing her thing." He closed his mouth at the end, and I stopped.

I waited.

He looked at me, his eyes darting inside.

I grunted. "Say whatever you got to say."

"She needs this."

His words came swift and without hesitation once I gave him the go-ahead.

I settled farther back on my heels. "Explain."

I was pretty certain I knew, but these guys were around us almost twenty-four/seven. They got time to sleep. We had the eight-hour shift set in place, but sometimes they chose to stay, and they did that because they worried, because they were almost family by now.

Just before Chrissy's murder, I had started to wean some of Bailey's regular guards and use them myself because their skill sets fit my purposes better for the path I was taking against Calhoun. But Fitz was one I kept on Bailey. He was one of her main guys. I trusted Fitz. He was good at his job, and his leadership was outstanding.

He was also a professional, and that meant a lot of his personal opinions, as with most of my men, were kept to themselves. So, hearing and seeing him wanting to express his own thoughts now, I was not foolish enough to not want to hear them. I welcomed it.

"I know you probably know what I'm going to say. She's awake again. That light went out after her mother died. It's been gone, but it's back, and the more she planned with Matt and the other one, the more that light grew. She needs to be a part of this fight, not on the sidelines. She needs it on a vital human level, and that's all I'm saying." A beat. "Other than to say, it's really nice to see her back again." He inclined his head. "I'm done now."

That meant I'd put the right guy on her.

I nodded and clapped him on the arm. "After this, you'll be getting a hell of a promotion."

He blinked a few times. "That's not why—"

"I know."

Josh and the others had already bypassed us, setting in motion their jobs, but I headed for the back door.

I could hear her.

The door was left ajar just an inch. It wasn't latched, but it was still closed for some privacy.

I opened the door and waited, taking her in, and it was just as Fitz said, but more. I doubted he had stepped back to watch her work. If he had, I would've gotten more of a speech. No, no. He said what he did because he saw her planning, but this, seeing her bending over, frowning, squinting at the computer like it was her personal opponent in backgammon, would've hit him in the same way but on steroids.

She was breathtaking.

Her hair was falling forward, and she wasn't tucking it back. That said she was more than distracted. She was obsessed.

Curses were falling from her mouth.

Her back was arched over.

Her fingers were typing like lightning over the keyboard, and she had pulled up her own laptop. It was plugged in. She was alternating between Camille's system and her own, back and forth, back and forth.

Then she was back to the main system. Her hand on the mouse. She was clicking through screens so fast that I couldn't make out what each screen was about. Clicking. X-ing. Bringing them back up. Cursing more.

She paused, her breath held.

She was reading, biting her lip.

Another curse, then she brought up a new screen and went back to typing like her life depended on it.

I intended to watch her a moment, then pull her away.

I couldn't do either.

I watched her and I couldn't stop.

I took in her pride, her stubbornness, her will to right the wrong—and she cared. I was remembering another time when I saw her hack, when she cared enough not to harm Seraphina, Cyclone, or Matt's accounts. She got in. She wanted to let Quinn and Peter know that she could get in, but she didn't harm them. She cared even at the start.

"You love."

She screeched and whirled around. Blood had drained from her face, but seeing me, she scrunched up her face in frustration. "No, no, no. I need more time." She wheeled back, taking a moment to press the bottom of her palms to her eyes. She lowered them, shook her head, and started back. "I need more time. This girl is crazy with her firewalls. She has like five backup systems, and I had to get them online in order to get everything from them."

I waited.

It was a minute later when she paused and looked at me. "What did you say?"

I knew where we were. I knew what she was doing. But this moment was important, so I was taking it.

I nodded at her. "I told you that you had siblings, and you loved them immediately. I gave you their files. I let you see their faces, see their names, and that was it. You sunk for them. Then I took it from you and said you'd be a stranger to them. I saw how that crushed you, but you did it anyways. You didn't cry or whine or become resentful. You didn't hate them, and you could've. Others would've. Most would, but not you. You loved them first, and you loved them pure. That never changed. You've been angry at your mother, and you were angry at Peter, and I know you were angry at me. The three of us, we could take it, but never at your siblings. You *only* loved them. You never let anything else in there when it came to them. No anger. No jealousy. Nothing. Only love."

I remained in the doorway. I knew she needed space, and I wasn't going to crowd her. I was going to do what I could to give her as much time as she needed, but I needed to tell her this much.

"It's that same love that's motivating you now. It's driving you. Marie misjudged you. Quinn insulted your upbringing. But when they did that, you knew it wasn't you being insulted. It was Chrissy, and that's what pissed you off the most, because in your core, you are all Chrissy Hayes."

Her eyes were watering. Her bottom lip started trembling.

I nodded at her. "Obliterate this bitch, because I know you're not just doing this for you, for me, for Matt. You're doing this for Chrissy." I inclined my head to her. "Thank you."

She sniffled, drawing in a deep breath. A tear fell and she wiped it away with the back of her hand.

She grinned, though it was still shaky. "You're not supposed to make me a blubbering mess."

"I'm not supposed to do anything except love, cherish, and protect you." I gestured to the computers. "Do your thing. We'll cover you until the last second."

Her eyes were clear again, locked on, focused, and when she looked back to the computer, I knew she was immune even to me being in that room. A circus could've thrown a show with elephants and she wouldn't have let them pull her concentration away.

Fitz had been on the phone with Matt, who reported that Camille Story was fast becoming drunk and that her lips were getting looser and looser as the night wore on. She'd started talking about Quinn, so Matt wasn't staying for Bailey anymore. He was staying because he hated Quinn more than anyone. When Fitz asked about her phone and if she was getting any alerts, he said she pulled her phone out once. She frowned at whatever she saw on the screen but clicked out of it and never pulled it out again.

He had a plan in motion to try to sneak it away from her because he saw the key to get in.

I was okay with all of it.

Josh reported they found the hidden cameras in the apartment and everything was pulled. "You think your girl in there could loop some background video and make it look like the place had been empty the whole time?"

"I'll ask her, but we need an ETA as soon as Matt calls when she leaves. I want to give Bailey as much—"

"*I'm done! Hell yes, you motherfucking bitch!*"

Josh and I both had to look down for a second.

Bailey continued cheering from the office and I nodded to him. "Call Matt. See if he can sneak her phone sooner than later. Have him erase any alerts she might've gotten."

"If she saw the first one?"

That was a gamble. "I'm judging by the fact that she stayed and chose not to worry about it. When it goes missing, she'll pretend she never saw it."

He grunted, nodding. "You think she's really that hard up for him that she'd choose to ignore a security alert?"

That was the gambling part. "I'm hoping that she never got any follow-up alerts and assumed it was a momentary glitch."

"Maybe your girl could put her spy stuff on this chick's system?"

Josh had been fully briefed on everything Bailey was capable of.

"I'll ask, but knowing Bailey, she's already ahead of us."

She proved my point when I entered the office again.

She wheeled around, all smiles and literally glowing. A sheen of sweat covered her face, and she jerked her hair up in a hair tie and gushed. "I got everything. Everything! It's all been transferred to an account that's off-line. Take that, you bitch. You want to fight by keeping shit off-line, I'll do the same. I cleaned everything but let her keep certain items that aren't harmful to any of us. She had a crap load on Quinn, things that will be helpful if we need to use it. And"—Literally. Fucking. Glowing.—"I uploaded my hacking program. It's the ghost program I was working on before."

Some of the glow lessened. She bit her lip, looking down. "I got the codes for her security system. I looped footage from earlier in the day, changed the time stamps and put them in. I also wiped two alerts she got on her phone. They showed that she hadn't seen it yet, so we're good on that account. Now we have to leave, and she'll have no clue we were here."

She started to wheel back but stopped. Her hand in the air. "Oh!" She pointed around the office. "Could you take pictures of everything in here? Just to have. When she has the computer on, I can watch her from there, but you know." Some of the glow was fading, and fading fast. She'd been on an upswing of adrenaline and emotion. She was going to crash soon. "The psych part of this office is probably off the charts."

I crossed the office and leaned down.

My arms went around both sides of her.

She looked up, her eyes wide and trusting—starting to cloud over, but still so trusting.

I stifled so many other things I wanted to say to her at that time. I brushed my lips to her forehead, tucked some of her loose strands behind her ear, and turned her back around. "Finish up. We'll take care of the rest."

Her shoulders slackened a second.

She was losing her steam at a faster rate than I thought. Her arms went up to the keyboard, but they looked like they were suddenly under a crushing weight.

Shit.

I brushed more of her hair back. Her eyes closed. She savored that touch, so I leaned down again. My lips found hers and I whispered there, "You did amazing."

She nodded, her lips finding mine, and as I stepped back, she had a little more gusto than just a split second earlier.

She was working again. It wasn't with the speed and force she had before, but it was steady. She'd be done before we would.

That meant I'd change our plans.

I waited, and as soon as she was done, I helped put her stuff in her backpack. When she stepped out of the office, I told her to head to Fitz. She did, and then I waved Josh over. The guys had been spot-dusting any places their fingerprints might've been left.

Josh watched her go with Fitz, then turned to me.

"Take photos of everything in the office. Copy anything left in the copy and fax machine. See if there's a history there we can get. Then close up. Bailey said she got the codes. Matt doesn't need to grab the girl's phone. Bailey did it all remotely."

"Got it, boss."

I left, and Fitz had Bailey in my car. I stepped around him, taking the driver's seat. He nodded, going to his car. He'd follow us back to the Chesapeake. Once on the way, with Bailey's backpack sitting in front of her and with Bailey curled in a ball on the passenger seat, already asleep, I called Matt. I relayed to him everything that happened.

Forty minutes later, Matt texted.

Camille Story was in a cab, heading back to her apartment.

Hoda and her other friend had left earlier.

Josh called.

"I got everything. Place is locked up."

"Take the night off."

Bailey would be asleep most of the night, but I needed her. I needed to hold her. I needed to be there in case she woke, because when she did, I knew she'd be hurting. It was always that way after a high that she was on. There'd be the low and then her haunts would slip in.

I'd be there.

She was back, and I intended to keep her back.

TWELVE

Bailey

I was falling.

I felt it.

It was a pull, tugging me down. I knew it. I knew the consequences.

I was back there.

The shots.

Matt tackled me.

They were bursting through the doors.

More shooting.

Trembling.

Weeping.

Shrieking.

The smell of burning and urine in the room.

Sweat.

Dust.

Then I was up. They were gone.

I was running.

"*Bailey!*"

"Mom!" A panicked breath in. "*Mom!*"

Chrissy.

I had to get to her.

Chrissy.

My legs were weak, shaking.

Chrissy!

I slammed into the wall, and then I saw them.

Outside.

He was dragging her.

He was looking.

He pushed her to her knees.

The gun was out.

He looked up, right at me.

And he smiled—my chest squeezed.

I'd forgotten.

I'd forgotten!

Bam!

I jerked upright. Someone was screaming.

It was bloodcurdling.

"Hey." A soothing hand. Down my hair. "Hey. Hey, Bailey. Baby."

Whispered and frenzied kisses.

I was rolled over.

There was still screaming. More shaking.

Then sobbing. Hiccups.

It was me.

I was the one screaming.

"Bailey!" I was pushed down, and a body came over me.

I froze, the same panic as before. My fists were up. I was fighting. Shoving.

I had to get free.

I had to get my—

"Bailey!"

A mouth came down over me.

It was Kash.

That was him.

It was his mouth kissing me.

That got through.

Everything quieted, except there was a pounding. A thumping sound.

I gasped as Kash lifted his mouth. He ran a hand down my face, a face that was sweating.

Sweat mixed with tears.

He didn't care, and I could see him now. The moonlight was outside, filtering in, and I was still crying.

Oh, God. It hurt. Everything hurt.

"My mom," I choked out. My hands were curled around his arms. "My mom, Kash."

"I know." Another whisper, of such understanding and pity and sympathy. It unraveled me.

I couldn't hold it back anymore.

I bent my head to his chest and gave in.

His arms tightened around me. I felt his kiss on my shoulder, and he was moving us. I was cradled in his chest. He pushed up, sitting against the headboard. I was on his lap, curled into a ball.

More tears.

More pain.

Slicing me.

He held me. He ran a hand down my hair, my back, sweeping up my arm and repeating.

He did it all night long.

I cried all night long.

She was there, all night long.

And right before I fell asleep—later, much later—I swear I heard my mom whisper in the air, *"My baby girl."*

THIRTEEN

Kash

Six A.M., and Bailey was finally sleeping.

It wasn't a restless sleep, but one where she was *out* out. No sounds were coming from her. She hadn't moved an inch for the last hour. The only way I knew she wasn't dead was because I felt her breath as I held her, but six meant I needed to get going.

I was coming out of our section of the house when Matt bypassed me, yawning widely.

He stopped, took me in, and let out an audible sigh. "What happened?"

I frowned. "You smell of martinis, cigarettes . . . and I'm hoping that last smell isn't what I think it is."

He frowned right back. "Fuck you. You weren't the decoy while my sister played at breaking and entering."

"I wasn't judging. I meant that I hoped you didn't have to do what it smells like you did."

"Oh." He blinked, bags under his eyes. "I'm tired."

He hadn't answered.

"Matt." I inclined my head toward him. "You didn't fuck her?"

"What?" His nose wrinkled and he stepped back. "No. That's what I smell like?"

I didn't want to test my theory and take another whiff. But, shit. Nope.

I knew what I was smelling on him.

"Matt," I was cautious here, proceeding slowly. "The last relationship you had was with a mar—"

"God. I know." He glared at me, rocking back on his heels. "You don't have to tell me, and no, to get ahead of this awkward-as-hell conversation you're determined to have with me, it's no one. It's not a thing or anything. Had an itch, knew someone who'd scratch it, and that's all." Another heated look from him. "You okay with that, Dad?"

"Stop with the jabs, dick."

"Prick."

"Asshole."

He blinked. His mouth twitched. "Fuckup."

"You wish," I deadpanned back. "You'd be loved more."

"God!" He burst out laughing, throwing his head back. "That one almost hurt."

My own mouth twitched.

His laughter faded, but he was still grinning. He jerked his chin up. "What happened last night? Did Bailey get what she needed?"

"She did good." And he had to know. "She was on a high."

He jerked, his eyes shuddering for a beat. "Wait. What? She was high?"

"No. When she hacks, she can get a high from it." I needed to spell it out. "And then afterward with how she is, with the grief . . ."

His eyes grew wide and alarmed. "Is she okay?"

"She's sleeping, but she went low. She remembered that night and woke up thinking I was Calhoun's men."

"Shit." His nostrils flared. A keen, murderous look entered his eyes. "If I had a gun, if your grandfather was here—why isn't he dead yet?" He was gone. All rationality checked out, and he was breathing fury. "That's your job. What's the problem? I know you know where he is at every goddamn minute of the day."

"It's not that easy."

I wished it were.

For a second, a minute, I considered it.

Could I just go? I could. I could get to him. I could even get him isolated, and I would have weapons at my disposal. I could kill him. It'd be so easy. I could do it slow, torturing him. Or I could merely slit his throat and watch him bleed dry. Or I could slice him all over, make his last breaths so painful, puncture his lung and have him choke on his own blood. That was a different type of dying that was its own hell.

But it was the after that I had to consider.

"Calhoun wasn't stupid. If he dies, there are policies set in motion. People will come after whoever killed him. He still has resources I need to turn against him. I'm digging. I'm trying to find everything."

He whistled. "He's a sick bastard."

"He has a contract out to go after not only me but also Bailey. Maybe you guys, too. I'm working on isolating him from all his assets, but it takes time. And money. And diplomacy."

"Yeah." His voice cracked, and he looked exhausted once again. The bags under his eyes grew in size just during our conversation. He rubbed at his jaw, swearing softly under his breath. "I'm going to collapse, man. I gotta hit the hay."

I nodded. "Before you do, did you learn anything new from Camille Story?"

He grimaced, his mouth twisting. "Yeah, actually. She said Quinn has someone else in her camp."

That wasn't good, and how the fuck had I missed that?

"Quinn is digging for information on us, right? Did you get that from her?"

He frowned. "Yeah. Sorry. I should've said that first. Camille admitted she was tapped by Quinn to get as much info from her as possible. Then they started a weird friendship, but Camille was asked to try and dig up more info on you and Bailey—Bailey specifically."

"Bailey? Not you?"

He shook his head. "No, and I pressed. She said she was only saying what she was saying because she was happy it wasn't me anymore. I don't think she meant to let that slip, but she shut up right after for a long while. She got a funny look on her face, like she realized she was saying too much. She tried to turn the tables and push me for information. Think that's the only reason she came, because Hoda said I was drunk. I was acting it up. She thinks I forgot to pay my bill, that we dined and ditched. I'm sure she's going to give Quinn that tidbit on me, but she said Hoda's a tapped well. Which makes sense; it's why she's letting Hoda move out without a fuss."

"Quinn wanted to scare Chrissy away from Peter. That was what started the whole thing."

Matt was nodding. "And it didn't work. It brought Chrissy closer."

"So Quinn wanted Bailey dead, thought that would push Chrissy away. That Chrissy would blame Peter."

"Which she might've, but it didn't happen."

"Evidence is solid on her. She was released on bail, but her trial is starting and she's got one person that we know looking into Bailey and myself. You're saying according to that same asset, Quinn's got a second in her pocket. Why? For her trial?"

Matt shook his head. "I don't know, but . . ." He was frowning, his forehead scrunched up. "Didn't it come out that the Arcane team did that, hoping it would get them in Calhoun's good graces? But Quinn said they were stupid, that he'd never have approved that move?"

"Yeah."

It didn't feel right. None of it felt right.

Quinn and my grandfather were together in my head, but

maybe they weren't really together. They weren't. I knew they weren't. So why did I keep putting them together? Were they working as an alliance? Against whom? Me? Was it something else? A different target? A different person?

"Okay." Matt clamped a hand on my shoulder, moving past me. "I'm exhausted. I had a whole night of faking the doughnut, and then I went and didn't fake the doughnut, but I need sleep."

"Do I want to ask who you didn't fake the doughnut with?"

Matt grinned. "No one special, but she's also no one married."

"That's something." I added, "You need a shower."

"That, too. Maybe later." He headed toward his section of the house, his hand in the air. "Let's save the world after I get a good twelve hours of sleep, yeah? Try not to slay too many dragons until I'm back awake. You and me, dude. We're Team Katt."

I snorted. "I don't want a team name for us. That's your thing with Bailey."

"You're right. You'd never be a part of Team Batt."

He headed off, and I looked up, seeing Marie stepping out from the kitchen hallway. She had a knowing look on her face, along with a steaming mug in her hand.

I started for her. "Is that for me?"

She held it up. "Three shots of espresso."

Thank fuck.

FOURTEEN

Kash

I was in Peter's study, working on some items.

Peter was working at his desk while I was on one of his leather couches in the corner. The door opened.

Peter looked up from his computer and instantly a loving smile lit up his face. "Come in, honey."

Seraphina darted inside, dressed in her robe and pajamas, her hair long and hanging free. I grinned at the slippers she was wearing, the flamingo pair that Bailey had given her. And it was one of those moments where I was thankful to be staying at the Chesapeake for the time being. If we weren't here, I wouldn't see that Seraphina wore Bailey's gift this evening, and that they were a permanent fixture on her feet every night when she dressed for bed.

"What's going on?"

Peter scooted his chair and Seraphina went around his desk, draping herself half on his arm. Her head lowered to his shoulder. She hadn't noticed I was in the room. I was thankful for that, too. Seraphina tensed around me, I'd noticed. I knew there'd been a moment when she had a crush on me, but I thought that was gone. I can't say I was a fan of her stiffening whenever I was around, either.

Peter glanced at me over her head and I shook mine, just slightly.

He blinked, the slightest nod to me, and he leaned back, lifting his arm. He rolled his seat and shifted his daughter so her back was to me. "What's going on?" he repeated his question.

It was warm in the study. A fire was lit in the fireplace. Peter's walls were floor-to-ceiling bookshelves, except for a loft set up in the top corner of the room. Another couch up there pulled out into a bed. He had a bar set in a corner of the room, and patio doors that led outside.

Seraphina was leaning heavily on one of his legs. Her mouth was close to his shirt, but I caught enough to hear "Bailey will be okay?"

His hand flexed before smoothing up and down over her back. "Are you worried about Bailey?"

Her head moved up and down into his shirt and shoulder.

"She's going to be just fine."

Her head lifted up. She looked at him. I could see her biting down on her lip from the side. "But what's wrong with her? She was doing better, and now she's not again. She's got the vacant look in her eyes."

I sucked in my breath, my hand jerking as I laid down the paper I'd been holding.

Of course they would notice. If Seraphina was coming to Peter, I knew she and Cyclone had talked about it.

I hadn't let myself really think about them in the midst of everything, but hearing the words come out of Seraphina's mouth hit me hard.

I had neglected them. Her and Cyclone both.

I kept a good relationship with them, until Bailey had come to the estate this summer. Then it had become all about Bailey, about Calhoun, and minimal policing of Matt's activities.

Was this why she froze around me?

"Emotions can be up and down. You can get happy, then you'll get sad, and it is a bit more dramatic with Bailey because she's experiencing such intense emotions right now. It's her grief, sweetheart. She'll be okay. She's already getting better," Peter said gently.

His hand kept rubbing up and down her back. He was smiling softly at her.

She laid her head against his shoulder, heaving a deep sigh before mumbling, "Yeah. Okay. If you say so."

"I know so." He jostled her playfully. "You doing okay otherwise?"

There was a pause before she replied.

"Yeah. I'm okay."

He frowned down at her, his eyebrows pulling in together. "What's that about?"

"Nothing."

"Hey." He tapped her softly under the chin. "What's going on? Let your dad in, let him know what you're thinking." He grinned at her. "I'm feeling cold out here. Let me in so I'm nice and warm."

She snorted. "God, Dad. You're such a dork."

His grin only deepened.

"Give your pops a bone. What's going on behind that beautiful face of yours?"

Another snort, but she was smiling. She jerked up a shoulder. "I'm just worried about Bailey, and . . ." The pause was pregnant.

A sniffle.

Peter's eyes lifted to mine.

I sat up straighter.

"What's going on with Mom? I mean . . ." She ducked her head again. "CanweseehersometimeyouthinkCyclonemissesher." She finished in a rush, and damn.

Panic flared over Peter's face.

Peter looked cautious before he moved farther back, leaning down so he could look Seraphina in the face. "Heya, cupcake."

Seraphina's response: "Heya back, pound cake."

"You're missing your mom?"

She didn't reply at first, then her head bobbed up and down. I heard a sniffle. "Yeah."

"You and Cy talk about your mom?"

Another pause. "Yeah." A third sniffle.

"Well, she's in a criminal trial. You know what that's all about?"

Seraphina didn't reply, not right away.

"That's 'cause of what she tried to do to Bailey, right?"

"Yeah." Peter was speaking so quietly now. He visibly swallowed. "Your mom wasn't thinking right, and she decided to do something to hurt your sister—"

"But that's why Bailey came to us, right? Because of what Mom tried to do."

"Yeah." His voice grew rough. Hoarse. "And because she tried to hurt Bailey again."

Seraphina pressed even closer to Peter, whispering, "But she wouldn't hurt us, would she?"

Peter froze.

He blinked at her. "Well. The thing with your mom is that I don't know. Something's wrong for her to try and do what she did to your sister twice. You can go and see her, but I have to go, or another chaperone has to be with you. The court won't allow her to be alone with you and Cyclone, not now anyways."

"What about Aunt Payton? Is she going to come back, too?"

Peter frowned again, his head inching back to take in his daughter's face more clearly. "Would you like Aunt Payton to come back?"

She nodded.

"You miss Aunt Payton?"

"She's nice." Her head went down again. She started scratching idly at Peter's armrest of his chair. "She draws with me, and she talks to Cyclone about his robots. I know he misses her."

A look flashed over Peter's face, his features hardening a second before he blinked and it cleared.

I frowned, seeing it.

"Okay." He coughed, clearing his throat. "I'll—um—I'll have a word with Marie and then give Payton a call. I'm sure she would love to come and spend more time with her favorite niece and nephew."

Seraphina giggled. "Dad. You're silly."

He chuckled, softening. "Only for you, cupcake."

"Thanks, Dad." She wrapped her arms tight around him, squeezing. "Thanks, pound cake."

Another chuckle as he watched her leave the office. She never looked toward my corner, and I was glad. She had an easier bounce to her step, and if she saw me, I knew that lightness would evaporate. I would need to dedicate quality time to Seraphina to find out the reason why I made her uneasy, and she was the most reserved of the Francis children. Handling Seraphina was like moving a delicate diamond found in nature. You saw the gem there, the beauty of it, but you needed to be gentle in washing away the dirt that it grew from.

Once the door closed, Peter let out an audible breath, leaning back in his chair. "Fuck."

I picked up my paper, feeling a bit tight in the throat myself. "Yeah."

He groaned, sitting up. "I could use a drink. Want one?"

"No, I'm good."

He poured some whiskey in a glass and shook his head, right before taking a drink. "Quinn doesn't deserve her children's love, that's for damned sure."

"But she has it."

"Yeah," he bit out. "She does have that, doesn't she?" His eyes narrowed, focusing on me. "What's up with you and Seraphina? You didn't want her to know you were here."

"I don't know." I spoke the truth. "That'll take time and a gentle hand to find out what's going on there, but she gets tense with me. I didn't want her to do that this time."

His eyes never moved from me. "And you're going to take the time to get to the bottom of that? I don't like having my little girl feeling a weird way about you."

I scowled at him. "Of course, I will. You think I enjoy it?"

He relaxed, swirling his drink around in its glass. "I know your concentration is pulled in a few other directions, but Seraphina's always loved you and looked up to you. I wouldn't want anything to get in there and put a permanent wedge between you two."

My scowl faded to a frown. "I can't help but wonder if it's something with Quinn?"

He grunted. "Damn that woman. The trial starts soon, too." He finished the rest of his glass and poured himself a second, taking it back to his desk and sitting down. "I'm going to have to talk to Marie. She'll have to learn how to coexist with having Payton here."

Wait.

"Payton's the reason Marie was sent on a vacation before?"

He nodded, wincing before setting his whiskey on his desk and turning to his computer screen. "It was Marie. She threw a fit that Payton was here, but I needed Payton here. Ser and Cyclone love their aunt. I figured it was better to have her here when Quinn was just arrested. Marie came back when I sent Payton away, which was for Bailey's sake. I know she looks so much like her sister, but everyone's going to have to deal with it all. Payton's a good woman. Bailey and Marie will both see that."

His eyes locked on mine. "Right?" That word came out as an ominous warning.

I shook my head. "Calm down, old man. You have no arguments about Payton from me. I've been around the woman and know she's nothing like her sister."

"You're right about that." He grimaced, leaning back in his chair. A haunted expression came over him. "Sometimes I think I did wrong in choosing Quinn. But I can't think like that, because I got Seraphina—" He cut himself off.

Then he just sighed. "Life is sometimes just a bitch, isn't it?"

I didn't answer. I didn't think Peter was talking to me.

FIFTEEN

Bailey

"It's been three weeks. That's a reasonable amount of time for me to give you space."

I was back at school. Correction: I'd been back at school for the last three weeks, but I was currently in the library. My computer was set up. My textbooks next to me. I had one ethics paper to write on cyber laws, and one cup of coffee to last me through half of it. I'd been on my phone, texting Matt to bring caffeine reinforcements, when Hoda approached my table in a huff.

Melissa was with me, and both of us looked up at Hoda's arrival.

She said her piece, dropped her backpack on the floor, and slumped into the chair across from me.

We were at our own table, set between the bookshelves to help with some privacy, but it wasn't lasting. Students walked past each aisle on the regular, though I did pick all the way up on the eighth floor. I was bound and determined to finish this paper before heading home.

I had plans.

Like helping Seraphina with her latest school project and prying all the details about her new boy crush. I wanted to help

Cyclone. Apparently his computer club was into AI enough where I was getting alarmed. They were talking about robots and the ramifications of how much they actually resembled conversations like the *Terminator* movies. And then after that, Kash was back from traveling abroad. When I asked where he was flying to, he only said Greece. That made me think of Victoria, and I knew Matt had talked about some party at Naveah this weekend. I had plans to skip it, but I wanted to scope out the lay of the land before Kash got home.

Meaning that if Victoria was back, because she'd been MIA since the Aspen trip from hell, then I definitely wanted to track her down and do my own sort of interrogation about what had happened in Greece with her grandfather. Kash had given me the CliffsNotes, but I still wanted to hear what Victoria would say.

I frowned at Hoda now. "What are you talking about?"

She looked at Melissa. "Do you mind? I'm not trying to be rude, and I'm aware I come off that way, but this is personal for me. I'd rather not have an audience when I make Bailey do something we've all taken oaths not to do."

Melissa's mouth was open. She was half gaping. "What . . ."

"Hacking. Or *un*hacking. I need her to unhack something."

Oh, crap.

Melissa's phone buzzed, and she read the text. A small and slight giggle left her before she bit down on her lip, looking at us. "You know what? This is perfect timing. I, uh, have something." She grabbed her books, put her laptop in her bag, and was ready to go in a flash. "I'll see you all later, then?"

Her bag was swung up on her back.

We watched as she pulled her other arm through the strap before Hoda turned back to me. She was being all fierce-like. "Our deal. I know you had a setback after you hacked Camille—and by the way, she has no idea. I'm living with Liam, but I talked to her yesterday. She didn't say a word, and I know her—she would've been blowing my phone up if she ever figured it out."

She slid her fists over the table toward me and uncurled them, her thumbs sticking up. "So two thumbs up for that feat. But back to me. You said you'd pull your program from my stuff." She was all business and no nonsense. "I want to watch you do it."

She was right. I'd had a setback, but it hadn't lasted too long.

Grief was a cycling tornado. It hit, and it hit hard. It left a trail to recuperate afterward. You recuperated, and then it swung back again for destruction.

Hoda cleared her throat, staring at me pointedly.

Right.

She was here. She said something. *Brain, go back, and what did she say?*

"I want to watch you do it."

Got it.

"Now? Are you sure?"

Her eyebrows arched up. "You can do it now? On your laptop?"

I nodded. "I have it set up to do it anywhere."

She groaned, closing her eyes. She lowered her head, folded her arms, and laid her forehead over her arms. "Why me?" She lifted her head and her eyes opened. "I had it all worked up in my head. You could break into accounts but you had to do it in a certain room, with a certain computer, and there were all these precautions you had to take. You had to at least work for it. Nope." She snapped her fingers, leaning back in her chair, her shoulders slumping. "You can do it here. Now. Just like that. With your freaking laptop, that you can take anywhere. Of course. Of course!" She looked upward. "Why couldn't I have been the genius in our program?"

I sighed. "Are we really back to this? This was so first semester."

"Of course." Her hand flew up, gesturing to me. "You're funnier, too. Agh!"

I waited.

I waited another beat.

She remained quiet, so I asked, "Want me to do it now or what?"

"Yes," she bit out, shoving back her chair. She stalked around the table and stood over my shoulder, her arms crossed over her chest. I glanced up. She had an annoyed scowl on her face.

Well. She was about to get even more annoyed.

I opened up my program.

Click.

Another *click.*

I typed in my password, which I know she saw, but I would change it the second she left.

Then I went to her file, pulled up her social media accounts.

She growled under her breath.

Twitter.

It opened right away. I saw everything, had total access to it. And I clicked out of it, dragged it to the garbage.

I did the same thing with her Instagram.

Her Facebook.

Tumblr.

She had three fan-fiction accounts.

All of them.

Six emails.

A video blogger account.

She had a Pinterest account.

Every one was opened, closed out, and I dragged the entire program into the garbage.

She remained there, letting out more disgruntled grunts, growls, curses, until I had emptied the entire folder. Once that was done, I took her entire folder (even though it was empty) and that went into the garbage, too.

The garbage was emptied.

Then I went to my hard drive, and since she knew the coding, she saw me wipe the backups.

After that, I went back into my program, pulled up her name, and wiped that, too.

I waited, letting her digest everything once it was done.

"How do I know you won't get in again?"

I looked up at her. "Go and change all of your passwords. Other than that, you'll just have to trust me."

She was visibly upset, and I got it. I did. But I didn't feel bad, not after how she had threatened me last semester, and how she treated me. Kash's conversation from Camille's office came back to me, and he was right.

Anything. That was my line for what I would do to protect those I loved.

"Fine." She stormed back to the other side of the table, grabbed her backpack, and hoisted it on. Just before she left, she placed a hand on the table. "I will report you if you ever do anything like that again."

I gave her a look. Camille Story. Hello?

She flushed. "I mean to myself or Melissa, or anyone else in our class. I will go to the school dean, and I don't care whose father donated that check, I'll take everything with me that I have on you."

Now I started to get heated. "That wasn't a threat, was it? Meaning you don't currently have anything on me." I paused, letting that hang in the air. "Because if you did, then you know me, and you know that I'd have to go and find it."

Her eyes were almost bugging out. She screwed her face up, her mouth flattening. A quiet scream escaped, sounding like steam leaving a teapot. "No! I don't have anything. Just, don't hack me. Ever. Or I'll go to the feds."

Hawking's dean. Now the FBI. I almost retorted, *Who's next? The pope?* But I refrained. She was upset. I understood it, and now she needed to maintain a semblance of control. Having the last word would give her that sense of control. So yeah. Whatever floated her boat. I kept quiet and she huffed off a second later.

Fitz came down the aisle. "Was I supposed to have fended her off?"

"No." I was back in my program, and I changed my password for the entire system. Then I went in and got into her phone. Call me a violator, but I needed to make sure.

A second later, she sent a text out.

Hoda: It's done.
Quinn: Are you sure? And you watched her the entire time?
Hoda: Yes. I told her I'd go to the FBI if she did it again.

My stomach dropped, but I was waiting, air suspended in my throat, and my fingers were itching to start typing away, when Quinn texted back.

Good. I'm sure with everything Kash and Peter are going through, that's the last sort of battle Bailey wants. Are we still on for drinks tomorrow night? I know how you can get Liam to sleep with you.

I wanted to puke. My stomach was churning over.

Hoda: Yes! Let's. Girls' Martini Night at the Ritz.
Quinn: You're on. See you then! 8 sharp.

I had meant to close out Hoda's text messages, too, but not now. And crap. Crap! I had wanted to believe Hoda had become somewhat of a friend. I truly did. But this changed everything.

Quinn.

Fuck.

I was going to tell Matt first about Hoda and Quinn.

I knew I should tell Kash, but I couldn't. I just couldn't, and I didn't know why. It was like when I tried to open my mouth, to tell Fitz that I should be going to wherever Kash was, the words wouldn't come out of my mouth. And my hands refused to pick up the phone and call him myself, or even text him.

Matt I could text.

I asked where he was. He said Naveah, so that's where we were going. I looked up at the front seat where Fitz and my driver were sitting, and for once I had something they didn't know about.

Once we pulled up to Naveah, I texted again.

Outside Naveah. Can you come out here? I don't want to be where Torie is.

He wouldn't question me on Torie, but he'd question me on where else I wanted to go.

Matt: Sure. Finishing, gotta pay. Can I bring Tony and Guy?
Me: No. You and me only.
Matt: Is this a Team Batt thing?

I grinned, typing fast, and more relieved.

Me: Oh yeah!
Matt: Sweet. Paying now. Out soon.

I put my phone away. "Matt's coming out here. He wants to go to Octavo instead."

I was lying.

Fitz frowned at me in the rearview mirror. "He does?"

I nodded. "Hmm. That's not a problem, right?"

Fitz didn't respond. He just stared at me until there was a commotion outside and the door was opening. Sounds from the street and the club filtered in. There was a line waiting to get into Naveah, and people began shouting, seeing Matt. Then he was sliding in, his guards coming up behind him, the door shut after him. His guards went to where Fitz was getting out to talk with them.

Matt saw that and looked at me, his eyebrows raised. "What's going on?"

I locked eyes with him at the same time I texted him.

I spoke, "I told Fitz you wanted to go to Octavo instead."

His eyebrows arched even higher, and his phone buzzed from me. He took it out, reading my text.

Go along with it. I'll explain there.

He nodded, putting his phone back and raking his hand through his hair. "Yeah." Fitz opened his door, his head coming inside. "Are you sure about Octavo?"

Matt dipped his head down, his mouth pursed as if he were bored already with this questioning. "Yeah, man. What's the problem? Kash knows the owners. We'll be safe there."

That was the point. Kash knew them. Kash did not own them. And for full disclosure here, I didn't know who owned Octavo myself. What I did know was that there was some form of mutual respect between the owner and Kash. He mentioned the owners, saying there were two of them, and I could tell from his tone that he was cautious about both. So, for what I wanted to talk to Matt about, I knew his only employees would be the guards, and they would stay a respectable distance away. That meant I could actually talk to him, without having anyone else, like Torie, dropping by, or any of Matt's friends. Or mine, now that I thought about it. I knew Melissa had taken to hanging out with Torie and Tamara at Naveah, too.

Fitz continued to stare at Matt.

"What's the problem?"

No response from Fitz, but he straightened, and a second later, he got back inside while Matt's guards left. "They'll follow us there."

Matt nodded, as if he'd been expecting all of this to happen.

When the car pulled away from the curb, he glanced down at me and both of us shared a look. His elbow nudged mine and he grinned.

Have I mentioned how much I love my brother?

SIXTEEN

Kash

We arrived at the warehouse, and I was about to step outside when my phone rang.

It was one of Matt's guards.

"Something wrong?" I answered, putting the phone to my ear.

"Bailey and Matt are going to Octavo."

"Why?"

"Neither would say, and we weren't told this until Bailey pulled up to Naveah. She texted Matt, and he went outside to her."

"Where are you currently?"

"Following Bailey's vehicle."

"And they didn't say why they were going there? Whose idea was it?"

A moment of hesitation. "They're both saying Matt's idea."

I waited.

He didn't continue.

"But?" I prodded, inclining my head.

"But Matt usually tells us when we're changing locations

ahead of time. He didn't say a word. Fitz was the one who said Bailey claimed Matt wanted to go to Octavo."

Ah. That I understood, and he was right. Matt usually was decent about cooperating with the guards—at least he had been since Bailey's second kidnapping attempt. So if the idea hadn't come from Matt, then it came from Bailey and they were both lying, which meant she didn't want me to know. Or she didn't want extra hearing ears at Naveah, and neither idea sat well with me.

I sighed. "Just do your job, and guard them both. Let them proceed how they want."

"Are you sure?"

No, I wasn't sure. And no, I didn't want this to happen. But if something was going on with Bailey, I did what I always did. I watched, and I loved, and I would try to keep her safe until I had to swoop in myself.

"Yeah." My words came out clipped, because fuck, I wasn't happy about this new development. "I have to go, but keep me updated on their movements."

"Will do, boss."

The call ended. I put my phone back in my pocket and got out of my SUV.

Josh and Scott both stepped forward.

"Everything's ready."

Scott added, "Everyone is here, too."

"Harden made the trip okay?"

Josh nodded. "He did. He's the only one inside. Said he didn't dare try and get any more of his men with him." He paused a beat, sharing a look with Scott. "Your guest is prepped."

Good. Finally. It was time.

On that note, I went inside.

I looked at Harden. He lowered his head, a greeting. I returned the gesture, then I went forward. In the middle of the warehouse was a lone man, strapped to a chair. He was gagged and blindfolded. I stepped forward and took the blindfold off.

Bailey wasn't the only one keeping secrets.

"Hello, brother."

SEVENTEEN

Bailey

Octavo was a dark club. That's the best way to describe it.

The outside was nondescript. It was a black building with a red neon light that said the name of the club in simple lettering. A single silver door. A bouncer. A red velvet rope that sectioned off the line waiting to get inside.

When we pulled up, we went to the head of the line.

Fitz got out. The doorman saw him and nodded. The velvet rope was already being lifted as we were getting out, and with Matt leading the way, we went inside. Fitz trailed. Matt's guards weren't far behind. There was a black bar set up as soon as we stepped inside, with red neon lights highlighting the bottom of the bar. That was the theme of the entire place.

Black.

Red neon color.

There were silver disco balls set up in the hallway, but as soon as we got a drink from the first bar, Matt's guards were inside and waiting for us. A woman came down from a back hallway, clad in a black leather top and pants. They molded to her form. She wore black stilettos and her hair was slicked back. She looked like an assassin.

She led us through a back hallway.

Each door we passed was a solid black door.

Small crystal disco balls hung from the ceiling, the only light in the hallway. The walls were covered in black velvet drapery.

We kept winding around the building, at a slight incline, until she came to a door and opened it.

Going through, we'd been shown to our own box. There was a large booth set up, all black. Red neon lights were under the booth and the middle was open. There was no table. Leading off from our private booth was a walkway that led down to the main dance floor, and set above everyone was the DJ. Same lighting coming from his booth. Red neon under his booth setup and around his stage. A grandiose disco ball hovered over him, and there was another, even larger one over the entire dance floor.

That's when I saw the people on the floor. They were in every color imaginable. Hot pink, purple. Flashing colors. Neon yellow, green. Everything neon. A few people were covered in body paint that was illuminated by the black light.

I was not normally a dancing person, but seeing that crowd made me want to get lost in them. I was hungry for it, and ignoring the reason we were here, I grabbed Matt's hand. "Come on!"

He frowned, stepping close so Fitz and the others couldn't hear. "I thought you wanted to talk or something?"

I moved so I could speak in his ear. "I do, but right now I want to dance. Let's dance!" I squeezed his hand, and pulling back, studying me, he gave a tight nod.

We finished our drinks and ordered another round right away. Once we got those in hand, we tossed them back and headed down. Matt led the way.

Fitz followed, standing at the edge of the crowd. I expected him or the others to pull us back, to not let us mingle with the regular crowd, but they held off. One stayed at the walkway leading to our booth. The other positioned himself at the other side of the dance floor. All three kept us in their line of sight.

Once we got onto the floor, something came over me.

I'd never felt it before.

It was cliché. It was campy. It was phenomenal.

It was exactly what I needed.

The bass picked up. The tempo vibrated through the floors. The DJ hit the right notes, and the energy swept through everyone. The entire dance floor grew more frenzied, and Matt pushed us until we were in the middle. Once there, I didn't stop to think.

I closed my eyes. I lifted my arms, and I began to sway to the music.

It hit me.

A moment built up.

Feeling unalive, vacant, dormant.

Then, suddenly, I wasn't empty.

Something trickled back in, and I was desperate for more.

Hungry. Starving.

I wanted to feel *more*, and I couldn't get enough of it.

Right fucking now.

The music. The darkness. The anonymity. Being there and knowing there wasn't a set of twenty eyes watching me, reporting on me. And that feeling—I craved it.

I grew frenzied for that feeling, and then there was a shift in the music. A sudden interruption. The bass was going *boom, boom, boom*. Pause. The break, and the music came back, but at a different pace, and suddenly it was *boom, boom, boom!*

And everyone went *nuts*.

Boom!

I moved. I gyrated. I circled.

Boom!

My head was back. Arms above me.

Boom!

I was losing track of time.

I was dancing.

I was sweating.

Boom! Boom! Boom!

The lights were flashing above, and I could see them through my closed eyelids.

And then, I was back there again in Aspen.

Boom!

The door crashed open. Matt was running inside.

"Bailey! Get down!"

Boom!

I jerked, my arms dropped back to my side.

A body over mine, knocking me to the floor.

Boom!

Screaming. Shrieking. Someone wailing.

"Bailey!"

Hands were on me. I was being shaken.

Boom!

Tears were cascading down my face. I felt them. I tasted them.

I was being shaken again, and my eyelids jerked open. Matt's face was in front of mine, tight with panic, and he was yelling over the music. *"Bailey!"*

His hands pulled me to his chest, he wrapped them gently around me.

He crushed me to him after that, his hand smoothing down my hair and back. "Jesus." He panted next to my ear, swaying back and forth, as if rocking a child to sleep in his arms. "Jesus." He pulled back, but his arms only loosened a little bit. He inspected my face, taking me in from forehead to chin before shaking his own head. He moved back. "You scared the crap out of me."

I thumped him lightly on the chest, moving to his ear. "What did I do?"

"You started trembling. Mid-dance. And you looked like you were having a seizure standing up."

Christ. I gulped.

I yelled into his ear over the music, "Let's go back to the booth."

He nodded, stepping back. His hand took mine, holding it tight, and he wound through until we got to the outskirts. Fitz took over, leading us past the other guard. Once upstairs, Matt went to the bar and got us both drinks before sitting next to me in the booth. He handed mine over. "Here. This might calm your nerves."

He leaned in, elbows resting on his knees. "What happened out there?"

I didn't want to talk about it, but . . . "I get flashbacks."

His face shuddered, his eyes suddenly looking hollow. He jerked backward, his hand tightening around his glass. "Maybe you should try counseling again?"

I gave him a look. I hated going the first time we tried that. "Let me think about it."

I was still trembling, but watching Matt, I leaned over. "You have them, too?"

He didn't answer right away. His shoulders lifted up, held, and he let out the breath as he took another long drag from his drink. His eyes found mine, and they weren't void anymore. They were stormy.

I flinched.

His mouth flattened, and he grimaced. "Let's talk about why you wanted to come here and not Naveah."

It was like he threw a bucket of ice water over me, and swallowing over a knot, I glanced over. Fitz went to the booth's door. The other two guards were on the edge toward the dance floor, the one remained at the bottom of our pathway.

We were good to talk.

I pulled my phone out and showed him Hoda's text messages.

He read them, his jaw getting firmer and firmer until he scrolled to the end. He clicked on something, and then hit another button before almost shoving the phone back to me.

I took it, already looking. "What'd you do?"

"I sent them to my phone."

"What?" I was scrambling. I hadn't expected that from him. "Why?"

"Because that shit is bad." He pointed a jabbing finger at my phone. "That shit can't stay between us. That's why you wanted to come here, isn't it?" His eyes were blazing and fierce.

I shifted away, letting out a sigh.

That was messed up.

He was right. I needed to tell Kash.

I leaned back, my head resting against the back of the booth, and there, I felt the club swirling around us. Everything was swimming. I felt the waves pushing down on me. I was lost, hearing the techno bass, feeling the heat of the lights, the smell of the dry ice in the club, and he was right. He was totally right. I mean, I knew it, but seeing my brother's reaction to Hoda's text messages, I knew I'd been wrong.

But craaap.

Crap!

Crap!

I tasted salt and opened my eyes, everything blurring.

I was crying. Again.

I hated crying.

A hand circled my neck and I was pulled in to a chest. Matt's arms wrapped around me again. He hugged me to his side. "Bailey. Man." His hand began smoothing hair back from my forehead. "Shit. I'm sorry. I didn't mean—Well, I don't know what I meant, but if this is about Hoda and Quinn . . ."

I shook my head, the tears falling even faster.

It wasn't. I wished it was.

He hesitated then, and finally, after maybe a minute of sitting there in silence, he spoke. "I think we should call Kash about this." The admission came out of him in a rush, almost rueful, like he couldn't believe he was saying what he was saying. His hand shook as he said those words, then he smoothed it out, letting it fall to rest on my shoulder.

He was right.

And why was I crying?

EIGHTEEN

Kash

The inside of the warehouse was completely silent.

I had a twin. A fucking twin.

This man, this *brother* of mine, was tied to a chair and had been kept captive for weeks until it was time to finally deal with him. Didn't say a word, either. I put my phone down, my wallet. I laid my gun on the table and I picked up tape. I wrapped it around my knuckles, flexing my hand to test how it felt. All the while, he watched me.

He hadn't been beaten.

He'd been fed. He'd been given water. He was put in a room that was deemed comfortable. A bed. An audio cassette recorder, with tapes if he wanted to listen to anything or record his own message. There was a bathroom just off the bedroom. The temperature was always comfortable. He asked for a fan once, and it was given. He gave no indication of escape, or wanting to hurt himself, or even plotting an escape.

He read. He listened to music. He exercised in his room, and when he asked, he was brought out to do laps around this very warehouse.

He was also kept away. The closest building was a thirty-minute drive, through woods and rivers and fields. All the time, nothing.

I watched my grandfather, but there was no report of him being worried.

"Is that supposed to intimidate me?"

His first words to me.

I looked at my taped hands before going and dragging a chair over. "These?" I flexed them. "No, no, no. They're to cover up a cut."

His heavy eyes just watched me, not missing a thing. He didn't react. There were no emotions flickering over his face—his face that resembled mine exactly. But no. Looking closer—and I had been; I'd been watching him on video this whole fucking time—there were differences, but they were slight.

His cheekbones were a little wider. His jawline wasn't as pronounced as mine. He had a slightly wider forehead. But his eyes were mine. His nose was mine. Our mouths were the same. I imagined we would've been considered identical twins.

All the time—since he broke into my apartment, since he was captured—I didn't know how I felt about his existence.

I leaned back in my chair. "Do you know why I've waited this long to speak with you?"

He didn't hesitate. "To figure out if I'm here because our grandfather sent me or if I ran from him."

He was intelligent. Good to know.

I leaned forward, my elbows going to my legs again. "Yes."

"And to have your girlfriend look into me."

There was no prompt for that one. I raised my eyebrows. "What do you know about my girlfriend?"

"She's smart. Gifted with the computer. I know *our* grandfather finds her a threat."

I watched him steadily. I was looking for any cracks, any break, but there was nothing.

Was he telling the truth?

"My girlfriend's been preoccupied."

A small flicker. There it was.

He reacted.

I continued. "The same day you got on a plane for America, *our* grandfather ordered a hit on her mother. My girlfriend hasn't been looking you up. She's been mourning the murder of her mother that happened right in front of her."

His pupils dilated. Enlarging. He looked away, blinking rapidly to cover up his reaction.

I saw it, though. He was surprised. I wanted to name that other flash, though it was so brief, but it looked like regret. Sorrow? I wasn't sure. It was gone when he looked back at me. His features completely schooled back so he was in control, but I knew what I detected.

Fear.

I narrowed my eyes. Was he scared of Calhoun? Of me?

He was looking right at me, but while I was tracking every iota of emotion that might be showing on his face, he was thinking. I couldn't tell about what, but I felt it. He was calculating, and a second later, his eyes took on a distant look. He began to speak, his voice sounding from afar.

"I can see that I need to change my options here. I'd been prepared for your girlfriend to search me, and that fact and the history she would pull up would vouch for me. Or vouch enough where you might be inclined to trust me."

I waited.

He stopped speaking.

My turn. "Did you grow up with him?"

His eyes refocused, centering on me. They cleared, as if a wall fell away. He frowned. "You *really* haven't investigated me."

"There's reports he has sent teams to search for something. Am I wrong to assume that 'something' is you?"

His mouth tightened. A vein stuck out from his neck, his pulse beating visibly. "I would assume so." Another frown from him. "Perhaps. I'm not sure. He's lost quite a few of his assets, all of those being stripped from him by you. So they could be searching for me, or he might think I'm still where I usually go to get away from him."

"And that is?"

"I have people in Thailand I care about."

"People he knows about?"

Another tic from him. That vein was now sticking out from the side of his jaw. And it was bigger, pulsing harder.

"No," he bit out. "I wish that to *remain that way*." He hissed those last words, and to the untrained professional, it would seem as if I had something on him. This should give me a sense of power, where I could get comfortable. Then I would relax. I would dangle that threat above his head, issue my threats, and he would needle me. He would get information from me, and I would give it, almost gloating that I had that "thing" over him and I was deemed safe.

It was all a game.

I knew it. He knew it.

This is where I would need to "loosen" my strings. I would start getting arrogant. I would have to choose which information to "slip" to him. And then, when I left, feeling drunk on power, he would pull the string.

With all the shit that happened in my life recently, I didn't have the energy to play.

"I don't have time."

He frowned, his eyebrows jerking forward before smoothing back out.

Now I knew how he looked when thrown off balance. I cataloged that in the back of my mind, because while he was testing me, stringing me along, I was learning how to read him.

His eyes flared.

His head reared backward, with enough force to make his chair scoot backwards, too. "You motherfucker."

I gave him the slightest of grins, showing my teeth. "That's the point, isn't it? Our mother and the fucker who killed her." I shoved up from the chair, starting to warm my arms up, then pulling each one across my chest and stretching it. I let them fall back to my side and shook them out, rolling my shoulders. "Were you the price she paid for freedom? Give up one of his kids and he'd have to let her go?"

He sucked in a hissing breath.

I began to circle around him, slowly at first, watching him the whole time.

He watched me as much as he could, his head twisting to find me as I passed behind him. He was cautious now. Wary.

Good.

I didn't know this kid. I had no clue he existed, until my team found him, sent his existence to me, and a month later he's breaking into my apartment. He was either a secret they unveiled or a weapon Calhoun planted. Either way, he was here and he was currently under my control.

I stopped and squatted in front of him. My arms were loose, my elbows resting on my knees, and I stared up at him from this position. Maybe it was time to start asking the hard questions.

"Who raised you?"

No flicker. No response.

His face was like granite.

Okay. Next one.

"Did you know our mother?"

He blinked this time, a slight wince, but he caught himself, covering his reaction. A second blink. And back to a face of impassivity.

One more. "Did you know our father?"

There was no reaction from that one.

"Calhoun had our aunt raped. Were you there?"

His shoulders jerked up, but nothing on his face.

"Did you hear her screams?" I didn't wait. I pushed up and stood over him. "Because I did. Those tapes were sent to our mother. She listened to them, and I heard them, sitting outside her door."

I walked forward. This was a risk, but I was going to take it.

I leaned down, getting into his space. My hands went to his armrests and I was right there, almost eye to eye.

"He tortured them both. Mentally. Physically. Sexually. Emotionally. He did it all, then he killed them both."

His eyes were blazing. He tried, he struggled to put up his wall, but it slipped. He couldn't keep it up, and he was glaring at me. He moved even closer to me, trying to get into my space, trying to make me uncomfortable.

"If you're trying to figure out if I hate our grandfather, let me save you the trouble. I hate him. I have hated him all my life. I have dreamed about killing him, putting the knife in him, and I want to twist it, run it through the rest of him. Up his stomach, though his chest, and then turning, pushing it directly into his heart. And I would savor that moment, watching the life drain out of his eyes." He paused, breathing harshly. His nostrils were flaring. "If I had the power, I'd bring him back from the dead only to do it all over again. You didn't grow up under his thumb. I did. If you want a tutorial on torture tactics, I'm the one who should be giving it to *you*."

"And yet you're the one tied up here."

His eyes went flat at the reminder. His hands jerked, but they didn't ball into fists.

They remained flat, resting.

I was looking at him all anew, thinking back on everything. How he hadn't fought. How he hadn't asked questions or made demands. He'd been perfect . . . but those hands.

They never balled into fists. Not once. He jerked his arms, but they still remained flat.

Understanding dawned, and I stepped back from him.

Like he was preserving his energy.

Like he was waiting.

Like he was looking for his chance.

He knew how to fight. I bested him in the apartment, but had I?

That small knife.

"You knew," I murmured.

Yes. He knew he would be taken captive.

He knew there were body scans.

He knew he'd have to go in weaponless or he never would've gotten in, but he needed to go in.

"You couldn't stand going in without anything to defend yourself. That's why you brought in the small switchblade. You hid it. We found the towel on you. You had it wrapped up, and there was tape. We had someone put it back together. You had the tape to cover the ends of it, to make it look like something else, not a knife at all." Shit. Shit. I saw the knife taped back up, but I hadn't thought about it.

I was thinking on it now.

I moved back another step.

He wasn't moving. He wasn't reacting. It was like he was just waiting for . . . what? For me to piece it all together?

And then I *really* thought about him, and about where he grew up.

Another step back, toward my gun. "I turned myself into a human living weapon, and that was just training in preparation for him. But you . . ." Yeah. I was right. I felt it. It was clicking all the way down to my bones. "You lived with him. You were under his thumb. He tortured our aunt. He killed our mother. Jesus. You were there. You endured that. What does that make you? No way could someone live through that and come out unscathed."

He had to be unhinged. Had to be.

His eyes twitched. Not his eyelids, or his lashes. His eyes

themselves. That was the real him. I was getting in there. I was digging all the way in there.

I just needed him to show his face, his real face.

I needed to see who I was really dealing with, because what I was seeing was a mask.

Had to be.

I kept on, my voice growing soft. "If he knew you were gone, he would be frantic. What was his plan with you? Because he had one."

He didn't talk.

His eyes flashed, then went dull. His head lowered. His shoulders slumped.

Fucking hell.

It was like I pushed a button and he was a robot, turning off.

Talking was done. I'd gotten the information I needed, and I grabbed my things, but I barked at Josh, "I want a tranq, now!"

I sensed movement behind me. While I was in the process of grabbing my gun, his head whipped up, and if I'd been questioning myself a second earlier, that was all gone. I was right. His eyes went feral and he simply stood up.

He simply stood up!

His restraints were gone.

My hands closed around the gun. I was swinging around, but then he was there. He caught at my shoulder, his hands going to my wrist, and he stopped me midswing. Then he looked at me and said, "You're wrong, and I'll prove it to you."

Shouting.

Shots were fired.

Guards were streaming into the warehouse, but he let me go. He turned, and before I could incapacitate him, he was gone.

The door banged shut behind him, and the guards were running after him. But me, I was left with another realization. Despite him running now and despite him not trying to hurt me, I knew it in my bones. He hadn't gotten free from our grandfather.

He'd been *let* free.

I had no clue why.

Then Josh was approaching, his phone to his ear. I heard him say, "I'll tell him." He put the phone to his chest, looked up at me. "It's Matt. Something's happened."

NINETEEN

Bailey

We were pulling up to Phoenix Tech and *not* the Chesapeake.

"What is going on?" I leaned forward, a hand to the back of Fitz's seat in front.

"We're meeting Kash here instead."

Matt was frowning, too, so I wasn't the only one in Lostville, USA.

We got out, following Fitz. Matt's guards fell in step right behind us. The front door of Phoenix Tech was opened. More guards were there, and we walked past all of them, all the way to the elevator and up to the top floor, and when we stepped outside, I was having a moment.

I knew where we were going, and I'd never been to my father's office in this building.

I would've fangirled so hard going in there before this summer, but then *the summer* happened. But right then and there, I wasn't the daughter of Peter Francis walking inside. Okay. Maybe there was still some fangirling happening in me. I was the little nine-year-old that got her first *Computer Weekly* with Peter Francis on the cover as a birthday gift.

I think my knees were knocking together.

Matt frowned at me. "What are you doing?"

"Noth—" Total nerd squeak there. I coughed, my tone lower and calmer. "Nothing. I'm good."

My stomach was still doing loop-de-loops, but okay. We were here, and I saw my father, and the moment was done.

"Hey." Matt went inside, dropped to a chair, and threw his leg over the armrest. "Why are we here?"

Peter's gaze was lingering on me before he pulled away, looking at his son. "Because—"

"Because there's been some new developments everyone needs to know about."

Kash walked in with those words, his eyes falling on me and holding there. I was pinned in place, and I felt a rush of heat, of pain, of bitterness, but also of flutters and excitement. A whole rush of emotions all blasted me at once, and I had to pull my gaze away just to try and get ahold of myself.

I was all flustered.

What the hell?

Matt stood, sounding a whole lot more reserved. "Like what?"

I glanced up.

Matt had moved so he was half blocking me. His hands were in his pockets. His shoulders were bunched forward. He looked casual, laid-back, but I knew better. Whatever exchange had just happened between Kash and me, Matt saw it, and he was protecting me.

My stomach was cramping up.

"Why are you shielding Bailey from me?"

Oh. Crap.

A sudden silence fell over the room.

I swallowed over a lump, shoving that down.

Peter coughed.

Matt didn't respond, not right away. He shuffled to the side, still blocking me. "What are you talking about?"

I almost snorted.

"You know what I'm talking about." Kash's voice went low.

Goose bumps rose over my arm, along with a shiver going down my spine. But I was hot, and feeling achy, and also wanting Kash at the same time.

"Bailey," said Peter, in a quiet voice, "can you enlighten us on what is going on?"

I shoved out of the chair and surged to my feet.

My heart was beating fast.

I took a breath and stepped around Matt. Seeing Kash, seeing how gorgeous he was, his piercing eyes, how all those hours in the gym and swimming had sculpted his body so that even just standing there he was the definition of graceful deadliness . . .

The hairs on the back of my neck stood up, but I lifted my gaze. Catching how stormy his eyes were, locked on me, pinning me in place again, but sliding inside and, as if he could read my thoughts, feel my feelings, I gulped. My own vision grew blurry at the edges.

"Bailey." A soft prompt from Matt.

I opened my mouth, but nothing came out.

My throat ceased working.

What was happening to me?

I was moving.

My foot went forward.

My next, right after.

I was going past Matt, around Kash.

"Bailey?" Peter called after me.

I should stop.

I should explain.

I did neither.

I kept going, into the hallway. Past the guards. Past the elevators.

Fitz was coming after me. "Bailey? What's going on?"

I couldn't stop.

I pushed through the door to the stairs, but I didn't go down. I should've gone down.

I went up.

All the way, all eight flights, until the roof access door loomed over me, and I didn't pause. I shoved it open. Fitz was right behind me. I could almost feel his confusion, but get in line, buddy.

I had no clue what I was doing.

My body wasn't answering my own commands.

I was on the roof and I went to the edge, and there, once there, I stopped.

My hands grasped the railing. I was staring out over the back parking lot, and I closed my eyes. I threw my head back and I gulped, taking in the fresh air.

I suddenly couldn't breathe.

I couldn't move.

Everything was pulsating around me, pushing down on me, pushing from behind, from below, even from in front of me.

Kash was here. I could feel him.

I wasn't looking, but I heard the crunch of footsteps on the roof. Fitz was leaving. I could feel him easing back and Kash coming forward. He was coming slow, and the door shut again.

I was tense, waiting.

Nothing.

He didn't say a word, demand an explanation.

I couldn't take it.

I was biting my lip.

He needed to say something.

He had every right to be upset with me.

Still.

He said nothing.

God.

Fuck him.

Fuck me.

Fuck everything.

I whirled, tasting a sudden warm explosion of metal, and I knew I'd broken skin. I bit down on my tongue, but I didn't feel the pain.

I should've felt the pain.

He was right there, watching, looking like a goddamn saint. Like he had all the patience in the world. Like *he* knew what was going on inside of *me*. But that was preposterous. Right? *Right?*

I meant to offer an explanation, or an apology.

But those words didn't come out of my mouth.

"She's gone because of you." *Oh my God!*

I reeled on the inside, my actual body skidding back and finding the railing behind me.

I said that? I couldn't have, but his face shuttered closed. "I know."

No.

No!

"Don't be the victim here." I was shaking my head again and couldn't control what was coming out of my mouth.

His eyes flared, surprised. "I'm not."

"Yes, you are." I burst forward two steps, pointing at him. "You can't do that. It was your grandfather. If you hadn't fallen in love with me, then he wouldn't have . . ."

What was I saying? Shit. I was cringing, but I couldn't stop myself and kept going.

"I can't even say if we hadn't had sex, because you're you. I have to say if we hadn't met, because if I met you, I was going to fall in love with you. So, you. It's on *you*. You loved me. You let him know that. He hurt me to hurt you, and he *took her away from me!*"

I couldn't—Those words!

I gasped, my hands clamping over my mouth.

I didn't think like this or feel like this. But these words, they were coming out of me.

My mom.

Chrissy.

She was gone, and I . . . And now there was nothing.

I wanted to stay. I wanted to go in his arms, reassure him I didn't mean what I was saying, apologize for them. I didn't do any of that.

I didn't leave, either.

He was just staring back at me. His eyes were dark and haunted.

He spoke, his voice so quiet. "You don't think I know this?"

"What?"

He took a step toward me. "Or that I don't think this myself?"

"Kash." A soft sigh from me.

"You don't think I hold you at night and curse myself, knowing I should let you go? That if I hadn't met you, and fallen in love with you, that she would still be alive?" Another step. He was close to me, and he was whispering now. "It's my fault. And it tortures me every fucking minute, Bailey."

His eyes were so fierce, staring into mine, but he didn't touch me. I didn't touch him. Cold, biting Chicago air swung between us, back and forth, back and forth.

"She's gone because I loved you. It's that fucking simple."

I couldn't look at him anymore. I couldn't see his pain because then I would feel it, and I *was* already feeling him, and it was doubling my own pain.

I closed my eyes and I looked away. The silence was deafening, and I didn't know where we could go from there.

"I have a brother."

My head reared up.

A brother?

He was staring at me, but he was closed off. "A twin. My grandfather raised him, and he came to me. I had him. I don't know the reason why he's here, but he is, and I thought you should know."

My mind was a mess. There was too much going on.

I needed to regroup. I needed to fix this.

"Do you want me to leave?"

My heart was squeezing, but I couldn't answer him.

I closed my eyes.

"No . . ."

I opened them, but empty air greeted me back.

I never heard him leave.

QUINN CALLAS'S DEFENSE WILL PROVE INNOCENCE

Quinn Callas's defense team claims innocence, sets motion to pick jury members.

In an unprecedented move, the defense team for Quinn Callas wants to hold a jury trial, claims Quinn Callas is not guilty. Sources say Quinn "left a very toxic home environment with the Francis family. She just wanted to get out of there."

We'll continue to follow this story.

—*Inside Daily Press*

TWENTY

Bailey

We were at Naveah, and it was wrong.

Everything was wrong.

I messed up. I totally and completely fucked up.

I was a horrible, horrible human being.

A horrible girlfriend.

A horrible lover.

A horrible sister—No. I looked at Matt. I was a decent sister.

But back to Kash. I needed to fix it. Fix things. Fix everything. Kash wasn't taking my calls, and I had tried. I'd been trying for the last hour while it was only Matt and me in the VIP booth.

"Do you want me to leave?"

What was going on with me?

Pushing Kash away? Because that's what I wanted to do. That didn't compute, not one bit.

"This sucks." Matt reached for his whiskey, downed it, and held up the glass. A server signaled from the bar, and yes, it'd come to this. We'd only been here fifteen minutes, but Matt had gone through two other drinks already. The servers weren't even circulating up here. Matt began just raising his hand and the bartender noted it and sent a replacement. I watched as the bartender was already pouring Matt's next one and then handing it off to a server. She brought it up, her eyes taking in Fitz and Scott, who Kash must've told to go with us for some reason, and she sidled past them. The glass was on a tray and she placed it down in front of Matt. Her eyes going to mine, a silent question if I was okay or not.

I tapped my full drink. "I won't need a refill for a while."

I'd shared with him what happened on the roof. Matt was taking it worse than me.

Matt shook his head with a savage motion. "He has a brother." He snatched his drink up, downing a good sip before swallowing, grimacing, and throwing back another drag. He put it back down. "What is he going to need me for? Nothing. I'm your brother, but I was his brother, too, and now I'm nothing. I'm going to be replaced. There won't be any more . . ." He frowned. "There won't be any more Mash." A pause. "That doesn't sound right. Katt?"

Matt was in his own world.

I was in mine.

We were drinking together.

He snorted, slumping back. "Our whole house is in chaos. Finding out that Hoda is still evil and in Quinn's clutches. Kash has a brother now. Payton coming back."

"What?" My voice cracked.

His eyebrows went up. "Cyclone and Ser's aunt is coming back to the house."

Quinn's sister.

Payton looked like Quinn.

Quinn.

Who had been there, always there, always lurking.

It was Payton, but not really.

A sudden lance of panic pierced right down the middle of me.

Kash was gone.

Gone.

As in "not there."

I couldn't have that.

What did I do?

I shoved to my feet, knocking into the table.

"Hey, hey." Matt steadied the table, shooting me a glare. "Let's not be hasty and knock stuff over that we'll regret losing here."

I ignored him. "Matt! I have to fix this."

"I know." He reached for his glass, lifting it and petting the sides of it. "There, there. She didn't mean to frighten you."

"He asked me if I wanted him to leave and he didn't wait for my answer."

"Okay." He moved farther over in our booth. He was cradling his drink. "Can we refrain from the sudden lurching? I'm on a mission to get drunk. Let me have this, please. Since you're being nuts and irresponsible, means I can't be, and I want one night before I have to take up the mantle. I have a right to a pity party here. *Brother.* He won't need me anymore."

"Matt." I glared at him.

He glared back. "Mantle!"

I raised my hands, making a wringing motion with them. "You're exasperating."

"I'm aware." He hiccupped. "I've not had to grow up, because when Kash stopped taking care of me, you came in, and you are way more mature than me. But when you lost your head on that roof, I know the time has come when *I* have to adult. I don't like adulting. I try to do anything except adulting, but now I'll actually have to step up." He held a hand up. "I'm making my complaint official. I'm doing this under firm protest."

"Noted."

"Good." Another glare before he took a swig from his drink. "Mantle."

I rolled my eyes and sat down.

Matt slid my drink back over to where I was sitting.

He raised his up, waiting for me. "I'm sorry, Bailey."

I sighed, picking up my glass.

"You're still grieving. He shouldn't actually listen to you. What was he doing, listening to you?"

I frowned because he was right.

He grunted. "Kash is gorgeous. I may be a male, but I can tell when women flock to certain guys, and yeah, yeah, it could be about his money, but come on. Even I can tell he's got the brooding dangerous smoldering look going for him. You bone him on the regular, so you know."

Pain sliced me. "Your point here?"

"Oh yeah." Matt swung his hand up in a wide arc before it came down and slammed on the table. "My point is that there's no way in this world that Kash would actually leave you. It's more like a Kashcation, because you're going to be here with me, plotting to wreak mayhem on Quinn, and he's off doing whatever murderous mission he wants to do." He burped but didn't miss a beat. "He'll come back. He'll walk into your bedroom, and he'll say 'Hey' and you'll say 'Hey' back. Then you'll melt and he'll sweep you off your feet, then fuck you hard. Voilà."

A second burp. His eyes were growing a little wild.

"Trust me. You and Kash, this is just a small hiccup." He picked up his empty glass and held it toward me. "The makeup sex will be off the charts, so can you please wallow with your brother, because I'm the one who should be wallowing here, not you."

Yes. Matt.

He wanted to wallow, so we would wallow.

But, holy crap.

Kash had a brother.

I picked up my drink. "You're right. Here's to wallowing."

"Drink up, Bailey." He raised his arm for a fourth whiskey, which the bartender saw, and nodded. And the same server sashayed up moments later for Matt, and turned, swinging her hips slow and seductively on the way back down. Matt was watching, but I didn't think he was really seeing her. He held his glass out for me, and knowing what he wanted, I clinked it with my own.

He said, almost sullenly, "I figure you and me, we're due a night. You're going to pretend you're upset about Kash, even though we both know he'll be back and you'll both be fine. And me . . ." He burped again. "I'm going to indulge and let my wild paranoia run free, because come dawn, I'll rein it in. You and me. Team Batt needs to step up to home base. Kash has a lot on his plate. We'll help out. It's up to us to take Quinn down."

He looked up.

So did I. And as if taunting us, the news was reporting on Quinn's trial. Footage of her walking into the court was showing on a loop.

Matt extended a fist to me. "Team Batt."

I met it with my own fist, and we pretended to blow it up.

"Mantle."

"Mantle."

TWENTY-ONE

Bailey

Six A.M. and Matt and I were struggling to even walk.

There were shots, more drinking. Dancing. Yelling. Chanting. We might've coordinated a cheer even, complete with starting a flash mob with strangers. Matt has a favorite hot dog place he likes to stop at after drinking.

All in all, the night was epic.

Walking through the Chesapeake hallways as Matt veered off into the kitchen and I headed for my room with Kash, I already knew this was a hangover day. I wanted to collapse in bed and never move. There might be Disney movies to watch later on, but still from bed. Or in the house theater, but in my pajamas. I wanted to embrace the theme for the day.

"Bailey."

Aw, crap.

I faltered, first hearing Peter and then hearing what could only be described as . . . a father's dismay? My heart soared for a split second because (a) Peter was acting like a dad to me and (b) I had forgotten how much I missed that "parenting" effect until Chrissy was gone. But that was quickly pushed out to make room for embarrassment, a good amount of shame, and nausea.

The nausea was winning out.

He was coming down a hallway, fully dressed to start his day. A newspaper in one hand, a steaming mug in his other. And he was looking me up and down. There was no real expression on his face, but his eyes and mouth were both flat.

He stopped in front of me and wrinkled his nose before raising his mug and taking a sip. "You reek of Matt."

I paused. "That's an odd cologne."

"And you speak Matt, too. What an unpleasant surprise."

I felt that one like a punch to my sternum.

"You're fluent in parental disappointment. Why am I missing Chrissy so much? I've got you as a replacement."

I winced even before I had two words out of my mouth.

Who was this person in my body? I didn't like her.

Peter looked like he agreed with me, and his mouth pinched in at the corners.

He looked me up and down before shifting his newspaper under his arm and raising his hand to pinch at the top of his nose. "I think it's time we had a talk." He nodded in the direction I was going. "Go. Shower. Change. Come back to my office in an hour."

My tongue weighed down on the bottom of my mouth. My throat swelled and I couldn't speak for a moment.

A flare of regret pierced me, jarring me, but he moved on.

Climbing the stairs, I pushed open our bedroom door and stopped just inside.

The encounter with Peter hadn't been good, but this, coming into this room, this was worse. So much worse.

The night out with Matt had helped distract me, probably part of his reason, and I knew there was so much going on, but I felt the room's emptiness inside of me. It was pushing out everything in there, and I was a void hole in its place.

I missed Kash.

I was an idiot. And a fool. I was a total and complete fool, and I needed to call Kash now. Like, *now* now. Not *later* now, but the immediate now.

But I couldn't.

Damn.

Shower. Change. My first lecture ever from my father. After that, if I was still standing and in one piece, I'd call Kash and grovel.

Sighing, I went to get this going.

Peter was on the phone when I stopped outside. The door was slightly ajar, so I knocked softly and stuck my head in.

He motioned for me to come in. "I have to go. My daughter just came in."

My daughter.

That was nice to hear, and the acid built. It made the whole "dad being disappointed in you" even worse.

Putting the phone back, he looked me over again. This time his eyes were a little kinder, and I hated seeing it. There was so much pity in there.

I sat in one of his chairs, sipping my coffee like it was my shield to the world. "You're going to lecture me." Taking a cue from Matt, I slunk down in my chair. If I'd still been speaking Matt's language, I would've thrown a leg over one of the armrests.

"No, actually."

My eyes squinted over the top of my mug. "Huh?"

A ghost of a smile flashed before he cleared his throat. It was gone, and a hollow look entered his gaze. "I'm in no position to lecture you. You've been through so much that I can't fathom how you're still standing. You going and having a Matt night, I'm shocked this was the first time it happened. Truth be told, I won't be surprised if it happens a few more times."

I didn't want understanding.

Anger blazed through me.

Peter gave me a sad smile. "I know something happened with Kash, but while I love you both, that's also not what I wanted to talk to you about."

"Oh." I frowned. "What then?"

"Payton."

I groaned.

Peter's faint smile came back. "I expected that response from you, but I had a talk with Seraphina. Your sister and brother need some structure, especially with Quinn's trial getting more coverage every day. Payton may look like Quinn, but she's not at all like her. If you're around her, you'll start to see her as herself. She's very loving."

Loving.

Right.

I didn't want it.

"Bailey."

"What?" I snapped.

He stared at me, long and hard, before choosing his words. "I don't want you to move out, but I also need to think of my other children. I need you to stay. I need Marie to stay. I need Payton to come back, especially because your mother isn't—" His voice cracked and he looked away.

It was the first time I was seeing his reaction to Chrissy's death. That hit me hard, too, smack back in the sternum.

I murmured, "I wondered how you were handling it."

He frowned, blinking rapidly before his eyes seeming to focus on me again. "Handling?"

"She told me right before they attacked that night."

His Adam's apple moved up and down. "Told you?"

"That you two were falling in love."

He breathed in through his nose. "I had no idea you were aware we had gotten to that part."

"You loved her." I put the coffee on his desk, hugged myself, and sank low in the chair. "But I get it. I understand why you didn't tell me."

Another swift intake of air. "I'm a parent before everything else. You had Kash, but you needed a father, and that is who I will always be for you. I don't think you know how much I love you, how I would do anything for you."

I lifted up a corner of my mouth, letting him see the sadness on my face, and then I noted, "But I do know. It's the same love you have for Ser and Cyclone. It's why you're bringing someone back that's the face of my kidnapper." He went rigid, but I stood. I leaned down, placed one hand on his desk, and flattened my palm there. My fingers were turned toward him. "You don't have to worry about me. If you say Payton will help my siblings, then I'll deal. I love them, too."

His gaze searched mine, studying me, and then he nodded. His shoulders lowered, and he looked decidedly relieved. "Thank you."

A dip of my head. "Yeah." I blinked away a few more stray tears. They were sneaky little bastards. "I'm going to head to bed, if that's okay?"

"Bailey."

I got to the door, but paused.

He was still sitting there, his face seeming to have aged just from our exchange. Or maybe he wasn't masking it anymore. "Whatever was said, Kash knows you're still mourning. If that is something you're worried about, you don't need to. He'll be back."

Yes. But I'm not there for him now, and I should be.

I tried to give him a grin, but I know it didn't reach my eyes. "Yeah."

TWENTY-TWO

Kash

We'd just touched down in Aspen, Colorado, when Josh brought a phone to me. "Scott."

I took it, continuing as we deplaned and got into the back of two SUVs. "Bailey?"

"She's okay. Got drunk with Matt, but she's at home, sleeping safely." He hesitated a second. "She seemed sad."

"Did she say that?"

"No. I was reading her body language. Peter had a talk with her, but what we could ascertain, it was about the aunt returning to the house."

"Yeah." I remembered now. "Peter's doing that for the younger ones." Everyone filed in. The little luggage we brought was a few bags, and they were stowed away. Josh got in next to me and we were off to the next location. "Were you calling to give an update on her?"

"No. Harden reached out. He said he has news you will want to hear about Bastian."

I needed good news, and at this point, any news was good news. Calhoun had been quiet and I didn't like that. "Have him call."

"He said it was news that should be heard in person, and he's unable to come to you this time."

Meaning I had to go to him.

I mulled over that information. Harden had a reputation that once he said he was on your team, he was, until death or an event close to death would separate him from your side. When he locked in on a mission, it was for life. But the paranoid part of me, the part of me that knew my grandfather was an anal obsessive bastard, also set off alarms inside of me.

Josh must've been thinking the same. "We can reach out to your intel-gathering team. They have military backgrounds, too, and could act as backup if it was needed."

"No." They'd been my first call after my twin took off. I pulled them from working on my grandfather, looking for my brother. Harden was now my only in-field asset on Calhoun.

We were getting closer, and that was why we were in Aspen.

It was time to bring in one of his last assets that he thought he still had. Griogos Maragos had a home here.

The drive was an hour through the mountains.

We ended the call with Josh being responsible for setting up the meet. He was briefed on the reason we were in Aspen. And exactly one hour later we pulled up to a log cabin-esque house. Three stories. Every single window was lit up.

Josh took the house in as we parked. "Don't think she was expecting us."

I hid a grin, but then it was go time.

We got out and the guards took off.

They would sweep the perimeters, then the interior of the house.

The first wave approached the house.

The security system was dismantled.

The door was unlocked and we entered.

I was the fourth man inside.

We cleared the first floor together, moving as a team.

Two went upstairs.

I was with Josh as we went downstairs.

The second floor was cleared.

The guys went to the third floor right as Josh and I kicked in the last door of the basement.

Everything was cleared.

The living room. Bathrooms. Bedrooms. Closets.

Any door was opened, the room or whatever it led to was swept through.

We came back together on the main floor, and guns weren't holstered but they were lowered.

Josh frowned. "Is she hiding?"

I looked at Derek. "Did you check the feeds?"

He already had his computer up and was typing. "Pulling it up now." He clicked. Clicked. He frowned. Clicked some more, and his eyes lifted. "There's a secret door behind the living room couch."

We were in the living room.

As one person, we turned.

The couch was behind us.

Jasper and Josh moved to the couch, lifting it clear from the wall.

Derek put his computer down. All of our guns were raised again, and he approached the wall.

Jasper moved in from the right.

Josh from the left.

A small hatch was in the wall, and Derek took point right in front of Josh. He grabbed the latch and opened it, hurling himself and the small door to the side. Josh rounded, his gun drawn. Jasper bent down, sweeping the bottom. Josh the top. Neither saw anything. Both went inside.

Derek looked at me.

I looked at him, then nodded to the computer. "Pull the active feeds. I want to see if that's a tunnel, if she's coming out somewhere else."

He holstered his gun, nodding at the same time, and hurried to the computer.

We waited. A minute passed. Two. Three.

There were no shouts.

The guys checked the perimeter and all radioed in. Everything was cleared out there, so that meant she wasn't out there somewhere. She was inside the house—or hell, she was in a tunnel for all I knew.

Josh's voice came over the radio. "Got her."

Derek stopped what he was doing, going to his own radio. "Where?"

"There's a back room. I think we're under the basement. Her grandfather had a whole system down here."

"Is she unharmed?"

A slight laugh from Josh. "Oh yeah. She's feisty, some cursing, but she's good to go. She'd been drinking, so I think she got lost in the tunnels. She trapped herself."

Over the radio, we heard a feminine voice, "Fuck you! Fuck who's out there. Is that Kash? Tell him to fuck himself!"

There were scuffling sounds next.

A thud.

Josh came back on the radio, his voice sounding strained. "Jasper needs a hand. We'll be out momentarily."

"Guys outside want to know your orders. They switched channels," Derek said.

I nodded, rubbing a hand over my face. I was exhausted and I hadn't even dealt with this girl yet. "Tell them to set the detonators. This is going to be a message to him."

Derek's eyebrows dipped before smoothing out. "Can I say something?"

"Yeah."

"What's the message of burning down this house? You already eliminated the owner, and he was one of your grandfather's biggest assets."

"The message is that he can't hide anything from me. I will find it, and I will destroy it. It's cat and mouse right now, but I've become the cat. He just doesn't know it. Me burning this house down, and the five others we're going to do by the end of this trip, is me letting him know. He's now the mouse. I want him scared and I want him doing what she did, messing up and trapping himself."

Josh and Jasper arrived back, stepping out from the small door, and in their hands was a struggling old lover.

I greeted her. "Hello, Victoria."

The guys hadn't lied. Her eyes were dilated, her hair a mess. She was wearing a robe over a nightgown. Her feet were bare and she reeked of booze.

"You mother fucker fuckerrr. I'm gonna—I'm gonna— aghrdd." She tried again, twisting around. "Im gont hurd youph. Yood aholed!"

I had to take stock for a beat, because the last time I saw Victoria, she'd been furious, but she hadn't been this Victoria. She was skin and bones.

"Boss." Jasper lifted her arm, shoving her robe's sleeve up.

Her veins were black and blue. Track marks.

I frowned, shooting an order out to Josh. "Go. Search the house. I want all the drug paraphernalia collected."

"*What?* Noooph. Im nod a drgge. I'm nod."

"Vic."

The nickname silenced her. She stopped struggling against Jasper's lone hold. He was behind her, one foot between hers so she couldn't kick back, and he had a firm grip on both her arms, keeping them slightly behind her.

Her eyes were wide, but damn, she was gone. Anything I said to her would be wasted. So instead of issuing the threats and the ultimatums that I wanted to, I remembered she was someone I used to care about.

I never loved her, but I cared for her.

I stepped close, sliding my hand under a strand of hair that was hanging over her face, and I moved it back. I tucked it behind her ear and I let her feel a gentle slide of my hand down her cheek, a slight cupping of her chin, before I angled her head to see me better.

"You're going to get clean." The words were firm and without reproach from me.

She took note and her eyes widened. Defiance started to fill, but I shook my head.

I let go and stepped back. "I'm not asking, Vic."

"You took away my grandfather," she whispered.

"But not you, Victoria."

Her eyes closed first.

Her shoulders fell.

The fight left her body.

It could've all been an act. It probably was, because she had the signs of a full drug addict. I wasn't going to give her an option.

"Take her outside," I told Jasper.

Derek was listening to his radio, and as Jasper led Victoria outside, he approached. "They're done outside."

"Okay." I nodded toward where Jasper and Victoria were going out the door. "Leave me the remote. I want you to go back with them and the guys."

"Will do."

A minute later, one of the men came inside and handed me the remote. He explained which button to use, how far we would need to be, and then he left.

Josh came down the stairs, a full bag with him, and he placed it on the dining room table. "I think I got everything. I'll do a sweep of the main level and the basement." He disappeared to the back rooms, and I moved to the far wall, which extended down the farthest hallway.

I was looking at the pictures when Josh finished, coming up to me. "Done."

I didn't speak. I kept looking.

He transferred his gaze, taking in the image. "Is that Victoria?"

"It's her and her father."

Josh looked at me. "Her father's dead, isn't he?"

"Yeah." That was a sad fact that I never stopped to consider until now. "My grandfather killed him."

Josh didn't react, but I felt his attention sharpen.

"I overlooked it. That was around when Victoria and I met for the first time, and looking back, there were rumors. I never questioned why. I never questioned the reason for it. If I had, then what? Would I have stepped in sooner? That's probably the time when he decided to use Victoria to get to me."

"That's what Griogos was talking about, that Victoria was supposed to marry you."

"Victoria was supposed to control me. That's how my grand-father thought. He wanted me tied to him. It was just one more way he was trying to control me."

"You and her *did* date."

I nodded, moving to the next picture.

They were smiling in it. I pointed at it. "This is Maragos and his daughter."

"The daughter who Calhoun was controlling, too?"

"He owned her. Griogos sold her to Calhoun."

But that wasn't the point of my trip down memory lane.

I was remembering the first time I saw Victoria.

The first flirt. The first kiss. The first date.

I came to the last picture, and Josh said under his breath, "Damn."

It was me, Victoria, Matt, and Tony.

I forgot that, too. The four of us were friends. We were the beginning of everything.

"You're so young in there."

I nodded, lingering on Victoria's face. Fuck. The bitterness was strong.

I had missed this.

I had missed it completely.

"This was another family he destroyed." I touched Victoria's face in the picture. She was thirteen. It would be the next year when Tony and Matt began drinking. It would be a few years years after that when Victoria and I started sleeping together. And in the midst of it all, I never thought about how Calhoun took her father first, then indebted her grandfather to him, and through all of that, began to own Victoria and her mother.

"Why am I getting the feeling you're changing your mind on her?"

"She was a friend first. She was an innocent at one point."

She looked like Bailey in the eyes. Both pure and both smiling.

I nodded, rapping my knuckles against Victoria's thirteen-year-old self one last time before turning to leave. "We're going to get her clean, and then we'll go from there."

We were two miles away when I hit the remote.

The sky lit up behind us, painting the sky orange and red.

TWENTY-THREE

Bailey

"I'm supposed to be hunting my grandfather."

I gasped, whirling around. Kash had been gone for a while now, maybe a few days. It felt like forever. I was coming back from a rousing game of bowling downstairs. Seraphina won because everyone threw theirs in the gutter. She loved it. Cyclone vowed to make a robot bowling ball so he'd win forever.

There'd been an ache in me because, well, because of who was standing in front of me.

"You told me you had a brother."

"You told me to go."

I winced, remembering. "I didn't, actually. You asked if I wanted you to leave, but I did hesitate on answering. I'm sorry for that."

He sighed, coming farther into the room. He was dressed casual—a Henley shirt, jeans, a ball cap. I didn't understand the need for a ball cap, but I'd never say no to it on Kash. It made his jawline and lips so delicious. Those high cheekbones, too.

"You weren't wrong. I am to blame—"

"No, you aren't. Your grandfather is. Not you. And you're also right. I need you to kill him. I need that, Kash. I shouldn't, but I do, because it was my mom and—"

He stopped me, coming forward, not stopping until he was right in front of me. He tipped my chin up so his eyes could rake over me. "I do not tell you enough how amazing you are." His hand slid to the back of my neck, his fingers threading through my hair, and he cupped the base of my skull in the palm of his hand. "You are funny. You are courageous. You persevere. You endure. You adapt. You look for the positive. You are allowed to blame someone for losing your mother, and you are allowed to blame me. I failed."

"Shut up."

He started to say something but stopped. "What?"

"Shut up." I moved in, spreading my hands over his chest and then around him, and I tipped my head back even farther. We were flush against each other. "I don't know why you came back . . ."

He groaned, his thumb moving to my bottom lip. "I had to."

"But I'm so thankful you did. I need you. I think I need you more than ever right now."

"Bailey." A sigh from him.

Not good. I recognized that sound, and only bad news was coming on the end of it.

I stood up, going to my tiptoes, and I looped my arms around his neck. I was ready to go full spider monkey on him if I needed to. I'd climb up his body, my legs and arms would wrap around him and become like glue. I didn't have real glue, so I'd have to meditate that I was glue. Power of the mind. I'd be embracing it real quick if he tried to disentangle me.

"No." I shook my head. "I'm going to have to do another 'shut up' moment here, because Kash, shut it. Seriously. You came back and I'm not letting this chance get by me. You have a brother." I gently shook him, smiling up. "A brother. That's huge news. And a twin. What's he like? Are we talking identical, and if we are, how identical? Why aren't you excited about finding out about this guy? I'd be doing cartwheels. I'm pretty sure I did when I found out about my family."

He'd been staring at me, a lightness starting in his eyes, until I brought up the brother.

The light went out then, and he stiffened. He reached up, taking my hands in his, and gently unclasped them from around my neck. "It's not the same situation."

He took another step back.

I tried not to be upset about the distance, but I was aching for him.

He needed me. He just wasn't letting himself need me right then and there.

He shook his head, his whole face sobering. "The problem with my sibling versus yours is that I know yours are safe. They weren't sent to break into your home and don't have the ability to kill your loved ones."

I stopped short. "Your twin can do that?"

His eyes flicked up at that, before a short laugh slipped out. "The thought of him hurting you . . ."

"Hey, hey." I went over to him, catching his hand. "Stop, okay?" First things first here. "Do you accept my apology for telling you to go away?"

"Of course, I do. But you can say that . . ."

Another squeeze to his hand. "You know that I love you, and I don't want you to leave my side again, even though I know you have to."

He opened his mouth to say something.

A third hand squeeze from me. "Just nod. We're getting in a cycle here."

A rueful grin from him, but he nodded.

We were moving forward. Blastoff.

"You know that I know you have to go and do scary things, and I'm okay with it, but I'm going to worry about you."

He groaned. "I don't want to leave your side."

I waved that off. "But I'm guessing you don't want to take me with you, either?"

"Want to? Yes. Hell yes. Can I? No. If something happened to you . . . I can't risk that. Not after everything that you've already gone through and suffered. I would be selfish if I did."

I nodded. "I get that. I do. But . . ." Team Batt. I didn't want Kash upset with me because of things I would be doing. "You have to understand that I can't sit and do nothing here. Right?"

His eyes narrowed. "Are you talking about your drunk night with Matt?"

I laughed, a lightness shifting in my chest. "No. I mean there might be a situation where we could do something to help you, here, on our end, you know . . ."

He gave me a dark look. "What are you planning?"

I shrugged. "Nothing. Just if a situation happens to show itself and we can do something to help out, I want you not to worry about me. Or Matt."

"Matt?"

"Or whoever might be around who can help me. You know."

There was a long beat of silence between us.

Kash was studying me. I was more trying to look at him, but also not looking at him, because he could see through me and I didn't want him to derail us from going after Quinn.

"Bailey."

"Hmm?"

"What are you planning?"

Oh, screw it. A whole rush of air left me and I capitulated. "I have to do something. Something! I'm going crazy not doing anything. You're off being all dark and dangerous, and well . . . let me help, too. Quinn is here. Her court case is happening, and we haven't gone after Camille Story at all. You handle big and scary Calhoun and we'll handle Quinn here. Deal?"

I held out my hand.

He stared at it, then at me, back to my hand, then to my face. His head tilted to the side and he raised an eyebrow. "I am not shaking on that." A whole whoosh of disappointment flooded me. "But do what you have to do. Just don't get in trouble, and my God, please listen to your guards. I have them on you for a reason."

Did he . . .

Holy crap, he just did!

"You're okay with it then? Matt and me going after Quinn?"

"I wouldn't say I'm okay with it, and I'm not sure about Matt, because he likes to get arrested a lot, but . . ." His tone gentled. "I know that you need to help and this is your way of doing it."

The lightness was in full effect. I felt like I was floating on air. "Really?"

"Really." He closed his eyes, his face shuddering. "I cannot control you, nor do I want to, but I am terrified for your safety."

"I won't take any risks that are stupid. I promise."

A stark look came over him as he stared at me. "Good."

I stared back. "Good," I whispered. "Do you need to process having a twin?"

He shook his head. "No, because I don't know if he's going to be good or harmful. For now, he just exists and that's all. He's a possible threat."

"That sounds ominous."

"I don't even know his name." He let out another soft sigh. "I need you. I need to hold you. I need to reassure myself that you're okay. But I think for right now I need to do something normal with you."

I perked up at that. "Normal?" Normal was my new thing of fantasies.

He grinned. "I could rent an entire movie theater for us. Any recent movie you'd like to see?"

A movie? The floor just moved under me. I haven't even thought about a movie since last May. "I'm sure there's a new superhero one out."

"Done." His grin shouldn't be as sensual as it was, but it was, and it was sending tiny little thrills down my spine. "Popcorn?"

Those thrills turned into tickles. "Yes, please."

"Chocolate candies?"

"Now you're making me want to jump you on the way to the movies."

"Oh no, no, no." He was being slightly flirty now, a little twinkle in his eyes. "We'll be as normal as we can be, and that means making out in the theater. I reserve time for that."

The tickling, thrills, and the whole floating sensation was overtaking me and I moved to him. "I'm really happy you came back even though you're in the middle of destroying your grandfather."

He smiled, his eyes so tender. "I'm just glad you love me. Promise me you'll be safe."

"I promise."

I was standing close enough to him so he tipped my head back, his lips lowering and giving me a soft kiss, before he said, "Now, change. I have a movie theater to go and buy out."

TWENTY-FOUR

Bailey

I wasn't supposed to like her.

I had seen her before. She'd been a person lurking in the background. Then she was lurking in the background when I was at the house, and, full disclosure, she was there, and she was quiet, but she wasn't really *lurking* lurking. I wouldn't have noticed if it was someone else, but the point is that she looked almost exactly like her sister, and it was her sister that I hated.

Loathed.

Despised.

I've digressed.

Payton. I wasn't supposed to like her . . .

But I did! Or, well, I didn't want to stab her. She seemed nice.

She came over and gave me a hug when she got to the house, but that was after a long look at Kash. And Kash being Kash, he watched her right back, until he finally spoke. "Hello, Payton."

She swallowed. "Hello, Kash. I didn't know you'd be here."

"Just for the night. I'm leaving soon."

She gave a small dip of her head before she turned to me for that hug. It was a gentle hug, too. She was soft-spoken, her head folding down a lot and her eyes looking away. She wrung her hands like it was a nervous habit.

Marie walked into the room and she sucked in her breath, actually taking a step back. The wall was there, so she hit the wall, but I got her drift.

And then—then!—Seraphina looked over at her, frowned, and took her hand. Seraphina was reassuring *Payton*, and the wall crumbled. Game over. I knew that I'd been wrong to not like this person. If Seraphina, one of the kindest people I knew, was trying to shield Payton, or at least comfort her, we were in the wrong.

Cyclone headed over next, wrapping his arms around her legs.

He pressed in, his head craned back so he could see her, and the brightest smile was there. Payton looked down, her entire face softened. She raised a hand up, a finger tucking a strand of Cyclone's hair back, and then she smoothed her hand through the rest of his hair.

He was loving it. He was living for it.

We needed to trust these two gentle creatures.

They were choosing her, and they were telling us something.

Humble pie, I believe I might need to eat you.

While she had the same wheat-gold blond hair, blue teardrop eyes, and high cheekbones as her sister, Payton looked more demure. Quinn's face was strong, her bones were more angular. They were defined better. Payton's face was softer, a little rounder, and her cheeks were more plush. She had slightly thinner lips.

Quinn seemed as if she demanded attention, but Payton got it with a second glance, then a third, a fourth, and soon . . . who was Quinn again?

Those were the more noticeable differences between the two, now that I was paying attention and not just insta hating. And during family dinner that night—with Peter in attendance,

Marie with a pressed mouth, Theresa who kept quiet but also kept watching her mom as if expecting her to explode any second, Payton sitting at the end and laughing quietly with Cyclone and Seraphina, both of whom were so happy that they were glowing—yeah, I was starting to pay attention.

Payton was not Quinn.

Matt showed up at the end, sneaking into a chair on the other side of me. Kash was on my right, and Matt made sure to pat him on the arm. We'd had breakfast together and Kash had given my brother a full lecture on being smart with whatever he and I were about to do.

Matt listened through it all, then leaned forward, plopped his elbows on the table. "Now, let's talk about how I'm not going to be replaced by your new brother."

He kept his voice low so no one else could hear, but the rest of the meal was full of Matt peppering Kash with questions, Kash not answering them, and Matt then asking even more questions. By the end, Matt seemed reassured he wasn't going to be replaced.

Matt slumped down now, grabbing the drink Theresa just sat in front of me, and stabbed his fork into my chicken. He sipped and chewed at the same time while Peter looked up, his nose pressing in. His eyes narrowed, lingering on his oldest before he shook his head from side to side, slowly, and reached for his own wine.

Matt watched the entire perusal and then smirked. "What's up, Pops?" He didn't wait a beat, his eyes sliding across the table to where Payton had stilled, half bent toward Cyclone, but biting down on her lip. Matt's smirk widened. "Look what prodigal reject swept in with the wind."

Payton sucked in her breath, her eyes blinking rapidly.

Peter instantly scowled.

Kash glanced at me, a small frown.

Marie was sitting with us, next to Peter, and her eyes widened.

"Aye aye aye," she muttered under her breath, making a point of looking down at her lap.

Theresa had been returning to the kitchen, but now she paused and swung back to glare at Matt. One hand on her hip.

Seraphina frowned, a tiny wrinkle in her forehead.

Cyclone burst out. "You shut up, Matt!"

Matt jerked back.

Payton's eyes rounded. I had a feeling that if she could've poofed in the air and disappeared, she would've.

Everyone else was as surprised as me.

And Cyclone was not done!

He pounded his fist on the table, sitting up on his knees. He lifted that fist and pointed at his brother with a finger jabbing in the air. "You're always so mean to Aunt Payton. Stop it!"

Out of the mouths of babes . . .

I swiveled my head until I was only watching Matt, the back of my head to everyone else. He seemed frozen in place until his eyes jumped and met mine. Guilt flared before he blinked, and then it was gone. His smirk remained, but it was much less, and he leaned forward. His fork was poised over his plate, just hanging from his hand. "I'm being mean, Cy?"

Cyclone's face got beet red and he sat back down. But his mouth was still tight and his chin jutted out. He crossed his arms over his chest. "Not always, but a lot of the times to Aunt Payton and Dad."

Matt's eyes started dancing. His smirk was more a flat line, but I had the impression he was holding laughter in. "Really?" He leaned forward, placing his fork down in an exaggerated move and smiled politely. "Well, *Dad*. I am sorry for being mean so much of the time." He sat back, nodding to Payton. His tone was more genuine and softer. "Payton."

Her mouth turned down at the corners, but she nodded back. "Matthew."

"I didn't mean that in a mean way . . ." He winked at Cyclone.

"But in a way where I was making fun of Peter Dearest, since, you know, he sent you away when the big guns came home." His eyes darted to Marie, holding, before he leaned back in his chair. His arm came up, resting on the back of my chair, and he turned to me, his look holding on me, too.

The back of my neck got hot. "You're being mean to me now?"

The smirk was back, and it was wicked. "I called you a 'big gun.' How is that not a compliment?"

I opened my mouth, but Payton beat me to it, and her comment came out way softer than mine would've. "Because it's not, but thank you in a backward way." She turned to me, then Marie. "When Peter asked if I'd come back, he explained both of your concerns." She looked from Marie to me and back. "I'm not here to disrupt anyone. I'm only here for Cyclone and Seraphina. I love both of them so much, and Peter said it'd be good if I came back. I do not condone what my sister did. If I did, I wouldn't be able to sit here. I *condemn* what she did. I no longer consider her my sister."

Cyclone stiffened, and it was noticeable enough for everyone to look his way.

Payton, too. "Oh, honey. You have to know that what your mother did was wrong. I can't love her back, not until she apologizes to everyone she's hurt because of her actions. To Bailey. Kash. Everyone she hurt. Right now"—she put her arm around Cyclone, drawing him to her side—"she doesn't think it was wrong, what she did. That's why you can't see her right now, not until she gets better."

Seraphina frowned, but she didn't say anything.

Cyclone's eyes were so big and wide, and heartbroken. My throat swelled up, seeing that last emotion, and then I heard him whisper, "Does that mean we'll never get to see her again?"

"Oh!" Marie's gasp was hushed.

I looked over. Peter seemed to be struggling himself, his Adam's apple bobbing up and down repeatedly.

A tiny tear slipped from Seraphina, sliding down her cheek.

Marie bundled her back to her, hugging her as both still watched Payton and Cyclone.

The only one who seemed not affected by his whisper was Payton, but her tone was soothing and so caring. "I don't know, bud. I hope you do. I hope I do. I don't agree with what my sister did, but that doesn't mean I don't still love her. You can feel what you feel. Anger. Hurt. Love. If you miss her, you can miss her. You can do that, but she's made some bad choices, and until she starts making better choices that don't hurt people, we can't go and see her."

"She's not in prison." That came from Seraphina. She was sitting straight up, her chin raised, her eyes defiant, and she was holding on to the table as if her life depended on it.

I tensed.

"But she should be." Seraphina sent a furtive look to Kash, and I felt him tense beside me. She turned to Cyclone. "We should never see her again. She tried to take Bailey from us. If Kash hadn't gotten there as fast as he did, we might not have her with us anymore. We *just* got a sister and then she wanted to hurt her and take her away permanently. That's not a good person doing a bad thing. That's a bad person doing a bad thing. And she was bad. She was mean to me, always. I was never enough!" Her voice rose. "Never good enough. Never pretty enough. I had to speak perfectly, act perfectly, think perfectly, and I hated it. I hated her! She made me drink vinegar if I messed up—"

"*What?*"

Everyone exploded, but Peter's outburst overrode the entire room.

Seraphina turned those defiant eyes his way. "She made me clean my mouth out with soap. She picked my friends, did you know that?"

My stomach rolled over.

I wanted to throw up.

"She told them to pick on me. She's the one who created that website where they ranked everyone in our class, and she knew I could see it. She's the one who put that my personality needed work. It would've gotten worse except Bailey hacked into it and my mom was too scared to type it in again. She thought Bailey would look again, see it came from her, and would show it to you, Dad. That never happened, but . . ." She looked at me, and I was bowled over. "Thank you for doing that. I never felt like I could really tell you how much it helped, but it did. Those girls weren't as mean to me as they were before. And Kash, I'm sorry that I liked Victoria. I know she was friends with Mom, and I know she was your ex, but I overheard that she was mean to Bailey and I'm really sorry about liking her. But sometimes . . . sometimes I didn't like her at all."

Kash leaned forward. "That's why you've been nervous around me?" he asked quietly.

She nodded, her head almost jerking forward at an awkward angle. "I felt bad. I'm really sorry."

I had no idea what conversation she had overheard, or when, but I wanted to just grab her and hold her forever.

"Ser."

She looked back up at him.

"You don't have to feel bad about anything. Okay? I think of you as my little sister, and that will never change."

"Never?" A whisper from her.

"Never."

She sat up a little higher, her entire face brightening up. "Okay." Still a whisper, but it was progress.

"Those girls aren't mean anymore because I told them what you did, Bailey," Cyclone said. He was looking at me, too, and I continued to be bowled over. "I made them scared of you, told them you could hack into their parents' bank accounts if you wanted, and no one would know."

Matt snorted in a choked-off laugh.

I ignored him, reeling from what both had just said.

One. Two. Both with punches, because both were looking at me with such conviction, such strength.

Cyclone kept going. "I told them that they better watch what they say. If I heard one whisper they were being mean to my sister, I was going to sic my other sister on them. I told them even the FBI knew about your skills and gave you a wide berth."

Okay. That was funny.

My mouth twitched. I heard a low chuckle from Matt.

Seraphina was gazing at her plate and her bottom lip was trembling.

I couldn't take it.

I shoved back my chair, was around that table in a flash, and I had both my arms around my little siblings. They were sitting next to each other, but moved in with me, hugging me back.

Cyclone let go first, and I heard a little giggle from him.

Seraphina wound her other arm around my neck. She whispered into my neck, "I love you, Bailey."

Oh. Damn.

I was gone. Blubbering.

A mess.

My bottom lip was the one trembling now.

I eased back and smoothed down her hair, smiling at her. "You are so beautiful and so kind and you have the best soul I think I have come across. Anything Quinn told you was wrong. If you need to fact check me, look at where she's at right now. Not here. Not with her family. She did that, no one else. She is not the victim. She is not misunderstood. She hurt people, and because of that, she lost the two greatest things she's ever done in her life. You two. What your aunt said is right. You can still love her. You know that, right? You can miss her. But she hurt people, and she needs to atone for that."

Seraphina's hands came up and gripped mine where they were resting on her shoulders. She squeezed them, saying gently, "I know."

Good Lord.

I loved this little teenager.

Cyclone's hand snuck into mine and pulled it from Seraphina's shoulder. He squeezed. "After dinner tonight, can you help me with a computer project?"

"Of course." I squeezed his hand back.

"I want to learn how to hack into my gym teacher's emails. I want to get a pass so I can join the next robotics class, and it's only offered during gym. It's not fair."

Matt said, "Maybe wait until you're not at dinner with the adults to ask that, bud."

"Why not?"

"Cyclone, your sister won't be helping you with your computer project after dinner. You and me, we'll be having a talk instead," Peter said.

"That's why," said Matt.

Seraphina giggled. "You got in truh-bull. Truh-bull."

She kept snickering, and it was contagious. Everyone was sporting a grin.

I think it was the best dinner I'd ever had.

There was only one person missing.

TWENTY-FIVE

Kash

I was back with my team, and over the last few weeks, we found the rest of Calhoun's hidden locations. Bailey helped us find them a lot faster than we expected.

Safe houses. Warehouses. His or someone else's that he used as his.

We destroyed them.

Each one was isolated and so off the grid that I didn't know when Calhoun would find out about them, but it would take time. I wished I could be there when he was told.

Josh came to the back of our motel room, sitting on the bed beside my table. He let out a sigh, unclasping his holster and putting both his guns on the other side of my laptop. "Derek called. He said Victoria's detoxed. Wanted to know what you wanted done with her?"

I hadn't trusted Victoria, so I sent her off with two of my guys. Their orders were to find Robbie, who would get in touch with Ace, who had more friends with places that were completely off the grid. She went to one of those locations, and whoever Ace trusted was getting paid a lot of money to not only detox Victoria but also to deprogram her, since she'd been brainwashed. She'd been spewing pro-Calhoun sentiments when we had her at our first headquarters. Deprogramming was the way to go.

"Is she still pro-Calhoun?"

He grinned, stretching his neck so it cracked. "I don't think she's pro-Calhoun, but she's still anti-you, if that's what you're asking."

I lifted my arms up over my head, clasping them, stretching them. Sitting in the motel room for the last two days put knots in places I didn't enjoy. "I can work with that. Is she showing remorse?"

"Over what?"

I dropped my arms, eyeing him. "Derek didn't say anything about that?"

Josh shook his head. "Ace was the one who talked to Derek, said your ex was done and ready to be moved for whatever you wanted for her."

I glanced at my phone. Bailey's picture was there, smiling up at me.

Josh fell silent.

I shoved up from the chair, grabbing my own gun and sliding my phone into my pocket. Josh was watching my movements but kept quiet.

"Have we gotten word about my brother or what Calhoun is planning next?" I asked, while holstering my second gun.

Harden had asked to meet in person, but when we got in touch, he said he needed more time. So that's what we were doing; we were waiting.

I was getting sick of waiting.

"Still radio silence from Harden, but the other team called earlier. They found someone who got wind of your brother, but I gotta say . . ."

I stopped in my movements and looked at him.

He was grim. "Your brother's like a ghost. He's like you, maybe better."

"He's laying low. I was a ghost, standing next to Peter Francis. He was a ghost when no one knew to look for him."

Josh stood from the bed as I was heading for the motel door. "You're not worried about him?"

I reached for the doorknob, but paused and looked back. "I am, but so far he's not going after the people I love." Bailey. Matt. The Francis family. "When he said he hated our grandfather more than me, I felt it."

Josh's eyes narrowed. "And about Victoria?"

"Let me think on her." I opened the door. "I'll be back."

We were in the middle of nowhere, a back section of woods in North Carolina. A perimeter was established, but I needed to move. I needed to exert myself.

I needed to punish myself.

I had to run, and like two days earlier, I just started.

It wasn't enough. It never was.

I sparred at home. I swam to tire myself.

If those didn't work, I would wake Bailey and bring her and myself to a climax over and over again. There was a drive in me, one I didn't want, one I cursed, one that was a blessing, one that kept me going and going and going.

It'd always been there.

I had trained that drive into a thirst against my grandfather. He was always the target. He morphed my life, and I let him. I used his image, his threat, to mold me into who I was today. Bailey said I was half animal. Maybe. A half monster, too? Probably. Either way, I had to move and go, and I had to sweat until I wanted to collapse, and at the end of that, I would keep going, because I always had more in me.

Always.

And tonight, I was just starting.

TWENTY-SIX

Bailey

"You know what I was thinking about today?" Matt was sitting next to me on a bench, and we were getting attention. He didn't care. He slumped down, almost looking bored.

Not me.

I was fully aware of how much attention was coming our way, but that was our plan.

We were sitting on a bench outside Quinn's trial. It was closed and we weren't allowed inside, on everyone's request, but Matt wasn't okay with that. Well, he wasn't okay with anything when it came to Quinn, so here we were, sitting on a bench, getting cameras and phones pointed our way for pictures and recordings. People wanted to know why we were there, but mostly Matt wanted Quinn to know we were there.

Me, I had my own plan, and it was dumb. It was really, really dumb.

We were doing it anyway.

"Bailey. You're supposed to ask, 'No, my Genius Brother. What were you thinking today?'"

"Right." I moved my head up and down in a clip. "No, my Genius Brother. What were you thinking?"

He smacked my leg, a full grin on his face. "I was wondering how long it's been since you got laid?"

I spit.

Whatever was in my mouth, it landed on someone walking by us. Gum. Spit. Water from a bottle I just drank out of and hadn't fully swallowed. It was all gone, and after throwing a distracted apology at the passerby, I turned to face my brother squarely.

He remained slumped down in the bench, lounging to be more accurate. His legs were out and he had angled his body so he was taking over half the bench. He was dressed in faded jeans, but they were still the expensive kind, sneakers that weren't available in stores yet, and a sweatshirt that had a logo celebrities were starting to wear on their social media. I knew what he looked like: a rich, cocky dick. And it was working. A few girls on the other side of the hall were watching Matt. They kept sneaking pictures and whispering to each other. But it wasn't like we were trying to be incognito. The whole point of us being there was to get recognized and get the word out that *we were there.*

My neck was hot.

Had someone put a heater on in the hallway? In the middle of the winter?

I fanned myself with my hand and scooted farther down on the bench from him. "Why's that your business?"

"It's not." His smirk grew even cockier. "But I was thinking you're not the type to step out, and your man's been gone, so . . ." He was eyeing me, studying me.

"What?"

"How cranky are you going to be after we do this thing to-day?"

"This thing" was our so-stupid and so-not-genius-like plan, and I knew we were dumb to even be considering it, let alone to actually be here. And once those doors opened and Quinn showed, I knew we would put it in motion. Matt looked laid back in whatever too-cool image he was displaying, but he was tense and alert and primed to attack Quinn.

"After? What are you talking about?" A thought hit me. "And where's Tony? You said he's the one who can pull this off."

"I did." At that moment, Matt sat up, nodding to a crowd gathering in the hallway. "He's here."

"This is so stupid," I muttered, my heart rate suddenly spiking.

I straightened up, too, rubbing my hands up and down my jeans, trying to dry the sweat off of them to no avail. That sweat was going to be there until we were done, in the car, and safe. Preferably not in handcuffs. "Matt." A sudden burst of newly frenzied panic hit me hard. He was starting to stand up, but I grabbed his shirt. I yanked him to me. "Let's not do this! We'll get arrested. We'll get—"

A presence had stepped up to us, and Matt pried my hands off of him, standing fully at the same time. Once I let him go completely, he stepped back and looked at Tony. "Cutting it close, Cottweiler."

Tony rolled his eyes, raking a hand through his hair. "Whatever, Francis. I didn't think you wanted people to know I was here. 'Cause, you know."

"No!" I stood, stepping up to them and perhaps raising my voice louder than necessary. "'*Cause you know* what? 'Cause I think I should know, know whatever it is that Matt knows that I don't know." Yep. I was now shrill. "What should I know?"

Tony's eyebrows went high. "Dude." He stepped back, crossing his arms over his chest. "She's freaking out." He inclined his head toward me. "You're not even doing shit. What's your issue?"

My eyes were bugging out.

I wasn't going to do shit?

What did he just say?

I wasn't—I *wasn't*?

Matt coughed, stepping into both of us and bumping us both back. He hissed under his breath, "Shut up, you guys. And dude, who do you think is doing the hacking? And Bailey, calm down. We have done this before, and it will be fine. Do not worry."

Do not worry.

Like hell, do not worry.

The crowd was getting bigger and bigger. That only meant one thing: they were finishing for the day.

"I cannot sit in the jail cell next to Quinn. I can't do it! I won't stand for it!" I hissed.

The doors opened, and it was too late.

I knew the plan. They knew the plan. And those doors opening set the plan in motion.

The crowd tripled in size. It was chaos. Flashes were going off. People were shouting questions. People were shoving. And for once, the attention was no longer on us.

I loved *that*.

Maybe this wasn't such a dumb plan after all.

But then Matt was shoving through the crowd.

I was still standing back, but he turned, grabbed my arm, and dragged me behind him.

I glanced for Tony, but he was already doing his part. He was skimming the back end of the crowd, and he was hunching down so I was close to losing him in the crowd.

Wow. He was good at this. They really had done this before.

Fitz was on the outskirts. He and Scott were both watching us. Both wearing slight frowns. Both looking resigned to letting us do whatever we were going to do. They'd been like that since Kash left, so I assumed either they hadn't been given orders to directly stop us from doing certain things or they were given the opposite order—protect from afar, but still let us do idiotic things.

Quinn's lawyers were leaving the room, Quinn right behind them.

I had another burst of fear and grabbed for Matt's shirt. He stepped out from the last edges of the crowd, and his shirt slipped right through my fingers.

Was that fate?

At first, they didn't see us.

They kept going.

Matt stepped even more out of the crowd, right in their way now.

The first lawyer guy had no option. He was blocked, but his glance was distracted as he began to move around Matt. Then recognition flared and he ground to a halt. He was raising his briefcase, but I was certain that was a reflex, because he didn't do anything with it, just held it up to his chest and looked at his partner.

They'd all seen Matt.

Eyes slid to his right, and there I was.

Now cameras were swinging back to us, because apparently they'd forgotten we were present, and I had a thought in the back of my mind that the whole reason we came ahead of time hadn't worked. Word had not gotten to Quinn, because both of her lawyers looked shocked to see us.

They were dressed in their sleek business suits. One lawyer had a head of white hair. The second lawyer was younger, his black hair combed back, and I wondered if he was sleeping with Quinn. Seemed like her type; he was very Drew Bonham-ish.

Then there was Quinn. She had paused behind the two lawyers. They closed ranks, as we knew they would, and the younger guy tugged at his collar.

"What are you doing here?" he asked. "There's to be no interaction between your family and our client."

Matt was talking.

I wasn't paying attention to his words, but I heard his tone. It was the same voice he used when he wanted to get a reaction, when he wanted to piss someone off. He was doing it amazingly, because the white-haired lawyer went all rigid. Quinn, too. Her gaze had been latched on me, but whatever Matt said, Quinn's head snapped to his and she began to step forward.

That's when it happened.

The guy in the black hoodie, his head slouched down, moved behind Quinn. There was a surge in the crowd, and I knew it had been created by him, but also by the press suddenly jostling forward to get whatever Matt was saying on camera, and Tony was there.

And he was gone.

It happened that fast.

Quinn had been jostled from the crowd, too, but it happened so smoothly that she never reacted.

Shit. Holy crap.

It was done. Already.

I gulped, looking around to see if anyone else caught it.

No.

No.

No!

We were in the clear.

All cameras were on us. Well, they were on Matt, then to me, and back to Matt.

I gulped again. It couldn't be that easy. Could it?

I kept looking, even to the people lining up on the sides of the hallway. All eyes were on us. I looked up, seeing security cameras up there, but no way. No way could they have gotten Tony on there. I looked, checking the group of people surrounding us, and we were encased. Quinn, too.

Crappity crap crap. Looks like the plan worked.

"—ley!"

"*What?*" I yelled, out of reflex, jerking at Matt's sudden shout in my ear.

But he wasn't in my ear. He was standing a normal distance away and he had been trying to get my attention.

I flushed. I was always flushing. "What? Sorry."

He was fighting a grin, but one of his eyebrows was arched up. He nodded to Quinn. "Now's your time. Say your piece to her, to the woman who tried to have you killed."

At his words, a new buzz went through the hallway. The press got excited. That sound bite was going to be played on repeat over the next few weeks.

I stifled my groan but looked at Quinn. I made eye contact with her, and the hatred that I expected to feel . . .

It wasn't there.

It wasn't there!

Why wasn't it there?

A burning was in my chest instead, and it was spreading. Growing. It was filling up my throat, tunneling down into my stomach.

No. I didn't feel hate for her anymore.

I smiled at her instead, and a few people in the crowd gasped, as if a smile was worse.

Quinn frowned, but she was waiting.

Everyone was waiting.

"I know the government cares what you tried to do to me, but right now, I don't care about me. I care about Seraphina and Curtis. They're the real victims here."

Quinn blanched. A sheen came over her eyes, making them glisten. I wanted to believe those were unshed tears, but knowing her, dust might've been thrown in her eyes.

"Stop hurting them. Do what's right, for them."

Then, turning, grabbing Matt's arm, I pushed him out of the building. He resisted, but I dug in. We were done. Show was over. And after a slight pushing match, he yielded. He led the rest of the way. Fitz was ahead of us, Drake right behind us, and the car pulled up.

Once we stepped outside, a guy was coming at us fast. Really fast.

It was Tony.

He bypassed us, and I knew that was the instant he handed the phone off to Matt. But it was so fast, so smooth, so good that I never saw it. I wouldn't see it until we were back at the house and Matt came to my room. He knocked, came inside, and brandished the phone.

There was a wicked grin on his face, and he tossed the phone on the bed. "Do your thing."

Right.

Now it was my turn.

TWENTY-SEVEN

Bailey

Quinn's phone was a joke. It was like she didn't realize who she had been married to, who she tried to have kidnapped, and whose son came out of her birth canal. Seriously. Not a clue. I hacked into her phone within thirty seconds. She used the most generic password ever. 0000. She needed to update to the one that uses her thumbprint instead. That would've been more of a challenge, but okay then.

I was in. And I was snooping. Well, first I turned off the locater so it couldn't be tracked. When we came up with this plan, the intention was to get in the phone, clone it, upload some spyware, and hand it back. That all got usurped because I pushed Matt out the doors. So yeah, that was my bad, but we could still do this.

I think.

Maybe not.

Probably not.

Crap.

She was going to get a new phone, and we'd have to do it all over again.

So maybe I didn't need to worry about spyware, but for some

reason I was still uploading it. I was in the middle of it, when suddenly the phone lit up. It was an unknown number, and then it suddenly stopped.

The phone froze in place.

Then lit up.

Then not. The screen went black.

Lit up again.

And—what was happening?

It was being downloaded.

Holy crap. Holy crap!

She was getting it cloned remotely.

My spyware was half downloaded.

I lunged off the bed, grabbed a cord, and plugged it into my computer. From there, I tried to get into the basic coding for the phone itself. The phone was ancient and Quinn was a moron for not updating it in years, but I could work with that code.

Whoever or whatever program was uploading the data, it was doing it fast. Quinn must've gone right to a phone store, and they were good. I had disconnected it from Wi-Fi, too, so they were using a different connection. I wanted to know what they were using, but I could analyze everything later. First, I pulled up my spyware and finished the code.

Once it was done, I looked over.

The phone was still being cloned.

Then, another flash on the screen.

The screen went black, and I waited, holding my breath.

It came back up, and I whooshed a whole breath of relief. Quinn's new phone had my program on there, so I turned to my computer and disconnected from her old phone. I pulled up a new screen, searched, clicked on my program, and sat back.

I had a live feed into her phone, and she was going through it, or someone else was—fast, too. They were searching to see what was changed.

They could find my program if they looked hard enough, but

I was hoping that when they saw nothing added or deleted or changed, they would think nothing happened.

One app was opened. Two. Three. They went through fifteen of her apps before the screen stopped.

The text messages were pulled up.

She was texting someone.

Who was she texting?

A number came up. She typed:

Quinn: I got my new phone. You can send the virus to the old one.

Quinn: Good try, Bailey. Better luck next time. *middle finger emoji*

Oh. Yeah. Hadn't thought that through, but made sense she'd figure it out.

Her old phone's screen lit up again, and there it was. I saw the virus being uploaded. Whoever was on the other end hit the final button and the phone went dead. RIP Quinn's old phone, because that sucker was dunzo.

I already had everything backed up on an external drive.

Matt and I would have to have a ceremony later to send off Quinn's phone, but until then, I opened another window and pulled up my program again. This time, I clicked on the ghost program and let it go. Anything new she did on her phone would be downloaded here, and that would be sent to the same external hard drive that I had set up with her old phone's data. Minimizing that window, I pulled up her old data and started going through it.

A hard knock came first, before the door was shoved open. "Yo!" Matt strolled in, a bag of chips in hand, and he popped a bunch in his mouth. "What's happening, hot stuff?"

I wrinkled my nose. "Don't quote pickup lines to your sister."

He blinked at me, blankly.

He didn't know.

"That quote is a pickup line from a movie."

A slow grin on his face. He laughed, putting more chips in his mouth. "It's like second nature to me. I don't even think about them anymore." He turned to the computer and nudged my shoulder. "What have you learned?"

"That she got in touch with someone who knows phones, right away. They cloned her old phone remotely and then killed it."

His head jerked back up. "Are you saying we got nothing?" His voice went hard.

"Where's the trust? Where's the Team Batt faith?" I nudged his shoulder. "I got the data already downloaded, which is here." I clicked on the window, showcasing it. "And . . ." I pulled up the other window and then we were watching in real time as Quinn was setting up a date.

"Whoa!" Matt leaned in toward the screen. "Who's that?"

The number wasn't saved, so there was no name.

hotel at 9 again?

Unknown number responded immediately.

yes.

Matt grinned at me. "Wonder who gets the room? Who's the bitch in this relationship?"

Three minutes later:

Quinn: Called. Room 314
Unknown number: I'll be there.

Snorting, Matt shoved up, his bag still in hand. "Guess we're doing another stakeout." He put his hand in the bag, then paused. "Wait. What hotel? She didn't say."

I was already on that, too. "Again, where's the love, brother? The Team Batt fai—"

"Yeah, yeah." He was back and peering over my shoulder.

I was pulling up the call history and looking back. Matt had his phone out. He was putting the numbers in and giving me a nod, then he hit Dial and we both waited.

"Coastal Hotel, this is Amanda. How may I help you?"

Matt hung up. He pivoted around, facing me square, and his head cocked to the side. "Who owns that hotel?"

I turned back to the computer and typed it in. A simple Google search and I looked back at him. "According to this company's name, the real CEO is Edward Nathans. Do you know him?"

He was frowning, and his hand came up. He began idly itching his cheek, thinking. Then his eyebrows surged even lower and he looked at me. "You're not going to like it."

I sat up, my stomach falling at the same time. "What?"

"I don't know the name, but . . . I think Kash might."

I pulled my phone out and dialed.

"Please tell me you're not already in trouble."

That was his greeting. Talk about—

I sighed. "Um. Maybe?"

"What's happened?"

Matt's eyes were bugging out, but I gave Kash the entire rundown, except, you know, about stealing the phone or hacking the phone. We didn't need to start this call on a bad note. Okay. I vagued-up a lot of it, saying we got an alert Quinn might be at this hotel, meeting someone.

"Do you know Edward Nathans, and if you do, please tell me this isn't going to be a problem?"

"I should ask how you got this alert, but in this instance, I'm not, though I'll probably regret not asking. As for Nathans, I do know him, but not well enough to call him about one of his customers. What are you guys planning?"

Matt had been eavesdropping, and he grabbed the phone from me, hitting the Speaker button. "We'll just do a stakeout. They have a bar there. We'll have a drink and maybe see who shows up. The guys will be around us. No one will be in danger. Just a stakeout."

"You won't engage?"

"Uh . . ."

"Matt."

"Nope. Just a new spot we'll try out for drinks. We'll go incognito. Disguises. Maybe? Just hanging out. Nothing else."

Kash's entire voice was tight from his end. "Matt."

"Hmm?"

"If you put yourself, the woman I love, or my guys in unnecessary danger, I will shoot you in the ass."

Matt swallowed. "Got it."

I snatched the phone back. "We're good to go then?"

Kash sighed again. "I'm sure it's five o'clock somewhere."

TWENTY-EIGHT

Bailey

Dumb.

It was an adjective that described Matt and me. Our dynamic duo wasn't so dynamic sometimes. Like now. We'd gone to the hotel, thinking we could grab a drink in the corner.

That was the problem.

We could not grab a drink and be incognito.

Scott was parked near the second entrance to the bar. Fitz was positioned toward the first entrance, but since he was sitting, I was supposing that was his helpful attempt at being incognito. There were two others in the lobby, but thank God they were new guys. Quinn wouldn't recognize them—or I was hoping she wouldn't.

But that reminded me of something. "Isn't Quinn on house arrest?"

"No." Matt said, as he lifted his glass for another slug.

He had the whole lounging look again, and I was noting that it worked. He looked bored, rich, and cool. I don't know how they all correlated, but they did. It's why there were three women eyeing him, because there were only three other women besides me in the bar. Wait. I caught the bartender eyeing him, too. Four women were eyeing him, four out of five.

"Ankle bracelet?"

"No." Another drag from his glass.

"Why not?"

"Hmm?" Another drink. He started eyeing the redhead.

I was going to grab that glass and pour it over him in two seconds. "Hey."

I got his attention.

"Sorry. I was slipping back to old and immature Matt. New Matt. Here. Mature Matt. What's up?"

"Her trial is for kidnapping and murder. Why isn't she on house arrest or wearing an ankle bracelet?"

"Because she made bail claiming she wasn't a flight risk because of her children."

I started wondering who we'd find coming to meet her. "You think it's Drew Bonham again?"

Matt tensed. "No. That dickhead is on house arrest."

"Why'd Quinn get out of it and he didn't?"

"Because she's a bigger profile and she's got money. Peter's. Better lawyers can do *a lot* against the law."

"Bonham's got money, too."

"Not anymore. He's fighting a nasty divorce. Quinn didn't fight her divorce. She settled fast, so it looks good for her defense." Matt shrugged, but there was a heated look in his eyes, and not a good heated look.

We had a perfect view of people coming in and out of the hotel. They had to walk past us for the elevators, but we were slouched down in order to not attract their immediate attention. I was hoping we were far enough in the back of the bar so no one would see us even if they took a second look. If they came into the bar, our shtick was up.

The hotel doors swooshed open.

A wave of cold air swept through the lobby, and I was ready for it, knowing it'd hit us in a second. The sounds of the city came in. Cars honking. A guy was yelling outside. We saw the front desk attendant nod at someone going through . . . It was her!

"What the hell?" Matt was scowling, and he shot up in his seat.

He leaned forward, peering closer, and then he was out from the table.

"Wha—Wait!"

My heart was pounding.

This wasn't the plan. Team Batt needed to have rules and guidelines and protocols so that we didn't ruin the entire reason we were staking this lobby out in the first place. Like seeing our target and storming right up to them.

And then I got a good look at who was waiting for the elevator.

I ground to a halt.

Not Matt. Matt kept right on going, and the doors opened just as she looked over.

Blood drained from her face, but Matt grabbed her arm and stepped into the elevator with her. "Bailey!"

I pitched forward as the doors closed.

I thought it was Quinn. Same face.

It wasn't her. It was worse.

Payton.

Maybe my first read on her was the correct one? She had been lurking, lurking and waiting, and what? She was here to report back to her sister about us?

Everything happened so fast that even the guards hadn't gotten to us.

Matt had Payton cornered, and he was right in her face. "Is Quinn already in the room?"

"How did you . . ." Her eyes went from him to me, and back to him. "What? Yes. She's up there."

"How?"

"She—uh—" She was blinking, trying to think. "A back entrance, because of the press."

"The million-dollar question . . ." He leaned down into her, getting in her face. She flinched. "Why the *fuck* are you here?"

Another eye dart from me to him. Her lips thinned, parting. "It's not what you guys are thinking."

"You don't know what we're thinking." I crossed my arms over my chest.

"That I'm here as her spy or something."

Oh.

I uncrossed my arms.

Then, maybe.

She kept on, her voice rising, insistent. "She thinks I'm on her side, but I'm not. Honest to God. I love those children. Seraphina and Cyclone. It's like they're mine . . ." Her voice shook. "I meant what I said at dinner. I condemn my sister. She called earlier, in tears."

She was lying.

"She told me what you said to her in the court building, and she asked me to see her. She thinks I'll help get her back in her children's good graces, and Peter's."

She was so lying.

There'd been no call. I had that data going to my own phone, so I saw that Quinn had placed calls in the last two hours, but none to Payton. The only correspondence had been the text, and once we got back to the house, I wanted to check the texting history between the two.

I had a feeling those would be enlightening.

Matt eased back. He wasn't saying anything.

She kept looking between the two of us, and she must've mistaken our silence as believing her, because she started breathing easier. She spoke calmer, and a laugh hitched in her throat. She pressed a hand there. "You guys scared me. Where did you come from? How did you . . ." Her voice trailed off.

She was thinking.

We were surprised it was *her* meeting her sister.

We knew Quinn was here.

She looked at the elevator panel. Matt had been the one who pushed the floor number.

If she didn't say another word, Matt would've led her right up to the room.

She swallowed, and her voice got suddenly quieter. "You bugged her phone."

I took note that it wasn't a question.

"How long?" Her voice was hoarse now.

I didn't say a word, but damn it, this wasn't good.

And then, even quieter, her head lowered, she said, "I won't tell her. I'm not here to help her. Honest to God, I'm not."

I ground out, "I don't like you anymore."

Her head lifted. Her face was pinched in. "I am not what you're thinking. I swear it. There are things you both don't know about, reasons . . . just . . . things you don't know. It's why I'm here. I *have* to be here. I have to play nice for my sister right now. Just right now, and then—" She cut herself off, swallowing. She looked in pain, her eyes closing slowly. "Please let me walk in there alone. Please let me see this through. You can wait for me. I'll ride back with you guys to the house. I'll tell you everything she says." Her eyes got big. "Wait! Look." She dug into her purse and pulled out a recorder. "I was going to use this tonight on her. I'll play it for you in the car."

Matt and I shared a look.

Should we? But then the elevator suddenly stopped. The doors opened, and it wasn't the right floor, but Fitz and Scott were both there. Both were glaring. Both stepped inside. The doors closed again, and yeah.

We were in trouble.

TWENTY-NINE

Kash

"They're there right now?"

Scott was giving me the latest report on Team Batt. It wasn't good.

He sounded frustrated. "I'm sorry. This is not professional of me, but Bailey and Matt are insane. They're out of control. We have no idea how they got their hands on it, but they got Quinn's phone and Bailey hacked it. Somehow that led them to this hotel, and we're sitting there, assuming they're doing the same thing they did at Octavo—letting loose in an establishment you don't own—until Quinn's sister swoops in. Matt takes off after her. Bailey darts after them, stops, and Matt yells at her. She jumps in the elevator with them and up they zoom. We're currently holed up in a hallway below where Quinn's sister was going to meet Quinn, and Bailey and Matt are huddling over some listening device. Every time we step close, they move away. We can't force them anywhere, but they're not letting us get close enough to overhear. I repeat," he said, extremely frustrated, "Bailey and her brother are out of control." He took a breath. "What's next? Getting arrested so we can protect them inside jail? I would not be surprised if somehow Quinn gets word what they did and sends patrol units to the Chesapeake."

I needed a minute to process all of that.

Processing done. I'd be shooting Matt in the ass at some point in the future.

"I'm coming back. Again."

Josh whirled back to me. He'd been stretching. "What?"

Scott got quiet on his end.

"I'll return with Drake. The rest will stay"—I was half speaking to Josh now—"and will take the meet with Harden, because he finally reached out."

Josh cursed, shaking his head. "He's going to be pissed you aren't there."

"Tough."

"Huh?" Scott asked.

"Not you. I'll do an international flight to the States. Get one of the jets up and going. Have it meet me in San Antonio."

"The last I heard, you were in North Carolina."

"That was two days ago. We're in Colombia now."

Scott fell silent again.

"You can coordinate from there," I commanded, before I hung up and put the phone in my pocket.

"We just landed. Ten minutes ago," Josh said.

"Drake!" I motioned to him. "Grab your bag."

He bent, grabbing his duffel. I was going through my own, because flying on normal planes meant stricter rules.

"Boss." Josh stepped to me, his boots on the ground next to my bag. "Kash."

I looked up, my hand going into my duffel. "What?"

"Harden specifically asked for an in-person meet. This has to do with your grandfather. If he is isolated, you can just finish him tonight. We can have this all done tonight. We can all be flying back. Give it twenty-four hours."

I shook my head. "You heard Scott. I've given you guys strict orders not to force any of your charges to do something against their will. I am firm on that line, so that means someone has to talk sense into both of them. We're not just dealing with Bailey here. This is Matt. I love the guy, but Scott's not wrong. Matt will get her arrested if they're as out of control as he's saying. I don't want my woman behind bars."

Drake was looking between us.

I motioned to him. "We're flying back commercial."

"Commercial?"

I nodded. He knew what that meant, and right then and there, both of us pulled out our guns, our knives, and any other weapons we had. All were handed over to Josh, who was glaring at first. A second later, he relented with a grumble. "This is stupid." But he took the weapons, finding room in his duffel for each one.

We handed the chambers over next.

Same thing. They were put inside his duffel bag, too.

Drake and I went through our bags one more time to ensure we wouldn't get pulled over or questioned in customs.

I looked over. "Passport?"

Drake froze, then expelled a deep pocket of air. He patted his top breast pocket. "I almost thought I hadn't brought it." He pulled it out. "All good to go."

Mine was in my inside pocket.

"Okay." I nodded to Josh. "You're in charge. Keep in contact. I want to know what's happening on this end."

Drake lifted two fingers in a salute.

Josh flicked his middle finger at us. "I hate this."

"Boss, what about Victoria?" Josh asked.

"Her deprogramming?"

"They said it's as good as they'll get her. We do more and we run the risk of that gray area."

I didn't feel right holding anyone captive, unless they shared my blood.

I made my decision, knowing I'd probably regret it. "Let her go."

THIRTY

Bailey

Despite the glaring, Fitz and Scott didn't say a word. Scott had to walk away for a bit, and during that time, we concocted a plan. It was more like blackmail, but the ends justified the means. We had Payton make a video in which she confessed to everything she'd told us in the elevator. The deal was simple. She went in that hotel room, taped her conversation while also having Matt's phone open in her pocket. It was put on silent so anything incoming wouldn't make a noise.

We listened to everything from my phone a floor below, and when Payton came back, the video was deleted.

It was easy-peasy.

Until we got home. Because once we got home, Peter was waiting for us.

Somehow Kash was told where we were.

Kash told Peter.

And Peter started laying into us.

All three of us got an earful, and after we got the basic general lecture, Peter called us all into his office for our own individualized and customized lecture. I knew this because each of us had to wait. It went Matt first, then me. Payton was last, and she looked more terrified than I imagined Seraphina would've been if she was waiting to be called into the principal's office. In Payton's defense, the meeting with Quinn had been exactly what she said—which was not told to Peter. We let him believe what Payton thought we believed, about how Quinn had called her. We knew it was only a brief text exchange, and that it seemed like it had happened before.

We were hoping it would happen again, or I was.

Matt and I whispered about it in the hallway, but Scott and Fitz kept trying to get closer so we had to stop talking. And if I were asked why we were keeping it a secret, I wouldn't have an answer. If we found something vital, we'd share. We'd have to. But so far we hadn't gotten anything vital from Quinn and I hadn't had time to go through her phone data. Which is what I had planned to do for the rest of the night.

Matt was waiting for me in a chair outside my bedroom window. There was another one set up, so instead of going into the room, I sank down and kicked up a foot on the windowsill. This corner window looked out over the back end of the golf course on the estates. Right now, it was all snow.

"How was he with you?"

I shrugged. "Not that hard. I got the Chrissy factor working for me still."

He grunted, running a hand over his face. "He lectured me on influencing you, and if it's the right thing to do, me spending so much time with you."

"What?" My stomach rolled over on that one. I didn't like it. A flare of panic started in me. "We've been fine."

We barely did anything slightly illegal.

He kicked up his feet, too, sliding down in his chair. "I should go to my room. I'm exhausted."

"Me, too." I slid down, mirroring him.

"Yeah. Your room is right there."

He closed his eyes.

"Yeah."

I closed my eyes.

Next thing I knew, sleep.

Kash

Peter was waiting for me when I got to the Chesapeake.

The interior of the house had the usual low lights they kept on during night hours, but none of the staff was around. Just Peter, and he had a coffee cup in hand. I raised an eyebrow. "You brewed that yourself?"

"It's four in the morning. Don't be a jerkface." He grinned. "Cyclone is teaching me the current insults. Dickface. Assface. I used the tamest one of those three."

I grinned back.

It was good to be home. "She's in bed?"

His grin got bigger, but the bags under his eyes told me he'd been waiting up the whole time. "You can see for yourself." He took a sip. "Do we need to have a debriefing before you go and do that?"

I frowned, lowering my duffel bag. "Not unless some form of emergency has come up I should hear about now."

He didn't say a word. I knew what that meant.

"Okay." I gestured ahead. "Your office, I'm assuming?"

"My office."

Peter filled me in on *everything*.

Bailey

I was dreaming about Kash, and it was a delicious dream.

I could smell him. I could hear him. I was feeling him.

He was carrying me. We were moving. Then there was warmth, more warmth, and I was in bed.

He wasn't there, though. I didn't like that, and I reached for him.

I was searching. The bed was empty. The bed shouldn't have been empty. And then he was back.

The mattress depressed under his weight, and his arms were around me.

I was being pulled back into his chest.

His legs were around me.

He was folding me into him, and his lips skimmed my shoulder.

He ran a hand down my face, his lips brushing my cheek, my lips.

A whisper from him. "Sleep. We'll talk later."

So, I slept again.

Best dream in a long time, but that night, it was my best dream ever.

Wait a second . . .

My eyes snapped open.

My entire body froze before I flipped over in bed.

Two very angry eyes were glaring right back at me. A very large and very rigid body was lying next to me, arms and legs wrapped around me.

Not a dream at all.

Kash was back.

Kash

She looked so *goddamn* good.

She smelled good.

She felt good.

Jesus Christ, she even sounded good.

I moved before I could stop myself.

I wanted to talk to her, question her, lecture her, but my mouth was on hers.

Lecturing would wait.

Multiple Witnesses for the Prosecution Missing

On Monday, the prosecution against Quinn Callas found themselves shorthanded when multiple witnesses did not show up for their testimony. The district attorney says investigations have been opened as to the whereabouts of each witness.

A GoFundMe page has been established to help support Quinn Callas's defense team. Sources say she "didn't fight her divorce to Peter Francis, leaving her with almost nothing."

—*Inside Daily Press*

THIRTY-ONE

Bailey

"We need to talk," he said as he came out of the bathroom.

God.

He was wearing track pants that fell low on his hips, and the rest of him was shirtless and barefoot. That body, those muscles. I could glide my hand over every dip and valley of his body and I'd never get enough. He had the V leading under his pants, and when he turned around, which he was doing as he was reaching for a shirt, I saw the back dimples, too.

Back dimples.

Time apart had made me an obsessed woman.

His words came to me, and I lay back down, closing my eyes. "I don't want to talk."

We had gone on a normal date, or normal for us, the last time I saw him.

I missed that. Making out in a movie theater. I wanted to do that again.

"Do you know anyone who had a normal childhood?" I sat up and scooted back to rest against the headboard.

Kash threw me a small frown. Henley in place, he was putting on socks and shoes. "Normal? Define 'normal.'"

"Two parents. Middle class. A home."

"That's your problem. I don't think we have normalcy any-more. I don't know anyone who had that and *only* that. Why are you asking?" He stood, coming to stand beside me. I expected him to sit on the bed, but he didn't. He remained standing, his head tilted to the side, and those eyes studying every angle of me.

I didn't know how to say it so I just waved my hand at him.

He frowned. "What?"

"I don't know." I lied. I did know, so I started to scramble off the bed.

He caught my hand as I did and pulled me back to him. "Hey."

God. I closed my eyes. He said that word so soft and quiet. It felt like a whole other caress from him, and he doubled down. His hand came up and he trailed a finger down the side of my face, lingering over my mouth, and then falling to my throat.

He murmured, so soft again. "What is it?"

I shook my head, coming out of my lusty daze. "You see every-thing." I looked away, feeling exposed once again, but this time I was doing it. I was explaining myself. I was exposing myself. "I— you see all of me, and sometimes I don't want to feel all of me. And I'm just having a moment, but it'll pass, and right after, I'll be flooded with appreciation because I know how amazing you are. I know how supportive, loving, caring, and I'm totally and completely aware of how utterly blessed I am to have you in it. But right now, I'm just having a moment."

I looked away.

And waited.

And waited more.

He was silent, and then a soft sigh came from him. His hand touched my arm and he tugged me to him. Drawing me into him, he looked down at me, and yes, into me. "If I'm looking at you in a way that you don't want to feel, then I get it, but I love you. I can't stop that. It's me trying to figure out what's bothering you and if I can do anything to help eliminate it. And for everything you just said, it goes both ways you know. You see me, too." He tucked a strand of hair behind my ear, his hand cupping and resting on the side of my face. "I'll never stop seeing you."

I moved into him, our bodies flush against each other.

My head went to his chest and I melted. I let go of tension that I hadn't even known was there. His hand came up, rubbing the back of my neck, then my shoulder blades, and he moved further down on my back. Oh yeah. That was the spot. I was almost crooning and swooning here. Then his hand moved to my ass, and he grabbed a handful of one cheek.

My eyes darted up and he was watching me back, but his eyes were dark and lusty, too.

That was enough for me.

A few hours later, I got a whole lecture about being smart, and safe, but it was later.

Matt was called in, and he got the lecture, too.

Kash asked to see Matt alone afterward, and I'm pretty sure he got *another* lecture. I asked him at one point how bad it had been and Matt just grunted. "Let's just say I'm not taking my ass for granted right now."

I couldn't stop hearing what Kash said, though.

"I'll never stop seeing you."

I smiled.

THIRTY-TWO

Kash

Bailey was half back to herself, but not all the way back.

Watching her now, as she was working on some project with Cyclone, I saw the vulnerability. It was on her, just under the surface, and it was thin. She was still struggling, but damn, she was getting stronger. Better.

"You here to stay now?"

Matt brought over a beer for me, taking the bar stool next to me. We were in the basement, with the wall section open between the bowling lanes and the bar area. Seraphina, Peter, and Payton were playing a game of pool. Theresa was up in the kitchen and Marie was in her office. I knew this because both came and checked in with me, hugging me, glad I was back.

Was I here to stay?

I had to be honest. "If I have to go, I'll go. But I'm back mostly because I'm scared what else you and Bailey are going to do." I gave him a pointed look.

He grinned, then shrugged. "Stay and love your woman or leave and kill your grandfather. What a choice to make." He gave me some side-eye. "But you're not infringing on Team Batt.

We can do Team Katt or you can do Team Kailey. There's no Team Bakatt."

Okay. My turn now.

I leaned toward him, getting in his space and not giving a damn who noted it. "What the fuck were you thinking? There was one time her phone could've been lifted. Who did it? My guys said Tony was there. I know he's got a juvie record. And then the hotel stakeout?"

Bailey's head lifted and turned our way.

I kept going at him. "If Quinn gets proof about who stole her phone? Who hacked it? If Payton tells her? She could fuck with Bailey's life, and you know it. She already has."

"Payton won't tell."

I grunted, easing back a bit. "You don't have a clue what Payton will do or not do."

"What?" He looked and stared hard at me. "You do? The great and knowing Kashton Colello? So, tell me, brother. Tell me what Payton will do to hurt my sister. Huh?" His voice rose and carried.

The whole room silenced.

Eyes turned our way.

I ignored Matt's question for a second, finding the woman in question. My gaze fell on her and she blanched. Her hands trembled, so she stuffed them behind her.

"I don't know, Matt." I spoke to him, my eyes on her. "I actually have no clue what Payton will do, but I would hope—"

"Kash," a low warning from Peter.

I ignored him, too, continuing, "—that since she's been brought into the fold, that since Seraphina and Cyclone love her so much and are so happy she's here, that she won't do anything to hurt anyone *they* love."

Payton closed her eyes, lowered her head. Her one hand came out, rested on the pool table, and then hit it. Her head came up. Her eyes opened and she had made a decision. "Like my own sister? What about her? She knows Calhoun. Did you forget that?"

"So do you."

Matt stiffened.

Peter swore under his breath.

Bailey was standing up, at a slow rate. Her head swung my way, then swung Payton's way. "You do? You know Calhoun? I knew Quinn did, but . . . Who else knows Kash's grandfather?"

"I—" The courage she had seconds ago looked like it was dwindling. She turned for Peter, but he was already shaking his head. She was on her own, and seeing that, Payton paled. "I would never do anything to harm Seraphina and Cyclone." She looked hurt. "You know that, Kashton."

She sounded hurt, too, but then she went on the offense. "Haven't *you* been gone?"

Got it. What place did I have in questioning her? The whole "being hurt" was a ruse. That was her shot at me.

I smirked at her, sliding off my barstool. "You're right, Payton. I do know you." My head went to the side. "I know that your father worked for my grandfather. He was in business with Griogos as well. And I know that before your father died, you and Quinn stayed at my grandfather's home for a summer."

Payton's pallor was getting noticeably whiter. "Everyone knows that."

Matt raised his hand. "Uh, I didn't. You stayed there? With him?"

She gave him a look. "He wasn't there, and that was before everything."

"Dad? Did you know that?" Matt asked.

Payton was looking at Peter, too, a deeper look being shared between the two. His hold tightened around his pool stick before he cleared his throat. "Uh, yeah. It's actually how Quinn and I got to know each other. She knew I was partners with Kashton's parents by then, and said we had an acquaintance in common."

"An acquaintance," Matt scoffed. "This is hilarious, and I

mean that it's *not* at all." His words were biting. "What the hell, Dad?"

"Matthew." Peter indicated Cyclone and Seraphina.

"Then maybe they should go to their rooms, because apparently there's some real adult stuff that needs to be dealt with, like the fact that *Payton and Quinn knew Calhoun Bastian?*"

"You knew that Quinn knew Kashton's grandfather."

Matt scowled back at his father. "Not to that extent. What the hell, man? Quinn stayed at your grandfather's house? You knew that?" The last questions were directed to me.

I nodded, everything in me growing cold. "It was when they were younger. I was told about it before my parents were killed. And when Quinn married Peter, she swore that she had no contact with my grandfather since." I turned to Payton. "Is that true? Is it the same for you as well?"

Did they know about my brother?

I looked at Bailey. Meeting her gaze, I felt punched by the look coming from her. I wasn't sure if it was a good punch or not. She was looking at me with this sudden new understanding. Her head tilted the other way.

"What is it?"

"I—you see all of me, and sometimes I don't want to feel all of me."

I suddenly knew exactly how she felt.

I rubbed at my chest, feeling her in there. It was a different sensation.

Whatever she saw in me, it got her moving. Whispering something to Cyclone and Seraphina before both ran upstairs, she began to walk my way. I ceased paying attention to the room. Payton was not my business to handle, but Matt and Bailey needed to know the extent of her connection. They did now. I hadn't intended to put Payton on blast. She really was not a problem for me to handle, and I could've mentioned it to them behind closed doors, but I was glad it got handled this way. It was in front of Payton. It was in front of everyone, and Payton got the message.

Stand on your own if you want to stay.

For as long as I'd known Payton and Quinn, Payton came only a few times. She never stayed long. She talked to Peter a little, to Quinn a little, and to Cyclone and Seraphina most of the time. She doted on both of them. It'd been Cyclone who took to her the most in the beginning, but that seemed like it was changing since Bailey was in the picture and Seraphina was getting older.

Then Bailey was in front of me, and she touched my chest. "You okay?"

Oh yeah. She saw right through me.

I moved away from the bar, ignoring anyone paying us attention, and drew her to me. An arm around her waist, I pulled her in. She fit perfectly, just how she was supposed to. I bent down, my lips resting just above hers. "Always." I felt her heart speeding up, it was in sync with mine, and damn I loved this girl.

Woman, I corrected myself.

I loved this woman.

She'd been through too much, dealt with too much. There was no more innocence in her. That'd been taken from her, and lifting my head, I peered at her. I touched her lip. "Could do with more time with you, though."

My hand slid around to the back of her neck.

I felt her whole body shiver, and her lips parted. Her eyes were dilating, darkening with lust.

"How about . . ." Two arms came around us both.

Bailey and I went rigid, but then Matt's head was forcing ours apart and he was smiling wide at both of us. Looking from one to the other. His arms tightened around us.

". . . we all have a night together? I think we're due. How about it, Kash? A night at Naveah? It's been a while since we all hung out together."

I frowned at him. "You're interrupting some Kailey time."

He stiffened.

Bailey tensed, and then a wide smile lit up her whole face. "I love it!" She moved even closer to me, almost letting me have her whole weight. "Yes, please."

"What? No. I want time with you both—" Cutting himself off, Matt took my hand from Bailey. He moved in, turning his back to me and put both his hands on Bailey's shoulders. He began backing her up, walking with her. "I'm making the decision. You. Me. My sister here. We're heading to Naveah. I'm making it happen." He kept walking her out of the room, saying over his shoulders, "I don't trust both of you being alone to get ready, so I'm walking her up there. She gets the bathroom first."

I was watching, counting exactly how long I'd give them before I followed, when I heard Payton behind me. "Why did you bring up my connection to your grandfather?"

I turned.

She was almost right behind me.

Beyond her, Peter was observing us. He remained at the pool table, a pool stick in hand.

Okay. Let's have this talk.

"Quinn employed a group of men to try and kidnap Bailey. There was one man on their team that's never been accounted for. There were rumors that that group of men were hoping to get into Calhoun's good graces by hurting Peter. Since then, I've also learned a girl I used to date was given a job to try and seduce me for my grandfather. That girl was brought into this house on a consistent basis by Quinn. Both are gone, and now who shows up? You. I don't think I'm being paranoid to bring up the connection and at least let Bailey and Matthew become aware of your background."

Her mouth tightened. She was getting angry. "You know about the hotel, and you know what Bailey and Matt did to me. They blackmailed me."

"Were they wrong to do so?"

She didn't respond; that was her response.

I looked over her head to Peter, lifting my chin up. "I need time with Bailey and Matt right now. You'll notify me if anything happens?"

He dipped his head down. "I will." His eyes cut to Drake in the hallway. "But you've had that handled for a long time by now. For what it's worth, Kash, you deserve a night off. Try and have fun tonight."

Have fun tonight.

I couldn't remember the last time I heard those words directed toward me.

DREW BONHAM FOUND DEAD

Wednesday morning, the body of Drew Bonham was discovered. Early findings suggest he died of a drug overdose. Bonham was charged, then took a plea for his part in the kidnapping of Bailey Hayes, Peter Francis's daughter. Bonham was released on home probation, and was scheduled to testify for the prosecution against Quinn Callas, the former Quinn Francis.

Sources say Drew Bonham had a history of being abusive and controlling of Quinn Callas.

—*Inside Daily Press*

THIRTY-THREE

Bailey

I was in front of the mirror.

Dark pink dress on, halter straps that wrapped around and tied behind my neck. I was wearing simple ballet flats, a muted silver color. My makeup was bare. My hair was up in a twisting French braid. A matching silver clutch in my hand, and I knew Torie and Tamara would've been proud.

Torie and Tamara.

A hollow ache dug into the middle of my chest and remained.

I hadn't talked to either of them in so long—too long, now that I was thinking about it. I missed them. I'd been at school, but it was different. Hoda was there, and I couldn't trust Hoda. Melissa was there, but she was such good friends with Torie and Tamara. I pulled away from them. I still had some study time with some of my classmates, mostly Melissa, but it wasn't the same. I did what I needed to do. My classes. I talked with my professors. I attended my meetings with Ms. Wells. And my internship, I hadn't even started. That got pushed off because of Chrissy's death.

I needed to start my internship, but looking at myself now, the desperation for work, for school, wasn't there anymore. I would still do it. I would still love it. But it wasn't the only me anymore. It did not define me anymore.

I didn't recognize who I was looking at. I used to be tank tops and jeans. Sweatshirts and jeans. Nothing dressy. Nothing flashy. Now the dress I was wearing was from a designer that sent me clothes. There was a whole closet of them. All items sent to the daughter of Peter Francis, and I knew the deal. They wanted me to wear it to get their name out there. I got it. I understood it, but this wasn't me.

Or it wasn't me back then.

I placed my hand on my stomach and realized how much weight I'd lost. Jesus.

It was time. I felt something shift in me, something old reaching up, connecting with something new in me. They were intertwining.

I was no longer the outcast I felt like this summer. I was no longer the novice in this new high-society world. Whatever I was, I was me. Just me. But I felt rooted. I was no longer just a Hayes. I was a Francis. I was half of Kash, too.

Kash.

I sucked in another breath and felt the emotions sweep through me, but these were good.

I did not lose Chrissy, because he loved me.

The universe would not take away someone if I dared to love more than one person. I would not give up Kash.

I had not given Chrissy up.

Calhoun Bastian took her from me.

He alone was to blame.

My fight was to love, and to know that I *could* love. I *would not* lose those that I loved because I loved them. I felt tears in my eyes and I swallowed a knot. I blinked back those tears and I raised my chin. I stared at myself in the mirror. Defiant. But more.

I was more.

I would be more.

Knock, knock.

The door opened. Kash looked inside. "Can I—" He stopped.

One look and I was back there, in his villa. Torie and Tamara in the background. My mom there, too. He came to get me before Peter's welcoming party. He had the same look in his eyes, but there was more now.

I stepped back as Kash came in. He came right to me.

We didn't talk.

I don't think we needed to.

He reached for me at the same time I was stepping into him. His hand came up around my neck, the other around my back, and he pulled me to him. I burrowed into his chest. He cradled my head and I felt his cheek resting on top of my head. He smoothed his other hand down my arm, and he lifted. His lips grazed my forehead, and he whispered, "You are so beautiful."

I couldn't talk. My throat was clogged up, but I hugged him back hard.

The hardest I could.

"God." Another whisper from him. "I love you. If anything, I hope you know just how much."

I did.

I do.

"I know," he said. "Are you ready? Do you want to stay?"

"I'm good. And I want to go. A night out will be fun. I think we've earned that."

His eyes darkened. "Definitely." His head cocked to the side. "You haven't seen your friends for a while. Are you sure you want myself and the guys there? We can do something else, or stay in the background? You can get your time with the girls."

"I'm good. Things have been different since my mom . . ." I still have a hard time saying it aloud. "You know, being with family has been more important to me. Besides, the friend group has sorta dispersed."

"If you want me to make myself scarce, give me a sign. I can always work."

"Sign? What kind of sign?"

He shook his head. "You decide." His mouth twitched up. "Any word you want to use."

"*Raccoon*."

His head moved back. "*Raccoon?*"

"Yes. *Raccoon*." I gave him a look. "Do you not know how obsessed I am about those animals? Have you looked at my Instagram? Do you know how many raccoon Instagram accounts there are? They are little, furry, adorable, curious creatures who are quiet but hilarious and I cannot take how freaking adorable they are. One rolls down the hallways. Rolls. Down. The. Hallway. And don't get me started on the YouTube videos of them, where they pick up snow to take and eat, and it melts by the time they put it down and they look for it. Freaking. Hilarious."

"I had no idea."

I shrugged. "I don't just hack, you know."

"Huh." He grunted. "Raccoons."

"I'm also a big fan of octopuses. Do you know that if you save them, they will come and hug your leg as a thank you?"

I was just getting started.

Kash needed to know about all things wondrous and adorable.

I had a photographic memory, so I had a lot to tell him.

THIRTY-FOUR

Bailey

Group text:

Melissa: Sorry, sorry, sorry, but I don't think we should invite Liam tonight.

Tamara: Which one is Liam again?

Torie: The athlete one right? Or the one that looks like he could be an athlete.

Matt: Why am I included in this?

Matt: I'm down with No-Liam.

Matt: Is this supposed to be a chicks' group chat? I don't see any other guys included.

Melissa: I would've included Liam, but since this is about him, I thought that'd be not good. Anyone heard from Bailey?

Matt: Good luck. She's with the Kashsters right now.

Matt: ;) if you know what I mean.

Torie: He's my boss, Matt. The wink wasn't needed.

Matt: But it got my point across.

Bailey: I'm here! Hoda's not invited as well.

Matt: WE ARE NOT DOWN WITH THE HODASTERS!

Melissa: I'm assuming. No one talks to her in class.

Tamara: Why isn't Liam invited? And what's going on with Hodasters? Matt, can I get a nickname?

Matt: You are now The Tam Tam.

The Tam Tam: ** thumbs up ** ** hands in the air **

Torie: I'm fine with no Liam, though if I remember right, he's a cool guy.

Melissa: He's roommates with Hoda now. Hoda is, like, somewhat of an enemy, isn't she?

Matt: Hell yes she is! WE ARE NOT DOWN WITH THE HODASTERS!

Melissa: That's what I thought! Okay. Bailey, are you okay with that? This is your night to hang out with everyone. Hoda's gotten weird at school, and I know you're not talking to her. But Liam is living with her and yeah . . .

Tamara: That's weird.

Torie: Agreed.

Matt: Why have I not been added to this group text earlier? Can this be a regular thing? I'm loving it.

Melissa: Bailey?

Matt: Told you. She's with the Kashsters. They're probably groping in the shower.

Bailey: Shut up, Matt! I know where you live and I will piss off Marie and Theresa and sic them both on you.

Matt: I mean, this is actually Cyclone. He hacked my phone.

Matt: This is Matt now. I got control over my phone again. Wtf is Kashsters? That's disrespectful and I have a respectable amount of fear of both my sister and Kash and I would never make a joke like that, now.

Torie: **handing you a wipe for your drool there**

Matt: Thanks. I'm handing it to Cyclone. Love you, B. A lot. Don't sic anyone on me please.

Matt: I'm still grateful for my ass.

Torie: Moving on before Matt remembers he's had too much to drink for this group chat. B, you okay with the no-Liam vote?

Bailey: I am. Thanks you guys for even thinking of that.

Melissa: Care about you! Also, I'm super excited for a Naveah night. Seems like forever since we had one.

Torie: Whoop for some drinking.

Matt: Whoop!

Torie: Not you, Matt. You've already been over served.

Tamara: ** snickering ** you just got served

Matt: I'm thinking I was added by mistake.

Melissa: Lol! You're fine. Everyone's fine. I just wanted to make sure about the no-Liam invite because tonight seems like a night where he might've been invited, but this semester's been different.

Bailey: I'm good and thank you! See you guys at Naveah. Matt, we're waiting for you downstairs.

Matt: See you in two snaps.

THIRTY-FIVE

Kash

"You two seem cozy."

That was Matt's greeting as he slid into the booth beside me. He'd just gone to the bar for another drink, though it was more to flirt with the new bartender, and now he was studying where Bailey was standing with Torie and Tamara. Her friend Melissa was there, too, and there was an uneasy edge to the whole group. It'd been worse when we first arrived. I'd kept an eye on it and it was getting better. A couple more drinks and they'd be laughing like times before Bailey had lost her mother.

"Bailey and me, or are you talking about someone else?" I nodded in their direction, turning to eye Matt as he continued to eye them.

He took a drag from his drink before putting it on the table. He slumped a little in the booth, but that was his way. He threw people off with that body language, but he was never not watchful and alert. Or he wasn't unless he had too many drinks or something else in his system, and so far, I was counting only two drinks.

We'd been here two hours by now, so that was a tortoise rate for Matt Francis.

"You and the B Master." He tipped his head her way. "She's happier now that you're back."

Well, shit. Here we were.

I grinned at him, cocking my head back a little. "We doing this?"

His eyes met mine, and he had his own answering grin. He sat up and leaned forward, resting his arms on the table. "I guess. I mean, why not? We didn't get to it before." He shrugged, his head falling down a little. "I am her brother, you know."

"You want to know my intentions towards your sister?"

Another half grin. "Yeah. I do." The grin vanished and he leveled a look at me, a hard look. "Don't leave again, fucker."

"There's a part of her that blames me. I needed to give her time and space to process those emotions, and you know it." I rested my head against the seat, rolling my head to look his way. He had slid down, mirroring me.

He let out a sigh. "Yeah. I get it. Sucks." A beat later, "But it was fun to spend some time with her."

I grunted. "If I'd gotten a call that she was arrested because of you, then you and I would be having a different talk."

He shook his head. "Whatever, jerkface."

I grinned. "Cyclone?"

He paused a second, then got it and laughed. "Should I say 'dickface' instead?"

"Please no."

His grin was there, but it grew more somber. "Just don't leave my sister like that again. I'm assuming you didn't get him yet? Figured there'd be a news bulletin out if you had. Did you get close, at least?"

I shook my head. "I was heading to a meeting when I got the call about you and Bailey. She's more important than him."

A grunt from him this time. "I get it. You had to come back. Your woman needed you."

"Yeah."

"Yeah."

Then we were done.

The talk was over, and we sat there, watching the woman we both loved as she relaxed around her friends. An hour later she was flushed, and curled up next to me in the booth. The night wasn't bad, or not as bad as I thought it'd be.

That was, until now, seeing who'd entered Naveah and was heading our way. I knew the good times were done.

"Aw, fuck." Matt sat up, throwing me a look.

I gave him a quick dip of my head. I saw.

Bailey hadn't, but she had heard her brother.

She lifted her head from my shoulder and looked up, a little drowsy. Then she jerked upright. "What is she doing here?"

Victoria was walking up the path to our booth. Fleur and Cedar right behind her. Since she was here, I had no doubt that the usual gang was about to follow as well. Chester. Guy. Cottweiler. It wasn't like Victoria to be in town and not rally support.

She knew I was here.

She was here to say something.

I sat back and waited.

"Hello, Kash."

Bailey

I was experiencing bad déjà vu.

I hadn't seen her since . . .

"He fucked me hard. He flew me to Greece, making me come over and over again on the plane. And it didn't stop there. He was insatiable."

I was tasting my own vomit. It jumped up in my throat.

"What's the problem, Bailey? Not enough for him?"

"What. The. Fuck. Isshedoinghere?"

The end of my question rushed out of me, because I was

pissed. I was ready to commit murder, and I was rising up out of Kash's lap without even knowing I was doing it. His hand clamped down. He held me still, but he was moving for both of us.

"Torie," he barked.

I knew what he was going to do, and I started struggling. "No. That's not fair."

But Torie came over, taking in everything, and I already saw her go from my friend to his employee. She was set, the epitome of a cool professional. "What do you need?"

"Take her. Keep her in my office until this is done."

I was pushed toward Torie, but I swung free. "No!" He couldn't make me. Torie couldn't make me. Scott and Drake were closing in, and shit. *They* could.

I found Kash, my eyes burning. "Don't. Do not shove me in a corner for this. I mean it, Kashton. She was there that day. She was taunting me. She's a part of that nightmare. Don't make me go away."

He wavered, and then Victoria was at the table. Her eyes were on us. She was watching and waiting.

God.

I hated her. I didn't wait for Kash to make his decision. I rounded him and went at her. "You were there that day. I know you lied to me, and I know what really happened, but what you said to me . . ." I choked off, my entire body feeling like it was squeezing in on itself. "Get out of here."

I cringed, hearing myself.

I sounded like a wounded, feral animal that was backed into a corner.

But no. That's how I *was* feeling.

She was here. She had come for me, sought me out, and she took a knife to my heart. With her words, she thrust that blade into me over and over again, only to leave, and then *he* sent them for my mother.

My mother.

I was shaking.

"You vile bitch. You are pathetic. You are hateful inside, and you have to spew that outwards. You have to hurt others so you're not hurting as much? Is that it? Or was it just payback? Because Kash didn't want you, so you flew back to damage the one he *does* want?"

She was silent.

Why was she so silent?

Why was this starting to not feel right?

No.

No!

I would not stop. I had a right to lay into her, and my entire body was writhing in fury. My vision was only seeing red. I wanted to hurt her. I wanted more than that. I wanted to destroy her. But she wasn't saying a thing. She wasn't reacting.

She wasn't reacting.

There was no anger on her face.

Oh, God.

She was—she was remorseful. I saw it. I saw it in her eyes, and no, no, no.

No!

"Stop it," I growled, advancing on her. My hands were in fists. "Stop. You don't get to be the good one now. You're not the victim here. You're not. You victimized. You hurt me. You hurt me on the same day I lost my—"

An arm went around my waist.

I lost it.

I couldn't keep—Jesus, why wasn't she fighting me? I needed her to fight me.

I needed it to breathe. I needed it to—There was so much pressure inside me. I felt like a balloon ready to pop, and I had to hurt her to make some of it go away.

That arm wasn't restraining me.

That arm was just holding me. A chest came up behind me, and I knew that chest.

Kash was standing there behind me, holding me, and his head bent. His lips were on my shoulder.

I was still trembling.

I hated Victoria. I hated her with everything in me.

She was the one who did all of this . . .

No.

I stopped, freezing in place.

That wasn't me talking in my head.

I smelled Chrissy. I felt her. I could hear her laughter, and I sagged in Kash's arms.

I was done.

Everything Victoria did to me, I was doing to her.

Round and round.

The train never stops. But I was hurting. The pressure was building, building, building. It was going to rip me apart, and right behind it was pain. Just pure and horrifying and paralyzing pain, and I couldn't feel that. I didn't want to feel that. I wanted to rip apart my skin, push my hand deep inside, grab that pain, and yank it out of me.

I wanted it out of me for good.

Bailey.

That was my mom again. I was hearing me, and I knew she wasn't there, but she was. She'd come back to haunt me.

"Mom," I broke, my head folding down. My knees gave out, and down I went.

Kash caught me and he lifted me.

I curled into him, just needing him, and then he was moving through the crowd.

"Here." That was Torie.

A door opened. We were through it. The club's music faded.

Kash was carrying me down a hallway. Then we were in an elevator. We were going up, and then another hallway.

"Sir." His guard.

A door opened, and then I was being lowered onto a couch.

I looked up, but the room was dark. There were neon lights flaring from a window behind him. He'd brought me to his office.

I hadn't been in this room for so long.

"Stay, okay?" He placed his hand on my shoulder, bending over me. Concern marred his forehead. "I have to go and talk to her. Will you be okay until I get back?"

Would I be okay?

I didn't answer, just lowered my head and curled in on myself.

I would always be okay by myself. Didn't he know?

I was a Hayes. That's what we did.

THIRTY-SIX

Kash

Victoria had been taken to Torie's office. I walked in, not caring when she blanched.

She should blanch.

"Are you kidding me?"

That was my greeting to her, with my nostrils flared, and she gulped. She'd been pale already. Some of that was from the state we found her in, the detox, but she was here, and I was regretting my moment of trying to be the good fucking guy.

"I'm sorry."

I cocked my head to the side. "That's all you have to say?" I took a step closer, growling, "What the fuck are you doing here? I told them to cut you loose and send you to a rehab. Funny," I clipped out, "my club doesn't look like the insides of a drug treatment center."

"I know. I know." She held up her hands, backing away a step.

Fuck that.

I wasn't in her space.

I wasn't pushing to be in her space.

I had taken one step toward her, then locked up, because

right now the woman I loved was crying in my office and I was down here, dealing with this one.

"Start talking, Victoria. You're taking time away from me being with Bailey right now and I'm not happy about it."

"Okay." She edged back another step.

"If you take one more goddamn step backward as if I'm the aggressor here, I will kick you the fuck out of Naveah so quick, your head will spin."

She stopped edging.

My nostrils flared again. "Out with it. Now."

"I'm sorry!" she cried out, her arms flinging outward. The dam broke. All the fearful crap vanished and she was dissolving again. Her chest was heaving. "*Okay?* That's what I came to say. I'm sorry for everything. Everything!"

I opened my mouth.

She kept going, "I'm sorry for being with you, knowing that if you fell in love with me that I would actually try to control you for your grandfather. I'm sorry that I never told you. I'm sorry that I was so scared of him and what he would do that I put my family and him first. I'm sorry about all the insanely bitchy moments I've had. I'm even sorry about little cutting comments I made to Seraphina. I'm sorry that I knew Quinn was a monster and I never said anything. I'm sorry that I cosigned with Quinn, using her and not even thinking about who she could hurt. I'm sorry Bailey was hurt by your grandfather. I'm sorry for what I said to her. But, I'm *not* sorry that I fell in love with you and I'm not sorry that I *still* love you, but I know that you'll never love me back." She stopped, breathing hard. The tears had left black makeup streaks over her face.

I closed my mouth.

Her head hung, but not before I saw the agony flash in her eyes.

She was sniffling, dabbing at her nose with a napkin. "You

saved my life, and you didn't need to do that. I would've died."
She looked up; that agony was there. It was right on the surface,
and it was enough to dissipate some of my anger. "Calhoun told
me to go to that house and hide there. I did. But he also sent me
the drugs. He sent enough for me to overdose on, and a part of
me knew it. I had it lined up. I was going to take it, and I knew
I was going to die. You got there in time." More sniffling. Her
voice grew hoarse, to a faint whisper. "You saved my life, and
then you further saved my life by helping me detox."

"Go to a treatment center."

"I am." A tear slid from her eye, but she let it go. She didn't
wipe it away, and resolve flared at me from her gaze. Her chin
firmed. Her shoulders straightened. "I came back to pack my
things and I have a car waiting for me. I didn't come in here to
upset anyone. I truly didn't, but when Fleur said you were here,
I came to say thank you. And . . ." her chin wobbled now. She
blinked rapidly. Her throat moved up and down as she swallowed. "And . . . and I know what your grandfather intends to
do with you."

I grew still.

"I know that you have a twin brother. I know that you know
about your twin brother, and I know that he's supposed to watch
you because he's supposed to replace you."

What . . .

I blinked. Once. "Say again?"

Her mouth pressed together, but that chin was firm again.
She lifted it. "Your twin brother is supposed to take over your
life. He's been studying you this whole time, observing you, and
when he's perfected you, he will kill you."

She paused another beat before she finished.

"He'll take over your life as if you never existed."

THIRTY-SEVEN

Bailey

"Bailey."

I'd fallen asleep. Crap. How had I fallen asleep?

A hand smoothed up my arm and he leaned over me. "Bailey. Wake up."

My heart spiked.

It was Kash, but it wasn't Kash.

That hand wasn't Kash.

The lights in the office were off, but there'd been a lamp on. I knew Kash left it on.

What was he doing? No.

"Bailey." A bit more insistent. His hand shook my shoulder harder. "Come on."

"What are you doing?"

I winced, hearing my voice. It was raspy and barely there.

"We have to go." Now his voice was more clear, louder.

He sounded like Kash.

His head moved closer, and my eyes were adjusting. He looked like Kash.

But he wasn't Kash. I knew it. I felt it.

"Who—" I stopped. There was a nagging in my mind, in the back of it. This guy . . . I knew him.

My heart dropped.

This was the twin.

Was it?

Wait . . .

No.

But.

This wasn't Kash.

He looked like Kash. He was speaking like Kash.

He was acting as if he was Kash.

But *he was not Kash*.

The realization hit me hard, in my chest.

I started breathing hard.

Sweat ran down my back, chilling me at the same time.

This was him.

The twin. I knew it. I so knew it.

Oh my God.

What should I do?

Kash! Where was Kash?

I froze, my entire body locking up.

"What's wrong?" he clipped out, impatient.

I had to try it. "Raccoon."

And I waited.

Nothing. No reaction.

Sooo not Kash.

So *seriously* not Kash,

But there was another thing bugging me.

It was in the back of mind.

It was there . . .

Something about this guy. Something *else* about this guy.

Who . . . What?

An alarm was blaring inside of me.

Screw all that.

What do I do here?

Lie. Be fake. Act.

I felt the answer as sure as if it'd been Chrissy speaking in my head. I even heard a hint of her voice in the air. My stomach still locked up tight, I tried to sound drowsy. "What's going on?"

"We have to go, babe."

Babe.

Kash called me that, but not like this. Not now. It would've been in a casual way, not in a way that he knew I would be alarmed. Or baby. He called me that, too, but in the throes, as he was moving inside of me.

This guy was really truly and ridiculously *not* Kash, but he pulled me up.

I didn't want him touching me.

I didn't want his hand on me.

He took my hand—but he didn't lace our fingers. *Thank God.*

Kash would've laced our fingers. And he was pulling me from the office. His head was kept low, but as we stepped into the hallway, the guards didn't say anything.

He was dressed like Kash.

Fitz was there, pushing the elevator button.

He glanced over Kash's brother, to our hands, and then to me as the doors opened.

I looked hard at him, and he frowned, but followed us inside.

Then there was that nagging in my head. Again.

I knew him, but I didn't.

Right?

Right . . .

That had to be it.

Two worlds. Colliding.

Why was I getting that feeling?

A bad sense of déjà vu, *again.* It was washing over me, giving me chills.

Was that why I wasn't saying anything? Fitz was here. He had a gun. I'm sure he could overpower him easily. But I knew this guy.

I couldn't shake this nagging voice in my head.

How did I know him? Was that just the likeness to Kash? Was it?

That didn't feel right.

It felt like there was more, something else here. Something I wasn't remembering—and I remembered everything!

Then we were at the bottom, and the elevator was opening.

I had to alert Fitz. I had to say something. Only Kash knew about raccoons.

Not Kash tightened his hold on me and walked forward.

Kash would not do that. He had carried me. He had led me places. He had guided me. But he never dragged me somewhere, not in the state he had left me.

"The street exit?" Fitz's question was directed to Not Kash.

"Yeah."

God. Even his bark was like Kash, the perfect pitch.

I tried to eye him better, to pick up any differences in the face, but he kept his face turned down and away. He was keeping it at an angle on purpose, but it was good. He was good at this, and a chill went down my spine, adding to my alarms.

I had to say something.

How did I know him? And why was that bothering me so much?

But Fitz was going to the exit door. He was opening it. There was a vehicle parked out there. I could see the red brake lights on. Someone was in there and waiting, and this was a setup.

I couldn't wait any longer, so I spoke, my voice coming out calm. "I know you're not Kash."

He froze.

I saw Fitz freeze, and then *bam!* Both sprang into action.

It took a second for me to comprehend what happened, because I expected Fitz to take him down. That didn't happen. In fact, pretty much the opposite.

Fitz's hand went up, but he went to his radio. He had the transmitter button pressed and was raising the unit to his mouth when Not Kash took Fitz down. Not the other way. Not the way I thought, because I fully expected it to be a done deal. I'd say the words and *wham!*, Not Kash would be unconscious at my feet.

Not what happened.

I was still processing that when he looked at me.

Oh.

Crappers.

Now it was just me, him, that door, and whoever was on the other side of it.

"*Ahhh!*" A bloodcurdling scream came from me, followed by, "*Helllpmeee!*"

His face twisted in fury and he began reaching for me.

I dove, and in the back of my mind, I now understood why Fitz went to radio for help—because he needed help! Because *I* needed help. I dove for his radio; there was a gun in his holster—Fitz's jacket had opened in his fall—and I reached for that, too.

In my head, I was going to dive, grab both, duck my head. I'd complete a full roll, like I've seen volleyball players do in their matches. Why I was remembering volleyball matches from high school, I had no clue, but anyway, that's not what happened.

First, Not Kash slammed his foot down on the radio.

Okay. I'd work with that, because it took him a second away from where he could've used that kick to knock me unconscious. Instead, he stepped on the radio and kicked it away.

And two, the gun was still in his holster. I grabbed it, tried to yank it free. It didn't come free. It remained in the holster.

How did these get free?

But then Not Kash was reaching for me, and that's when he messed up.

His touch was gentle. That told me he didn't want to hurt me. I could work with that. So when he went gentle, I became a snarling dirty street fighter. Or I was doing my best impression, because then I finally did finish my roll (just not with the gun or radio), and the movement yanked me out of his hold. But instead of scrambling and running, I twisted around and went for his ankle.

I was the personification of an ankle biter.

I bit his ankle. Literally.

"Fuck," he growled, then he grabbed my hair and I was being yanked away.

He was fast losing the whole "gentle" approach, but he didn't pull me to my feet, and I used that to my advantage, too. I kicked out at his legs, and the movement helped propel me out of his hold again. But then I was on my butt and he was looming over me.

I was out of options.

Our eyes met, and I opened my mouth.

Another scream was coming out of me.

He knew it. I knew it. We were both about to hear it.

But then he lunged, grabbed me, dragged me up, and I was pushed against the wall.

Déjà vu. For the *third* freaking time.

His hand slammed over my mouth, and he bent low, whispering into my ear, "Shut up!"

Except I wasn't hearing that. I was hearing, *"In two minutes, men will break into your home and take you hostage."*

It was his height.

It was his eyes.

It was his voice, now that it was more rough and he wasn't trying to disguise it.

There was a sixth sense where you shouldn't know but you just do. You just know it, and that feeling was inside of me. I *knew* this guy.

My lungs stopped working.

Everything stopped working.

Recognition crashed into me, overloading my everything, and I swear I heard the circuit breakers in my brain frizz and snap as they stopped working, too.

I knew this guy. I so knew him, and I had known I knew him, and I stopped thinking about what I was doing. I slapped his hand away, grabbed his shirt, and hissed, "I know you!"

Articulate genius, I never claimed to be.

His eyes widened, but I was still going. "It was you! You're Chase."

"You got the upstairs, right, Chase?"

Arcane team member Chase. Chase who broke into my house, told me he was supposed to rape me and I was about to be kidnapped. That Chase!

"He better have, or was the two pumps not long enough?"

Their sick laughter. I was hearing it all over again.

I was back in my house.

I was arching my back and screaming, *"Aahhh!"* A breath. *"Heeelp me!"*

He went still, staring at me. It was like I had captured him and he was being held hostage. Then, "Shit" slipped from him.

Shit?

Shit!

Shit?

I frowned. "What do you mean, 'shit'?"

A door opened down the hallway. The nightclub's music blared loud, and someone said "Hey!"

Not Kash/Definitely Chase cursed again, but the door was pushed wider and we heard more shouting, then a stampede was happening, and all the hallway lights were switched on, and he was gone.

I mean, it didn't happen just like that. He didn't vanish.

His whole face pinched in on itself. He took two steps back, grabbed the door, opened the door, and was out the door. The SUV's back door was shoved open and I surged forward.

I had to see. I had to see.

I saw—and my lungs seized.

They stopped working, too, because there was no way.

I was seeing a ghost.

Chrissy Hayes was staring right at me, and there wasn't a flicker of recognition on her face.

My mother was alive.

THIRTY-EIGHT

Bailey

"Bailey!"

Kash was there and his arms were around me, and he was carrying me back inside the club.

It was pandemonium all around me. Guards were running outside. Kash's arms were tight around me, but he was barking orders at the same time. Guards were sent to every exit. Every floor. Every room. They were checking the entire club, and then checking the perimeter around the club. I knew all this, heard all this, because Kash refused to let me go.

We were in the stairwell.

Kash was bounding up them, two at a time, still with me in his arms. He was carrying me like I was a baby, and then we were in his office. He laid me back down right where the imposter had woken me. I kept that to myself, knowing Kash would further lose it.

So I sat, and I waited.

Fitz ran in, took Kash aside.

"What the fuck happened out there?" Kash growled.

Fitz's head went down and he was talking, but in a rushed,

panicked way. I knew he was giving Kash a report on what happened, and with a searching look at me, Fitz nodded when Kash told him to go. I didn't hear his instructions for him, but I knew there were some. The rest of the arrivals started.

Torie first. Melissa was right after.

Tamara came with them; she started fixing my hair. Her eyes were worried. She was biting down on her lip in a fierce way, but she couldn't sit. And she couldn't stop touching me, so my hair was fixed one way and then another. My shirt was righted. She swept over my top, making sure the creases were all smooth. When she went to my ears, to fix my earrings, she had to pause. I didn't have earrings, and she shot me a wry look.

"Oh God, girl."

I held my arms up and she crumbled. She buried her head into my shoulder, her arms wound around me tight, and I held her as she cried.

Torie came over, reaching around her roommate and took my hand. She was blinking back tears, giving me a shaky smile, and I saw the concern from her, too.

I mouthed to her, *"I'm fine."* I patted Tamara's back. "Help her?"

Torie blinked away more tears, clearing her face before she patted Tamara's back. "Hon. Tam. We gotta go."

Tamara let go of me, reluctantly, but she was nodding as Torie grew more insistent. "Yeah. Okay." Tamara eased up from the couch but looked back at me. "If you need anything—*anything*—you'll call us?"

I nodded, my throat swelling.

I think I'd been in shock, but now emotions were starting to swarm up.

I rasped out, "I will."

Melissa came in, but she just gave me a quick hug. She cupped the back of my neck and whispered, "I'll see you later in class, but hang in there. I'm here if you need anything. Call me. Promise, please?"

Again, my throat was damn near choking me. I whispered, "I promise."

Matt was next.

He pushed inside, Chester, Guy, and Tony behind him.

At the sight of the last three, a growl came from Kash, who was standing halfway between me and the door. He was surrounded by guards. Matt and the guys all stopped short. Everyone stopped short.

The growl was primal sounding. Savage.

Matt's eyebrows went up, but he indicated for them to hold back. He went to Kash first. Their heads bent together. After a nod from Kash, Matt headed over to me.

"Hey." He sat next to me, pulling me into his arms.

Okay. It hit me then.

Not the emotions. Those were there, but I was stuffing them down.

All these people coming up here, they were the emotional ones. They were the ones needing to be reassured I was okay. They were coming over, hugging me, and that was all for them. Kash was ready to rip someone's head off, but I knew he was handling business until it was just him and me. As if he could sense I was thinking of him, I felt his eyes on me. Looking over Matt's head, I met Kash's gaze, and whoa.

Pinned. Down.

His eyes were smoldering.

He swallowed to get control of himself.

"Oh, Bailey." Matt pulled me closer and shoved my head into the crook of his shoulder and chest. He started petting me. "I'm here for you. I'm here for my sister. I'm so sorry. That's so scary."

Yeah. It was. But my hands started shaking.

It was building in me. Fury.

I was *pissed*.

My mom was alive, and I hadn't said one word to anyone. Kash caught me up, whisked me here, and I'd been too stunned to start talking. Everything happened at a whirlwind pace, but now thoughts and emotions were catching up together. They were syncing, and I was livid.

I tore out of Matt's hold. "I need my computer."

I swung around.

The room had gone quiet.

I said to Kash, "Raccoon."

His eyebrows snapped down together. He took one step, made one bark. "Out! Everyone out."

Everyone scrambled.

In two seconds, we were alone, except for Matt.

He lingered, standing slowly. "Uh, guys—"

"You, too." Kash nodded toward the door.

"But—"

"Matt."

My brother pointed between me and him. "We're Team Ba—"

"*Not* the fucking time!" Another one of those growls.

"Okay." He turned for the door. "I'm going, but honestly." He whirled one last time, his hand on the doorknob. "Are you okay?"

I was already standing, but I felt myself rising inside.

I tipped my chin up. "I'm good."

He paused, then nodded. "Alright. I'll leave it at that." He pounded the door with his palm before leaving, then the door was shut.

Kash moved to lock it. "What's going on?"

I felt alive.

My body was trembling with the feel of it, and I was fighting to stop from pouncing on him. We didn't have time for that.

"Remember that guy that tried to kidnap me with Arcane? The one who was in on the first attempt but not the second?"

His frown was fierce. "Chase, right? That's the name you told the police."

"Well," I locked eyes with him, "your twin brother is Chase, and my mom is alive."

THIRTY-NINE

Kash

This was the moment I had feared.

I couldn't shake it, and hearing that my twin had come in, that he had touched Bailey, gotten near her, this was my fear. Calhoun had taken everything from me. Both my parents. He had taken my own brother. I didn't know of him before now, but it didn't matter. He was stripped from me. And now that same brother had impersonated me, tricked my own men, got through to one of my buildings, and I heard Victoria's warning.

It was a fucking premonition of sorts.

He wanted to replace me.

This was it. This was what my grandfather always wanted. This was why he had allowed me to live so long, because it never made sense to me. He had allowed me to live.

"How are you handling all this?"

Detectives Bright and Wilson came as soon as they were called. My guards were all debriefed on my twin brother, who to look for, and since then we'd been sequestered inside my office while Bailey gave the FBI a formal report. This wasn't a local kidnapping attempt, not anymore. This was so much more, and I wanted answers.

I would fucking get answers.

Instead of answering Bright's question, I pivoted with one of my own. "How was an entire body taken into evidence and processed and no one reported that it wasn't *Chrissy Fucking Hayes?*" I ground out, my teeth grinding against each other. "How is it that Bailey witnessed her own mother get shot in the head and now she's seen alive and well?"

And in the backseat with my goddamn enemy?

"Well . . ." Bright's eyes flashed before she got ahold of herself. She ducked her head, glancing back to where Wilson was writing on his notepad, sitting on the couch beside Bailey. "Are we sure she actually saw her mother?"

I nodded my head. "She saw her."

"How do you know?" She edged closer, lowering her voice. "M.E.'s report was solid. DNA matched Chrissy Hayes, along with her own daughter's eyewitness testimony of seeing her mother executed."

Jesus.

I ground my teeth again.

If Bailey had heard that word. *Executed.*

"You'll watch how you talk about Chrissy Hayes's supposed murder when you're in the presence of her own daughter." My tone was scathing, and her head whipped back. Her eyes widened.

She got the message. Respect or get out.

"We're running road cams, all the typical stuff we'd be doing. We need to verify what Bailey saw is who she actually saw and not a play of shadows or something."

"It wasn't."

I knew it in my bones, just like that other feeling. The end was coming.

"We have to make sure—"

"It wasn't."

"Your girlfriend's been in mourning. It makes more sense that she wanted to see her mother and so her subconscious produced what she wanted."

"She didn't and *it* didn't. She saw her mother."

"How do you know, Kash?"

I heard the inflection in her tone.

I rounded on her. "Because I know Bailey. That's not a daughter in mourning anymore. If there was doubt, she wouldn't be looking like that. Look at her, Bright." I nodded toward Bailey.

Bright turned.

I kept talking. "She's ready to set fire to the earth and burn with it. If there was any chance she didn't see Chrissy or she doubted herself, none of that would be there. She'd be curled up in a ball, because trust me, it's been a long process to get her uncurled from that ball. No." A decisive shake of my head. "She's itching for you and Wilson to get out of here, and then I know she's going to launch herself into whatever and however she can help to find her mom."

And we were wasting her time.

I cursed again.

Bailey wanted to hack. Hell, that wasn't even it anymore. She *needed* to hack. I could see it pulling at her. She wanted to fuck or fight. It was the most human part of us, and taking her to bed wasn't prudent right now. That meant fighting.

Which meant hacking for Bailey.

I needed to get these FBI agents out of here.

"Are you sure?" Wilson was repeating some question to Bailey, whose eyes were flashing from annoyance.

"I'm sure!" Her tone was snapping.

That was enough.

I started for them.

Bright's hand touched my arm, stopping me.

I looked at it, looked at her. "Get your hand off of me. Now."

She did, jerking backward from the severity of my tone. She tucked her own phone into her pocket and her lips parted, glaring at me. "We will handle this, Kash."

"You are on retainer for her father."

Her hand clenched into a fist. I saw it before she caught herself and lowered it back to her side. Her head ducked, but her eyes remained on me. They were in slits. "That's for special favoring. Not for us to look the other way on a case. We have to verify what Bailey is saying. Look, it won't be hard. There will be things to be covered up if her death was faked. It's easy if no one is looking. Once someone's looking, there'll be traces. We'll catch the traces, but let us do our job."

My own eyes were narrowed, and I leaned into her space, saying quietly so she could hear just how clear my promise was, "Then work fast, because once you leave, I'm letting my girl go. If I find that anyone in your department is being paid by my grandfather, they will be taken down."

Her lips parted again. "Is that a threat?"

One last skewering look before I straightened and started for Bailey. "It's a promise."

She gave me another warning look but sighed and headed for her partner. Wilson and Bright left, and then it was just Bailey and me.

Her eyes were wide and clear.

I flinched. They were so clear.

"I need my computer," she said.

I was already nodding and going for my keys. "We'll go to your father's office for this. He has the best technology."

She stood, but her hand touched my arm, pausing me. "You believe me?" Her gaze darted to the door. "They didn't."

"I believe you."

My chest was tight. I wanted to pull her into my arms. Instead, I just cupped the side of her face, my thumb tracing her lips. "Let's go and find your mom."

She blinked, startled, and then her mouth tugged up in a smile I hadn't seen for months.

Right there. That was worth everything.

FORTY

Bailey

I felt awake.

It's not something someone can explain, because it wasn't waking up from a sleep or a nightmare. It's not the drowsy state, clambering out of bed, stumbling into the bathroom, and hoping you can hit the snooze button for another hour, then crawl back into bed. It's not that type. It's not even the type where suddenly the world is clearer, brighter, and you feel magic in the air. I was riding next to Kash in his car, because he needed to drive, because he needed to feel in control, and I was awake. That's all I could think about.

I felt the texture in his hand as he was holding mine. I felt the ridged grooves of his fingers. The roughness of his skin. The strength of his palm as it rested against mine.

I felt the texture of the seats.

I smelled the leather in the car. Heard the crispness from the cold in the air.

But I felt a nagging sensation. It was zooming down my spine. It was coursing through my body.

I was thirsty.

I was ravenous.

I wanted to dance.

I wanted to laugh.

But I wanted other things, too.

I wanted Kash, and my finger skimmed down the side of his hand.

He tightened his hold over mine, meeting my gaze through the side of his eyes, and I saw the answering desire there. He wanted me, too, but not yet.

My heart was pounding.

My legs were restless, starting to tap on the floor of his car.

I was soon a bundled ball of nerves, barely able to contain myself.

I was focused.

We didn't talk once during the ride.

Not one time.

Our hands never moved from one another.

He pulled into the Chesapeake, and I hadn't realized we were going to Peter's personal office. I thought we'd be going to the Phoenix office. But Kash was right. This one held Peter's best computers. This was the right place to be. But once we had parked and turned the engine off, once we should've gotten out and didn't, I looked at him.

He was already watching me.

"This can't come back on Peter."

Kash's eyes darkened before he leaned down. His lips just an inch over mine, he said, "It won't. I won't let it." Then his lips grazed mine, a soft nip, and he pulled away. It was a promise for later, probably much later.

He got out on his side.

I got out on mine.

"What do you need?" he asked, as the door opened for us and one of the guards stepped outside.

I was striding through the hallways, Kash having to keep up with me. "I need my headphones." I was listing everything off.

"I'll use mine if you can grab them, or any with a thirty-six-inch cord. Coffee. Energy drinks. Snacks. I'll take chips. Anything with sugar. Lots of sugar." And what else?

I felt electrocuted. I was so energized.

I glanced down at my outfit. I was wearing a dress. I couldn't hack in a dress.

"Clothes," I remarked.

"Clothes?"

I pushed open our bedroom door. "I'll change, but can you grab my headphones and the rest?"

He nodded. "Your father's office . . ."

I was already in the closet, tugging my shirt off. "I know where his office is."

He came to the door, his voice closer. "No, you don't."

I paused, hearing a tone in his voice I'd never heard before. The shirt was off and I let it hang from my hand. "What?"

He was taking me in, his eyes almost black. "The office he uses for what you're about to do is not in the office you're thinking about."

My lips parted.

My dad hacked?

I flushed. Of course my dad hacked, but . . . Peter hacked?

"He still hacks?"

Kash grinned at me, a slow tug from the corner of his mouth upward. "He hasn't in a while, no, but you get it from someone, you know."

Another flush. This one I felt on the back of my neck. I knew that, but hearing he still did—it got my stomach doing all sorts of somersaults.

"His office is downstairs. The wine wall in the bar."

"Yeah?"

"It's behind there."

My eyes were like an owl's and my mouth was hanging open.

"Right." I snapped it shut. My hands went to my pants. "I'll finish. Let's meet in the basement."

The other side of his mouth curved up, and he came over. A finger under my chin. He tipped me up and he bent down. He said, as he always did, right before touching his lips to mine, "It's nice to have you back."

A shiver went through my whole body, but I was grinning. It was a good shiver. I replied back, my lips moving against his. "It's nice to be back."

He groaned before lifting his head. "I'll meet you in the basement."

I grabbed a tank, sweats, and put my feet in some fuzzy slippers. I left the hair and makeup how it was, and at the last second, grabbed my own bag. It housed my laptop, and the headphones were already in there. I found Kash waiting at the bar. He had a few items there, but when he saw me scoping them out, he said, "I'll get you started, then get the rest."

Right. That was smarter.

He went over to the wall, removed one of the bottles, and pushed in the wine bottle holder. He stepped back and the entire wall shifted outward, then glided to the side.

There was a hallway behind it.

Kash walked in, put his hand on a scanner, and another door opened.

I was in hacker nerddom love.

Beyond was everything I could've wanted in life—except for, you know, Kash. But everything else, hell yes. I went inside.

Kash touched my shoulder, indicating a side door. It had a red EXIT sign over it, and it looked just like the exit doors at a movie theater. "Bathroom is through there."

Right. *Exit* meant "bathroom." Got it.

"I'll be back with your other items."

But then I was thinking again, and I rounded as Kash was leaving. "Wait. What about everyone else?"

Kash held his phone up. "I will send everyone away, don't worry."

"And you . . ."

"I'll be right here." He nodded to a couch in the corner. "I can work just as well as you."

I liked that. I liked that a lot.

"What about Matt?"

"He is going to be told to take his friends on a three-day trip." He smirked at me. "He will get the jet."

I laughed as he left, and I repeated to myself. "He got the jet."

I focused on the computers and sat down.

First things first, I had to hack into my dad's personal computer, and then his system. Again.

FORTY-ONE

Bailey

I had two objectives with where I started. One, the location, and two, the players.

I did what the FBI said they were already looking at, but I was going to do it better. I wasn't going to wait and get permission from local store cameras. Yep. I hacked 'em. All of 'em. I didn't feel one iota of guilt. Some of these systems were so easy that I was almost doing them a favor. If they realized they'd been hacked, they would get a better system.

But that wasn't a justification, because I didn't feel guilty.

Within an hour, I had two photos of my mother. Two.

One was of her in the backseat. Okay, it was more an image of a woman in the backseat of the SUV. But I knew it was her, so I was counting it as one of them. The second one was pure luck. Kash came over once to refill my coffee and he pointed it out. "Reflection."

One word. That was it.

Mind blown.

I completely forgot about reflections, and then I was cursing myself because I had to backtrack over all the work I had already went through.

I found one, but it wasn't enough. She was blurry. Too many shadows. It was just a glimmer, a hint of who was inside that SUV. I recognized her. I knew that was my mother, but no one else would, and that's why I was doing this. I had to find proof. I had to ramp up the fight for her.

Four blocks around the club and I was able to find the SUV's trail. Then I just kept doing that. Over and over and *over* again. I worked every single system in a four-block radius, mapping out the SUV's path until they hit the interstate. After that, it was the street cams, and thank goodness, they were so much easier. I panned out, and once the SUV stopped showing up, I rerouted back to the last exits, from where I lost them to where I last saw them. It took me twenty minutes to find them, because the first turn did have a camera but the second turn didn't. It wasn't working. So after that, I had to redo all the same work I'd already done. I panned out in a four-block radius until, an hour later, I found them.

After that, it was hit and miss.

And slow. So much slower.

They were getting into suburb territory. The street cams were more sparse, with a few on the major streets. I hit those first. Hacking in. Scanning. Not finding anything. So I had to go back, again. I took each street, in every single way they could've gone.

Chicago suburbs had a lot of streets.

Four hours.

Four freaking hours.

I was getting a headache, and I didn't want to count how many personal systems I had hacked, because by then some of the guilt was trickling in. Some. Not a lot. I reminded myself who I was looking for—Chrissy Fucking Hayes.

My focus grew firm again. Crystal clear.

I was back on it.

I was being Kash with his business deals. Ruthless and calculating.

It was another two hours later when I got a hit, and I cried out, because I couldn't help it.

"You found her?"

Oh. That's right. Kash had no idea what I was doing.

I shook my head. "I'm still trailing the SUV."

He came to stand next to me. "Give me the license plate number. I have another team on standby. They can help you."

Another team?

I frowned up at him. "What? Who?"

He was scanning the video feeds I had up on the screen and, distracted, he replied, "I have two teams working for me. One does computer stuff like this."

My mouth dropped. "You're telling me this now?"

"Yeah." He glanced down, back to the screen, and did a double take back to me. His eyes narrowed. "What? What's wrong?"

"Who's doing the computer stuff? Do you know them personally? Do you trust them? Why haven't you told me any of this?"

He took a step back, straightening up. Both his eyebrows arched up. "Uh." He shook his head, his eyes blinking a few times. "I—I didn't know you wanted to know this stuff."

"Of course I do! Why wouldn't I?"

His mouth opened, hung there, then closed. He lifted up a shoulder. "I don't know. You were adamant about only doing grad school—"

I shoved back my chair, and my hand flew out. "That was last semester! Things were different last semester."

"Uh. Yeah . . ." He frowned, then scowled, then just looked confused. He raked his hand through his hair, and when it fell to the side, he did it again. His whole palm ran down over his face. "I'm sorry. When was I supposed to fill you in on all this?"

"From the beginning." I huffed that out.

"The beginning?"

"Yeah. The beginning."

"You were in counseling, trying to process the second kid-napping attempt . . ."

He was muddling things for me, and I shook both my hands in the air. "Stop trying to rationalize things."

He bit out a laugh. "It's called rationalizing things."

"Oh!" Now my eyebrows went up and both my hands were in the air, palms turned toward him. I leaned back. "Now I'm being irrational?"

"What?" His mouth hung open again. "Wait. *What?*" He was shaking his head. "I'm lost here."

"Well, that makes two of us." I crossed my arms over my chest, one more huff coming from me. I was all heated. My blood was rolling, but damn. I should've known. So I told him that. "You should've told me."

"One, I think I actually did. Two, when? You went from only focusing on grad school, trying to bury yourself in your school-work, to then mourning your mother and trying to process wit-nessing her murder!"

I flinched.

"Okay!" My hands flung up in the air and I sat down, whip-ping my chair back around to the computer screen. "I got it. I was a mess."

He was quiet behind me.

I didn't care. Or I was telling myself I didn't care?

I went back to work, pulling up another security system, un-til I realized that there was a camera at the intersection, smack above the stoplights. I'd missed that one, so I started working to get into that one, too.

"What just happened here?" He sounded so cautious.

I let out a sigh, getting in and then getting the angle. I clicked over the time period, fast-forwarding and waiting for a big black blob. "We had a little tiff."

"We did?"

I wasn't doing this.

I flicked my eyes upward, still speeding through until the time frame when the vehicle should've gone past. I slowed the time. "It's a couple thing."

He sat in the chair beside me, rolling it to face me squarely. "We did a 'couple' thing?"

I paused, my hand on the mouse, and glanced sideways. "Yeah."

His eyes were intense, fastened to me. "That's an okay thing?"

"Yeah." I frowned. "Isn't it?"

He frowned at that question and leaned back in the chair. His hand came up, raking over his head before he let it fall to the desk. "I have no idea. I just don't want to upset you, and you seem to be doing good, with all . . ." He wavered, his hand gesturing to the computer. "You're doing your thing, and you seem good. You're good, right?" His brows furrowed together and he leaned forward slowly. "Are you good?"

He was nervous.

I blinked a few times when I registered that.

I'd never seen Kash nervous. Kashton Colello. The great and intimidating and sexy Kashton Colello, who could kill if he needed to. The billionaire boyfriend who was menacing, protective, and dangerous.

He was still talking. No. He was rambling, his hand going over his face again.

I noted how tight his shoulders were, and then I started grinning.

All the mess, all the dysfunction and crisis in our lives, and in the midst of me breaking the law, of him assisting me breaking the law, we were doing a normal couple thing.

He noticed my smile and stopped talking. "What? What's wrong now?"

"Nothing."

He nodded, his shoulders loosening.

"Just . . ."

His shoulders tightened back up.

"This is nice."

His eyebrows shot up once again. "This is nice?" He waved a hand between him and me. "Us? Right now?" He included the computer screen. "Committing felonies? That's fun?"

I hid a grin, going back to work. "No. *This* as in you and me in the same room, and being normal." I thought about it. "Kinda. Sorta." Okay . . . "Not really. But you know what I mean."

He expelled a ragged breath. His hand thumped down on his armchair and he lounged back. "I haven't got the first clue about what you're talking about. I'm just," he hesitated, choosing his words, "I just don't want to lose you."

My breath stopped in my chest. It held there.

He was looking down, shaking his head. "I was so fucking scared." His voice grew thick. Hoarse. "I thought I would lose you. From the kidnapping attempt, to when Victoria ripped into you, to after you lost your mom. I didn't think . . ." He lifted his head, and there was no wall there. No mask. He was more naked with me than when we made love. "I don't think I've breathed until now, and I had no idea." Another layer slid away, and he was hurting. The pain was raw and pulsating.

I went to him. His face tightened in agony and I was there. I was in his lap, and my hands were cradling both sides of his face. "I love you."

He drew in a breath. "Are you sure?"

God.

He was so raw right now.

"I'm sure."

He moved his head, up and down, just slightly. My forehead went down to rest against his, and he closed his eyes. "My grandfather, I didn't deal with him when I was young—"

"And what? Become a murderer?" I lifted my head, and I tipped his chin up to meet my gaze.

My chest was squeezing together at the sight of his suffering.

He was ripping me in half, but I kept on. "You couldn't do anything except live in fear."

I found his hands and laced our fingers together. Resting our hands on his legs, I moved so I was straddling him. "I'm going to find my mother. We're going to get her back. Then I'm going to help you destroy your grandfather, once and for all, and figure out what to do with your twin brother."

I bent down, finding his lips, and I lingered, just needing to feel him.

Once I had my fill, I slid off his lap and went back to the desk.

FORTY-TWO

Kash

All night long. She never wavered.

She took my breath away.

Every minute. Every hour. She was nonstop. She wasn't going to stop until she found Chrissy.

This. This felt good. This felt refreshing.

Hell. This felt necessary.

She worked past the next day shift.

The staff was sent home, paid day off. The minimum amount of guards stayed on.

I told Peter to take the kids away for the day, and I brought Bailey licorice and energy drinks.

It was that afternoon, after too many hours of working, when her hands shoved in the air and she pushed back her chair. She took a victory walk around the room, pumping her fists in the air.

"*Scooore!* Bailey Hayes *wins again!*" She turned to me, fists in the air, and the brightest smile I'd ever seen on her face. "I found her. I got visual. And I got in their neighbor's security system." A strand of hair fell down her forehead. Her cheeks rounded, and she puffed it back up. She never lost that smile. "I found her, Kash. I found my mom."

Her hands still in the air. Red in the face. Her eyes wild and dilated.

I smiled back. "I knew you would."

I stood, slow, so she could see my purpose.

She did, her hands starting to lower. Her eyes widened, and I heard the air catch in her throat. "What are you doing?" But she was excited. I heard that, too, a whisper at the end of her statement.

My grin turned wolfish. I went full force, knowing my eyes were smoldering and intense, and knowing how she reacted to that.

"You know what I'm doing." A slow step toward her.

She was getting flustered, and her chest rose, holding. Her hands started fluttering in the air, and I didn't think she knew she was doing that.

Another step to her. "I've been watching you do your thing all night, and most of the day. Do you realize how sexy you are?"

She was captivated, her eyes holding to mine, and I slowly reached for her.

She was coming down from a high.

I drew her chest to mine, my hand sliding under her shirt and up her back. She murmured to me on a sigh, "I found my mom, Kash."

I bent down to her, my lips over hers. "You did."

She smiled, a tear slipping from her eye. "I'm so happy right now." Then a crease showed in her forehead. "It always goes away after. It can't go away this time." Her hand went to my arm, sliding up over my bicep. "I won't come back this time if it goes away."

That wouldn't happen.

My lips touched hers, and I murmured back, "It's not going anywhere. I won't let it."

No matter what I had to do.

FORTY-THREE

Bailey

"Are you insane?" I hissed at Kash, my mouth gaping.

After we closed everything down, I wiped any security feed of us and then cleaned everything up on the hardware. I had broken so many laws, and just thinking about a ballpark of them made my legs wobble.

He was on the phone, shirtless, and standing facing the windows.

I wasn't actively listening to him until I heard the words *wait*, *team*, and *swarming the house*. Then I focused on what he was actually saying.

I shot up to my knees, and my mouth was still gaping as I listened while he was arguing with someone else on the phone about waiting to go in and get my mother. I'd heard enough to get my blood boiling by the time he finished the call.

He turned, saw me, and stopped in his tracks.

"Are you insane?" Here's my hissing part. "I *did not* just hear what I heard."

He took me in, his mouth closed, and his jaw firmed. His shoulders lifted and rolled back, and his chin went up.

Oh yeah.

We were going to fight.

He tossed his phone onto the couch before turning back to me and folding his arms over his chest, and I wasn't distracted by how his muscles moved and shifted from that movement. Or how he looked all hot and moody. And my loins weren't stirring.

Nope. Not happening.

I coughed, clearing my throat. "You did not just tell whoever was on that phone that you need *time* to go and *get my mother*, did you?!"

Because that would be absurd.

That was preposterous.

That was going to make my blood pressure go from a good sizzle to a boil to exploding the blood pressure cuffs off of me.

I'm sure steam was coming out of the top of my head.

And all the while, Kash lowered his head, his eyes on me, and he shifted his feet apart. Oh boy. He was taking a fighting stance. This was going to happen. We were going to fight about this.

I said it quietly, but clearly. He had to hear how serious I was. "I want my mother."

"You'll get your mother." Almost as quietly, just as clearly, and he was locked in.

We were going to battle.

"I want her now."

"You'll get her."

He didn't say "now." He needed to say "now."

"Kash." A warning from me.

"Bailey." His eyes cooled.

"Kashton!" A low growl started in the back of my throat.

His shoulders rose and held. He was tightening up. "I do not want the authorities to get my brother. *I* want my brother. And I have a team that can do it, but it's going to take time."

"A team?" I remembered what he said last night. "How many more teams do you have?"

He blinked a little, like I'd thrown him with that question. He raked a hand over his head. "Like I said, I have one team helping with research, whatever that entails."

Research. Whatever that entails.

Why did that not sound legal? Though I was *not* judging. At all. If I did, I might as well start sharing a cell with him.

"And I have a specialized team on my grandfather."

My eyebrows skyrocketed up. "Are you *kidding* me?" More hissing from me. I shot to my feet, my voice rising. "*You know where he is?*"

He didn't respond, not at first. Then a grudging nod. "I've known for a while."

"Kash!"

His jaw tightened. "You have been in serious mourning. I've been doing everything I can to make sure I can move against my grandfather, but I can't be stupid. I can't go in without covering all my bases, and some of those bases are finding out if he has a death policy or not."

Wha . . .

I sat back on my heels. "Death policy?"

"My grandfather has been in the game a long time. He has allies built over allies. Allegiances. Fucking plans on what happens if he dies. And while you've been grieving, I've been unearthing all of it. It's a lot of shit to unearth." Again that jaw was tightening, then flexing. "I'm close. I'm so close. But finding out about my brother was new, and every stone I turn over, there seems to be more under them. But I'm close. I can feel it."

I swallowed over a lump.

I was getting it now.

"And this team you have on him, that's the team you're pulling for my mom?"

He nodded, his eyes cast off. "Yeah."

Wow. I was really getting it now.

"You're doing that for me?"

His jaw clenched again. He lowered his head, turning away. "I'm doing it for my brother."

But he wasn't, and I knew it, and he knew it.

I crawled over the bed, reaching for and catching his hand. I tugged him over to me, sliding to the edge of the bed. I moved in to stand in between his legs and looked up at him. "Thank you."

He was giving up his grandfather for me.

"I'm not just doing it for you."

But he was, and he was lying so I wouldn't feel bad.

Kash was moving heaven and hell to help me find Chrissy.

I rose up on my knees, and holding his eyes, I pulled my shirt up and over my head. After our second round, I'd pulled on underwear and a top to sleep in. I was naked in front of him now, except for my underwear, and he took me in. His eyes darkened, lust filling them, and he moved forward, just beyond touching.

He pinned me down with his gaze. "Underwear. Off."

The underwear went off, and then there was touching.

There was kissing.

There were moans, groans, and thrusting.

But mostly, there was nothing but good happening.

Finally.

FORTY-FOUR

Kash

The phone woke me, and I rolled over to grab it.

Bright calling.

I turned the light on, sat up against the headboard, and knew this wasn't going to be a good call.

"Yeah?"

Bailey rolled over, lifting her head. She was blinking at me, still drowsy.

Glancing at the clock, I added, "It's four in the morning."

"Your girlfriend messed up."

Fuck.

Throwing back the covers, I stood and went to grab my pants. Pulling them on, I grabbed a shirt and threw it over my shoulder.

"What's going on?"

I headed for the hallway, but mouthed to Bailey, *"Go to sleep. I'll be back."*

Her eyes were troubled. I doubted she'd go to bed.

Going out into the hallway, I headed for Peter's study. "Hold a second."

"No." Bright's tone was snarling. *"You* hold on. We know

what you and your girlfriend did. We also know you didn't call when you could've called."

Coming to the office, I left the lights off and went to stand at the windows. The golf course lay just beyond and the lighting was on, but dim, so anyone walking could still see.

This place had been my home for half my life.

With this conversation, I was now wondering if I'd be getting a different home for the rest of my life.

"You found the house."

"We found your twin and Chrissy Hayes!" she snapped. "Why the fuck didn't you give us a heads-up?" She pressed on, not letting me answer. "And don't even give me some bullshit story where you wanted to handle it yourself, because you know that'll give you so many felonies that we could lock you up for the rest of your life."

My hand clenched tight around my phone. "I take it that this call is not as someone who has been paid heavily for favors from the Federal Bureau of Investigation."

She laughed. "You bet your ass it ain't. What were you *thinking*? Your girlfriend left a trail a blind semi driver could find. She did not cover her tracks, and we are working our asses off and finding our own tails behind our rears, but the second you found Chrissy Hayes, you should've called us. The *second*!"

I remained silent. There was no response that she'd want to hear.

She heard that silence and sighed. "Oh, dear God. What were you going to do?"

Again, silence from me.

"We picked up a transition call from someone at your location to a location in Greece. Tell me that wasn't you, and tell me that wasn't you either calling in a team or you making plans to go and get your grandfather. Tell me that wasn't also Calhoun Bastian's coordinates."

I just let my chest rise, air went out, and it lowered.

"Fuck!" She swore into the phone, the vehemence almost rattling. "Shit, shit, shit. You are going to ruin my career. You are a right bastard, aren't you? What were you going to do, Kashton? At least tell me that."

Now she was coaxing?

My hand went into my pocket and I tipped my head up, thinking. "What are you doing, Agent Bright?"

She wanted me to say the words.

Fuck.

She was trying to trap me. On the phone.

Fuck.

Someone was listening.

Fuck!

She was no longer an asset to me.

They were moving against me.

"I take it that you are calling me to notify me that you have found my twin brother, and also Chrissy Hayes? Was that the purpose of this phone call?"

"Shit." A low curse under her breath. "Yeah." She was resigned. She knew I knew. "We have a team moving in as we're speaking, and I'm assuming we'll be taking your brother into custody momentarily." Another pause of hesitation. "You can wait for another call from myself. We'll let you know if we find Chrissy Hayes alive or not."

She ended the call, and with that, I hung my head.

The hold I had over Bright and Wilson was done.

She'd been trying to entrap me, which said they were putting together a case against me. Whether they moved on it or not was a different situation, but now I knew, and I'd be covering my bases. Not letting myself contemplate the loss of that professional relationship, I went to Peter's safe in the office and took out a phone I didn't use unless it was absolutely necessary.

I called my team. "Delete everything. Feds are now looking."

Then a second call. "Have you left yet?"

"No."

"Stay. They've moved on them already."

"Will do."

I had one thing at least. I still had my grandfather within my clasp.

"What's going on?"

Peter Francis was standing inside the office, his eyes alert and alarmed. It was a stark contrast from the bags under his eyes, or the exhaustion emanating from him.

"The FBI found Chrissy Hayes."

FORTY-FIVE

Kash

I had limited time.

Peter was told everything, and as he fell to his couch in shock, I strolled right past him. I was an ungrateful asshole to him, too. I should've taken the time, softened the blow, been there for him while he was coming to grips with everything that'd been uncovered in the last thirty-six hours.

I didn't.

I walked right past, texting Matt.

Kash: Fly back. Chrissy Hayes is alive. Your father and sister need you.

My phone buzzed a second later.

Matt: WHAT? WHAT? WHAT?

Kash: Bailey will fill you in. Come back. I have to circle the wagons, don't have time for more.

That was it. He was texting me back, but I ignored his calls. What I said was true. I'd lost Bright and Wilson from my pocket. They were looking at me as an adversary, trying to find charges against me, and, well, they'd have a fight on their hands. I hadn't intended on adopting the mantra that if I went down, they'd go down, but since they were flying around me, I was taking that mantra on now.

Game on.

"Hello?"

"I need you to pull up anything and everything on my two FBI assets."

"Not to incriminate you, I'm assuming."

"Correct."

If they took payments from me, guarantee there was a whole closet of other payments, other bribes, other times they had looked the other way. They looked the other way when Bailey was first brought in, and they did it without blinking. There was a pattern, one they'd been doing for a long time, and there was a trail. There was always a trail.

"You don't want your girl to look into it?"

I paused, just briefly, as I considered it. "No." Bailey needed to be as clear from this as possible. "They said she left a trail when she found them. I need to know if she did."

"She didn't."

My hand tightened on the phone. "Are you sure?"

"She left one system open, the neighbor's, but that was it. And I only know it was your girl because you told me what was going on. I'll look, but I didn't see anything they could trail back to her."

"They found the house."

He was silent on his end.

I could read between the lines. I doubted they would've found the house on their own, not as fast as they did. That meant something happened. They had followed—

He interrupted my thoughts. "They might've put an alert on your location, figuring you'd hunker down and have her look."

"They can do that?"

"They can do almost anything, but if she erased her trail . . ."

"Could they still have it?"

He was silent again. A long second. "I don't know."

Fuck.

"Can you break in? See whether they have anything on her?"

"They're saying they do?"

"Yeah." I hated that word. I hated that admission.

"I'll look, but once I do, they'll trail it back to me. Our own location will be exposed."

I couldn't risk Bailey.

"Start packing up. Do it remote, if you can," I responded, still walking down the hallway to our room.

"On it."

I ended the call as I got to the room, and going inside, I saw Bailey hadn't moved. Her eyes were big. She was clutching her knees to her chest. I cursed, seeing how pale she was.

"What's happened?"

I checked the clock. I was figuring I had one hour, if even that.

"Feds found the house. They called; they're trying to pull me in. My guess is you'll be getting a call from them to notify you that your mother is alive this afternoon."

"Wait. *What?*" She scrambled off the bed, following me as I went into the bathroom.

I stripped, turning the shower on and stepping underneath.

Bailey waited, just outside the shower door. "What's going on, Kash?"

I stepped under the spray, my eyes finding and holding hers. "I'm in trouble."

She drew in a breath, but she didn't waver. She didn't look away. She knew the risks we'd both taken the night before.

"What can I do?" she asked.

Relax.

Sleep.

Rest.

Smile.

Laugh.

Comfort her father.

Be herself.

"Nothing. Stay here, and wait for my call."

She nodded.

My chest was tight. I didn't know what was in store for me, if anything would even happen, and I needed one more touch. One more taste.

As she turned to go and change, I caught her hand. I pulled her in, my hand sliding behind her neck, and tugged her into my chest. My arms went around her. Her hands slid around my back, raising up, and she held me right back.

We both savored this time.

I *loved* this woman, but I didn't have time to say the words.

We didn't talk.

Moving to the bed, I held Bailey, and fifty-three minutes, twelve seconds later, the call came through.

Feds were at the gate.

FORTY-SIX

Kash

Bright was pissed.

Her eyes were flat, her mouth just as flat, and if she could grind up acorns and spit them out like chew, she would've. I wasn't being brought into their questioning station with handcuffs or zip ties around my wrists. I was being brought in with two federal agents as my "guides," two agents not Bright or Wilson, and as a "courtesy."

Their words, not mine.

Which meant they didn't have what they claimed they had, or they wanted to use me still. I was willing to bet money they'd be circling the conversation of me helping them bring my grandfather in.

We rode into an underground parking lot.

Once we parked and got out, Bright and Wilson flanked me. They led me through a door, showing their credentials, and I had to give up a fingerprint. A pass was printed right in front of me. It was taken by a staff member, stuffed into a lanyard, and Wilson put that over my head.

Then we were walking down a hallway.

There were doors on either side. I heard murmuring from inside each room.

"You have my brother here?"

Bright's head snapped to mine. She scowled. "We are not happy with you."

Interesting.

She was pissed and showing she was pissed.

I had to smile. "What happened, Bright? I had to imagine you tried to keep your affiliation with me hidden. Yet here you are and here I am. Are they holding your activities over your head?"

Her mouth got tighter the more I talked. Her shoulders grew more rigid.

"Shut it and just follow. You're here to watch your brother."

Even more interesting.

I wanted that opportunity, but not here. Not with them. Not this way.

They led me to the basement, and to a back corner. A staff member came through a door, and I saw the stairs there, but they weren't showing any EXIT signs. This building was not following basic code.

This was a black site, one they used to do interrogations they didn't want the public to know about.

That wasn't good.

"What if I were to tell you that I have a tracker on me?"

Bright braked and whirled to me. Her eyes were searching, but so were mine. I saw the quick panic there. She was alarmed, but then she concealed it. Her mouth went back to that scowl. "You don't."

She started to go ahead.

I didn't. I remained, and she had to stop and look my way again.

I raised an eyebrow. "How do you know?"

Her hand flexed over my arm, gripping me hard, but it was a reaction she hadn't been able to hold back. "Because you wouldn't tell us if you did." Her head went forward again. "Let's go."

She jerked me after her.

They took me into a room, but it wasn't a questioning room. It was a watching room, and inside the next room, which I could see through a two-way mirror, was my brother.

He was at the table, head bent, arms handcuffed flat to the table. He was wearing a T-shirt that'd been ripped at some point, and dried blood had seeped through it, mostly over his right shoulder.

I remembered how easily he got away from me. "Did he fight when you took the house?"

I was watching my twin. My gaze never wavered, but I noted two movements. One was Bright looking at me, seen from the corner of my eye, and the other was my twin lifting his head. Just slight. Just enough. And then he lowered it back down.

He knew I was here.

How I knew it, I didn't know. But I knew it.

"He didn't have time. We took them both by surprise. He was in the kitchen."

"I doubt he had blood on him when you took him, all peaceful-like." I should ask about Chrissy, but I didn't. "What was he doing in there?"

"What?"

"What was he doing in there?"

The answer came from Wilson, who sounded as if he was leaning against the wall behind us. "He was cooking eggs."

Eggs.

He was making food.

"Who else was in the house?"

Bright made a growling sound.

Wilson answered, almost sounding bored. "Him. The driver, who we're still identifying. And Chrissy Hayes."

This told me three more things. One: Wilson was not alarmed. He would've been, if their heads were on the chopping block. Two: that meant they were safe, but Bright was frustrated. She didn't want me to ask these questions, and she didn't want to give me the answers. And finally, Wilson was answering, so that meant either Wilson was doing a damn good job at playing the good cop or they were ordered to give me information.

They needed me.

That's the only scenario that could be at play here.

That gave me cards to play. That gave me some power.

Now I asked, because I needed to, "Where's Chrissy?"

Bright answered this one, her features softening. "She's in medical. Once she's cleared, and we get her statement, she can be reunited with her daughter."

My teeth ground together.

Her pity told me she felt bad for Chrissy, which meant Chrissy hadn't been in good shape when they found her.

"I'm assuming she's been questioned." I peered more directly at Bright. "What was her state?"

Bright hesitated. "She doesn't remember a lot, and the psych doctor advised against pushing her. As for physical, she'd lost weight. She'd been traumatized, but she was coherent when we found her. She could walk and talk." Another hesitation. Her eyebrows pinched. She flattened her lips together before she nodded at my twin. "She wasn't scared of him."

I looked toward him, and his head had raised. It wasn't all the way up, but it was halfway up. He was listening.

He shouldn't be able to hear us.

My eyes narrowed back at Bright. "How do you know?"

"There was an incident. We were taking him out and had to pause because a van was going down the street. We held him back. Word did not get communicated to her team and they brought her down the stairs from where they were keeping her. They looked at each other, and her handlers said she didn't react."

"Was she in shock? She didn't know what she was seeing."

"No. She said his name."

His name?

I wanted to ask, but I didn't.

"There was no fear. Her body didn't lock up. One agent had been holding her pulse, it was just habit, and he said there was no spike. How she said his name, it was as if she was worried about him."

I turned to inspect my twin once more.

His head was back down.

They wouldn't get anything from him. He was good. Too good. And there were things happening I didn't know, and I needed to know. So, weighing the pros and cons, I decided to pull my card.

"I want time with him."

Both agents reacted. Bright's head snapped around to me, her eyes wide and unbelieving. And I heard Wilson's swift intake of breath.

"No." Bright shook her head.

"Yes." I leaned toward her. Before she could make more protests, I laid out my argument. "You will get nothing from him." They didn't know he could hear us, but I did, and so this message was twofold. I wanted him to know what I knew, and then I would go from there. "I had him before."

Neither knew.

I felt the tension fill the air.

They were not happy to hear that.

I kept on. "I did not know about him until he showed up at my apartment. He broke in. We caught him, but he let us take him. He was testing us. He was testing me. We waited to ques-

tion him. I wanted to see Calhoun's reaction to his disappear-
ance because all three of us know that he came from Calhoun.
There is no other explanation for his sudden appearance and his
identity not being known before now. Once I ascertained what
I needed to know, I went in. The questioning lasted five minutes, and he was gone. He's remained hidden until his move on
Bailey. He had Chrissy Hayes in his possession. He's good, and
you all know it. You won't get anything from him." Now was my
card. "But I will. Let me talk to him."

"No!"

I looked at Wilson. His gaze was wide and alarmed. He was
skirting from Bright to myself, and back again.

"Wilson?"

He hesitated.

Bright turned to him, her arms folded over her chest. "No,
Wilson. No. No way."

His phone buzzed.

Wilson pulled it out.

Bright stepped toward him, her hand outstretched. "Don't
answer that. We can't let them near each other. Not any more
than this."

I studied Bright, hearing her wording: "Them." "Near each
other." She spoke as if . . . I frowned. She was talking as if we
were *together*? A team? Or was it the twin thing? Did she believe
in twins?

Was *she* a twin?

But he answered. "Wilson." He waited, listening. It wasn't a
long call. He sighed, hanging up, and looked at me.

I saw the capitulation at the same time Bright started sputtering, "No!"

I smiled.

Wilson nodded behind me. "Go ahead."

I hesitated for just a second.

Chrissy Hayes wasn't scared of him. I knew Bailey's mother enough to know this was not enough time for her to be brainwashed, so if Chrissy wasn't scared, that gave me hope.

The second was up.

FORTY-SEVEN

Kash

Each time I'd been in the presence of my twin, something new was revealed. The first was just that he existed. The second was the first inkling of a connection. It shouldn't be there. We didn't grow up together. He was a stranger to me. And yet it'd been there.

He knew I was coming.

I knew he knew I was coming, and when I opened that door, his head was up.

I came in, and this time he was wary of me.

Roles were reversed somehow. Maybe he had heard me earlier, on the other side of the wall, and he knew that I knew more than he wanted me to know? Or maybe it was because he was caught in a way that he couldn't get out of here?

Was that it?

Still, as I stepped inside and shut the door, neither of us looked away.

"Was he going to have you undergo plastic surgery?"

I bypassed the chair, content to lean against the mirror behind me. My head was down, and I watched him steadily.

There was no reaction, but I knew, I knew in my gut, he knew what I was referring to.

"Yes."

My nostrils flared. "What were you doing with Chrissy Hayes?"

Why wasn't Chrissy scared of you?

He darted a look to the mirror, then shrugged, his head lowering. "I was getting to know my future mother-in-law."

He looked up, a small grin at that, and he saw my eye-roll.

He snickered, then sobered. "I'm kidding."

"Ass."

Another grin from him. "I know." He swallowed, looking at the door. "We can't, you know." Those eyes—my eyes—came back to me.

Yeah.

I nodded. I knew what he was talking about.

"But I would. If . . ." His eyes darted behind me again. "You know."

Well, this was anticlimactic.

He was telling he *would* talk, but not *here*. And that was putting me in a position I didn't want to be in.

I pulled out the chair and sat. Rubbing my jaw, I dipped my head and raked my hand through my hair before I leaned back. "What's your main goal? You have to tell me that."

If I was going to risk everything, I had to know it was worth it.

He sobered and dipped his head down before lifting those eyes again. "Not hurting others. That's my main goal."

That told me nothing.

I had to remember.

He was not my twin.

He was a guy. A stranger.

I shook my head. "I already have a brother, you know."

He saw it, and his Adam's apple moved up and down. A light that started to shine in his eyes diminished, and even though his hands were still cuffed to the table, he was able to lean back. He put distance between us with that motion.

"I know. Matt Francis. Chrissy told me about him." He

paused, his gaze darting to the mirror behind me. "She told me about Bailey, too."

Everything went flat in me. "Don't say her name."

He shut that down real quick. A nod. His eyelids clasped closed a second. "Yeah. Okay."

I knew I should keep the real questions to a minimum, and this next one was as real as they were going to come. But did it really matter? The authorities knew about him. They knew about Calhoun. They knew about me. Not much was still secret, so I had to ask, because it'd been bothering me since he first broke into Bailey's sanctuary.

"Were you the payment?"

He drew in a ragged breath, his own nostrils flaring.

I leaned forward. "Did he allow our mother her freedom because she gave you up? Or did he kill her because he found that she'd hidden one of us from him?"

Fury lit up his entire face.

He jerked forward. His throat contorted.

His features twisted, sharpening.

One brief second before he caught himself. He forced himself to relax. Then he lounged back. He swallowed. His shoulders loosened.

He rolled his neck, back in control.

And he smirked. "Wouldn't you like to know."

I waited.

Nothing.

I frowned. That was it? That was his comeback?

My frown deepened, and feeling some of my monster railing inside of me, I leaned farther over the table and showed him my teeth. "That's all you have? No smart retort? No jab? No insult?" Were his social skills less developed? "I don't know what your life was like, but I have to ask: Do you know what mine is like?"

He blinked, and I got him.

There was a sense of wonder there.

I leaned back again. Victoria said he was supposed to study me. She said that's what he had been doing, what Calhoun thought he had been doing.

If he had, he would come back with something. Anything. Even an old insult that Matt might've used. A little quip. But I was getting nada from him.

He hadn't been studying me.

"What were you doing?"

His eyebrows flew back up.

He saw it. He knew I had him, but he didn't cover it up. He didn't slam a wall down. Instead, he let me see him, and then he said, "I won't." His head lowered closer to the table, closer to me. "Not here."

Oh yeah.

We were doing the twin thing, already.

I got his message loud and clear.

I nodded, standing up from the table.

I left that room knowing one thing: I needed to break him out of FBI custody.

Bright and Wilson were waiting for me in the hallway. Both were not happy.

"What the fuck were you two talking about?"

Wilson was glowering. "I've seen videos of twin babies talking to each other. They make no sense to anyone. A bunch of gibberish, babbling, but each of them knows exactly what the other is saying. I swear, I saw the adult version in there."

Yeah. Maybe. Thinking back on our conversation, I'd think the same thing.

"He doesn't know anything."

"Bullshit."

Yeah. Bullshit on me. I was lying through my teeth.

I exhaled. "It's true."

Bright raised an eyebrow. "And how do you know that?"

I glanced at Wilson. "Guess it's a twin thing."

Bright cursed, reeling backward and walking a few feet away. Her hands were in her hair. She grabbed a handful, bent over, and let out a yell. Letting go, she strode back to me. "I swear, if you are lying to us, if you are lying to the government, we will swoop in. We will hurt you and you'll never recover."

My chest tightened up.

She read my face. Her tone grew quieter, more lethal. "You don't get it, Colello. We won't come after you. We'll come after *her*. She's the one who hacked everything. She's the one who found them. We can prove it, and that's what we'll do. We'll take away your little girlfriend, and we'll never let her near you again."

Wilson grunted. "You know what kind of place this is. We have these places as prisons, too. Public doesn't know about them. Public doesn't have the right to know about them."

"That's where we'll stick your girlfriend. So once again, what does he know?"

I stared at each of them, knowing I had to make a choice.

Fuck.

FORTY-EIGHT

Bailey

I was curled in a ball, sitting in the chair in the entryway, and I knew they were coming back.

Kash called. He had her.

He had her!

And he was bringing her here.

To me.

Heaven had answered my call. Hell rescinded its try. I got my wish.

So soon.

Since Kash's call, I had not moved.

I camped out, and no one even dared to come over to me.

Curled in a ball, face forward, eyes trained on the door. I wasn't budging an inch, because the same part that was so scared this was all a delusion, all a prank, was the same part of me that feared that if I dared look away, she wouldn't return to me.

She had to return to me.

I had to have her again.

Life wasn't over for us, for her.

I wasn't leaving this seat until my mother actually walked through the door.

Then the buzz happened.

I heard Peter on the phone from the gate.

They were coming.

That would've been security calling them in to the house, even though Kash had clearance. They still would've called, because they knew I would've wanted to know.

So I sat up, my entire body one big heartbeat at a time.

Thump.

I moved.

Thump.

I scooted to the edge of the seat.

Thump.

They were coming.

Thump.

My feet touched the floor.

Thump.

My hands curled around the chair cushion.

Thump.

Peter went to the door. He opened it.

I heard the crunch of gravel under the tires.

They were there.

They had parked.

Thump. Thump. Thump.

The doors opened.

My heart stopped. My whole body froze.

I heard Kash's voice, and then—a woman's voice.

I tore out of there.

Thumpthumpthumpthump.

I sprinted past Peter, through the open door, and she was climbing out of hers.

She was there.

She was thinner.

More frail.

But it was her.

It was Chrissy.

It was my mom.

She looked up. Her eyes trailing up the stairs, to me, and there she was.

"Mom!"

"Honey."

She was sobbing.

Tears were probably streaking down my face.

I waited. I still waited. I needed an indication that if I went down there, I wasn't going to break her.

Her arms lifted, and that was all I needed.

I flew down the stairs, and I was on her. Arms around her neck. Around her waist. I kept hugging her. Burying my head in her neck. Smelling her.

She wasn't a figment of my imagination anymore. I wasn't smelling her ghost.

She was real and alive. Flesh. Blood. Bones. Ligaments. The whole bit.

Chrissy Hayes just rose from the dead.

"Mom!" I couldn't let her go, no matter how tight I was squeezing her. I couldn't. I wouldn't. No one could make me— but no one was trying to.

She was holding me back just as hard, and whispering to me, "You are so beautiful, honey. So beautiful and kind and strong. And I love you. Your mother loves you so much. You sweet, sweet girl. Oh, my goodness." She pulled back, framing my face. Tears were glistening over her entire face. She didn't care. She was taking me in as I was taking her in. She breathed as if she were afraid to let go of the air. "If it was possible, you have gotten even more stunning." She was blinking rapidly. Her hand cupped the side of my face. Her thumb swiped over my cheek. "Oh, honey." She melted, and her forehead moved to rest against mine.

I was holding her.

She was cupping the side of my face, and she was smiling at me.

Our eyes were so close our eyelashes were almost touching, but neither of us cared. We were breathing each other in, we were that desperate.

"Mom," I whispered, biting back tears. "What happened?"

"Oh, baby." She lifted her head, winding her arms around me, and she tugged me to her. She held me gently in her arms now, as if already shielding me from what she needed to tell me. "We'll get to that. I promise."

I felt her head lifting. Turning.

She tapped my arm softly. "You tend to your man, because you're not the only one who saw a ghost today." She stepped back, but her gaze was trained over my head, toward whoever had been waiting for our reunion to finish. She squeezed me once more before stepping away. "I need to see to my man, too."

She was the one who ran this time, going up the stairs toward Peter.

His hand hadn't moved from the doorknob, like he was scared to let it go. But then she was in front of him, and he leaned back.

She stopped.

I found myself waiting, holding my breath.

My mom lowered her head, as if she were suddenly shy. She was saying something. I couldn't make out the words, but whatever she said, it worked.

Peter surged for her, wrapping his arms around her, and he lifted her in the air. He let out a roar before burying his head in her hair, smoothing one hand down her hair, and as I watched, he kept touching her. They hugged a long time, maybe even longer than she and I had, but he never stopped touching her. Even after their hug was done and she moved back an inch, their heads were together. She was saying things to him. He was nodding; both were crying. He never stopped running his hand down her arm, over her shoulder, down her hair, smoothing over her cheek.

I felt Kash behind me, and my body was already sagging into him.

He caught me, but it wasn't a big catch.

I felt him, and my body gave out. He merely stepped in behind me so I was resting on him. His hand came around my stomach. He nuzzled down by my ear and neck. "You okay?"

I nodded, but reached up. My hand slid through his hair, clasping the back of his head, and I looked to him. He was observing me, his eyes hooded, and I remembered my mom's words. "Are you okay?"

His chest rose and held.

Something was wrong.

I turned around to stand facing him. His hands fell to my waist, then moved around so one of his palms lay flat on my back, tunneling up under my shirt.

I continued watching him, touching his chin. "What happened?"

His eyes went from my mouth to my eyes, and I saw he was conflicted.

"Kash."

He frowned, a sadness shining from him. "I had to make a choice."

I caught my air again. "Between?"

"You and my brother."

I flattened my hands on his arms, my lungs still ceasing from relaxing. "And?"

"And . . ." He drew in another sharp breath. It sounded painful. "You're not going to like it."

FORTY-NINE

Kash

Three weeks.

We waited while the family got used to having Chrissy back.

There was a media shitstorm over Chrissy's "back from the dead" situation. How that news got leaked, I didn't know, but it was on the list to find and punish.

For three weeks, people were afraid to ask Chrissy what she went through.

Bailey did try, but Chrissy folded into a nearly catatonic state. She stopped talking for two days. It was enough to scare everyone, so for the rest of the time, Bailey basked in her mother's presence. Peter got laid again—a lot, judging by how he was the one glowing all the time. Seraphina's laughter didn't echo in sadness anymore. Cyclone was living up to his name; he was literally a cyclone again, running everywhere in the household.

Payton looked nervous when she saw Chrissy, and I made a point to check in with Marie.

"It's like she's been trained to be invisible. She's here. She's spending time with the kids. But the second Chrissy shows up, Payton scatters like a scared mouse. I'm now fine with the lady, realized I was wrong to get all up in my feelings the first time, but yeah. It's the oddest thing."

Chrissy never balked. Bailey never said a word. So Payton was excused from my mind.

She wasn't a problem.

Another person that wasn't a problem: Matt. He was hanging out and seemed to be stabilizing. He mentioned an idea for a company and wanted to talk to me about it later. He also mentioned a girl had caught his eye, but that'd been the only mentions of either.

It was during those three weeks that we all chose to forget about Calhoun and Quinn's trial, and we all chose to forget that Chrissy was home after enduring something so horrific that a mere question about it would paralyze her.

It took them that long to finish questioning my brother, before they were content to move him to a different holding facility.

After I told Bailey my plan, she wanted to help. I didn't want her to incriminate herself any more, but I had to be honest. I couldn't lie to her, and that meant she did it without my knowledge. I woke one morning and she was sitting there, cross-legged and beaming at me. She was waving a piece of paper in the air. "I have what you've been waiting for."

"Tell me you didn't."

"I did." She sounded so smug. "And don't worry, I *really* made sure nothing could be traced back to me."

I was afraid to ask what else she'd done.

She heard that they were able to trace her and hadn't liked it, not one bit. But they didn't realize that the choice was always going to be Bailey.

So, I was waiting.

In the meantime, I pulled my team from Calhoun.

Once we got the signal, I was moving in to grab my twin.

I sat up. "When and where?"

She handed over the paper. "He's being moved at one tomorrow morning and that's the address. I looked it up. It's a house. But from what I hacked, it sounds like they're only holding him there for the night. Then he'll be driven to another safe house outside of state lines."

"Can you track where the second house will be?"

She paused, biting her lip, before she shook her head. "I don't know if I'll be able to. I've looked at other trips where they've moved a high-priority subject, and some messages weren't relayed over the internet or technology. Coordinates were given to one agent, who then traveled to the house and gave the message face-to-face."

That meant we had one opportunity. And that also meant they'd be watching.

Her hand fell to my arm. Her thumb stroked over my pulse on the inside of my wrist. "It'll all work out. We have Chrissy back. You can grab Chase, and then maybe you can find out everything you need. You can move in on your grandfather, finally."

That was the hope, but I was tired. I was tired to the bone.

"Tell me you wiped everything, because they're going to come after you."

She nodded, her teeth sinking into her lip again. "I did. I will."

No one else was looped in.

"You'll have to stay back." I exhaled sharply, bending forward so my forehead was resting on her knee.

Her hand came down on the back of my head and held me there. Her fingers slid through my hair, and she began massaging the back of my scalp.

"It'll be okay."

I grabbed her shirt and fisted it. "It's not. Leaving you behind is never okay."

"But it's necessary."

I lifted my head, knowing she could see how heavy this was

weighing on me, but I wasn't shielding myself from her. Not any-more, not with what I was about to put us both through. "Is it, though? Is there another way?"

"Your brother won't tell you what you need to know while he's in custody. You have to take him. You have to know what he knows. He's the one putting you in this situation."

I looked at the paper.

I looked at the address.

I looked at the time.

I had thirteen hours.

Witnesses to Be Called for Quinn Callas's Defense Team

After weeks, the prosecution has rested their unfair case. Circumstantial evidence is weak, there is a lack of witness testimonies and holes were found in their timeline. The head attorney for Ms. Callas says they have a strong argument to present to the court. They are confident their client will be rightly acquitted.

—*Inside Daily Press*

FIFTY

Bailey

"Why are we doing this again?" Matt asked, his head inclining over mine as we were weaving in and out of Naveah.

Matt didn't know what was going down tonight. And we only had a small window to get into place. I was outside the door, almost on Kash's heels as he left for his top secret mission. My guards were with us. Kash wouldn't be alarmed if we went to Naveah.

But from Naveah is where we needed to lose the guards.

Yes, yes, I know.

How stupid of me to lose my guards. They're on us for a reason. Blah, blah, blah.

But I figured I already knew where the bad guys were. Calhoun was somewhere in Greece. Kash told me that, and I doubted he would've traveled back in the few days since Kash had pulled his guys from Calhoun. And the other bad guy was Kash's twin brother. We all knew where he was; that was the whole point of tonight.

So, one night. I was willing to risk it.

Matt just didn't know any of this.

We were fast coming to the time when I would have to clue

him in, but before that, I marched over to Tony, who had a girl gyrating on his lap.

His hands were on her waist and he was leaning back, a lazy smirk on his face, watching her. His eyes trailed to us and I noticed the caution coming over his face.

Be scared of me, buddy. Be very scared of me.

That gave me a warm feeling.

My hands found my hips, and I nodded at the girl. "Get rid of her."

He frowned, his eyebrows lowering. His hands kneaded the side of her waist. "Why?"

"Do it. Now." I was not messing around.

He noted it, and nodded, patting her on the bum. "Get lost."

Such kindness from such an asshat.

She glared at him. "Are you kidding me?"

He wasn't even paying attention to her anymore. "Yeah. Get lost. Team Brainiac makes me soft anyways."

She harrumphed, flicked us a look, then saw Matt, and a sultry smile came over her face. "Hey there."

Matt wiggled his eyebrows at her, waving his fingers, too. "Hey there."

Tony sat up. "Really?"

Matt snapped back to attention. "Right." He jerked his chin toward the dance area. "How about you go give me a dance out there? I'll watch from here."

Her eyes lit up, her smile turned even more seductive, and her hips were swaying as she walked down to where everybody else was dancing.

Once she was gone, I motioned to both of them. "We have to go."

Tony and Matt shared a look, but Tony was getting up. He was doing it slow, but he was doing it. "What the fuck, Hayes?"

"You need to do something for us, and we're not going to owe you. You're not doing it for any other reason than just to help us, and because you owe us."

His nostrils flared, and his head moved back. "I owe you? Your math is wrong. I've now done you two solids. You owe me."

I leaned in, making sure he knew I wasn't messing around. "No." I clipped that word out. "You owe us. You owe me. You owe Matt for being a bad influence on him."

Tony's eyes darted over my shoulder, and I couldn't see Matt's response, but I heard his, "Um . . ."

I didn't care. I kept going. "You owe me for being a douche-bag, for having girls touching you, blowing you, and doing all the disgusting sexual things you've been doing. Not for doing them, though. I'm sure the girls might have something to say about that. No. For me. Because you did them right next to me, when you know you shouldn't have done that. You enjoyed making me uncomfortable, and because of that, you are going to do this and you aren't going to ask questions. You'll never talk about it again. You won't even think about it again." I waited. One beat. "Got it?"

I couldn't say that there was fear in Tony's gaze, but there was definitely a new uneasiness.

I cocked my eyebrow, and he nodded. "Fine. What do I need to do?"

"You are going to set up a distraction for us, and then you're going to drink with us for the rest of the night."

Except, that wasn't exactly how it was going to go.

As plans went, this one was simple. That was the genius of it, in my opinion.

There was no real thought put into the selection of our stand-ins. Tony walked up to two people, a guy and girl, and told them to go to the back section. They were told to wait, and that showed the power these guys had over normal people, because they did it, no questions asked.

It hit me then how much I had grown accustomed to this

world. I didn't see Tony as the intimidating guy I had when I first
saw him. I didn't see Matt Francis as *the* Matt Francis. He was my
brother. Tony was annoying. That's who they were to me. But
when Tony approached those two strangers, their eyes were sau-
cers, they gulped, and they jumped when Tony told them "Go."

I would later process this. Later. Not now. I did not have time.
But this very interaction would remain in the back of my mind.

The plan was put in action.

We went to a dark corner and as the guards were watching
us, the three of us slipped into the booth. This booth was chosen
for a reason. It was far enough away that the guards would see us
go in, and from there, they knew three people were partying in
the booth. The shadows and the club's dark lighting would help
camouflage our stand-ins. The guards were ordered to remain at
the bottom of the walkway to keep people away from us. It was a
bit of a diva move, because we were taking up an entire section
of the club, but it was necessary.

We got into the booth.

We ordered drinks.

The guards all saw this, then turned their backs as they took
their positions. One glanced back to make sure we were there,
and I allowed that we could waste five minutes. That was it, and
then Tony called in his distraction.

I don't know who he asked or how he got them to do it, but
exactly three minutes in, there was a burst of fireworks in the
front corner of the club. One guy stood with sparklers, and when
those went off, all eyes were on him. He was in plain sight of
everyone. A few people shrieked. Most laughed. And the club's
security guards took him out.

Everyone relaxed after that and went back to partying.

In that time, Matt and I slipped out of the booth. The guy
and girl slipped in. As they picked up our drinks, Matt and I were
tiptoeing out an exit door that was hardly used. There would be
security footage of us, but it wouldn't be caught until later.

Matt and I slipped out this side door as our guards remained inside. They wouldn't look for us if they thought they knew where we were.

Then we got in Matt's car and drove away.

Easy, right? The hard part was going to be next.

FIFTY-ONE

Kash

Both my teams came in.

The computer team was set up. They knocked out any surveillance within a three-block radius, which included street cameras and personal security systems. The other team stood next to me, all of us in our spots, taking up the perimeter around the house.

It was a lone house.

There was nothing special or distinguished about it. That was why they used it. Just another suburban neighborhood home.

I didn't want anyone to get hurt. I didn't want anyone to die. But when you send in a team to take over eight agents, I knew there was a high risk of someone getting a bullet in their body. Setting this up, thinking over everything, from every angle, I used what we had to use.

Me.

"All clear." A voice came over our coms, and that was the signal. "I have control of their system. You are good to enter the east door. We have three minutes before they realize they're not in control."

That meant all clear for us.

My team was made up of the best of the best. They moved in

on the house as if they were a part of the shadows. They were approaching without sound, leaving no trace, and unless someone was watching us, they were ghosts.

We were ghosts.

There was a small team of three in front of me, and a team of four behind me. There were more approaching from the other side of the house. We came in from over the neighboring dividing fences.

A door was unlocked.

We slipped inside.

The men before me spread through the side of the house.

"Heat signatures have two at the front. Two at the back. Two upstairs. One in the kitchen. Two in the basement," came from our coms.

We'd gone over the blueprints. There was no easy entrance. "There's no way they'd keep him in the basement. If they're attacked, they'd want at least two escape routes," Harden argued. He pointed at the plans, his finger digging into them. "If there are heat signatures in the basement, I guarantee you that it's a decoy. He won't be kept there. My guess is that if there's a heat signature upstairs, that's him. They can take him over a balcony or climb onto the roof. Two ways to escape, other than the obvious."

Harden spoke with confidence, but it didn't feel right to me.

Now we were moving to the kitchen.

We were supposed to draw one guard out at a time. I was the decoy for that trap, but it didn't feel right. None of this felt right.

Two at the front. Two at the back. Two upstairs. One in the kitchen. Two in the basement.

We were in the east side of the house, so we had three options: front, back, kitchen.

The front would be too vulnerable to a frontal assault. The same with the back end of the house. But the kitchen . . . I wished I had Bailey's memory. I tapped Harden's shoulder in front of me. He held his hand up. The rest of our group paused.

I typed out my thoughts on my phone and held up the screen. It was turned on night mode and dimmed, so when he read it, none of us were worried a sudden flash of light would alert anyone else in the house.

Does the kitchen have two exits?

He frowned.
I pulled my phone back and typed again.

Two are in the back. They're surrounding the kitchen. Above, below, behind, in front.

He knew what I was saying. My brother was the one in the kitchen, but instead of replying or making a decision, he raised my phone so the computer team would be able to read it. The camera was hooked on his night vision goggles.

A second later, we heard in our ears, "The kitchen has two exits. A door and hallway connects to the garage. There's also a door leading to the backyard. The two heat signatures are on the back patio."

The voice added, "You have one minute to get out. Decide and go."

Harden made a hand motion, signaling to the rest of the team.
The four behind me moved ahead.
We'd decided.
Harden had a hand on my shoulder, and he held me in place. Once his men were lined up against the wall, he walked me past them. At the opening, he tapped me twice on the back.
I was to go.
He raised a hand in front of his camera. In sync with his motions, the voice in our ears said, "Three. Two."
I walked out.
"What the—"

It was enough.

The guards in the living room were alerted first, but they were confused by the sight of me. My men used that second. They rushed forward, getting the jump on them, and I ran into the next room. When I went into the kitchen, I understood their shock. Chase? We still hadn't been officially introduced to each other, but Chase was handcuffed to a chair. He had restraints around almost every part of his body. Looking at him, I searched for signs of abuse. I saw nothing. He looked fine. No bags of exhaustion under his eyes. No gaunt look around his mouth to show he was hungry. His skin was fine, so he was hydrated. He was merely held captive.

His eyes cut to mine as shouting and shots erupted in the air behind us.

I darted to him, but paused right before trying to cut through his restraints. "If you make me regret this"—I placed the edge of the knife to his throat—"I will find you and I will finish this job. Do you understand me?"

There was no reaction from him. He didn't blink. He only said, "Yes." His gaze held mine steadily the entire time.

Another second, and Harden came in yelling. "They've dispatched more agents. We have to go *now*!"

"I need help."

Harden holstered his gun and dropped to his knees. A second later, another man joined and we were hurrying through the restraints.

Harden cursed. "We can't wait."

I looked up. We'd only gotten through four of the restraints. "What do you suggest? Because I'm not leaving him behind."

Harden's eyes flashed at me right before he took a step back, brought his gun up. He shot through the two back legs of the chair. Wood exploded in the air. I had enough time to jump at the same time the second man grabbed my vest and hauled me back, too. The momentum kept me clear from any shards getting into my skin.

Chase wasn't as lucky. He winced, readying himself, his head lowered and bracing.

The guy let me go, grunting as he passed me. "Minor scrapes. The trajectory sent the wood in your direction."

Good to know.

Chase was glowering at both of them. "This is who you had on him?"

Him. Our eyes met. We both knew who he meant.

Harden grabbed the back of the chair and answered for me. "Yep, and your granddaddy didn't have a clue. If you're thinking of complaining, save it. We don't have an HR department, if you know what I mean." With that said, he lifted.

The second guy lifted the other side.

The back door was shoved open. A guy appeared and yelled, "We have to go now! Now!"

"We know. We're coming!" Harden yelled back.

The third guy saw the dilemma and his eyes got big. "Clear some space! They're bringing him out strapped to a chair."

They carried my brother out the back, going through the door being held open by the third guy. All of us darted over the backyard. Men were working behind us. There were a bunch of flashes as the third guy ran next to me. He took my arm, guiding me into the second vehicle. I saw them taking my brother to the first vehicle.

"No."

The guy's grip tightened.

I knocked it off, twisting out of his hold, and at his look of surprise, I snarled back, "Do not attempt to force me. I know your skill level. You don't know mine." He let me go. I took advantage and moved around him.

They were loading Chase into the back. I jumped in next to him. They were going to shove him in and shut the door. I got in right as they were reaching for the door.

The guy saw me and paused. "What—"

Harden shot me a look, but commanded, "Leave him. We have to go."

After that, they got in. Doors were closed. The rest of the guys streamed out and loaded up. We were off.

I waited until we got one block before speaking. "Did you kill those agents?"

Chase seemed to tense next to me.

There was no going back if they had. All of this would've been for nothing.

Harden turned around from the front seat. His eyes locked on mine and he shook his head. "Not one. They were tranqed. That was it."

Good. I didn't need the feds coming after me for murder.

We'd gone one more block before we heard in our ears, "Uh, guys?"

Harden pressed his com. "What is it?"

"Feds are going the opposite way of you."

Harden twisted back to me, frowning.

He wasn't the only one. I leaned forward. "How?"

"Someone broke into our system and took control," the voice in our ear answered,

"How did that happen?"

The voice was in disbelief. "Remotely. Someone set up at a close enough distance, got in, took our signal, and they're leading them away."

I knew.

I *knew.*

Anger, hot and pulsating, rolled through my body, and I growled out an order. "You take that hack back and you send the feds anywhere except after that car."

"I'll try, but they're moving out of range. I don't know if I can stop it."

"She's smart. Trust your woman," Chase said.

Trust her? I half growled right back at him. "Are you kidding me? You don't know her."

A glimmer of a smile flashed at me, then it was gone. He coughed, the exhaustion now seeping in, and his head bobbed up and down. "You're right. I don't."

He seemed to dissolve in front of me.

What I saw in the house had been what he wanted those agents to see. Now he was here, and the mask was slipping. It was falling fast, too.

"Wait. The signal is gone," said the voice in our ears.

I didn't necessarily believe it, but I was praying. I was praying hard.

"We're good. The feds are turning back to the house. The signal is totally gone."

Thank God. Bailey was safe.

Still, I touched my radio. "I want a car sent to where that location was. Find her, follow her from a distance."

"Got it." And then, "A car has been dispatched. I got control again and went in to clear out the memory data or anything missed. But it's completely gone."

Harden shook his head. "What do you mean it's gone? There should still be some feed there. You said you couldn't loop over and replace their feed, but you could halt it from going to them and then go in and erase it."

"That's what I was going to do, but there's no system left. She destroyed it all."

"Jeez," said one of the men in the vehicle.

Another laughed. "Can we recruit her?"

We drove the rest of the way in silence, taking back roads, and the only person who was making a sound was my brother. He was laughing.

"I like your woman. A lot."

"Shut up."

FIFTY-TWO

Bailey

I was coming out of the shower when the bedroom door slammed shut. A second later, the bathroom door was shoved open. In strode Kash.

Correction.

I'd been reaching for a towel, and my hand grabbed it, drawing it to me, but my concentration was all on what was coming toward me. He wasn't coming at me light and casual. Oh hell no. He was heated. His eyes were flaring with some unnamed emotion, an emotion that was sending serious shivers down my back. And he wasn't striding to me. There was no "stride" about him.

He was stalking me.

Kashton was in full-on predator mode, and I drew back just by instinct.

I pulled the towel farther to my chest, but then he was there. The towel was ripped from my hands, tossed to the floor, and he was crowding me in. Hands to my hips. Eyes pinning me in place, he eased me all the way back to the shower wall. He was fully clothed. I was fully naked. But it didn't matter.

He. Was. Pissed.

My heart sank.

"I did it to help you."

"Who asked for your help?"

The words were clipped out, though it wasn't really in a question form.

I gulped.

He was fighting for control, but it was slipping.

Kash had darkness inside him. I knew it. I'd always known it, and I used to salivate over feeling that side of him, especially in bed. He could make me forget weeks, all just begging for the feel of him inside of me. My body was addicted to him. I'd always been desperate for his touch. A fevered rush would come over me. I would be frenzied for him. But he'd never directed that side of him toward me outside of the bed, and as he drew up to me, pushing against my body, I wasn't sure what was happening here.

I didn't know if he was so mad that he was going to punish me . . . Well, correction, I knew that was the case.

Another shiver went up my spine this time.

I swallowed over a knot, half of it forming from fear and the other half already reacting to the proximity of his body. I was leaning into him when his hand grabbed mine. He pushed it gently against the wall behind me, his hand over my wrist, and he leaned down, all the way in my face.

"What the fuck were you thinking?"

I blinked a few times. "I wanted to help you."

"*Why?*" His growl was more savage this time, more primal.

I was feeling it all the way between my legs, and I was beginning to throb.

"Because . . ." I licked my lips.

I wanted him.

Now.

Not later.

Not in a minute.

Now.

I began rubbing against him, and he was already hard. He was really hard. "Kash," I murmured.

He grasped my other wrist and pinned it above my head.

His head still pushed so he was breathing on me, he angled his hips back.

I mewled, wanting him back where he'd been.

"You seem to mistake the position you're in here."

He was cold.

My eyes snapped to his face.

A whole slew of shivers moved through me.

The rational part of me, the side that thought, was telling me to proceed with caution. He was starting to lose control, a little edge at a time. But the feeling side of me, the body part of me, was starving. It'd been twelve hours ago when he left me in bed, and my mission to help had already been made up in my mind. It'd been the only thing that held me back and let me watch him leave the room. If I hadn't decided that, I couldn't have let him leave. If he had gone or not, neither of us would've known the outcome of that fight. But it was what it was.

Some of those memories were splashing reality on him. I was sputtering in the cold, and I searched his gaze again and felt chilled to the bone.

"You wouldn't hurt me," I said, not thinking.

His eyes flashed.

I knew he wouldn't. But in bed . . . yes. He would hurt me there, in a good way. He would punish me.

A raw snarl ripped from low in his throat, and his hips slammed against me.

"I told you not to push me."

I was pushing.

"Bailey," he rasped out.

He was losing his restraint.

Please.

Yes.

I was moving before I knew I was moving.

My hips were grinding against him. My legs lifted and he had to catch me or I would've fallen. He let go of my pinned wrists, his hands catching me under my thighs as my legs wrapped around him. My breasts were flush against his chest, and my hands raked through his hair.

Our mouths met.

We both knew where this was going.

Our tongues were battling.

He was loose. This monster in him. My monster.

He was out and he was in my arms, and I was stroking him, further inflaming him.

Kash gripped me, his mouth owning me before he dropped me to the floor. My feet hit the ground with a thud, but his hands caught my hips. He held me, not letting me drop farther. I was flipped around.

My wrists were caught, raised, and pinned above my head.

I was trying to rub against him, but there was another growl as he shoved my hips forward, holding me captive against the wall.

I heard a zipper.

His pants fell.

I felt the whoosh of them in the air.

A hand slid up the inside of my legs. He found my middle, one finger went in, and he bent me upward for him. A stroke. A thrust.

I was already panting, already dripping.

And then his hand left and he shoved inside.

Hard. Deep. Rough.

He was not gentle.

I did not want gentle.

I wanted these strokes, how hard he was going. I wanted to be punished.

I swear that I blacked out from the pleasure. It was pulsating, throbbing. It was so strong, so powerful, that I could only cry out as the first climax hurtled through me. It tore me on the inside and I hadn't been ready for it.

Kash wasn't done.

He kept thrusting.

He was becoming more forceful with each slide inside, until it wasn't enough. The angle wasn't doing it for him, and he pulled out. He lifted me in the air. I felt as if I were flying for the brief second, then he was inside me again. He pushed up and all the way.

My legs were wrapped so tight around him I felt the back of his hip bones gliding with his movements. His back muscles were all coiled and smooth, lithely rolling as one motion as he pounded into me, and I wrapped my arms around his neck. I was back up, my hands raking through his hair, and I yanked him back. This wasn't just a one-way street.

I felt a second climax nearing, and I dragged his mouth to mine.

That was another battle. He was trying to control me. I was fighting him right back, my tongue sliding against his, invading his mouth.

A grunt from him. His hand began kneading my thigh.

I didn't need him to help me stay upright. I was doing it all on my own. He was my own pole and I was working him right back.

His free hand slid between our bodies, pushing in for room, and he found where I was throbbing the most.

I lost it.

I started thrashing as wave after wave hit me, searing my body, and I was shaking from that last climax.

"You ass," I hissed against his mouth.

He nipped my lip. "Yeah." Then he took control once more, holding my head prisoner, and as he owned me there, he owned the other part of me, and he came with a roar.

I wasn't sure who won, but there was no mistake that there'd been a full battle between us. I also wasn't sure what either of us was fighting for, what the stakes were.

Once his body stopped trembling, he let go of me.

My feet hit the tile with a muted thud, and before I could muster something to say, his pants were up and he was turning. He was walking.

The door shut a second later, a soft *click*, and I didn't need to look. He was gone.

I fell back against the shower wall, sliding down to sit, and I pulled up my knees to my chest. I had no clue what had just happened, but him leaving wasn't good.

FIFTY-THREE

Bailey

I had tugged a hoodie over my head and slipped my feet into some shoes when there was an abrupt knock on the door.

My head lifted. I was expecting Kash, but Matt shoved through, his hand covering his eyes. "I can't wait for permission. Tell me you're decent, but we have to go."

His voice stopped everything.

He was scared and panicked.

"What's going on?"

"Can I look?"

"Yeah."

His hand dropped and the terror in his eyes had me paralyzed.

"Where's Kash?"

"I—What?"

"Kash. Where is he?" Matt's voice rose up. "Have you seen him?"

"I—" I looked at the bathroom. "Yeah. He was just here."

"But he's not now?"

"What's going on?"

"Where's Ka—"

"He's not here!" I stepped toward Matt. "What is going on?"

"Feds," he clipped that word at me, some of the panic easing. "They're here for Kash."

Oh no.

"You think . . ." Our eyes caught and held.

He shook his head at my question, the question that I couldn't get out. But I noted his response and it was slow. He wasn't sure.

"I'm assuming our alibi will hold up unless they ask to look for the club's security tapes," he said.

A whole litany of curses went through my head. I was loath to hack again. I'd been doing it too much, and too often.

"They threatened Kash."

"What?" His eyebrows pinched together. "When? Threatened how?"

"I might've . . . done something. They might've . . . I don't know." I looked away. I'd been so rushed that night. I'd been desperate to find Chrissy. "I don't know if they can prove it. They're here for Kash?"

We had driven to the house, but we hadn't left the car. I was able to remote hack into their system, and then we tagged a passing car with the signal. I had them following that car until it was far enough away that I knew Kash and whoever he'd gone inside that house with had time to get away.

"There's no way they can prove anything," he said, almost in a daze.

Right.

Well.

We couldn't go on the run.

"Let's go."

"What?"

"Let's go. Let's see what they have to say."

"They're looking for Kash."

"I know. You told me. Like, four times."

"He's not here." It came out as a statement, but Matt was more making sure that he was correct.

I nodded. "Yes. He left."

But where had he gone? He could've just gone to the office he used here, but this was Kash. He would've known the feds would come here. He would've had a plan.

"Let's just go and see. I mean, we can't do anything else."

"Right."

Matt agreed with me, but he didn't move.

Neither did I.

We had to go, though.

I had a feeling. Dread. Something bad was about to happen; something worse.

We walked down to the sight of my father in handcuffs.

Agent Bright had him turned toward the door, his hands behind his back and her hand on his back. "Peter Francis, you are being arrested for cyberterrorism."

FIFTY-FOUR

Kash

"You have to appreciate the irony, right?"

My brother was annoying me. He'd been annoying me since I slipped away from the Chesapeake, jumped in our car, and the four of us took off. Me. My brother. Josh. Scott. No one else was with us. Fitz was ordered not to leave Bailey's side, along with four other men. We took Scott's personal car.

We were now walking into a cabin an hour outside of Chicago. It was remote, off the grid, and had been purchased with cash, through a third party, so there was no trail leading back to me unless people got creative with their searching.

I ducked inside, dropping one of the backpacks in the corner, and shot him a look. "Shut up."

He smirked, snickering, and came in behind me with another backpack on his shoulder.

He started to scan the interior, but a fire was blazing in me and had been the whole time.

"Wait. No."

My brother stiffened, hearing my tone, and turned. I saw a wariness flicker in his eyes—and *good*. I liked that. I liked that a lot.

"*Chase*, right?" I bit out, that flame in me just building and building.

His eyebrows dipped low. Oh yeah. More wariness flashed and he eased back a step. He lowered his own bag, but moved slow and cautious.

"Yeah. Chase."

I snorted. "Right. *Chase*. It's nice to meet my fucking twin brother who's already been a pain in my ass. And please, tell me. Enlighten me on the irony of this situation?"

He opened his mouth.

I clipped my head in a shake. "I don't give a shit what you have to say, because trust me, I am fully comprehending that I had to choose *you*, break *you* out, hoping you'll have some fucking answers for me, and all the while, the rational side of me is saying this is one huge fucking trap. Calhoun sprung this whole thing, me going on the run, me having to choose someone over the people I love, and any second he's going to send in an attack squad for his first wave." That's when I dropped what little mask I was still holding on to. I reached behind me, grabbed my gun, and brought it up.

Movement ceased in the cabin.

Josh and Scott had been bringing in the rest of our gear, but both paused.

Chase, my *brother*, went still. His eyes went to the gun, to me, and he let out a sigh. He raised his hands up. "Okay." He was speaking cautiously now, too. "I heard it in the car. I know that the FBI went in and arrested—"

I cocked the gun. "I know what they did."

He kept on as if I hadn't interrupted him. "They arrested Peter—"

"Again," I growled, moving forward two steps, raising the gun higher, "I know this, you little fuck."

He paused, frowning slightly. "How'd you know that would happen? They threatened your woman."

"It was Peter's office, Peter's equipment, Peter's computer. It was all Peter's. And I wiped the room clean. The only person who's been in there since has been Peter. They can *only* arrest Peter."

Yeah. I was a dick.

I chose this moron over someone who was like a father to me. Self-disgust flared high in me.

"You better start talking to make this all worth it, because if you don't, I will shoot you in the head right now. I'm starting not to give a fuck about whatever you have to say," I gritted out.

His eyes widened.

He hadn't expected this from me, and that gave me satisfaction that I couldn't even fathom trying to measure.

I cocked my head to the side. "What? Did you underestimate me?"

His eyes flashed.

He had.

This arrogant piece of shit—breaking into my home, giving me the slip, being a ghost, then appearing to try and take Bailey out from under me?

I was seeing red.

I snarled, my top lip curling up. "You think I don't know your play? You've been on offense this whole fucking time. You think I don't know the power in that? 'Cause you got the control. You know where I am. You know where my anchors are, because I'm always going to come back for them, for the people I love. Who do *you* love? Who's *your* anchor? Tell me who your fucking weakness is and I'll ghost, then try to take them out from under your watch. Let me slip away and do some fucking offensive play. *You* be on the defense. You tell me how that feels!" My voice was rising. "Now this last stunt? Where I'm jumping through *fucking* hoops to get you out? Start goddamn talking, motherfucker, or I'm going to blow a hole in your brain, then go find Grandpops and do the same to him. I'm at my end, so start. Fucking. Talking!"

This was no idle threat. This wasn't a bluff. I was dead serious, and my brother saw me, looked deep, and read me right, because his hands lowered and he moved back one more step. He was still cautious, but he was losing some of the smirk on his face.

"Okay." His voice was gentle. The smirk was gone. He was dropping the walls.

Fin-*fucking*-ally.

I placed my second hand on the gun, steadying it, and he let out a sigh as I took the position. My feet readied themselves, becoming my foundation.

He noted that, too. His Adam's apple bobbed up and down. "Okay. Okay. I get it. You're done with this dance. I'll tell you everything."

I didn't move, but I waited.

Then I arched an eyebrow. "You slow in the head? Need my guys to set a timer so you know when your time is running out?"

At that comment, two more guns were raised and cocked.

His hands dropped down to his sides. "Okay. Okay! Just . . . Jesus."

"You think you know me," I started up again, giving him my last piece, and I was speaking it low and quiet, but I knew he was hearing the dark promise in my words. "You don't. Start talking."

He straightened up, and all pretense was gone.

Sitting on the edge of the couch, he leaned forward. His elbows rested on his knees, and his head was turned toward the floor.

"All of this, everything that our grandfather has done, has been for one thing and one thing only. Money." He lifted his head, his gaze finding mine. I saw the loathing in him. "Our mother gave you that inheritance and that's what Calhoun has wanted this entire time. He gets his way by two methods: control and destroy. Our mother was first in power of the inheritance. He couldn't control her, so he destroyed her. You were next, but

you were a child. He wanted to first control you through women."
A mocking, bitter laugh slipped from him. "He believes they're
only good for sex or as a tool to use sex to control their target."

I knew all this. None of this was new.

"You went after his assets, but you didn't see the two assets he
had in your camp, under your nose. Quinn and Victoria."

I knew about Victoria. Quinn? I knew she knew Calhoun,
but *working* for him?

"Victoria was supposed to seduce and control you. Quinn was
sent in to control your environment. She targeted Peter, seduced
him. She cemented her hold on Peter by having Cyclone."

Wait.

I frowned. "But not Seraphina?"

He shook his head, his features tightened, as a haunted look
flared in his eyes. "Calhoun is old. He doesn't respect women. He
looks at people how he can use them, and the only use he could
see for a daughter is as someone to sell for further gain later. He
only believes in sons. Calhoun didn't trust Quinn, thought that
she didn't have as much control over Peter as she claimed she
did. All that changed when she had Cyclone. Only then is when
Calhoun eased back and gave Quinn some freedom to just live.
She brought in Victoria to seduce you."

My irritation was flaring. "Keep talking. As of now, none of
this is surprising me."

Surprise flashed over his face before he covered it up. "He let
me loose because he wanted me to observe you. I was to transition and take over your life. That was his plan for me. But when
I got on that airplane from Thailand, I never had any intention
of doing anything to harm you. I know you don't have to believe
me, but it's the truth. I've been living under his control until
you, until you started fighting back. Then I saw my chance."

"Your chance?"

Now his nostrils flared. "For freedom." The haunted expression came back, coupled with an almost dead look at the same

time. "I'm tired of hurting people. You want to keep your loved ones alive; I just want to *have* a loved one. I want the chance to live a normal life, as long as I can."

"You were going to defy Calhoun?"

"I didn't think it would happen, but you kept fighting him and you kept winning. He's so far hidden and isolated right now. I've never seen him this vulnerable. You did that to him. He's a cornered animal now. I made my move when I went in and took your woman's mom from her guards."

Now *this* was new.

"Explain why Bailey still has nightmares seeing her mother's head getting blown off."

He winced. "Theatrics."

My nostrils flared. "Explain better."

"Bailey did see Chrissy, but it was a blank in the gun, and they rigged this pouch on the back of her head. When enough air punctures it, the contents inside explode. They use it in movies. Chrissy would've fallen forward from the impact of it, and they would've dragged her body out before Bailey could've registered what she was actually seeing. I've seen it. It's . . . traumatizing."

Jesus. All that for what? Why? "Tell me more."

"I didn't get to her in time. They were starting to brainwash her. They were going to use her to do something for them, and I know it's altered her. She'll never be the same woman, but she's fierce. She's strong." Pride and respect rang from him. "I'd be damned proud to have her on my side, and she knows what side I'm on."

I stilled at that.

Chrissy never said a word . . .

As if reading my mind, he kept going. "We had to keep it quiet. When the feds took us in, I knew they'd release her back to the Chesapeake. And I knew they'd keep me. I tried to prolong it, give her as much time as possible."

"Time?" I was standing, slowly, every nerve in me stretched thin. What had Chrissy done? What was really going on? "For what?"

"Time to turn."

"Turn who?"

Chase didn't answer right away. He waited a beat, then said the last piece, the part that I knew I'd been blind to. "The new asset."

"*Who?*"

He didn't answer that, but still continued. "Calhoun messed up, easing from Quinn. She started to actually love Peter, got obsessed with him. Got obsessed with never losing him. When she sent Arcane in after Bailey, she did that on her own accord, but she never got Calhoun's permission. She was supposed to get permission to do anything. That's how he thinks. She's only been given the go-ahead to fuck her man and be a mom to the kids. Our grandfather got wind something was going down, ordered by Quinn, and that's why he sent me in."

I was reeling.

He was sent in?

"Where?"

"With Arcane, the first time they tried to take your girl. That was me. That's why they thought Calhoun was really behind the job, why they let me in on their team. I was sent to see what they were doing. I was supposed to report back to him what *Quinn* was doing, but I didn't want anyone to get hurt. I'm the one who told Bailey that men were coming in to kidnap her. I was trying to help."

Bailey had reported all this to Bright and Wilson.

"Keep going," I grunted.

His head dipped once. "Have you been keeping up to date with Quinn's trial?"

That was from left field.

"No." I scowled. "Why?"

"Because Quinn made amends with Calhoun when she was arrested. They're going to help get her acquitted. After, she's supposed to set up a meet with you. She's supposed to kill you, and I'm supposed to transition into your life. You asked if I was supposed to have plastic surgery to make us completely identical? I was. The surgery was supposed to happen last week."

"How were they going to get Quinn acquitted?"

"They'd need to blame someone else."

Someone else.

I had a feeling who that was, and I wasn't liking it.

"They killed the Arcane team. Every last one of them. Drew Bonham was killed a month ago. That guard, also dead. Only two people remain alive that were at Bailey's kidnapping: Quinn and"—another beat of hesitation—"Bailey."

I sucked in some air because fuck him.

Fuuuck him.

I was getting what he was saying. I was seeing it all now.

"They took Chrissy to set Bailey up. It was always planned for Chrissy to come back and reunite with her family, but she was supposed to be brainwashed. I got her out, but I'll be honest, I don't know if it was in time. She started saying to me the shit they wanted her to recite to the public, and that was that her daughter had made it all up. Everything. She was never kidnapped by Quinn. She never saw her mother get murdered. Chrissy Hayes is alive, and she was supposed to say instead that the two kidnapping attempts took a toll on her daughter. Bailey was mentally unstable, had hallucinated the whole thing."

The facts were all swimming in my head, getting muddied around. "But there were too many other factors that still would've helped Bailey's statement."

"Court of law, it wouldn't have mattered. If they had a mom who said, instead, that her daughter attacked her, stuffed her in a car, and had her taken away by strangers, and she waltzed into a court to testify to that, that's all they would've needed. Quinn would get off. Her charges would be dropped and there'd be no hold for why she couldn't still see her kids, and that means, she'd still have an opening to get back in with Peter."

"But why?"

I was ignoring the bullshit about setting Bailey up and focusing on the endgame.

Chase shook his head. "It's simple. Money."

Jesus.

All the pieces. My grandfather had thought of it all.

But there was one more piece missing.

"Who's the other inside person?" I asked.

Chase gave me a hard look. "The next person who I'm fairly certain is about to be called as a character witness for Quinn, who's supposed to also collaborate against Bailey's case, saying she saw Peter's estranged daughter doing weird shit, maybe even attacking her personally."

If they had been successful in turning Chrissy, then added a second witness to testify to the same argument, it would work. Quinn would walk free. Bailey would be implicated, at least in public opinion, because those transcripts would get out. Press was there. Quinn's lawyers would throw a press party.

"Who is it?"

"Quinn's sister. Payton."

FIFTY-FIVE

Bailey

"All rise."

We rose as the judge came in, then sat when we were allowed. I didn't understand why today was the day Chrissy insisted we come to Quinn's trial. I'd not been allowed in the other days, and most of it had been kept hush-hush. They talked about it on the local news every day, but that'd been the extent of my knowledge. But today, for some reason, was the day Chrissy was adamant we attend. She put everything in motion, arguing with the lawyers until finally it was allowed. On any other day, yes. I would've loved to go. I would've been curious about what was being said, what was happening. But today? Peter was arrested the day before, and not for something he did but for something I did.

That was more important.

Chrissy was arguing with our lawyer for us to come here, and right behind her, I was arguing with him about why he wasn't doing more to get Peter released from custody.

Apparently, the whole thing *took time*. Those were his words.

But we were here, in court, definitely *not* sitting behind Quinn's side.

Since I was here and thinking on all of this, I gave my mother a side-eye, because when had she decided to take up the torch for anything? I mean, post her not-murder/kidnapping? Because she hadn't been like this since Kash brought her back home. She'd been traumatized and quiet. Now I saw it in the way she was sitting firm and upright. I saw it in how her eyes were fierce and focused. Her mouth was set and determined.

Her chin was tight.

Her focus was entirely on someone else.

I followed her gaze, until it landed on Payton Callas.

That made me pause, too, because why? Why would Chrissy suddenly care about Seraphina and Cyclone's aunt so much? As far as I knew, there'd been no interaction between them at the house. If Chrissy came into a room, Payton left. Whatever the case, I had a feeling the whole building could burn down around Chrissy and Payton and still my mother's attention wouldn't waver from Quinn's sister.

Weird.

Eerie, too.

The first witness was called.

"The defense calls Payton Callas to the stand, Your Honor."

"Motherfucker," Matt hissed next to me. He shot me a look. "We let her go. She met Quinn and we didn't say a word."

Matt leaned forward next to me, his elbows on his knees.

Quinn's team, not the prosecution, had called Payton. What was happening?

She walked up, and I hadn't noted what she was wearing earlier. I hadn't cared. But I sure cared now. A trench pencil skirt. The colors were dark orange. Her blouse was the same color, with a black blazer over the top. Her hair was up in a bun, set behind her head. Her makeup was on, but muted. She had the natural look going on. She was demure.

Then again, Payton was often like that. She was a quiet, in-the-background kind of person and always had been.

That was, until she got on the stand.

When she climbed up there, was sworn in, there was something more to her. A spark? No . . . I was thinking on it, watching how she looked at my mother and swept her gaze to Quinn. Looking at her sister, her head lowered back down. Her shoulders slumped forward.

"Miss Callas, what is your relationship to my client?"

Payton wet her lips, leaned forward, and spoke into the microphone. "She's my sister."

It was the expected answer. The lawyer nodded, looking down for his next question.

"Um . . ." Payton's throat moved as she swallowed. Her mask faltered, just for a bit. Some of the strength slipped, but as if she needed to think of something to harden her again, she did. Her whole face grew tighter, more resolved. She cleared her throat, speaking more clearly into the microphone. "We don't get along."

The lawyer went rigid.

Someone gasped. A whole buzz went through the room.

Quinn shot forward in her seat, but I couldn't fully see her face. Two of her lawyers blocked her from view.

I glanced at my mom. Her eyes were trained on Payton. They were narrowed now.

"Excuse me?" This from the lawyer. He clipped out those words. "Can you reiterate?"

"We don't get along."

He stared at her, hard.

She stared right back, just as hard.

A power battle was unfolding right before us.

"Miss Callas, didn't you agree to testify today on behalf of your sister?"

"I did, yes, but that doesn't mean we get along."

The lawyer turned, looked at Quinn, then glanced at the rest of his team, which was having a silent conversation about whether he should continue questioning her.

But one of the lawyers gave a small nod, and the questioning lawyer turned back to Payton. "Miss Callas, isn't it true that you have chronic depression?"

She bit down on her lip before jerking her head in a nod. "Yes, I do."

"And it's so bad that you've had to be hospitalized a dozen times over the last ten years."

"Twenty."

"Twenty times?" God. He was so condescending.

"No. Twenty years." She wasn't affected, still speaking clearly. There wasn't a flicker of remorse on her face. "Since I was a child, I've struggled with depression. I've been hospitalized for it thirteen times over the last twenty years."

"And is that something you're proud of?"

Her nostrils flared, just slightly. "It's who I am. I can't change me. I've been trying; that's the purpose for those hospital visits. I'm proud that I've sought help."

"Right." The lawyer sounded dejected, as if he wasn't sure where to go from there. A cough. He leaned forward on the podium. "Miss Callas, tell us about your relationship with Bailey Hayes."

Another rip cord of reactions snapped through the room, and I knew it, because I felt it. It landed on me, smacking me hard in the chest.

This whole case was about me, but a trickle of dread slid down my spine, pooling at the bottom.

Payton found me in the room. Her eyes narrowed, briefly, before sliding to look at my mother, and whatever look they shared, Payton suddenly looked like she was on a mission. Her eyes grew keen. The corners of her mouth turned up, just slightly.

"I don't really know Miss Hayes. Bailey Hayes."

The lawyer's head jerked back, and his hands clenched around the sides of the podium. He didn't look at his team this time. His head inclined. "Excuse me?"

She repeated, "I don't really know Bailey Hayes." She went

on to explain, "Bailey wasn't living at the Chesapeake when I was first called to come and help take care of Seraphina and Cyclone."

"Cyclone?"

"Curt Francis. Cyclone is his nickname."

"And the Chesapeake is in reference to . . ."

"To the Francis family's main home. It's a large estate and it was given a name."

"I see." But the lawyer's tone wasn't sounding sure. His head twisted, taking in his team once more. His papers were in his hand, his fist clenching around them for a moment. "Your Honor, we're done with the witness."

The judge nodded, turning to the prosecution. It was now their turn to question her, and they did. The district attorney hopped up, and her first question was out even before she got behind the podium. "Miss Callas, please tell us more about your relationship with your sister."

"Objection!"

Before the judge could rule, the district attorney spoke. "It was introduced in their questioning. I can explore it."

The judge nodded, looking as if he was going to say the same thing. "Overruled. Proceed, counselor."

She cleared her throat, taking on the same posture that the defense lawyer had used—hands tight on the podium, head forward—but with her, it was a whole different feel. She was eager. Her next question came out and you could hear her salivating for the answer. "Payton, please tell us about your relationship with the defendant."

"Quinn and I have never gotten along."

"How so?"

"She's not a good person."

"Objection!"

The two sides argued over this point until the judge sighed and asked Payton to keep her personal opinion of her sister from her answers. "Only facts, Miss Callas. That would be more help-ful."

She nodded, her eyes earnest. "Okay, well then . . . fact. My sister would lock me in the closet when she wanted to spend time with her friends."

"Objectio—"

The judge raised his hand. "She can testify. It's why you called her here." He nodded to Payton. "Proceed."

"Fact." She didn't miss a beat. "Our father was a gambler. He was old-school. To pay off his debt, he sent Quinn and myself to live in Greece with someone, and when we were there, Quinn became a big partier. That's when she'd lock me in a closet, but . . ." Her mouth parted and she faltered.

"But what, Miss Callas?"

Payton's eyes were glued to Quinn now. "But . . ." She blinked rapidly and her head raised up. "But I think she did it somewhat to protect me."

Quinn's lawyer had started to stand, but hearing the rest, he sat back down.

The DA glanced over, her eyebrows up. "Protect you from whom, Miss Callas?"

"From the men who were there where we were staying."

Oh no.

I got it.

It was all coming together, and I slid down in the bench.

I didn't think I wanted to hear this.

My stomach began tightening up, knotting.

"Miss Callas, whose place was it that you and your sister were staying at?"

She didn't answer.

A look came over her. It was a slow slide, and her eyes closed, but I saw it. Everyone saw it. Terror. I knew who she was going to say, but for a moment I didn't think she was going to do it. It was all leading there, to him.

"Calhoun Bas—"

"Objection! This line of questioning has nothing to do with Ms. Callas's case. I move for the entire line of questioning to be stricken and tossed out."

The DA didn't waste time, either. She shot back, "Miss Callas was brought as their witness. They opened the line of questioning by asking about her relationship with the defendant. I think it bears exploration, Your Honor."

The judge was silent, taking in both lawyers before his gaze searched the room.

He found me, his eyes narrowed. His head raised. He was scanning the entire room.

Matt leaned over, whispering, "I think he's looking for Kash."

Right. My lover, who was now "on the run," though I hadn't had time to digest that, either. I didn't know what to say, so I didn't respond.

"I'm going to allow it."

"Your Honor!"

He raised his hand up, silencing the defense. "I want to see where this goes." He nodded to Payton. "Keep going, Miss Callas, but bailiff, I'd like more security guards added to the room."

Two men left the room and Payton closed her eyes.

"Miss Callas." His tone was gentle.

She opened her eyes.

He nodded, his entire demeanor softening. "You're safe. You can say what you need to say in here."

Her head dipped in an abrupt nod back, her eyes glistening. She closed them, then reopened them, and she swiped at her cheek quickly before leaning forward.

She started, and once she got going, she told everything.

She and Quinn were "sold" to Calhoun when they were young.

They were raised in Calhoun's main house, but he treated them almost as if they were his daughters.

Quinn had been angry, rebellious. She partied, acted out. Not Payton. She withdrew.

She learned that Quinn had begun working for Calhoun. She was taken from the home and she didn't see her sister for two years.

"Where did you see your sister again?"

"In California."

The DA's head straightened at that information.

Even the judge looked shocked.

Payton continued, "I was sent to live with her, but Calhoun asked me to watch her."

A chair scraped against the floor over at Quinn's table. There was a hissing sound, and the judge fixed them with a glare. "Silence, Ms. Callas. Counsel, control your client."

He gave Payton another nod.

"She—uh—Quinn was different when I went to live with her. She was more smooth, I guess. More seductive. We lived there for a few years, and that's when she met Peter Francis." She stopped, a sudden stricken look coming over her. She jerked back in her seat.

"Miss Callas?" This from the DA. "How was your sister when she met Peter Francis?"

"Um, my relationship with my sister was almost nonexistent once she married Peter. I remained behind in California and she moved to Chicago to be with him."

"Miss Callas, weren't you instructed to watch your sister for Mr. Bastian?"

"I was, but Quinn wouldn't let me come with her, and Calhoun never contacted me. I don't think he really put much stock in me."

"Why do you say that?"

"Because he never did. He only gave Quinn attention." Her cheeks got red and her head ducked down briefly. "She's prettier than me. That's mostly all Calhoun cared about, a woman's looks."

No one commented on that, though to be fair to Payton, she wasn't not pretty. She was. She just wasn't stunning like Quinn, but if she'd said this in a room where I could've spoken up, I would've told her it was more than that. Payton looked submissive. She *was* submissive. Someone like Calhoun Bastian would've disregarded her as anyone or anything useful to him.

"Miss Callas, I'd like to ask the reason the defense called you as a witness today. What were you supposed to say for them?"

"Objectio—"

"Overruled." The judge's tone was flat and final. He wasn't messing around.

"I—" A sheen of tears came into her eyes, and she searched me out. Me? I felt zapped by her look, not understanding it. An almost apologetic look flared before she looked at Quinn, the same sheen of tears just thickening then. "I'm sorry, Quinn. I know you thought I was going to come in and testify for you, but I can't." Her voice grew hoarse. She looked at the DA. "Quinn's team wanted me to testify that I'd seen Bailey Hayes abusing her mother."

Shock spread through me, piercing me in the chest.

I couldn't breathe for a second.

A whisper went through the room, but Payton was continuing. "Since Chrissy Hayes was found alive, I was given orders to discredit anything Chrissy Hayes would say. I was supposed to talk about how I saw her daughter hit her on three different occasions. I was supposed to talk about the language Bailey would use with her mother, how I had overheard Bailey blackmailing her mother into being a loving and doting mother."

The DA didn't respond at first. She was just as stiff as I was. Then she coughed, and her voice came out strangled. "And for the record, have you observed any of these events?"

"None. Not one."

"And what was the reason you were given for providing those lies to the court today?"

"I wasn't told the reason, just that that's what I was supposed to say." She flinched, her eyes so bleak for a moment, before she turned to her sister and said, "I can't do it, Quinn. I can't say it. I can't incriminate Bailey or Chrissy because you and I both know that you *did* try to kidnap Bailey Hayes. Calhoun was upset with you, I get that, but he also doesn't know the truth. You shouldn't have lied to him, and you shouldn't have underestimated a mother's love for her son."

"Shut up!" Quinn sprang up, starting to go over the table. "Shut up—"

All hell broke loose in the court.

Guards streamed in from every corner of the room. Four of them surged on Quinn, getting her under control.

"Miss Callas, can you please explain your last statement to the court?"

"Quinn was always supposed to seduce Peter Francis for Calhoun Bastian. But he didn't trust her to keep her 'charge' in control until she had Cyclone, Curt Francis." Both head lawyers were standing, but Payton took over. She dipped her head down so she could be heard better through the microphone. "Calhoun Bastian only sees males as important, but Quinn couldn't get pregnant after Seraphina. She lied to Calhoun when she told him that Cyclone was hers. He wasn't."

A pause.

A surreal feel came over the room, as if everyone knew what she was about to say was going to change lives, and an awareness spread. Everyone quieted. Everyone waited.

I was starting to stand.

Payton's eyes found me. "I'm not letting my sister anywhere near him because Cyclone is mine. He's *my* son."

The court was pandemonium after that.

Reporters were rushing from the room. I wasn't sure, but I could swear we could still hear Quinn screaming. Fitz appeared at our side and cleared his throat. "You need to go."

"Right." Matt stood up. "It's probably not safe, huh?" But as he said it, he was dazed.

I was dazed.

Chrissy—I didn't know what she was, but she seemed in a daze, too. I slipped my hand in hers and squeezed once. "Did you know?"

"What?"

Those dazed eyes blinked, looked at me, and I had a feeling she wasn't seeing me.

I nodded toward the stand, where Payton still was sitting, but the prosecution lawyers had surrounded her. "Cyclone. Her revelation. Did you know?"

"I—" Her mouth opened. Her lips did a goldfish impersonation, and she closed them. "I didn't know. I had no idea. I—she was never going to turn on us. I could see it now. I'd been worried. I had . . ."

I frowned. What was my mom talking about?

"Mom?" I edged closer to her.

I cocked an eyebrow. She was saying that like it was a revelation to her.

"I thought . . ." She didn't finish.

Fitz came up behind her, herding her forcibly, and me with them, to the side door and out. Some of the court guards had fallen in line to help, since we'd only been allowed a certain number of men in the court. We were led out, down a hallway, and we swept through a side exit. There was a handicap ramp, which we hurried down, and then we climbed into the waiting vehicles. Two SUVs today. Once inside, Fitz got into the front seat but turned around to us.

"I got the call moments ago."

I nodded. "About Payton?"

He frowned. "From Kash."

Matt jerked forward. "*What?*"

I was experiencing déjà vu from all the bombs being dropped, but my whole body grew warm. It was also riddled with tension because there were too many factors happening right now. I couldn't keep up.

Chrissy, though, had jerked out of her glazed-over state. "Chase is with his brother?" she asked calmly.

Fitz paused, growing eerily still, as he took in my mom and what she had just said. His eyelids dipped low, matching his tone. "Yeah. They're talking to the FBI."

"Good." Chrissy nodded, sitting back. She turned to the window, folded her arms over herself, and nodded again. "Good. It's done then." Her words were soft, as if something monumental had happened and we all escaped unscathed. A smattering of tears fell to her chest, but she didn't wipe them away. She let them fall, and I was experiencing, yet again, one more weird, alternate-reality feeling.

It's done? What was done?

"What are you talking about?" My voice broke. What was going on here?

"Kash brought his brother back to the FBI, where he's agreed to actively cooperate and assist in their search for Calhoun now. In exchange, no charges will be brought against Kash, and your father has also been released from custody," Fitz explained.

"I was supposed to turn on my child."

I reeled. What?

Chrissy's head was turned toward the window, and she sounded like she was speaking from far away. "They underestimated a mother's love. Payton. Me." She looked at me, her eyes flashing, and they were hard. She grasped my hand and squeezed. "You think I don't remember what they did to me. I do. I did. I remembered every second of that hell, until Chase got to me."

She stopped, her bottom lip trembling before she smoothed it out.

"They were trying to brainwash me. I was supposed to come back, testify to back up everything Payton was supposed to say.

Her word. My word. Quinn would've gotten off, and I have no idea what they would've tried to do to you, but it's all over. Chase got to me, he helped me.

"After we were found, I had to get to Payton. Every time I cornered her, someone would come into the room or she'd leave. The few times I did get a word with her, she never gave me any indication what she was planning on doing. I was so worried today, but if she had said what she was supposed to say, I would've had the district attorney call me as a witness. I would've testified that everything she said was a lie, that I was kidnapped, that they tried to brainwash me. I would've testified that they should've never fucked with a mother."

She stopped, turning back to the window, and her next words were so soft. "And if anyone had come for my baby, I would've killed them."

Chills went down my spine.

She meant every word.

FIFTY-SIX

Kash

It was four thirty in the morning when the feds finally let me go.

I was now walking inside the Chesapeake, feeling as if it'd been a full month since I was here last, when it had only been a day. I'd gone a few steps before Peter came from the kitchen, his morning coffee already in one hand and the morning paper in the other.

He wasn't dressed for the office, but he wasn't dressed for bed.

Peter sipped his coffee. "Want some?"

I shook my head. "I want to try and crash with Bailey for a bit."

"Then let's get to it."

"No."

He frowned. "No?"

"No. I know what happened in court yesterday and I'm done. Family meeting. Everyone can know then, except Cyclone and Seraphina, but they should know some of it. No more secrets, Peter."

His lips thinned.

I doubled down. "No more secrets, not about this."

He sighed. "Fine."

I did grin. "I hear congratulations are in order. You have a new baby mama."

He snorted, but I could see a small flush appearing.

He rolled his eyes. "I have my faults, and one of those was women. I am making amends this year, but I won't apologize for keeping Cyclone's mother a secret. She was in and out of hospitals almost every other month, and she was bad. She got so bad, Kash. So low. She tried to kill herself eight times. Eight. Times." He let out a long sigh. "We didn't keep it a secret to be malicious. We thought we were doing the right thing."

"*You* thought," I corrected him.

"What?"

"Quinn didn't think. She was setting you up. But *you* thought you were doing the right thing. It's a difference that needs to be acknowledged. You were trying to be a good father at that moment," I said, before another thought hit me. "When are you going to tell Cyclone?"

"As soon as he wakes up. Figured that's best, so he doesn't hear it from someone else." His response was swift. He'd already thought long and hard about it. "Like you said, no more secrets. I do worry what this will do for Seraphina, finding out she's the only child from Quinn now."

"I'm worried what Bailey's feeling, knowing that you chose to keep her out when you brought Cyclone in."

"That's not . . ." But he stopped, his mouth gaping. A groan came from him. "I didn't even think about that." A pause. He shook his head. "But it's different. The circumstances were different."

"Yeah, and a part of that genius brain of hers will know that. She'll understand it. But the daughter in her might not feel the same."

"What do you suggest I do?"

I shrugged, a full yawn working its way out of me. "Just be

honest. Truth might hurt, but in the long run it's always what heals, too."

He nodded, sipping more of his coffee before nodding at me. "Go, Kash. We can talk about the rest with the family later. Be with your woman, because I know you're one of those on that same list, too. She'll be a lot happier once you walk into that room."

"'Night, old man." I threw him a quick grin.

He smiled. "'Morning, son."

FIFTY-SEVEN

Bailey

The next morning, Chrissy took center stage first, sitting on the couch in Peter's study, surrounded by all of us.

For some reason it felt more intimate, more private. Peter was sitting next to her, holding her hand, and Seraphina was to her left, nestled between her and Marie.

Everyone was silent as Chrissy spoke, focusing her attention on me. "When they took me, I didn't know what was happening. They told me later what they made you see, but I didn't really understand it. Not until they showed me a videotape."

Jesus.

I had to stand. I couldn't do this while I was sitting.

Kash caught me, but he only brought my back to his chest and wrapped an arm around my front. I leaned back on him.

"I saw what you saw and I was horrified. Bailey." Her voice broke, a hand going to her chest. Seraphina scooted closer, wrapping both her arms around Chrissy's free one. Peter closed his eyes, his head hanging down. He had an arm resting on the couch behind Chrissy.

"When I think about what you must've thought, what you went through . . ." Her voice trembled before she paused and came back clearer. The emotion was tucked back. "Never again, Bailey. Never again. I won't let it."

"And when Chase got you?" The question came from the side, from where Matt was leaning back against one of the bookshelves.

"Who's Chase?" Cyclone asked, perched on Payton's lap on one of the other chairs. Peter had told him and Seraphina about the final family secret that was revealed in court yesterday. It wasn't done in a family meeting setting, but more privately. I wasn't there, but I heard about it. Seraphina had gasped, then started crying. Cyclone hadn't reacted.

Chrissy had been in the hallway, and she's the one who told me about it. "He didn't say anything. What do you think that means?"

"I think he just needs to process it. A quick reaction wouldn't be normal. I think this is normal." And seeing him firmly huddling on his real mother's lap, it seemed maybe I was right.

Payton had stress lines all over her face. Her eyes were panicky, like if she made the wrong move, Cyclone would leap from her lap and declare her a horrible mother or something. She had the whole deer-in-headlights look, and it wasn't going away. I was half expecting to see her sweating buckets within an hour.

Peter turned to Kash, who tensed behind me, a slight curse under his breath.

Peter grinned. "You said no more secrets."

"He's not a part of this."

Matt gestured to the couch. "Thinking he is, since he's the one who saved my next stepmother."

Peter's head whipped over. "Matthew."

Matt shrugged. "What?" He grinned. "No more secrets, Dad."

Seraphina sat even further upright. Her arms dropped from around Chrissy's arm, but they were still linked around her hands. "Wait. What?" She looked between Chrissy and Peter. "You two?"

Cyclone snorted. "Even I knew that much, and I'm ten and three-quarters." He looked at Kash. "Who's Chase?"

I drew in a deep breath.

Kash said, "He's my brother."

Marie sucked in another breath.

Theresa, who was also in our meeting but had been quiet and in the background, muttered.

"You have a brother?"

All eyes went to Seraphina, who was no longer holding on to Chrissy at all. Her hands were resting on her own legs. She had scooted to the edge of the couch. Her gaze was firmly latched onto Kash. "Like a real brother?"

"What's that mean for me and Matt?"

Kash's eyes swung to Cyclone, then back to Seraphina. "I have a brother. A twin, actually."

Seraphina's mouth fell open.

"*You do?*"

"Madre de Dios." That was Marie.

Chrissy coughed, clearing her voice. "Kash's brother is the one who rescued me from the men that had taken me. He, uh, he helped me remember things." She looked at me again, her eyes piercing. "He showed me a video of you."

My heart skipped a beat. I'd been holding on to Kash's arm in front of me, but now my fingers sank tight into him. "What videos?"

"You at my funeral."

Another skip.

"You at some ceremony at your school. You had a dress on that I knew you hated wearing." She smiled, but her eyes were so sad.

Skip.

"You at a bar with a couple of people."

I was clinging to Kash's arm, and my knees were starting to knock against each other.

"At your school. In your library. At other times you were with Kash, with your guards. There were more pictures. With Matt. None here. I don't think he could get close enough for a long-distance lens." Her head folded down.

That's when I saw she was clinging to Peter's other hand in her lap.

"I saw in the pictures as you were coming back to life. I was glad, Bailey. I was thankful." Unshed tears lined the bottom of her eyelids. She swallowed. "You didn't let him win. I was proud of you. Damn proud."

I couldn't stand.

My knees gave away.

Kash caught me, an arm sliding around my waist, and no one could see, but he was holding me up.

"Those videos and those pictures helped me, too. He didn't win with me, either."

But it was costing her to say these words.

For a moment, no one said a word.

"So you're saying there's two of you?" Cyclone was back on the Chase thing. He had scooted further up on Payton's lap so he was standing, and more leaning back against where she was sitting. "Are you him right now? Are you guys *that* identical?"

Kash chuckled.

The tension broke in the room.

A few laughed.

"No, I'm not him." He squeezed me, rocking me gently from side to side. "Bailey would know. She did know."

"Hold up *again*." Seraphina had a hand in the air, and she was standing in front of the couch. "You've met him?"

Her question was directed toward me.

I nodded. "I did." I did not tell her the circumstances.

"Wha—Huh?" She gaped again, rotating to Cyclone and back to me, and then to Peter. "Not fair! We don't know anything that's going on. Chrissy's dead, then she's alive. Payton is actually Cyclone's mother. Kash has a twin brother. What about me? Do I have a secret mother, too?"

Oh.

Oh, no.

The hope in that last sentence broke me.

I started to pull away from Kash, but he held me back. "They need to do this. Not us," he murmured in my ear.

Peter edged from his couch, and he knelt in front of Seraphina. He took her hands in his. "Quinn is your mother, Ser," he whispered, though all of us could hear.

"But . . ." Her head folded even farther down, her chin resting against her chest.

Peter scooted all the way up to her, taking her gently into his arms. She went with him, her hands still in fists as her arms wrapped around his neck. "What's wrong with me? Why is it always me?"

I strained to get free.

Kash kept me back.

I knew he was right, but I just wanted to grab my sister, hold her, say anything I needed to say to take away what she was feeling, and I had no idea what she was feeling. I just knew she was hurting, and it was a hurt that could change a person.

"Honey." Peter eased back, smoothing the hair down the sides of Seraphina's face. He framed her face in his hands. "Nothing is wrong with you. Nothing. You know why your mother was how she was with you?"

"Why?" A hiccup-sob.

"Because you were what Quinn knew she needed to be. You're kind. You're loving. You got all the goodness from her and from me. They mixed together and made you."

"Dad." But she grinned.

He grinned, too. "It's true."

"You didn't get a crazy brain, Ser. We might be smart, but sometimes it sucks. Do you realize how hard it is to shut down this thing?" Cyclone pointed to his own brain, looking and sounding frustrated.

It worked. Seraphina's grin got a little bigger. "I'm not smart like you guys." She looked to Cyclone, me, and finally back to Peter.

"Honey. Sweetheart." Chrissy leaned forward, touching Seraphina's arm. "Take it from someone who lived with one of those 'crazy smart' brains, you have something they don't have." Chrissy's gaze swept up, spotting me before she looked back to my sister. "I've seen what you can do. You have a genius that you've not even shared with the world. Do they know?"

Seraphina's face got red, and real quick. "No." Her head ducked down again.

Peter cast a questioning look at Chrissy, who made a show of pressing her lips closed.

"I know!"

"Cy!" That was Seraphina.

"I won't say anything. I mean, I won't tell them to look in your drawing pad, because then, you know, they'd know."

Matt suppressed a snort.

Marie and Theresa were both fighting back grins.

Kash buried his face into the back of my neck, his shoulders moving up and down.

"Smooth, Cyclone." I gave him a thumbs-up.

His grin stretched. The little shit knew exactly what he just did.

Seraphina was now beet red. "Cyclone!"

"What? I didn't say a word."

"Well . . ." Peter hugged his daughter once more before moving to rest his back against the couch, next to Chrissy's legs. "Whatever is in your drawing pads, I'll be eager to see when you choose to share with the family."

Seraphina and Cyclone had more questions about Chase, about when they would meet him. Kash was firm, that it wouldn't be until much later—much, much later. The questions weren't as quick with Chrissy, about what she went through. It seemed as if they knew to tread gently, as if they were scared of what question would unearth a new minefield.

"Why didn't you say anything?" Cyclone asked.

It took a second before someone clued in.

He was staring at Chrissy. Then I caught a backward glance over his shoulder to Payton, and I figured it out first.

"You know what happened at the court yesterday?"

He looked at me. "Yeah." He flattened his mouth. He wasn't going to share *how* he knew. That meant he had known who Payton was before Peter told him this morning, too. Or I was guessing. There was a look in his eyes, a deeper understanding than my little ten-and-three-quarters-year-old brother should have, but it was there nonetheless.

He had known.

"You want to know why Chrissy never said anything about being held captive?" I asked.

He gave me a quick nod. "She said she didn't know, but she did. She just told us she did."

Chrissy's mouth had been open, but it shut with an audible snap. "Oh." Her face tightened, stretched. Her mouth pressed down before it returned to a flat line. She angled her head to the side, speaking in Payton's direction. "I couldn't tell what side you were on."

Payton sat up in her seat. "I didn't know, either. I knew they had you, and I knew what they were capable of."

Cyclone was looking between the two mothers, leaning against one of Payton's legs. "So you both didn't know and you couldn't tell, so both of you didn't say a word? That makes no sense."

Seraphina started giggling.

"Where's your brother now?"

Kash glanced to Cyclone. "He's at the apartment Bailey and I lived in."

"What's he going to do there?"

"He's going to stay there, and he and I will work with the FBI to help find our grandfather. You know when they took your dad into custody?"

Cyclone nodded, his eyes still glued to Kash.

"That was the deal. We help them, and they release your dad."

Another nod from my little brother. Then, "Can we have pizza tonight?"

Cyclone just solidified my theory.

That was the gist of our family meeting. It was pizza for the rest of the night, and bowling.

It felt almost normal.

FIFTY-EIGHT

Bailey

Three months later

Life didn't go back to normal after that day, but there was a sense of weird peace that settled over everyone. The household, too. Maybe it was because so much had been unearthed, we all needed time to digest. Or maybe it was because we were all just exhausted.

I knew I was.

I knew Kash was. Seriously. Kash was *really* tired. That night, he crawled into bed and held me. By the time I rolled over, slid a leg in between his, and worked my arm around to hold him back, he was already asleep.

He didn't wake for a whole twelve hours.

Peter spent the next month being with his family. I think he did work, but it was mostly in the morning. Kash told me that he had his "debrief" meetings with Peter in the morning, at an ungodly time of the day, but once we all met for breakfast, Peter's phone was never brought out. He was with the family.

We'd all taken to eating breakfast together before Cyclone and Seraphina headed to school. It was something they needed, but I think we all needed it. At first, Seraphina and Cyclone were both clingy with all of us. They weren't super choosy about whose side they were sticking to. They'd go from one to the other as if they were scared one of us would disappear.

After the first month, that got better.

They returned to skipping into the room, eating at their own table, and then giving each adult a kiss on the cheek and a hug before being taken to school.

Matt moved back into his penthouse.

I returned to school. Not that I had really stopped going to school, but there'd been a definite couple weeks in there that I skipped. And I was in graduate school, so skipping was a stupid thing to do. I made up the time. The professors weren't happy, but they understood. I was to start my paid internship with Phoenix Tech the next week.

As for the rest, Payton decided to move permanently to Chicago, but she was moving into her own apartment. It was in one of Kash's buildings, and I knew he offered her the free housing more because he wanted to watch her than for any other reason.

It was still a kind gesture, just with invisible strings.

Quinn was found guilty and sentenced to prison for twenty-five years.

After the second month, Peter returned to his job again, and soon the family was hosting banquets and events at the house again. It reminded me of the summer when Quinn hosted them, but I realized this was normal life for everyone who was not a Hayes. Chrissy helped with the banquets, but they were mostly Peter's deal.

Chrissy returned to working part time at a private clinic not far from the estate, and stayed living at the Chesapeake.

She was happy.

Matt returned to his evenings at Naveah, with Tony, Chester, Guy, and the girls. I went, but not often. If I went, it was for one drink with my brother and then I would head up to spend time with Kash. If he was working or needed to remain working, I would do my schoolwork on his couch or curl up and take a nap. It was our new normal.

The other thing that went back to normal was Kash's notoriety.

He returned to having his picture taken by local gossip sites.

Word hadn't leaked about Chase, but we all knew that was coming one day. I, for one, wasn't excited for it to happen. The world would find out there was two of them, and the world would go nuts. There'd be a frenzy.

I didn't want that, but I *totally* understood it.

FIFTY-NINE

Bailey

We were celebrating tonight.

Our last day of classes was today. We had a weekend, and then my classmates and I were starting our internships on Monday. So tonight, we were doing a whole Long Island theme night. Everyone came together after being off doing their own thing.

Melissa roped in Torie and Tamara, and everyone had started with the same bar/club crawl as we'd had for our girls' night so long ago—or it seemed like so long ago.

We went to the biker bar first.

Then we went to Octavo.

Now everyone was ending the night at Naveah, and I'd requested ahead of time to get the VIP booth for our group. Torie helped push that request through, mostly by marching up to the booth and shooing Tony, Guy, and Chester out of there. They weren't happy when they saw that we weren't alone. We had our guy classmates with us. Liam was back to being approved, since he moved out from living with Hoda.

Hoda.

I'd forgotten about her. I hadn't seen her on campus or at the library at all. Team Batt maybe needed to do some investigating. The other thing new: Melissa and Liam came in holding hands.

Dax, Shyam, and the rest of the guys were with them when they all arrived.

"Hey, sister." Matt bumped my shoulder next to me. "Where's your man?"

"He's with his brother tonight."

"Really?"

I nodded. I was having another Long Island, and I was right at the stage of alcohol where I wanted my man with me, but I was reining it in. I didn't want to be one of *those* couples, who couldn't spend an entire day away from each other.

Nope. Not me.

But yeah, I missed Kash. I wanted to see Kash.

Fine. We were that couple. All gooey and cheese and mushy.

Matt sighed. "I can already tell you're going to be moping tonight. Go, sister."

"What?"

He shook his head, flicking his hands in the air. "Go. You want your man, so go and get your man. Go. Find him. Drag him away from that brother."

"Oh no. I'm good. I'm with friends tonight."

"Go. To. Him." He spelled it out, rolling his eyes. "It's your turn, sister. Be selfish."

"You sure?"

Matt mock-glared at me. "Now you're pissing me off."

I laughed, finished my drink, and grabbed my purse before sliding out of the booth.

"Where are you going?" Torie called out.

I waved at her. "Gonna go find Kash! 'Night, guys. Don't drink too much." I grinned, because the guys were almost falling over by then. Melissa was buzzed, with Tamara drunk. Torie was the only one sober. I wasn't sure what Matt was, but he hadn't joined us until Naveah. He didn't get the boot like the other guys. As for myself, I was *definitely* buzzed.

Fitz moved in when I walked down the pathway. "I want to see Kash."

It had been a whole battle.

Fitz on one side.

Me on the other.

He was all like *"You should stay, be with your friends."*

And I was like *"No! I want my man. Take me to my man,"* in my drunken state.

Fitz lost, and now we were outside my old apartment building and he was going in first. He said the coms weren't working for some reason, so I stayed behind with Drake. Kash had taken to keeping Josh and Scott with him at all times, which I understood, but I missed the guys. When Drake got the notice to send me in, I was expecting to see Josh or Scott at the door.

I assumed they would escort me upstairs, but it was a no-go that night.

The building was probably on lockdown, so I headed up myself.

I was just leaving the elevator when the door to our old apartment opened. Out walked Kash, alone.

He was looking at his phone, but then looked up and stopped in his tracks.

"What are you doing here?" He looked beyond me, his face darkening. "Why are you alone?"

"Where's Scott and Josh? They weren't at the door."

"Who cleared you to come in?" His hand grabbed my arm, and he began pulling me toward the apartment.

I went with him, frowning. "Fitz."

We were at the apartment, and he shoved open the door, pushing me in first. "Where's Drake?"

"In the car."

He hurried me inside, throwing the door shut. The lock was next, then the whole barrage of locks. He went to the security cameras next, cursing under his breath. "Chase!"

Oh boy. What had I walked in on?

Kash's brother came out from the kitchen. "What's going on?" He saw me, and he started to smile—then his brother spoke.

"We're under attack."

"*What?*" That was me.

"Who?" That was Chase. He was much calmer; more efficient, too.

Kash was looking at the cameras, then he called down. "Scott, Josh. Go to the east side. Twenty men are coming up the main elevators. They'll come for us, but I want you guys to sweep in from the east, move slow and cautious." He hit a different button. "Fitz? Come in, Fitz."

Chase was now waiting along with me.

Kash was searching the security cams. He must've switched calls again. "I'm looking. My guess, our grandfather." A pause, cursing. He hit a different button on his phone. "Drake! Move. Drake!"

Chase disappeared into a room.

He reappeared later with three vests in hand and a myriad of weapons in a bag in his other hand. I was pretty sure he wasn't supposed to handle any of those guns like that, but he did, and he dropped them on the table way rougher than was necessary.

"Base, this is Kash. We're under attack at Chase's apartment."

It was Chase's apartment now? He was staying here permanently?

While Kash kept talking to whoever was at base, Chase touched my arm, pulling me over to him. His eyes were serious, his face tight. "Lift your arms."

I did, and then because I'm me, I made a joke. "In two minutes, men will break into your apartment and take you hostage."

He paused, and the side of his mouth twitched before he finished strapping me into a vest. "Kash." He picked up one of the other two vests and turned, tossing it in the air.

Kash was coming over, his phone pressed to his ear. He caught the vest, putting his phone on speaker and placing it on the table. He put his vest on as he spoke. "ETA for the authorities?"

Chase froze, midreach for his own vest. "No."

Kash didn't spare him a look, putting on his vest.

"There's a patrol three blocks away."

"No. We don't know how many are here. Any cops could get killed," Chase hissed.

I spotted a laptop on the kitchen counter and went over to it.

Kash ignored his brother again, speaking over him, "We'll do what we can, but warn the police about who they're going against. Let them know we're inside and we'll be defending ourselves."

"Got it, boss."

Kash finished his vest, picking up one of the guns to check the barrel, and he reached for his phone. "What do you mean, 'No'?"

"I mean no. I want him."

I was typing fast, hurrying to break into the security feeds.

"Bailey, what are you doing?"

"Hacking." My fingers were flying over the keyboard. This was my own system, too, but someone had changed some of the firewalls. The coding was different. Someone had hacked *me*? "Carry on with your fight."

Kash sighed, but turned to his brother. "If you want him, you get him before they get here."

"*I* want him."

"Then you get him."

Chase growled. "You're not hearing me."

"I am hearing you, loud and fucking clear. *You're* not getting it. These are Calhoun's men, coming in to get you, but I'd be shocked if he was actually here. He's not here. He's tucked away somewhere safe where no one can put a bullet in him. Also, Calhoun alive is what the feds want. It was our bargaining chip so both of us don't get arrested. Remember that time I broke you out of their custody? I got into a ton of trouble for you."

Another growl erupted from his brother. Something pounded the table.

I was still working to undo some of this new coding, so I didn't look. I was guessing it was his fist and not something else, like Kash, if they were going to start duking it out.

"He deserves to die."

I heard more clicking sounds. Glancing up, I saw both were prepping their guns. A box of ammunition was open on the table between them.

"Bailey," Kash called.

"Yeah?"

"Are you in?"

"Not yet. Someone changed my entire system. I have to figure it out." I bit down on my lip.

Now. This is the time when I should've been freaking out. I should've been, but I wasn't. An eerie and unnerving calm had settled over me. As I continued going through the system, section by section, I couldn't help but marvel at the oddness of my situation.

I was in an apartment, one that I used to love living in, and now I was here with a secret twin who was fighting with the man that I love over the chance to kill his grandfather.

I wasn't freaking, and the only reason I could think why was that this was no longer new to me. I'd been through too much. If they were going to be successful and get me, I'd freak out then.

I had fought back at round one.

I had been drugged at round two.

I had been paralyzed, then hysterical, at round three.

This was round four, and I was somewhat finding myself

wanting to vote with the secret twin. It was time to end this, and Calhoun dead was a viable option. There'd be no more rounds after this.

Then I got into the system and booted up all the security feeds. "I'm in!"

Hoda! I recognized her coding from school. She had a distinct style.

The floor rocked under my feet, and I looked, belatedly, if we really were in an earthquake. No. Nothing was falling off the walls. That was me, having everything swept out from under me.

Hoda must've been holding back, or learning hard over these last few months. I never knew what side she was, not really. Now I knew, I guess.

"We can go there." Kash pointed to a screen.

Chase grunted. "The next one."

They both looked.

Kash growled, "No."

Chase growled back, "Yes."

"The third one."

"No."

"Yes!"

They were both silent, both studying the cameras.

Chase gave in. "Fine. That sixth one."

No clue what he was relenting to.

A sigh from Kash. "Fine."

No clue about that, either.

"Good." Both nodded together and looked at me.

"What?" said Kash.

"I have no idea what you guys just said to each other."

Kash bit out a curse at the same time that Chase hid a grin, looking away. They moved around me. Kash took my arm, dragging me with him. They both reached for a gun and began filling shoulder holsters that I'd not seen them put on.

"Babe."

I didn't like the sound of that. "What?"

Kash was taking me to the back bedroom, grabbing the computer and handing it to me. "You know that time we had a conversation where I needed you to trust me? That you might not want to do what I needed you to do, but you just needed to do it anyways?"

"No."

We were in the bedroom. He was leading me to my closet. "Well, we just did." He swept the hanging clothes aside, ones that I'd left behind, then opened one of the drawers and touched a button. The back wall swung in, and my mouth was hanging open.

"What is *that*?"

He pushed me inside, hitting a light switch.

I was in a room. It wasn't a big room, but it was a room. There was a chair. Blankets. A caddy of water and those bars that could be eaten as a whole meal. In the corner was a bucket with a heavy blanket over it.

Ew. I didn't want to think why there was a bucket, but I knew. Some things you don't want to know and you just know. That bucket was one of those things.

"This room is an escape room."

I grunted. "No shit."

"The door is bulletproof. Once I close this, the edges will reseal. No one will know it's here."

Oh.

Whoa, whoa, whoa.

I tried putting on the brakes, but I was already in.

Kash pointed to a panel. "If we die, you can get out of here with those buttons."

"*What? Die?*"

He bent, his mouth finding mine, but before I could swoon, he was gone. "I love you." Then the door was pulled shut behind him.

"Kash!" I was there, pounding on it. I reached for the handle—there was no handle. Why wasn't there a handle? I could hear him slide the clothes in front of it again, and then . . . was that footsteps I was hearing? I moved to the other wall. What was on that side?

Eyeing the room, I was wondering whether, if worse came to worst, could I dig myself out through the walls. Okay. That was a bit dramatic for me, so I opened the panel and pored over all the buttons. They were labeled. I could call the front desk, the Chesapeake, 911, or I could unarm the door. The door was armed? Then the bottom button was "Exit."

Okay.

That whole eerie calm feeling I'd been having before? Vanished. Evaporated. It was gonzo and I was panicking.

Calm, Bailey. Calm.

I went to my deep-breathing techniques. I was not claustrophobic, even though this was a tiny room with no windows. I turned around. There was a screen!

And a remote under it.

Now I was talking.

I grabbed it, turning on the screen. Oh, hell yeah. There were cables in the corner. I hurried over, plugging the computer in to the larger screen and I was in business. A small desk and chair were in the corner, but I wheeled the chair over, pulling the desk right afterward. And sitting down, I was now in my own personal computer headquarters room.

I could watch and help this way.

Or so I was telling myself, but the truth is that I didn't do much.

I did sit. And I did watch. And I mostly marveled at how Kash and his brother seemed to work seamlessly together.

They were magnificent.

Both moving with precision, going fast. It was as if they had grown up together, as if they had been trained together. One went low, the other went high. One went right, the other went left. And it wasn't that one moved and the other followed. They moved at the same time.

They were almost a perfect mirror of each other.

"Bailey?"

I jumped, screaming. That voice came from . . . I whirled. Where?

"Bailey!"

The feeds.

I looked up. Kash was staring at one of the cameras, scowling. "Bailey!"

He had a headset and was connected into the system. I raced for the laptop and hit the sound button. "Yeah? I'm here."

He nodded to the screen and pointed ahead of him. "We need to know how many men are in that room."

I looked. "Four."

"Guns?"

My heart sank, then shriveled up. "Yes. But they aren't aimed at the door." I gave him their locations using the clock system. Noon. Three. Six. And ten.

He gave me one more nod and turned back to Chase.

Both went together.

Noon and Ten were shot at the same time.

Three got off a shot, but then he was clipped and went down.

Six was last, turning to run.

Chase tackled him, and rearing back up, he brought his fists down. He just kept punching. I heard Kash cursing as he went and yanked his brother off the guy.

The guy was unconscious.

"Rein it in," Kash snapped at his brother, moving ahead of him for the next room.

They kept going until I told them who was in what room. In the last room, they found Josh and Scott. Drake and Fitz were there, too.

Kash went over, checking Josh's pulse. "He's alive." The rest were alive, too.

I breathed easier after that.

"*Shit!*"

I jumped, my head jerking to where Chase was standing.

His hands were on his hips and he was looking around the room. "*Shit!* He's not here. He's *not here!*"

There was a buzzing and I clicked through the screens.

My finger was fumbling when I hit the button, and I couldn't speak, not at first. I couldn't believe what I was seeing.

"Kash!" I screamed, but Chase was still yelling.

"*Kash!*"

"Shut up," he snarled at Chase, then lifted his head. "Bailey?"

He was there, hurrying down the stairs, through the parking garage door. He was alone.

"He's here." I could not speak. What the crap? *Now?* Seriously. "Your gran—*Calhoun is here!*"

Both went still.

Then they leaped at the same time, rushing out of the room and down the hall.

Kash yelled out, "Where, Bailey? We need direction."

"Downstairs. He's in the garage." My mouth was so dry. "He's alone, you guys."

I couldn't believe it, but at my words, they shared one look before they were both sprinting even faster. Chase went down one set of exit stairs, but there was another set on the other side of the floor.

I looked back to the garage, seeing Calhoun was hurrying to that other side.

"Kash! Take the other stairs."

He veered away, around the door, and was gone in a flash.

I was holding my breath. I was there, with them, soaring down the stairs alongside them.

But wait. I wasn't.

I was still in this damn closet.

I needed to get down there. I had to.

I looked around. The panel of buttons. Kash said I could get out that way.

I started hitting every button there was.

SIXTY

Kash

Bailey said to use these stairs for a reason.

Because of that, I hit the door hard, slamming it open, and I was through it just as he was moving past me.

All this buildup, all the years, all the fears and worries and tears and threats, every fucking minute I spent in the gym making myself into this weapon, and it was here. Finally. I reached for him at the same time Chase came hurtling in.

"Don't!" Chase yelled.

I turned, not seeing the flash as Calhoun had whirled around to me.

I felt a searing burn on my side, but fuck . . . I couldn't think what that meant. I saw the gun at the same time he was raising it back up, but Chase was there. Chase swung in, hitting Calhoun on the side. The gun went wide, clattering over the floor, but after that, the fight was almost done.

Almost.

Calhoun had nothing left, that was obvious.

Chase growled, shoving him back against the vehicle.

Laughter.

I paused.

It was spilling from Calhoun.

I barely recognized him from the old surveillance pictures that Harden had given me, before I pulled the team to help get Chase free. He'd had a healthy weight the last time I saw him in person, but this man was old, haggard. His skin hung from his bones, sagging, and he was so skinny. Gaunt. His hair had been salt and pepper before. It was all gray now, some ends of pure white. He hadn't shaved, I was guessing, in months. His stench said he hadn't showered, either.

This was it.

This was the end, but fuck . . . I felt the pain slicing through me and I reached for my side. Blood coated my fingers, and I was feeling the burn now.

That shit had shot me.

Chase had him against the vehicle, slamming him into it over and over again. "You think this is goddamn funny?"

A savage growl ripped from me and I surged in, grabbing Calhoun from Chase. I tossed him to the concrete floor. He was rolling, trying to get free, but that laugh. It sounded like an evil character's laugh, and it was making me grind my teeth even more.

"Shut the fuck up!"

He kept rolling, and I grabbed him by the ankle. I twisted him over and bent his leg back until he couldn't move anywhere. Then I kept on bending until I heard him scream instead. A little more. *Pop.* I felt it. Only then did I let it go, stepping back and standing over him. He had one good leg now, but I was looking him over. He'd had one gun. There could be more.

A presence was coming in from my right, but I moved, slamming Chase back. "Stop!"

"You stop." He shoved me back. His eyes were wild, feral. He was almost salivating. "I want him dead."

"I want answers."

"Fuck the answers."

Chase started for him again, but I was seeing red.

In the back of my mind, I knew we each had our own cross to bear here. Both of us had been terrorized and threatened by Calhoun all our lives, but in different ways. I didn't care. Each man for himself, as far as I was concerned. And because of that, when my brother started for him again, only seeing Calhoun, I pounced. I couldn't bring myself to knock my brother out—I didn't know why, and I'd maybe think on that later, but as he stepped forward, I kicked out his leg. When he fell, I was there, my arms wrapped around him, and he toppled forward. I went with him.

I had him in a headlock, my legs preventing him from fighting back. He couldn't fight me. My arms had his locked up at an angle that he would've needed to break a shoulder—*Pop!*

Fuck.

He did.

Chase rolled out from my hold and was up on his feet the next second. "You fucking *kidding me?*" He was roaring at me, his voice echoing through the garage. "This kill is mine. You didn't live with him, under his thumb, being turned into a—"

I rushed him, trying to lock him back down.

He was the emotional one. Not me, not this time. I wanted justice, but I wanted my hits, too. Chase, he just wanted to kill. That made him irrational, not thinking clearly, and I was going to use that. He wanted me off and he wanted a clear path to Calhoun. I wasn't letting him get that.

He swung, batting me away, but his punches were pulled. He didn't want to hurt me. Fine. Guess I'd be the asshole here. I moved back, letting him think his punch worked, and he turned, already going for Calhoun again. I did an exact repeat of my first move, but this time, as I kicked out his knee, I kicked it harder than was needed. I heard another tear and I winced, knowing I was doing so much damage to my twin, but he fell and I fell with him with my legs wrapped tight around him so he couldn't move. I waited, praying, praying, praying.

He paused.

He fought.

He twisted.

He roared.

His head lashed around, trying to find mine, to make contact. I gritted my teeth, tightening my hold around his neck until I felt his body go slack. I still waited, loosening my hold on his neck so he could breathe. He did. I felt his chest move, but he didn't try to get out of my hold.

He was unconscious.

Still cautious, breathing harder than I thought, only my panting filled the garage now. I unwound from his body, kicking him over so he was on his side in case he vomited, and when my brother was okay, I lifted my head.

Calhoun was sitting up, watching us.

He hadn't moved. He hadn't tried to retreat. But then I saw why.

He was holding on to his own shoulder. Blood was pouring down from him. He'd been shot. But I looked around and didn't know what gun—

"Chase shot me."

He jerked his head to the side, where I saw a gun lying there.

I stood, my panting still echoing around the garage, and looked over my grandfather more carefully. One of his legs was crushed. Chase had shot him there, too.

"I can't use it."

He sounded resigned to his fate, and he grunted, half laughing again. A shake of his head, his beard barely moving, he let out a deep burst of air.

"Bested. Bested by my two grandsons."

Another half laugh, half grunt and he looked where Chase was lying. "That pathetic piece of shit was supposed to be my ace. I wanted him back. If I got him back, I could turn everything around. Slap him around, lock him back up until he was ready to come out and play like the soldier he was supposed to be. Didn't think I'd ever see the two of you team up. Pieces of shits, both of you."

My teeth were grinding.

"I know it's over. You . . ." Those eyes came back to me now, and hate filled them. Derision. Disdain. His mouth curled in a sneer. I was scum under his shoes. "Should've tossed you both out like pups, in a tied bag. Let you drown. But I had a weak spot for your mother. What a fucking cunt, all of you. Her sister, too. She was worthless. Then you, you should've been aborted when I found out she was pregnant. You both . . ."

I was letting him spew, and he kept saying the same shit.

He wanted us dead. He should've killed us when he had the chance.

His daughters were worthless, both of them.

And back to the beginning.

"Why'd you kill my mother?"

He stopped on a gargle, his eyes glazed over from the pain. He stared at me, long and hard, as if he couldn't see me. Then he hiccupped, and some blood sputtered out of him. "For the money. Bitch had my money."

"Your money?"

"Her inheritance from her mother. That was supposed to be mine. All the fucking stupid courts and their fancy lawyer. Your grandmother left everything to her. Not her sister. Not me. *Her.* She didn't have to die, though. She could've lived. But no, no. In the end, the bitch turned on me and had to go. Stupid. She was so stupid. That man, too."

My father.

Calhoun spat, "He was a worm. Nothing but a slithering, slimy worm. Losers. And you and your brother, you're the worst of them. You're just like your mother."

He kept going, the blood seeping from him as he said the same shit over and over again.

"You killed my mother for money? Why not kill me?"

He stared at me again, as if confused that I had even dared address him. "Because you wouldn't take your money. And you were a minor. Knew my daughter. I hated her, lost all respect for her, but knew her. She would've had something written up that if you died, everything that should go to you would've gone to that computer nerd. I knew his weak spot. He crumbled. Get good pussy around him and he'd have to grab it. Young. Beautiful piece of ass and he'd do anything to get his dick wet. Easiest thing I ever did, sending Quinn to him. She worked him. She could pump him. She told me all about it. We'd laugh about it, and then I'd get *my* dick wet. Best ass I'd touched." He started smiling. His yellowed teeth were caked with blood.

"I had to wait for you. Took you long enough. Couldn't understand it, why you were doing what you were doing. Who'd turn their back on the money and power you'd be inheriting? Then I got word that you finally stepped up. Quinn helped with that. Said she sent that journalist pussy what she needed to out you, said it was only a matter of time. Said that if you were outed, you'd step up and you'd take control over what your cunt of a mother left you. Knew then it was time to start moving."

He quieted, breathing harder now. He was staring at Chase, but I didn't think he was seeing him. His body was weakening before my eyes. The blood loss was affecting him, making him more pale.

He murmured, softer, almost faint. "I never had time. He has a daughter in Thailand. I was going to kill her if he ever turned on me, but he hid her. Now I don't have anyone left. All my friends. They turned their backs on me, or you killed them. You destroyed everything. I have nothing. I have no one. These guys weren't my normal guys—even those guys abandoned me. You took everything from me, everyone. Even Quinn refuses to contact me. I made her who she is today. The other one, too, worthless. All of them. They're rats, and they scatter when there's a little bit of fire. Stupid fucking fire. I hate fire. I hate . . ." He lifted his head again, but it was straining him. "I hate you. I die, and your woman is going to die. I have a guy. He promised me that he'd kill her for me. And you don't even know who he is, that's the kicker."

He had no one left.

I had drained his resources, destroyed everything he could've used against me.

The government froze his accounts.

He didn't have the capability to get to what accounts he could still use.

Yeah. I had a guess who he had asked to kill Bailey.

I went over to him, kneeling down before him. "That man who was supposed to kill my woman, his name Mike Harden?" That was his death policy. Calhoun had entrusted the one person he had left, but Harden was my guy.

Surprise lit in his eyes, and his mouth parted. "You know him?"

"Yeah." I was going to relish this. "He works for me."

His eyes went flat.

I smirked. "He always has."

"Wha—" he choked out, blanching, before a whole new fury started in his eyes.

Chase was starting to stir behind me. I felt the first groan from him, so I started to move, when suddenly I heard Bailey scream, "*Kash!*"

Calhoun was bringing up a gun. An ugly and harsh laugh ripping from him as his finger moved to the trigger.

I lunged.

Bailey had a knife, and in a split second she threw it toward me.

I flung myself out of the way.

Bam!

The gun went off.

Boom.

I felt like I was punched, but I was submerged in water. Everything was dull, happening in slow motion, and I reached, catching the knife from Bailey. I grabbed it at the handle and a little over the blade. It cut into my skin from how tight my hold was, but I fell to my knees and I lashed out. It all happened in three seconds.

Bailey yelled.

Bailey tossed the knife.

I jumped.

Reached for it.

Caught it.

My knees hit, and my arm made a horizontal slashing motion, right across his throat.

Then Chase was up and he was throwing himself at us.

Calhoun was sitting there, blood cascading down his throat, but he was trying to raise the gun again. He was trying to turn it. He would have shot me, but Chase grabbed it and threw it away. It clattered away like the other one.

Chase staggered back, falling into the vehicle. He glared at me. "So stupid. You don't let him talk. Ever." He bent forward, picking up the knife. He gripped it, turning it over. "You gotta put him down. That's how you handle someone like him."

"Chase, don't!"

Bailey was running toward us, but *boom!* The door burst open behind her. Bodies swarmed inside, guns raised, shields in place. Red and blue lights filled the air. The cops had arrived.

It was over.

Chase let out another roar, but I moved, catching him in the chest. He would've stabbed Calhoun in front of the police. I slammed him back, feeling pain with every shift I was making now. The adrenaline was starting to wear off, and I knew I'd be in worse pain after this.

"Colello!"

Bright was heading our way, holstering her weapon. More cops were streaming up the stairs. They'd check out the entire building. Paramedics were already coming in as well, bringing their stretchers.

"I called them. Gave them all a body count of guys I thought were dead and who I thought was just injured," Bailey said.

Bright nodded at her. "We know exactly where to go, but we still need to clear the building." Her gaze fell over me, Chase, and Calhoun. Our grandfather wasn't moving. "Is he dead?"

He coughed, but his head bounced once and went back to not moving. He was sitting up, but I had no idea how. "He needs medical attention if you want to take him alive."

Two police were by him, checking him and cuffing him. Once the cuffs were on, Bright waved and two paramedics ran in. They had him loaded, working on him at the same time, and he was rolled out within seconds.

"We are highly motivated to take him alive. He knows a lot of powerful men and dictators, and he could be very useful to our government."

"Fuck that," Chase spit out. His anger was palpable.

Bright cocked her head. "You have a problem with that?"

"He should be dead. You don't keep things like that alive."

A slight glimmer of a grin hovered over her face, and then she let it vanish. "Yeah, well, you'd be surprised which pieces of shit turn out to be super helpful in the end. He'll be singing like a canary, I'm sure." She looked me over. "There's an ambulance outside. You should let them take you in. I'm sure you could afford the charge."

Bailey stepped in and I slid an arm around her shoulders.

I sagged, and she caught me, her hand going to my chest, but she hissed under her breath. "You are bleeding everywhere."

"Bullets went through him, both of them. I watched," Chase told her.

His gaze met mine. That last one wouldn't have.

He had saved me.

I didn't thank him. I would, but not yet, not today. He wouldn't hear it. I had hurt him, taking a kill away from him, and he had saved my life in return. There wasn't anything I could say to make that right.

"Come on." Bailey sighed. "Surface wounds or not, I'll sleep better knowing you were looked at by a doctor. I will also breathe easier right now if you let me grab two EMTs and let them put you on a stretcher, even though I know you can walk on your own." She wasn't asking. She was telling me.

I noted that with a small grin, but she didn't see it. She was already stalking off to do just what she'd said.

Bright had stepped aside, having a word with another detective. She came back, looking both of us over. "Okay. Both of you go in, get yourselves looked at, and report to me tomorrow. I want full statements, and I'd send two police to sit outside your rooms, but I know you both will get pissed and probably vanish like fucking ghosts. So, since I don't want my time wasted or yours, both of you promise to come down to my office tomorrow morning. We will need a full debrief from you, separately."

Chase didn't respond.

I nodded.

Bright skewered Chase with a look. "Don't piss me off and make us look for you. My tech guys are already in my ear, telling me there is video of you trying to kill your grandfather. That's a violation of our agreement. If you push me, I will put out an arrest warrant on you and we will hunt you down like a fugitive. Got it?"

He just glared at her.

She started to leave, but then wheeled around. "Get cleaned up, both of you. I'll talk to you tomorrow."

I saw an elevator open and a stretcher came out, holding Josh. Another elevator, with Drake. Scott. All of my men were accounted for. Bailey was coming back with a stretcher for me, and I had to wonder what kind of circus it must look like outside.

Then I remembered what Calhoun had said.

"You have a daughter?"

"Fuck you."

He stalked off, his one good arm holding his bad one.

"Kash?"

I turned to Bailey, bending toward her. The EMTs were there, wanting to work on me, but I needed one touch from her. One beautiful touch in the midst of everything we just went through, and it was enough to tide me over. "I'm good."

"Colello."

Bright was coming back from one of the stairs.

She was looking at Bailey, and I stood, feeling the EMTs trying to get me to sit on the stretcher. "Don't start with her," I said. "You can get her statement, but not till tomorrow. You'll have to send a detective to the house for her."

"Colello!"

I cursed. She was going to fight this, but then she softened her voice. "We found a body."

In Loving Memory, Another Francis Friend Victim

A memorial service will happen this Saturday, at one in the afternoon.

Hoda Rai Mansour's family will be gathering to share favorite memories and stories as they remember the great person Hoda was.

She will live on in our laughter and tears. Please join us, her family.

On behalf of *Inside Daily Press*, our staff sends their condolences.

We will remain vigilant in our coverage of the wrongful conviction of Quinn Callas. Her attorneys remain confident Miss Callas's case will be appealed.

Click here to help support Quinn Callas and her innocence.

—*Inside Daily Press*

SIXTY-ONE

Bailey

I forgot about the footage until Matt brought out the latest *Inside Daily Press* article, and to say it was an article was being gracious. It was a local "news" website, and they were biased. Heavily biased. Case in point, the way they had been reporting on Quinn's trial. It wasn't all the time, but it was enough, and they got enough views to be a headache for my family's publicist.

This recent article came out the day after Hoda's body was found. The police were able to piece together how she had been involved. They explained that she received a call from an unknown number. Security footage found her walking outside her apartment building, where she was forced at gunpoint to get into a nondescript van. After that, they could only guess that she'd been an unwilling participant in Calhoun's attempt to kidnap his grandson. From their questioning of some of Calhoun's men left alive, their orders had been to kidnap Chase Bastian and to execute Kash Colello if given the chance.

I shuddered at the plans Calhoun must've had, to try it once again. Then this article came out and, well, my world wasn't falling apart anymore. Besides grieving someone I wasn't sure if I cared about or not—but still grieving that she had been pulled into my world's chaos and destruction—I decided it was time to find out who the hell was behind *Inside Daily Press*.

The result shouldn't have been shocking.

I hacked into Quinn's old phone, since she wasn't using it anymore, and sent a text.

Meet me at Octavo. Friday night. 9 p.m. Back booth under the stairs. I'll explain there.

Then I waited.

"Why are we here again? You know Kash isn't too happy we're not at one of his establishments." Matt sidled in next to me at our booth.

"We're here because she'd never go to one of Kash's establishments."

We'd been here enough. I picked this booth because until you actually slid into the one side, you couldn't tell if anyone else was sitting in it. She'd see my side profile, and I was hunched over, so I was hoping she'd see a female trying to hide her identity and guess the wrong person. But she'd slide in, and voilà, there would be Matt.

"No, I'm not," Kash said.

We weren't Team Batt right now.

Matt groaned. "Still saying this. I am not a fan of Team Ka-Batt."

I grinned.

"Tough shit. And you're in a nightclub whose owners I do know, but I don't know them well. I can also say that you will not be attending this nightclub without myself in attendance again."

"But—"

"Ever again, Matthew. These owners have Mafia affiliations,

and that's all I'm saying about that topic. Drop it and tell me instead the plan of what you're saying to this reporter."

Matt snorted again. "She is not a reporter. She's barely even a blogger. She's—"

She slid into the booth at that very second, and froze, hearing Matt's voice.

She took me in, took in Matt.

I didn't think she saw Kash yet.

She started to bolt.

She got as far as the edge of the booth before Kash was there, and he was glowering down at her. She'd worn a white silk shirt, her hair was plaited in two braids. She almost had a schoolmarm look going on, with her glasses, her red lipstick, and the black skirt she had donned for this meeting.

She froze again, head up, mouth hanging open, before she cursed under her breath. "Oh, no."

"Slide in." Kash's command was not an option.

She gulped before she did what he said.

Matt started, because I knew he would. "Oh, fuck indeed. Camille Story, aka Quinn's bitch, aka Hoda's puppet master, who probably gave her name up to Kash's grandfather." He leaned forward, hissing, "You got her killed. Take ownership of that."

Her eyes got bigger and bigger, the more he talked. She also got smaller and smaller in the booth, until she was almost shrunk half under the table. "I am not. What?" She pushed back up. "The only person I gave Hoda's name to was Quinn. What she did with it, that's on her. Not me."

"Right. You're so innocent."

"I'm not saying I'm innocent, but what do you expect? Your family tried to ruin me. You tried to ruin Hoda. I know you ruined Quinn—"

I burst forward. "Quinn is guilty! She tried to have me killed. You're on the wrong side here if you think you're some vigilante blogger."

She startled, pushing her glasses back up.

She looked at Kash, who was scowling at her. Then at Matt, who was also scowling, but he had more of a glare, and he raised his eyebrow at her.

"Are you serious?"

Matt snorted. "You're unbelievable. All that evidence. Calhoun's men killed your friend! Don't you care?"

"I feel bad about Hoda, but this is war. And in times of war, there are casualties—"

"Would you like to be one?"

The question came from Kash, and it was said quietly, but damn, chills down my back.

Camille was feeling the same, because I caught the shiver before she swallowed once again. "Are you threatening me?"

"No," said Matt.

"Yes," said Kash.

"Dude! She probably has a recorder on her."

Kash looked down, picked up her purse, and dumped it out on the table.

"Oh my God! That's personal property. You can't do that."

Kash was starting to look through her things. "Report me."

She sat back, her eyebrows pinched together and her whole mouth pursed. "I'm not okay with this, with any of this. You are going through my things. You are threatening my well-being. You are holding me here against my will . . ."

And I was done hearing her complaints.

I slid a picture over the table to her.

She looked down, saw it, and gasped. "What—How— You—*Oh my God!* You invaded my privacy."

Matt's head fell backward. "Are you freaking kidding me? That's all you do to us!"

Her face pinched in on itself. "I thought . . . I thought we had a good time the other night."

Another groan from him. "That was forever ago, and it was

so my family could get inside and figure out what the fuck you had on us."

I pointed to the picture. "That's also when I installed a program to watch you."

I let my statement hang between us.

The image was of her doing something *very* illegal.

"I have the trail to back this picture up, along with audio and video footage over the last month."

"You can't do that. What you did was illegal!"

She was white around her mouth, matching the blood draining from her face. She couldn't stop staring at the picture.

Yes. What I did was just as illegal. I didn't care.

"Prove it."

She looked up, her eyes so dilated that it took a second to focus on me. "You bitch . . ."

"I have mercenaries on my payroll."

She turned, looking at Kash, and she visibly shrank back again.

He stared right back, his voice level. "I wanted to give them your name, to tell them to 'get rid' of you in any way they chose. I'd be very kind to Bailey right now. She overrode my suggestion."

Another gulp. This time it was audible, and that said a lot since we were in a nightclub. Flashing lights and techno music was an automatic with these places. And dark corners, thank goodness.

She crumpled up the picture, her gaze back on me. "What do you want?"

Now that we got that out of the way, I slid over my next item. It was the latest piece she wrote about Hoda. "This is you."

"No, it's not."

I shook my head, not understanding why she kept trying. "By now, you should automatically know that I don't bluff. If I say I have it, I have it. If I say I know it, I have a trail of online evidence to back me up. Stop. We're not even here to do anything to you. Just shut up and listen."

Her mouth clamped tight.

"Finally." Matt sighed.

"You *are Inside Daily Press*. I ran all of the articles, and they're all from you. They all generate from your four computers. And yes, I know about the fifth one you keep in the back closet. I know all—just make that your mantra by now. Bailey knows all, so stop arguing with me. You're only going to piss me off to find more shit on you, and I have a ton already. I have enough that we could hand it over to two FBI agents, who would be happy to do with it what they wanted. I don't think you'd get away with the warning we're going to give you."

Matt was annoyed. I could feel it in the air.

Kash was having fun. Since Calhoun was locked up and taken away to a black site prison, one that we were promised the public didn't know about, he'd been almost whistling Broadway tunes. He was a new fan of *Hamilton*. But he was enjoying making Camille Story squirm under our threats.

"What do you want?"

"Stop writing this shit about Quinn. It's biased and it's lies. It's all lies."

"But—"

"*Stop it!* She tried to kill me. Forget all the shit we have on you; we could sue for libel and slander. We'd win. Why do you keep backing her story? The evidence against her is unquestionable."

She opened her mouth, stopped, gaped at me, and closed it. She looked down.

We waited, and ten seconds later, she looked back up. "She was a friend. I don't have friends."

Matt snorted, but I elbowed him in the side.

"Oof."

Camille's eyes narrowed and she lifted up a shoulder. "Quinn came to me. She told me all these things about you guys, and I believed her."

Matt growled but kept his mouth shut.

I sat back. "You told her about Hoda?"

She nodded. "She was looking for allies. I knew Hoda was your classmate and she didn't like you. Hoda actually found me. She commented on a couple of my posts, and then I dug her up, finding out who exactly was commenting. I reached out after that, and the rest was history."

"My grandfather's men knew about Hoda. Was that from you?"

"I . . ." Her eyes suddenly bulged out, and what color had come back to her completely drained again. "Oh no. Oh no!"

"We're getting that." A mutter from Matt.

"*Oh no!*" She surged forward, sitting all the way upright. "Quinn emailed me, asking how to get in contact with Hoda. I'd told her that Hoda had moved out, but I never thought about it. She said she wanted to send Hoda a card or email. I . . . It was me." She slumped back down. "She must've sent an email to Hoda and then to them, and that's how they knew where to find her. I . . . I never thought."

We waited, letting her process that.

Matt's hand shot up. "Can we move forward? I don't have any sympathy for her finding out she helped get a girl murdered. She's been consorting with Quinn this whole time. She's innocent of shit."

Camille's eyebrows furrowed up. "That's not fair."

"We don't care," said Kash.

I coughed, sitting up. "Moving along. This is what we're going to do. I have no interest in turning you over to the police. You'd have to explain how I got all of this, and frankly, I could delete everything and erase my trail, but that's a pain in the ass. I mean, I'll be erasing my trail anyways, but going through the hoops of proving that to the cops, I don't want to do that. And I have no doubt that if Quinn gets word that you've been arrested, she'll know you could turn evidence on her and she'll probably try to figure out a way to hire a hit on you."

"Oh my God!"

I ignored her. "So instead I want you to stop reporting anything and everything on our family. That is it. If you hear of a story brewing about us, you will merely type on your computer screen CANARY and I will know to get in contact with you. Creepy, yes. I don't care. I want you to know that I'm going to continue watching you because I don't like you. I don't like how much you have hurt my brother, myself, my family, and Kash. You can do whatever you want, but you will help us instead. For the rest of your life. And if for some reason you decide you're sick of being our puppet, remember that I'm only one hacker in my family. There's one more and one coming. I also have a photographic memory, so anything I read, I never forget." A pause for dramatic effect. "Are we clear here?"

She'd lost all color again but jerked her head up and down in a stiff nod.

It was good enough for me.

We left and headed to Naveah.

Once inside, and once we were sitting in our VIP booth, Kash watched Matt head to the bar. "You think she'll do it?"

I shrugged. "I don't know, but if she doesn't, I really will turn all my stuff over to the authorities. Bright will love me forever."

He grinned, then grew serious. He was still watching Matt, who was now flirting with Torie. "I'm thinking of turning Naveah over to Matt."

"He'd buy you out?"

"He'd manage it for me, and yeah, if he wants to buy me out later, I'd let him do that. What do you think?"

"I think that's a great idea, but he'll be pissed he can't drink here socially anymore."

Kash smirked. "I know."

"You think he's ready for something like that?"

He nodded. "I do. He's been quiet about it, but he's gone back to managing the Francois Nova, and he's doing well. There's been no complaints. I talked to a few of the employees and they're happy with him, said he was a new and improved Matthew Francis."

I was pleased to hear that, and proud. "He never told me."

Kash's grin was slow and warm. "We've kinda had a lot going on ourselves."

"Very true. And back to your idea, I think it's a perfect fit for him."

"Good." He leaned over, a finger under my chin. "I don't know about you, but I'm ready to go home." He kissed me, making it slow and delicious, and it sent tingles through my whole body. "Do you want to stay?"

"After that kiss?"

A low chuckle came from him. "I was hoping you'd say that."

EPILOGUE

Kash

Two years later

Everyone heard the laughter throughout the church.

I was standing at the front, my arms folded in front of me. Peter was in the pew and shaking his head. A space was next to him for Chrissy. Matthew stood next to me, dressed all fancy in his tuxedo. Chase was next to him. Cyclone was my last groomsman.

The girls hadn't started coming down the aisle yet, but they were back there.

Everyone was listening.

They'd been boozing it up since Torie brought half the bar with her. Seraphina was standing just beyond the door, peeking in. I couldn't hear her, but I knew there was a wedding planner back there. She'd been up my ass with financials since Bailey insisted on hiring her. Little did I know it was all a ploy.

Bailey didn't want to plan the wedding. She knew I didn't, either, and she didn't want to let Chrissy loose on the job; hence, a wedding planner, who I'd seen running around, her hands in the air, a permanent look of exasperation on her face, and no one blamed her. Bailey had taken to making a game of evading her.

So she was either back there, hissing at them to hurry up, or they got her drunk right alongside them.

"Anyone else jealous of the bridesmaids?" Matt said under his breath, straightening his collar. "Also, why didn't we sneak some booze ourselves? Note for your future best man."

Cyclone started laughing.

Chase's mouth moved, curving up.

It'd been a long road for Chase and me, but I was glad he was back, and I was glad he was standing up for me today. As if feeling the "twin thing," he caught my eye, and his own flashed. He dipped his head down to me.

Yeah. A long way.

"They're coming," Cyclone whispered, rolling his shoulders back. He had shot up in height over the summer, looking almost like an eighteen-year-old. With a small Mohawk happening. I heard Bailey groan almost daily about the girls sending her little brother private messages on his accounts.

How she knew, I wasn't asking. Everyone knew.

We just let her do her thing, because who was going to stop her? She'd appointed herself the cyber guardian over the entire family, Marie and Theresa included. Payton as well. All three of them that were in the back, too.

Then the music started.

The girls were lined up.

And Seraphina was the first down.

Melissa was next.

Torie and Tamara walked together, since Bailey couldn't make up her mind. Matt loved the idea of having two bridesmaids on his arm.

The music changed.

Everyone stood.

The back doors parted, and there she was.

Stunning. Beautiful. My life.

Bailey was smiling so wide, she was literally glowing.

Chrissy was walking beside her.

I was about to cry.

She started toward me.

Three years after that

"I hate you!"

I cringed, holding my wife's hand as her legs were pulled up into stirrups, spread wide. A sheet was over her legs, with the doctor's head angled between them.

"Push again. Almost there, Bailey!"

"I'm almost there. Did you hear that?" She squeezed again, glaring at me, gritting her teeth. Sweat was rolling down her face. "*I'm almost there.* Famous fucking last words. Pretty sure that's the same words you said nine months ago."

I sighed, running a thumb over her hand. She could crush it all she wanted.

I closed my eyes, knowing it was a matter of seconds, and then . . .

Our son's wails filled the room.

Then Bailey remembered she loved me, and we named him Matthew Curtis Colello.

Two more years later

Chase Peter Colello was born.

Three years more

Christina Seraphina Colello entered the world.

Another ten years even later

"Come on. Don't be shy."

We were sparring at one of my gyms. We had reserved it just for this afternoon, the two of us. Chase had just flown into town and I wanted some time with him. Matt would join us later, but only to heckle us, and he'd talk us into having a drink at his new bar. It was our routine.

Bailey was doing her thing, but unlike the days when I knew what she was doing, she no longer could tell me. The government paid her well to keep creating more programs, though she didn't do it for that reason. She did it for the thrill. A year after she graduated with her master's degree, she wrote a cybersecurity program that became the top seller among cybersecurity experts. She kept perfecting it, and once she sold the license for it, her net worth nearly rivaled mine.

The kids were with their grandparents, so we had all day if we wanted.

Bailey had plans to meet up with the girls, so I knew we'd be joining them at either Naveah or Matt's newest club. We'd find out wherever the girls went and would just go there, but they were always at one of our places.

Drake and Josh were still with us, and they'd send a text to report in. As usual.

I stopped and glared. "Are you kidding me?"

Chase smirked back, his taped hands up, and he bounced back on his feet. "Nope. Don't be shy. I know it's been ages since you've—"

I struck out. My hit was clean and it got him right across the face.

He hissed, bent over from the force of it. "Damn." He looked back up.

I smirked. "I might be getting old, but I still fight on a regular basis. Unlike your ass."

He laughed, wiping away some blood that trickled down from his mouth. "Whatever. No holding back, brother. You ready for that?"

Was I ready for that? Always.

We found the girls at Naveah, and some of Matt's old friends had joined as well.

I paused before going up.

Bailey was standing at the edge of the group, laughing at something Torie was saying, and then she saw me. She smiled, and like the first time I ever saw her, I felt a kick to my chest. She was in there. She tunneled her way inside and she never left.

Thank God.

I went up to her, slid my arms around her waist and pulled her into my arms.

"Hey." She relaxed back into my arms, her head tipping up to see me, and that same glow was with her. It rarely left her.

I bent down, my lips finding hers, and I said back, "Hey."

This.

Fucking perfection.

"Did you have a good time with your brother?"

She always asked. She always cared.

I nodded, tightening my arms around her, and I took in the scene. We had family. We were surrounded by friends. We had our own little ones. This was something that I had never thought I could have, but she came into my life. Bailey. Brainiac Bailey. And everything flipped upside down.

She did that.

I never expected it, but I was damned grateful to have gotten it.

She took in my face, tipping her head back. Reaching up, a palm to the side of my face. "What's in your head?"

"You."

She smiled. The sight was radiant and took my fucking breath away, and I knew that would never end, either. "Good," she said simply. She pulled me back down for another kiss, and I knew it'd be one of a million.

We had a long life ahead of us. A long and happy one.

Bailey

Sometimes having a photographic memory could suck, but to be honest, that was rare. And times like this, times when he was staring at me like he won the lottery, these were the times I was thankful I'd never forget.

Like when I held Matthew Curtis Colello for the first time.

The first time I held Chase Peter Colello.

The first time I held Christina Seraphina Colello.

And the first time I knew I loved Kash, and every single time since then.

We had a long life ahead of us. A long and happy one, and I'd remember every single moment of it. I'd have it no other way.

ACKNOWLEDGMENTS

Oh boy! I have so many to thank here! Crystal. Kimberly. Monique. The *entire* staff at St. Martin's Press. You guys were all so amazing to work with, and I was honored that you took a chance with Bailey, Kash, and me. Thank you, Amy, Serena, Chris, Paige, and Kimberley. Thank you, everyone in my reader group. Your constant posting helps in so many ways. Thank you, Debra Anastasia, Helena Hunting, and Rachel Van Dyken just for being you guys: always amazing and supportive and there for me if I need an ear for anything.

Thank you, Jason for helping and supporting me. And a thank-you to my Bailey at home, my little guy that's my anchor.

I truly hope you all have enjoyed the ride with me from *The Insiders*, *The Damaged*, and now *The Revenge*. I hope you'll keep with me on future rides I'll be writing!

May you find love, happiness, and miracles in your own corners of the world. I thank you from the bottom of my heart.

ABOUT THE AUTHOR

Tijan is a *New York Times* bestselling author who writes suspenseful and unpredictable novels. Her characters are strong, intense, and gut-wrenchingly real with a little bit of sass on the side. Tijan began writing later in life, and once she started, she was hooked. She's written multiple bestsellers, including the Carter Reed series, the Fallen Crest series, and *Ryan's Bed*. She is currently writing to her heart's content in north Minnesota with an English cocker spaniel she adores.